D1051565

HIGHLAND PROMISE

ALYSON McLAYNE

sourcebooks
casablanca

Copyright © 2017 by Alyson McLayne
Cover and internal design © 2017 by Sourcebooks, Inc.
Cover art by Paul Stinson

Sourcebooks and the colophon are registered trademarks of
Sourcebooks, Inc.

All rights reserved. No part of this book may be reproduced in any
form or by any electronic or mechanical means including information storage and retrieval systems—except in the case of brief
quotations embodied in critical articles or reviews—without permission in writing from its publisher, Sourcebooks, Inc.

The characters and events portrayed in this book are fictitious or
are used fictitiously. Any similarity to real persons, living or dead,
is purely coincidental and not intended by the author.

Published by Sourcebooks Casablanca, an imprint of Sourcebooks,
Inc.
P.O. Box 4410, Naperville, Illinois 60567-4410
(630) 961-3900
Fax: (630) 961-2168
sourcebooks.com

Printed and bound in the United States of America.
LSC 10 9 8 7 6 5 4 3

For Ken, Maddie, and Cooper.
I love you guys—like crazy and forever.
Your hugs, laughter, and kisses fill me up.

Prologue

GREGOR MACLEOD STARED DOWN THE LONG WOODEN table at the five Highland lairds seated in front of him and resisted the urge to smash his fists through the wood. Blackhearts, every one of them.

Drawing a vicious-looking dirk from within his linen sleeve, he leaned back in his chair. His legs stretched out in front of him and his plaid fell open to reveal brawny thighs. Firelight from the hearth danced along the dagger's blade as he slowly played with it.

The lairds watched...waited, revealing little in their expressions.

They expected to die.

The thought pleased Gregor and he smiled. "'Tis my right, and the right of every member of this clan, to cleave your heads from your necks, to feed your bodies to my hounds. Though in truth, I doona think they'd have you—treachery and cowardice sours the meat."

He flipped the blade in the air, caught it, and dug the tip into the wooden table. "So I'll take your sons instead."

Stunned and outraged faces stared back at him. His smile widened.

He would foster a boy from each laird and make their sons his sons—bond them to him and to each other so they became brothers, united their clans, and kept the people safe.

It had been his dear Kellie's wish to her dying day.

"You mule-loving devil. I'll not give you my son!"

Gregor glanced to his left, at the red-faced man who had spoken: Laird MacLean, father of Callum MacLean. A terrible laird, he had brought disorder and hardship to his clan. Still, Gregor suspected the man loved his son. For that, and only that, he commended him.

The lad, seven years old, was the youngest of the five Gregor wanted and already showed signs of reason and intelligence—the opposite of his undisciplined father. Callum would make a good laird if his skills could be paired with honor and loyalty, traits Gregor intended to instill in all the lads.

"I'm afraid, Laird MacLean, no is not an option. This isna a debate. You have lost and I am reaping the spoils—your sons. One from each clan who came together and dared attack me. That is the cost of your treachery."

MacLean swore loudly and grumbled under his breath but didn't offer any further resistance.

Gregor waited for the next laird to speak.

"And if we doona comply?"

The question, soft and measured, came from Gregor's right. He stared at the man two seats down from him:

Laird MacKenzie, father of Darach MacKenzie. A tall man, strong of mind and body, the laird was resolute and disciplined—traits Gregor had seen in Darach, the second-youngest of the lads, at eight years old.

"If you doona comply, Laird MacKenzie, you will be hanged, and I will still foster your boy."

"He'd revenge me."

"He could try."

The laird nodded, still calm, but his cheek twitched before he raised a hand to cover it.

At the end of the table, Laird MacKay roused himself. His voice was low, the words halting. He took a labored breath. "I willna give you Donald, but you can have my Lachlan. Donald will be laird by Christmas. He is needed to unite my clan. Lachlan is close to his brother, looks up to him. 'Twill be a good alliance."

Gregor met the laird's eyes. They were tired, troubled. The eyes of a dying man.

Having met both lads, Gregor suspected Donald would make a good laird, but Lachlan would be great. At nine years old, he already recognized his mother's manipulations and duplicity, and refused to play her games.

"Aye," Gregor said. "I'd be happy to take Lachlan and support Donald as laird."

The MacKay laird closed his eyes and nodded. When he opened them, they were wet. Gregor found himself pleased to ease the man's burden, despite being his enemy.

He switched his gaze to Laird MacKinnon, who sat in the first seat on his right. The big, tough, blond man had crossed his arms over his chest and glowered straight ahead. Another man who loved his son.

"You ask too much," he said when he noticed Gregor watching him. "I canna do it."

Gregor waited.

"Would I e'er see him again?" the laird asked, his voice breaking.

"Aye. You may have the lad back at harvest, but if he's not returned, I'll consider it a grievous breach and act accordingly."

MacKinnon grunted and still scowled, but his arms relaxed. Gregor knew him to be a man with a big heart, loyal and fair. All good qualities in a laird, but he lacked the necessary discernment to use them wisely. His son, Gavin, ten years old, mirrored his father in many ways. He could be taught to look beyond the obvious and see people's hearts, judge with his head as well as his emotions.

"I agree," MacKinnon said and leaned toward Gregor. "But if I e'er discover you are abusing my lad, MacLeod, I swear on my life, I will kill you."

Gregor nodded. "As I would you if you harmed my own." He held out his hand to the laird. "I will teach your son well, MacKinnon." The big man hesitated before taking Gregor's hand. MacKinnon would consider it an oath between them until his dying day. Gregor was well pleased.

Last, he turned to Laird MacAlister, seated two down on the left, father of Kerr MacAlister, who was the oldest boy and also ten. He suspected Kerr might be his most difficult charge, but the most rewarding if all went well. He'd never met the lad, but Gregor had heard he stood up to his father, who was a mean, controlling bastard.

MacAlister had instigated the attack against Gregor's clan, persuading or threatening the other lairds to go along with it. Gregor had known in advance they were coming and had trapped his enemies. 'Twas a gamble that had paid off.

"Naught to say, MacAlister?" he asked the last laird.

"You've no sons of your own. Will you be choosing one of the lads to succeed you when you die?"

Gregor was not surprised by the question. "You've already tried to kill me and failed. Doona think you'd be any more successful a second time."

MacAlister shrugged, his greasy, dark hair sliding forward to hide his eyes. "You misunderstand me—"

"I understand you, all right." Gregor pulled his dirk from the table and flung it past MacAlister's ear. A lock of hair drifted down as the knife embedded in a wooden shield mounted on the opposite wall. "As always, you want my land. MacLeod land. You canna have it. Maybe one day your boy will have it, maybe not. I give no promises to anyone here."

He looked around the table at each laird, his gaze hard, unblinking. Finally, he came back to MacAlister. "You will give me your son, or you will give me your life. Choose."

MacAlister's nostrils flared before he nodded.

Gregor placed his hand palm down on the middle of the table, and the lairds followed suit one by one until five palms lay over his. MacAlister was last.

The ache in Gregor's heart eased just a wee bit. His Kellie would have been proud.

One

*Gleann Afraig (Fraser territory)—The Highlands, Scotland
Twenty Years Later*

DARACH MACKENZIE WANTED TO KILL THE FRASERS.
Slowly.

Lying on the forest floor, he peered through the leaves as his enemy rode single file along the trail at the bottom of the ravine. Midway down the line, a woman, tied belly down over a swaybacked horse, appeared to be unconscious. Rope secured her wrists, and a gag filled her mouth. The tips of her long, brown hair dragged on the muddy ground.

In front of her, Laird Fraser rode a white stallion that tossed its head and rubbed against the trees in an attempt to unseat him. The laird flailed his whip, cutting the stallion's flanks in retaliation.

To the front and behind them rode ten more men, heavily armed.

The King had ordered the MacKenzies and Frasers to cease hostilities two years before, and much trouble would come of helping the lass, let alone killing the laird. Still, the idea of doing nothing made Darach's bile rise.

"You canna rescue her without being seen."

The whispered words caused Darach's jaw to set in a stubborn line. He refused to look at his foster brother Lachlan, who'd spoken. "Maybe 'tis not the lass I want to rescue. Did you not see the fine mount under the Fraser filth?" Yet his gaze never left the swing of the lass's hair, her wee hands tied together.

"Fraser would no more appreciate you taking his horse than his woman."

"Bah! She's not his woman—not by choice, I'll wager."

They'd been reaving—a time-honored tradition the King had not mentioned in his command for peace—and could easily escape into the forest unseen with their goods. They'd perfected the procedure to a fine art, sneaking on and off Fraser land for years with bags of wheat, barrels of mead, sheep, and horses.

Never before had they stolen a woman.

He glanced at Lachlan, seeing the same anger and disgust he felt reflected in his foster brother's eyes. "You take the stallion. The laird willna recognize you. I'll get the lass."

Lachlan nodded and moved into position while Darach signaled his men with the distinctive trill of the dipper—three short bursts, high and loud pitched. The MacKenzies spread out through the heavy growth, a nearby creek muffling any sound.

The odds for a successful attack were in their favor. Ten Fraser warriors against Darach, the laird of Clan

MacKenzie; his foster brother Lachlan, the laird of Clan MacKay; and three of Darach's men: Oslow, Brodie, and Gare. Only two to one, and they'd have the element of surprise.

As his enemy entered the trap, Darach mounted his huge, dark-gray stallion named Loki, drew his sword, and let out a second, sharp trill. The men burst through the trees, their horses' hooves pounding.

Two Frasers rode near the lass. Big, dirty men. Men who might have touched her. He plunged his sword into the arm of one, almost taking it off. The man fell to the ground with a howl. The second was a better fighter but not good enough, and Darach sliced open the man's side. Blood and guts spilled out. He keeled over, clutching his body.

Farther ahead, Lachlan struggled to control the wild-eyed stallion. The Fraser laird lay on the ground in front of Darach, and Darach resisted the urge to stomp the devil. He would leave the laird alive, even though he burned to run his sword through the man's black heart. Fraser's sister's too, if she were but alive.

In front of Darach, the mare carrying the lass thrashed around, looking for a means of escape. The ropes that secured the girl loosened, and she began sliding down the beast's side.

Just as her fingers touched the ground, he leaned over and pulled her to safety. Dark, silky hair tumbled over his linen lèine. When the mare jostled them, he slapped it on the rump. The animal sprang forward, missing Fraser by inches.

Damnation.

Placing her limp body across his thighs, Darach used his knees to guide Loki out of the waning melee.

Not one Fraser was left standing.

～

They rode hard to put as much distance as possible between them and the Frasers, and along game trails and creek beds to conceal their tracks as best they could. When Darach felt they were safe, he slowed Loki and shifted the unconscious woman so she sat across his lap. Her head tipped back into the crook of his arm, and he stilled when he saw her sleeping face, bruised but still lovely—like a wee dove.

Dark lashes fanned out against fair cheeks, and a dusting of freckles crossed her nose.

She looked soft, pure.

God knows that meant nothing. He knew better than most a bonny face could hide a black heart.

Slicing through the dirty gag, he hurled it to the ground. Welts had formed at the corners of her mouth, and her lips, red and plump, had cracked. After cutting her hands free, he sheathed his dagger and massaged her wrists. Her cheek was chafed from rubbing against the side of the mare, and a large bruise marred her temple.

His gut tightened with the same fury he'd felt earlier.

Lachlan rode up beside him, the skittish stallion tethered behind his mount. "If you continue to stare at her, I'll wager she'll ne'er wake. Women are contrary creatures, doona you know?"

Darach drew to a stop. "She sleeps too deeply, Brother. 'Tis unnatural. Do you think she'll be all right?" Oslow, Brodie, and Gare gathered 'round. It was the first time they'd seen the lass.

"Is she dead, do you think?" Gare asked, voice scarcely above a whisper. He was a tall, young warrior of seventeen, with the scrawny arms and legs of a lad still building up his muscle.

Oslow, Darach's older, gnarly lieutenant, cuffed Gare on the back of the head. "She's breathing, isna she? Look at the rise and fall of her chest, lad."

"I'll do no such thing. 'Tis not proper. She's a lady, I'll wager. Look at her fine clothes."

Lachlan snorted in amusement and picked up her hand, turning it over to run his fingers across her smooth palm. "I reckon you might be right, Gare. The lass hasn't seen hard labor. 'Tis smooth as a bairn's bottom."

Darach's chest tightened at the sight of her wee hand in Lachlan's. He fought the urge to snatch it back.

"She has stirred some, cried out in her sleep. I pray to God the damage isna permanent." Physically, at least. Emotionally, she could be scarred for life. His arm tightened around her, and she moaned.

"Pass me some water." Someone placed a leather flagon in his hand, and Darach wedged the opening between her lips. When he tilted the container, the water seeped down her cheek. He waited a moment and tried again. This time she swallowed, showing straight, white teeth. Her hand came up and closed over his, helping to steady the flask.

A peculiar feeling fluttered in Darach's chest.

When she made a choking sound, he pulled the flask away. Her body convulsed as she coughed, and

he sat her up to thump her on the back. Upon set-
tling, he laid her back down in the crook of his arm.

"Christ, we doona want to drown her, Darach—
or knock the lungs right out of her. Maybe you
should give her to one of us to hold for a while?"
Lachlan's laughing eyes told Darach his foster
brother deliberately provoked him. Another time-
honored tradition.

Gare jumped in. "Oh, aye. I'll hold the lass."

"You?" Brodie asked. "You canna even hold your
own sword. Do you think those skinny arms will
keep her safe? I'll hold the lass." Brodie was a few
years older than Gare and had already filled out into a
fine-looking man. He was a rogue with the lasses, and
they all loved him for it. No way in hell would he be
holding her.

"Cease. Both of you," said Oslow. "If anyone other
than our laird holds the lass, it will be Laird MacKay.
If she be a lady, she'll not want to be held by the likes
of you."

Darach glowered at Lachlan, who grinned.

Then she stirred, drawing everyone's attention. They
waited as her eyelids quivered before opening. A collective gasp went up from the men, Darach included.

He couldn't help it, for the lass staring up at him had
the eyes of an angel.

They dominated her sweet face—big, round, innocent. And the color—Darach couldn't get over the
color. A piercing, light blue surrounded by a rim of
dark blue.

A shiver of desire, followed by unease, coursed
through him. He tamped down the unwelcome feeling.

"Sweet Mary," Gare whispered. "She's a faery, aye?"

All except Lachlan looked at Darach for confirmation. He cleared his throat before speaking, trying to break the spell she'd cast over him. Not a faery, but maybe a witch.

"Nay, lad," he replied, voice rough. "She's naught but a bonny maid."

"A verra bonny maid," Lachlan agreed.

Her throat moved again, and Darach lifted the flask. Opening her mouth, she drank slowly, hand atop his, eyes never leaving his face. He couldn't look away.

When she'd had enough, she pressed his hand. He removed it, and she stared up at him, blinking slowly and licking her lips. Her pink tongue tempted him, and he quelled the urge to capture it in his mouth.

Then she raised her hand and traced her fingers over his lips and along his nose, caressed his forehead to the scar that sliced through his brow, gently scraped her nails through the whiskers on his jaw.

A more sensual act he'd never experienced, and shivers raced over his skin.

Finally, she spoke. "*Par l'amour de Dieu, etes-vous un ange?*"

❧

Caitlin stared at the beautiful creature gazing down at her. He was magnificent, with flashing brown eyes and a fierce scar. Wavy, chestnut-colored hair framed his face and glinted with red highlights in the sun, emphasizing his tough jaw and soft, touchable lips.

For some reason, an overwhelming sense of peace spread through her. She must be in heaven, and he was a warrior angel. Maybe Michael or Gabriel, sure to wreak justice upon the men who'd abused her.

"*Non, ma petite. Je suis seulement un homme.*"

A man. Her angel said he was but a man.

Beneath her, a horse moved, and she realized she sat on the warrior's lap. The man's strong arms and powerful chest cushioned her. Protected her. She felt like a child held close to his big body.

Nay, not a child. A woman.

He watched her quizzically, and she realized something was amiss. Where was she? Had she been taken across the sea by the man her uncle had given her to?

She glanced at the forest above her. Afternoon sunlight poured through the leaves, but the air was still crisp. "Am I in France?" she asked. The words spilled out in her native Gaelic.

The man looked surprised, then replied in kind. "Nay, lass. You're in the Highlands of Scotland."

"But you spoke French."

"Only because you spoke it first."

"I did?"

"Aye."

Why had she spoken to him in French and what had she said? She tried to remember, but her head ached. Pain radiated down her face. Oh, aye—she'd asked if he was an angel.

"I spoke French because I couldnae remember Latin, and Gaelic seemed too coarse for an angel. English even worse. What angel in his right mind would appreciate being spoken to in English?" She stopped when she realized she was babbling.

The man smiled, and to her delight, a dimple formed in his cheek. "What angel, indeed."

Then a thought occurred to her, and she frowned. "Maybe a fallen angel. He would like the English devils, now wouldnae he?"

Another man laughed, and she realized they weren't alone. Shifting her gaze from the warrior's face, she found herself looking at another handsome Highlander astride a horse. Tall and broad shouldered, his light-brown hair was tied by a leather cord at the nape of his neck. Dark-blue eyes smiled at her from a finely formed face—though not nearly as fine as the man holding her.

"Doona startle her, Lachlan. She's still confused," her savior said gruffly.

"I'm all right, angel. Doona fash."

A young lad leaned forward on his horse, as skinny as he was tall, with a face covered in pimples. "Why'd you think him an angel, lass?"

Two other men on horses gathered 'round. Every one of them stared at her, concern etched on their faces. For the first time since the fire, she felt safe, even though they were strangers.

"Because he saved me. You all saved me." She swallowed and took a deep breath. "And he's so bonny, of course."

The lad went from looking proud to horrified. "Our laird isna bonny. He's fierce and intimidating."

"Oh, aye, I'm sure. But he has such bonny eyes, doona you think? And his hair glints red in the sun. 'Tis verra pretty."

The man named Lachlan laughed again, causing

her warrior's brow to furrow. She reached up and massaged it with her fingers. "Doona glower so. 'Twill cause lines. You doona want to look fierce all the time, now do you?"

The man's eyes widened and the wrinkle disappeared. He appeared uncertain, an emotion she was sure he found bewildering. For some reason, it pleased her.

"What's your name, lass?" he finally asked.

She hesitated, not wanting to give too much away. "Caitlin. What's yours?"

"Darach MacKenzie, laird of Clan MacKenzie." He indicated his men. "This is Oslow, Gare, and Brodie. You're safe with us."

The truth of his statement settled in her bones with a certainty, and the fear and anxiety she'd been living with for the past three years slipped away, leaving her almost giddy.

She could barely contain her happiness as she waited for him to introduce the other man, the one he'd called Lachlan. A familiarity lay between them that did not extend to the others, and she wondered if they were related.

When it became clear Darach had forgotten, she asked, "Are you his brother, then? Lachlan MacKenzie?"

"Aye, we're brothers. Foster brothers. Two of five reared together by the great Gregor MacLeod. But I'm not a MacKenzie. I'm Lachlan MacKay, laird of Clan MacKay." Then his eyes twinkled. "Do you want to ride with me, lass? It's been suggested Darach may be getting tired."

Caitlin clutched Darach's lèine. "Am I too heavy for you, Laird MacKenzie?"

He made a loud, dismissive sound and tightened his arms around her, telling her in no uncertain terms where she would ride.

"I'm not your laird, Caitlin. You will call me Darach."

"Oh, aye. Darach." It was a good name. Soft yet hard. Strong yet gentle. Worthy of the warrior. And the way he said her name—rough and deep—caused warmth to spread through her chest.

"What clan are you, lass?" he asked. "We'll make sure you get home safely. How did you come to be so abused by the dog Fraser?"

The heat inside Caitlin turned to ice, and she stiffened. He wanted to give her back? Nay. 'Twas unthinkable. She'd just escaped.

She closed her eyes, knowing they were the windows to her soul and allowed anyone to discern her thoughts.

"Caitlin?" The worry in Darach's voice compelled her to look at him. "Are you all right?"

She nodded, lips pressed together lest she blurt out the horrible truth and they took her back to Fraser. Or her uncle.

Her clan, her real clan, was dead. That was the truth. By all that was holy, she didn't belong with her uncle or Fraser. She belonged…she belonged… Where did she belong? Maybe she could find her mother's people in France?

Surely she'd be safe there. Her uncle and Fraser wouldn't travel so far to find her.

"I doona rightly know," she said, her heart skittering as she shifted her eyes downward.

"Is it your head, lass?" Oslow asked.

"Aye. 'Tis thumping like a rabbit's back foot when the fox nears."

It was true enough, and she heaved a sigh. Surely exaggeration would not be considered a mortal sin. Besides, she could barely keep her eyes open.

She peeped at Darach through her lashes to see he watched her skeptically. Aye, just like her da—although he didn't feel like her father. And at times he had a look in his eye she'd never seen in her father's eyes. It made her want to burrow into his embrace.

"I've seen these things happen," Oslow continued. "Men taking a blow to the head and not rightly remembering. The lass may ne'er remember, Laird."

Darach exchanged a glance with Lachlan. The MacKay laird shrugged, and Darach returned his gaze to her, expression bland.

"Is that what's happened, Caitlin? You canna remember anything? Other than your name, of course. And how to speak French?"

"Well, things are a bit foggy. Maybe in the morning, my mind will be clear."

Darach stared at her before answering. "Maybe." Then strong fingers gripped her chin and tilted her head.

To her surprise, his eyes had darkened. He released her and traced his fingers over her face, following the same path she'd taken earlier on his face. Her heart swelled and something filled her deep inside.

When he spoke, his voice was grave. "I promise to keep you safe, sweetling. You'll come to no harm while there is breath in my body. I pledge this on the honor of the MacKenzies."

Two

DARACH WANTED TO KILL THE LASS—OR AT LEAST TOSS her in the loch and end his misery.

As weak as she'd been yesterday, today she wouldn't sit still, rubbing her soft ass against the vee of his thighs as she squirmed in front of him on Loki, craning to look at the view through a break in the trees, turning to talk to the others, reaching for the stallion they'd stolen from Fraser.

He was in a state of perpetual arousal, and it was apparent she was oblivious to it, unaware she excited him something fierce when she touched his thigh or leaned forward to whisper in his steed's ear. If they were alone, and if she were willing, he'd lift her skirts and plunge deep inside.

She wriggled again just as he imagined her soft, wet channel surrounding him, and his cock swelled so tight it was all he could do not to cry out.

Aye, he would tup her good and hard till she stopped squirming and moved her hips with his. Or maybe he'd spread her so wide she couldn't move at all, just accept his hard length until she reached her peak and convulsed around him.

And she would. He knew it as surely as he knew his own name. Caitlin was a very curious woman.

They'd camped last night beside a loch high in the mountains, taking a long loop back through the forest in hopes of confusing any trackers. The conflict would come—Darach longed for it to come—but for now, he would take the time to see Caitlin safe.

She'd succumbed again to that unnatural sleep right after he'd given her his pledge, failing to wake even as they dismounted. He'd wrapped her in his extra blanket and laid her by the fire, then settled close to her. When she cried out in the night, flinging wide his blanket, he reached for her immediately. Her limbs trembled and heat poured off her body, her dress soaked in sweat. She looked around, unable to focus, her big, blue eyes glassy.

"Darach!"

"I'm here, lass."

"Darach!"

"Hush, Caitlin. I have you. You're going to be all right."

A strong smell issued from her body—an herb of some sort. He'd smelled it many times in the sick-rooms after a battle.

Christ Almighty, not only had they hit her, they'd drugged her too. The devil help them if they'd raped her. He'd kill every one of them.

"We need to cool her. The fever is too hot," Lachlan said.

Lifting her gently, Darach hurried with her toward the loch. Removing neither his boots nor his plaid, he splashed into the icy water, then lowered her beneath the waves.

He'd taken off her shoes earlier but had left on her hose and arisaid for warmth. Now the wool dress was soaked. She'd need something dry in the morning when she recovered—and she would recover. He'd given her his oath to keep her safe.

Unfastening the brooch on her breast, the pleats came loose. The garment floated away, leaving only her linen chemise. He removed her hose, gathered her arisaid, and tossed them onto the shore. Gare and Brodie picked up the wet clothing.

"Hang them to dry by the fire and bring me a blanket." His men returned to camp, leaving Lachlan on the narrow beach.

"Shall I join you, Brother?" he asked.

"Nay, Lachlan. She's barely decent. She wouldnae want another man to see her like this."

The lines of her body showed through the garment that covered her. He distantly noted how wee she was, although she was long past the age of childhood— twenty, maybe younger. Her breasts were well formed, with dark areolas and protruding nipples, her waist small, her hips rounded. Her woman's mound showed against the wet chemise.

He concentrated on her flushed face, tilting her head back to soak her hair. The dark strands floated around her like she was an ancient sea nymph. Seductive. Alluring. His fingers ran through the silky tresses as he murmured all would be well, she'd be safe with him at clan MacKenzie. Cupping his hand, he scooped up water and trickled it over her brow.

She gasped and looked at him, her eyes focused.

"Darach?"

"Aye, love. I'm here."

Her fingers clutched his chest. "Doona leave me."

"I'll not leave you, lass. I promised you, aye?"

She gazed at him a moment, then relaxed. Her eyes closed and her breathing deepened as the heat left her. Darach caressed her face. She turned her cheek into his palm.

Once more during the night, he did this. She was sick too, emptying what little was in her stomach. By sunrise, her color was better and her eyes bright. She slept late into the morning, waking with a hunger to rival Gare's, demolishing a good share of apples, cheese, and oats as she sat by the fire.

"Even the porridge tastes good," she said, her smile lighting up her face. It drew him in like the blazing sun. "My mother made pastries that puffed up as they cooked, but she always made me eat my oats first. For a good constitution, aye?"

He could do naught but nod in agreement. She had a childlike enthusiasm that endeared her to the men, somehow seemingly unaffected by her treatment at the hands of the Frasers.

A sweet, pliable lass...until she had seen Fraser's white devil-horse tethered at the edge of camp. With an excited yell, she'd run toward it. Darach's heart pounded as he raced after her. He caught her just as the stallion reared and slashed at them with his hooves, missing her by inches. He pulled her back, blood coursing through his veins.

"By the love of Christ, lass, are you trying to kill yourself? Or me? My heart nearly stopped."

"Cloud would ne'er hurt me."

"Cloud?"

"The stallion. He rose up because you were running behind me. You gave him a fright. He's a verra sensitive horse."

The lass blamed *him* for almost getting them killed?

"And 'tis most ungodly to take our Savior's name in vain. 'Tis a commandment, doona you know?" She placed her hands on her hips and tilted her head to look him in the eye. "What will you do when you're standing in front of Saint Michael? Tell him you're a blasphemer?"

His men, including Lachlan, had stopped to watch, eyes wide and, in Gare's case, jaw dropped.

Darach heard Lachlan laugh, then mutter, "Christ Almighty."

Caitlin heard as well, for she spun toward him. "Laird MacKay, didn't your mother teach you anything? The angels desert you every time you curse. I hope for your sake they're still there when the devil comes-a-calling."

Darach would have let her continue just to see Lachlan on the receiving end of her pointed finger, but they'd tarried long enough.

"Caitlin, hush." A command he knew he'd be repeating often. "We're leaving now."

She gazed at Cloud and stepped toward him. Darach blocked her way. He gave her a stare that had intimidated the fiercest warriors. "You willna touch the stallion. You ride with me."

She looked over at Loki, standing proud in the morning sun, his coat glossy, his mane and tail a darker gray than the rest of him. "He's certainly a bonny lad," she said, then walked over and leaned into his side, waiting for him to acknowledge her. Finally he did, and when he huffed at her, she huffed back. He swished his tail and she laughed. "What's his name?"

"Loki."

Her eyes widened. "After the trickster god?"

"Aye, he was a mischievous colt. You had to stay one step ahead of him like Odin with Loki, or disaster would strike."

"Surely not." When he nodded, her eyes danced. "Are you Odin, then?"

He tried not to smile. "Maybe." Moving beside her, he laced his fingers together for her to use as a step. "Mount up, lass."

She did, putting her foot in his hands and swinging her leg over Loki's back. Darach averted his eyes as her skirt rode up her leg, but he couldn't help glimpsing silken hose over a slender calf. He grabbed the reins and quickly swung up behind her.

That's when the real trouble began.

Half a day of her squirming on Loki in front of him. Smelling fresh and clean like the loch with a touch of woodsmoke, like the flowers and leaves she picked from the trees along the way. Smelling like a woman. Like Caitlin.

'Twas a god-awful torture.

"Verily, Lachlan, you donna care to marry?" Caitlin leaned around Darach as she spoke to the MacKay laird, nudging Darach's shaft as she did so. It pulsed eagerly, and he gritted his teeth.

"Nay. 'Tis not in the stars for me, lass."

"But surely you like women?"

Lachlan snorted. "Aye, I like women."

"You willna speak on this with the lass," Darach interrupted, pushing a branch out of the way so it wouldn't scrape her. "She's too innocent for such talk."

"I'm not that innocent, Darach. I grew up on a farm."

His arms tightened around her of their own accord, thinking of what she might know about tupping. She leaned back against him. It surprised and pleased him to hear her humming a light, happy song. Surely a lass who'd been carnally abused wouldn't be so merry.

"I am lucky you found me, Darach. I wouldnae have liked being with the Frasers. They treated me poorly."

Darach's heart stilled. "Aye, lass. But you were unconscious for most of it, were you not?"

"Aye. But they dragged me along, and the laird hit me about the head. 'Twas not a pleasant experience. But if it led me to the MacKenzies, 'tis a blessing in disguise." Her arms covered Darach's as they held her around her middle, and she absently caressed him. "I am verra pleased to have met you. 'Tis an honorable clan you lead. I will do my best to be worthy of you all."

The swelling in his chest caught him by surprise, and he had to clear his throat. He glanced around and saw the other men so affected.

When he spoke, his voice was rough. "You are worthy, lass. No matter what might have happened to you, you are worthy. Doona e'er forget that. It will honor us to punish the men who dared touch you."

Caitlin slowed her caress, then stopped. She made a sound of understanding and her cheeks flushed. "Och, doona fash, any of you. They did not do what you're thinking. I have ne'er been…violated in such a way. I was too valuable a prize. And if I had, I would certainly not blame myself, though it warms me to hear you speak so."

Relief crashed through Darach, and a heaviness lifted from his heart. He heard the others sigh and knew they felt the same. Anger soared again when he thought about her ordeal, but this time it wasn't weighed down by the dread of rape.

"We will still punish the blackguards, aye? You were fair sick last night. You might ne'er have woken."

Gare rode up beside them. "And they hit you right hard, lass. Your face is swollen like a dead dog."

Darach ground his teeth at the lad's idiot remark. Caitlin lifted a hand to her cheek. "Is it that bad? I would hate to meet your clan looking like a poor, deceased animal."

"Aye, it is most unsightly." Then he caught Darach's gaze and lost his smile. He hurried to the front of the line.

"'Tis not true, Caitlin," Brodie said, ever the charmer. "You look like a bonny lass with a wee bruise, that's all."

Oslow patted her knee. "Aye, and it will rouse the heart of every MacKenzie you meet. 'Tis a badge of honor, lass."

Caitlin smiled. "'Twas my good fortune you were on Fraser land. Were you visiting?"

"Nay. The Frasers have been our enemy nigh on eight years, e'er since our laird's father died. They are lying scoundrels and broke an alliance, causing death and hardship to many MacKenzies. But Laird Darach, even as a young man of only twenty, saw through their treachery and saved us."

Caitlin turned to Darach. "Twenty? You were scarce older than me. Much too young for such responsibility."

"I was not a lad, but a laird. I had my people to protect."

She nodded and squeezed his thigh with her fingers. He suppressed a shudder as heat spread out from her touch.

"As you protect me. You are a fine laird indeed, Darach MacKenzie."

Pleasure welled at her words, but he suppressed it. It didn't matter if the lass found him worthy. He had given Caitlin his pledge to protect her, nothing else. Since it was obvious she didn't care to return to her clan, that meant keeping her—and keeping his hands off her.

But he needed to know what had happened that she'd come to be in Fraser's brutal care. She'd lied to him about not remembering, frightened to give too much away, and he'd let it be. But those lies may put his clan in danger, and that he couldn't let be.

She stopped chattering, and the ensuing peace was much welcome, but after a while, he began to worry. It was not like her to be so silent, to sit sedately in her seat. He jostled her, but she said nothing.

"Are you sleeping, lass?" he whispered.

She didn't answer for a time. When she did, she sounded wistful. "Nay. I was thinking if you've been laird for eight years, there must be a lady and bairns in your home."

Oslow snorted. "Our laird no more wants a wife than Laird MacKay. 'Tis a right fankle."

Caitlin spun around, and he suddenly regretted rousing her.

"You doona want a wife either?"

"Nay."

"But why e'er not? Surely you jest."

"Nay."

"But 'tis your duty to provide an heir, wouldnae you agree?"

"Nay." His voice was firmer this time, discouraging further conversation. Her mouth dropped open and Darach could see her small, pink tongue. Never had he found a tongue so enticing. Then she started lecturing. She had yet to understand he wasn't a man to be pressed.

"But you must. Think of your family. Think of your clan."

He fisted his hand on his thigh. His desire for a wife and child had almost destroyed his clan eight years ago. He would never make that mistake again. Fraser's sister, Moire, had led him by his cock as well as his heart, and he still fought the shame of it.

Women were all right in general. They had their place—preferably beneath him—but he didn't want one beside him ever again. He would pick his successor from one of the fine, young MacKenzie men he'd trained.

"A good wife is essential for your happiness," she continued. "Someone to love and lean on. She'll take care of your heart as well as your home."

Darach stopped listening. The idea of leaning on anyone made him shudder.

He decided to go on the offensive—a trick he'd learned from the MacLeod. "What clan are you, Caitlin?"

She hesitated, eyes darting from his. "What?"

"You said you were raised on a farm, so you must remember something." It was well past time he had some answers.

"Oh, well, that's not important now, is it? We were talking about you."

"Nay, you were talking about me. I was asking about your clan. What's your father's name, your mother's name?"

She lowered her gaze, and he saw her chin tremble. "My father's name was Wallace. My mother's was Claire."

"Claire isna a Scot's name. Is that why you speak French? Did your mother hail from France?"

"Aye."

"And have they passed?"

"In a fire when I was sixteen. They ne'er made it out of the cottage."

Darach's arms tightened around her. "I'm sorry, lass. 'Tis not easy to lose a parent."

She sighed. "I'm sorry too. I shouldnae press you on your marital decision, howe'er misguided it be. 'Tis not one you would make lightly, I'm sure."

He suppressed a grin. "I'm sure."

It was well into the afternoon when they stopped for a rest in a clearing near a small loch. Caitlin groaned as she slipped off Darach's stallion and rubbed her bottom.

Entranced by the sight of her kneading the tender flesh, he couldn't look away. She noticed, and a blush covered her cheeks. "It has been many moons since I've ridden such a distance."

Even her embarrassment enticed him. *Idiot*.

"Stay close so we can hear if there's trouble."

Her gaze strayed to the stallion, fighting with Brodie for dominance by a thicket of trees.

"And doona touch the devil-horse." When she nodded absently, he suppressed a sigh and wheeled Loki toward the loch. It was all he could do not to look back.

At the water's edge, he wasted no time dismounting, lifting his plaid, and walking in up to his waist, desperately needing respite for his privates. He knew he could take himself in hand—it would have been easier—but it somehow seemed wrong.

As the hardness and heat seeped from his loins, his breathing eased.

"Trouble, Brother?"

Darach checked to make sure Lachlan was alone on the shore before answering. "Aye. You try having that sweet arse rubbing between your thighs for half a day."

His foster brother laughed so hard he bent over at the waist and had to gasp for air. Grinning, Darach waded back to the rocky beach. His plaid lay flat for the first time since Caitlin had mounted his horse.

"If you like, I'll ask her to ride with me."

"You'll do no such thing."

Lachlan erupted into laughter again. Darach perched on a rock and waited for his foster brother to control himself. They had important matters to discuss.

"Are you through?" he asked when Lachlan settled down.

"Aye. And she does have a sweet arse."

"You've no idea."

It was another five minutes before they could talk seriously.

"What do you make of it?" Darach asked.

"Fraser either kidnapped her or she was given to him—maybe as a bride. Either way 'twas foul."

"Aye. Makes me wonder who did the giving. She doesn't care to tell me her clan, so 'twas likely her laird. I've heard such stories."

"You could force the truth from her."

"Maybe in time, but I want the lass to trust me enough to tell me on her own. If I'm to be her new laird—"

"I thought you didn't care to be her laird?" Lachlan wore a sly grin.

Darach grunted in response, then sighed. "'Tis a conundrum. All I know is we'll prepare for battle— her clan or the Frasers may try to force her return, and she doesn't wish to go back."

"Aye." Lachlan tossed a stone into the loch. The sound echoed forlornly around them. "'Tis a shame she lost her parents. Do you think the fire was deliberately set?"

"I've seen much evil in this world. It wouldnae surprise me."

Lachlan tossed another stone. "Have you thought on marrying the lass? She needs a home. A protector. And you seem sorely taken with her."

"I'll marry right around the time you decide to marry."

Lachlan grinned. "Maybe I'll marry her and then you'll be forced to marry someone else."

He no longer found his brother amusing. "You'll do no such thing."

'Twas also becoming a frequent command.

Sitting on a stump in the woods a wee distance from the clearing where they'd stopped, Caitlin dropped her head to her knees and squeezed her eyes shut. She needed a good cry. Her mother had taught her to never bottle her emotions, and indulging in a self-pitying sniffle now and then always made her feel better.

Ever since she'd thought on Darach being married with bairns, her stomach had churned, and it hurt to take a deep breath. Then to find out he didn't have a wife because he didn't want one had thrown her into a right fankle. What kind of a man didn't want a wife? Her father had adored her mother, although he often said that someday Caitlin would cause a young man as much trouble as her mother had caused him. But he'd never been angry when he'd said it. Nay, usually he would kiss her mother afterward.

She remembered those days fondly. It was only after the fire things had changed.

Her uncle had taken her to the keep and set a guard on her. In the beginning she didn't care; her grief had been all consuming. She'd wished she'd died with her parents. Certainly she'd desired such an end when she'd been handed over to Fraser in exchange for gold—contracts signed in the devil's own blood, no doubt.

Now she was glad she'd survived her ordeal.

She pictured Darach staring down at her from Loki—his wide chest, muscular arms, and strong thighs beneath his plaid. Her fingers twitched as she remembered playing with the hair on his legs and forearms—the fascinating feel of him, rough and smooth. Her fingers had often found their way to his exposed skin.

In her mind's eye, he smiled, and that dimple in his cheek sent her stomach dipping. Heat washed over her, and she shook her head. Darach had offered her help, not love and marriage—and even if he had, she couldn't accept. Fraser and her uncle had killed those dreams.

Nay, she had the right of it yesterday. She needed to find the only family she had left—in France. Make a home with them, preferably as far away from her uncle as possible.

If she could get to Inverness, then she could cross to the mainland and begin her search. She knew her mother's maiden name—surely someone would remember a young Claire Fournier from Lyon marrying a Scot named Wallace MacInnes.

A muffled chirping caught her attention, and she looked up. The sound came from the bottom of a tall tree. She hurried toward it and pushed aside twigs and pine needles to reveal a baby bird lying on the forest floor.

The poor dear peered up at her, its cries pitiful.

She knew just how it felt.

Wanting desperately to hold it, she put her arms behind her back. Her mother had taught her never to touch a baby bird if she could avoid it. Instead, she should use something to return it to the nest and hope its mother would continue to care for it.

The nest was up high, and no branches grew beneath for her to climb. She could stand on Cloud, but even then she wouldn't reach.

Cursing her wee size, she lifted her skirts and ran back for Darach, praying the little bird would stay safe till her return.

When last she'd seen her warrior, he'd been heading toward the loch on the other side of camp. Topping the rise, she saw him on the shore speaking with Lachlan, and her heart lifted. They looked up as she careened toward them.

"What's happened? Are you hurt?" Darach roared, rushing to meet her.

She shook her head but couldn't get enough air to speak. Instead, she grabbed his hand and pulled him back the way she'd come. Lachlan followed, and they ran into Gare, Brodie, and Oslow.

"What troubles you, lass? You must speak to me," Darach demanded.

"'Tis a… I need… You must…" She tried to complete a sentence but had no breath. The other men fanned out vigilantly and Darach pulled her to a stop.

"Nay," she said. "Come with me. Hurry."

She tugged again on his arm, and he complied. They reached the spot in the trees where the bird had fallen. Letting go of his hand, she crouched down to check on it. It chirped and looked up at her.

"Ah, wee birdie," she said between breaths. "'Twill be all right. Darach's here now." Turning back, she smiled at him. "It fell from its nest. I canna reach. Perhaps if you stand on Loki you can see it home safely."

Darach stared at her, disbelief etched into every line of his face. "A bird? This is about a bird?"

"A baby bird," she said. "It needs our help."

He closed his mouth. A tiny muscle jumped in his jaw. "MacKenzies, to me!"

The bird chirped with alarm.

"Shush, Darach. You're frightening it."

Turning away, he fisted his hands on his hips. The MacKenzies and Lachlan appeared from the forest.

"Caitlin has found a bird," he said, voice clipped.

"A baby bird," she corrected.

His shoulders tensed, but he didn't turn around. "Apparently it has fallen from its nest."

Gare came forward to squat beside Caitlin on the damp ground. "Och, it be a baby all right." He reached a finger toward it and Caitlin slapped his hand.

"Doona touch! The mother willna like its smell."

Lachlan snorted, and she looked up at him.

"'Tis true, my mother was a healer of animals and taught me well. 'Tis best if we place the bird in the nest without contact."

Darach turned to her. She smiled at him. He didn't smile back.

"And how do you propose we do that?" he asked.

"Well, you're a big man. You can reach the nest if you stand on Loki."

He took a while answering. "What I doona understand is why you didn't tell me this at the loch?" His voice rose, and he stopped to take a breath. "Why were you running like brigands were on your heels and wont to steal you at any moment?"

"'Tis a baby. It could have been eaten."

"Makes sense to me, Brother." Lachlan leaned over the bird for a closer look. "I'll do it for you, Caitlin. Verily, I'm as tall as Darach and much stronger."

"I'll do it," Darach snapped and pushed Lachlan out of the way. "Gare, fetch my horse."

"Aye, Laird."

The lad ran toward the clearing, and Darach crouched beside Caitlin, sifting through the leaves. "Are you going to save all the creatures we come upon?"

"Nay. Just this wee birdie."

He made a skeptical sound and picked up a hard, wide piece of bark that was concave in the center. "Will this do?"

Upon her nod, he gently wedged it beneath the chick and passed it to her. Gare returned with Loki, and Darach mounted beneath the tree, then rose to his feet. The stallion huffed, but it was too well trained to move. Caitlin handed the bird to Darach, who stretched as high as he could, but he was just shy of the nest.

Caitlin expelled her breath heavily. They needed a taller horse.

"Doona fash, lass. We'll save your chick. I havnae come this far to be defeated."

"What if you were to stand on Cloud? He's taller than Loki."

"The devil-horse?" Brodie asked. "He'd not stand still for a mare in heat."

Oslow scratched his head. "What if you were to toss the bird? Surely you wouldnae miss?"

"Nay! I forbid it," she said.

The MacKenzies turned to her, dismayed. Darach looked resigned. Lachlan smiled.

"You canna forbid your laird," Gare said.

She raised her chin. "I just did, and he's not my laird. He told me so himself."

"I wasn't going to toss it, Caitlin, but if I had, I wouldnae have missed."

The men turned away to contemplate the situation. Caitlin knew they were going to make a muck of it.

No one noticed when she hurried back to the clearing and approached Cloud. He danced around some, then settled at Caitlin's soothing words. A food pack stood nearby, and she fished out an apple. The horse's ears perked up. Caitlin had fed him treats whenever she could at her uncle's stable.

She untied the halter from the tree and led him toward the men. Truly, she was pleased with herself.

Darach was the first to notice her. "Nobody move," he said, voice low.

The men looked around, and sounds of concern filled the air. When Cloud stamped his feet, Oslow said a quick prayer to the Virgin Mary.

"Caitlin, step away from the horse," Darach said.

"You just told me not to move."

"Step away from the horse. Now."

Caitlin stepped toward the men and Cloud followed, snuffling her shoulder for more apples. She stroked his nose. "He's taller than your mount, doona you see? If you stand on him, you could reach the nest. I'll hold him for you. I'm sure he willna mind." She turned her head to the stallion. "Will you, love?" The horse nuzzled her again.

Darach slid from his mount and approached her slowly.

"Let him get used to you," she said. "He doesn't like men. My uncle brutalized horses."

When he reached her, he pulled her close. She turned

in his arms, back toward Cloud. The stallion whickered nervously, and she placed a piece of apple in Darach's hand, which he hesitantly raised to the stallion's mouth. Cloud responded by huffing and throwing his head.

"Doona fash," she said to Darach. "The calmer you are, the calmer he'll be."

She felt Darach's chest expand against her back and the tension ebb away as he released his breath. Cloud huffed again and took the apple.

"See?" she said with a laugh. "He's really just an angel."

After feeding him another piece of fruit, Darach grasped the reins. "All right. We'll try it your way."

Brodie moved Loki and they led Cloud beneath the tree. Holding the stallion's head, Caitlin spoke soft, gentle words to him as Darach mounted.

After dancing around halfheartedly, Cloud calmed and looked for more apple. Gare handed Darach the chick, and he easily placed it in its nest, then came back down.

He pulled Caitlin away from the horse. The stallion tried to follow, but Lachlan distracted him with treats. Darach placed her on his mount's back and climbed up behind her—all without speaking. Hardly even looking at her.

Unease whispered up her spine. "Darach, I—"

"Doona speak if you know what's good for you."

"But I—"

He twisted her around to face him, eyes narrow, mouth drawn tight. "I told you not to touch the stallion. I told you he was dangerous. Have you any idea what it did to me to see you standing there with him at your shoulder?"

Releasing her, he urged Loki into the clearing. The other men had mounted and were waiting. They silently fell into line and headed along the trail.

Caitlin was hard pressed not to cry, and a familiar panic tightened her chest. She'd caused nothing but trouble from the moment she'd met the MacKenzies. Like as not, Darach would return her to her uncle the first moment he could. 'Twas a grim imagining, and she choked back a sob.

She couldn't go back.

He sighed and his arm came around her, gentle and comforting. She leaned back into his embrace, and her anxiety eased. Maybe it would be all right. Maybe he would still help her get to Inverness and on a ship, so she could find her mother's family.

"Darach," she whispered.

"Aye."

"I'm sorry I worried you. I promise I'll ne'er cause trouble again."

Three

SHE FOUND THE KITTENS THE NEXT MORNING.

The first anguished meow reached her ears when she was picking wild berries for breakfast in the valley where they'd slept. Four kittens, about five weeks old, hungry and scared, crawled over their mother's dead body beneath a crumbling log.

'Twas a pitiful state that Caitlin well knew. The MacKenzie castle was but a half-day's ride. It'd be no trouble to take them, no trouble at all.

Hovering on the edge of camp with the full cape of her arisaid bunched together in the front and the kittens inside, she searched for Darach. She couldn't see him or Lachlan anywhere.

A purr vibrated through her chest, and unable to resist, she peeked inside. The kittens roused, mewing and tumbling over one another. Her heart swelled as their wee tongues and soft paws tickled her face, their fur soft as velvet. She'd longed for a pet all those lonely nights at her uncle's home.

"Caitlin."

She jumped and turned to find Darach and Lachlan

standing behind her, looking big and brawny in the sun. The kittens batted against her arisaid.

Lachlan cocked an eyebrow at the commotion.

Darach's brows slanted inward. "Nay."

"What do you mean, nay?" she asked with growing alarm.

"I willna have cats in my home. I doona like them."

"I doona have any cats."

He stared at her a moment, then reached forward and tugged open the folds of her arisaid. The kittens blinked in the bright sunlight.

"Nor will I abide deceit."

"'Tis not a falsehood. They're kittens, not cats."

"Kittens need their mother. You will return them to their den."

He turned and strode into the clearing toward the horses.

Caitlin ran after him, dogging his heels. "Their mother is dead, and the kits are too young to survive. I'm taking them with me, Darach. 'Tis the godly thing to do."

"The godly thing to do is to leave them to their fate—survive if they can, provide sustenance for other animals if they cannot."

She stopped, aghast. "I'll not abandon the babies to die. If you leave them, you'll leave me too."

He turned. That muscle jumped in his cheek. "They're not babies, Caitlin. They're kittens. They smell and skulk around. I doona like animals that skulk."

"Have you ne'er had a cat? They're loving and playful. And verra useful in a keep."

"Nay."

"But—"

"My dogs will eat them."

Relief flooded through her. He was just worried lest they be hurt. "Doona fash, Darach. I willna allow your beasties to hurt my babies."

He made a disbelieving sound she'd come to know quite well. "How do you plan to stop them?"

"With training and discipline. Same as all animals."

"You think you can train my devils? They're bigger than you."

"Size doesn't matter. They will want to please me and therefore do as I ask."

"That sounds familiar," Lachlan said from behind her.

She ignored him, but Darach did not. His shoulders tensed further. He glared at her another moment then mounted his horse. The others did the same.

He looked down at her. "Choose, Caitlin."

"What?"

"I said, choose."

Her heart beat like the wings of a tiny bird caught in her chest. How could Darach do such a thing? "I canna."

His hands fisted on the reins, then he wheeled away from her. "We ride!"

❧

Darach kneed Loki, and the stallion cantered across the green meadow. She would call him back. Any minute now, Caitlin would cry out his name. He would even be charitable and allow her to take the kittens. Maybe give them to the miller or house them in the grain stores to catch the mice. Truly, he did not like cats and would not abide them underfoot. A demon of a cat had dwelled in his home when he was a child. The beast would stalk him around the dark passageways. It was a happy day when the fiend finally passed over to its devil father.

His arms were empty without Caitlin riding with him, his body cold. He wanted to turn back, reassure himself she was all right, but he gritted his teeth and kept forward. She would call him back. She had to. Slowing, he gave her more time, let her see them leaving the glen.

The lass could not be allowed to ignore his wishes. He was laird, a warrior, not some lowly kitchen boy. To ask him about the kits was one thing. To tell him, another. He would not be led by the cockstrings ever again.

When they reached the edge of the glen, his stomach twisted. He sweated with the strain of continuing to move forward. She would call him back.

"Lachlan?" he asked through clenched teeth.

"She's all right," he responded. "Right where you left her, still holding the kits. More than likely crying her eyes out."

His chest squeezed. *Damnation.* He would not be led by the heartstrings either.

Oslow moved up beside him. "Darach, lad, 'tis all right to yield to the lass. She's not Moire. She will cause you trouble, all right, but not the same kind. There isna a bad bone in her body. I think she's learned her lesson."

"I saw wolf tracks," Gare said. "The crying will draw them to her."

"Or the Frasers," added Brodie. "And she doesn't have a horse to get away. If you'd at least left her Cloud, she might have a chance."

Still Darach rode, leading the party into the woods.

"Och, for Christ's sake, go get her," Lachlan exploded, no longer amused. "You've lasted longer than any of us would have. Didn't I tell you women were contrary? She's going to win no matter what. It's the curse of men. We're bigger and stronger, yet one wee lass can topple us all."

Darach stopped but didn't turn around. His stomach was a mass of knots and his heart thundered in his chest. If she had just called him back.

Lachlan suddenly tilted up his chin and howled like a wolf.

The sound gutted Darach, and he glared at his foster brother. He lasted one more second, then spun his mount toward the glen and Caitlin. Relief at seeing her standing in the field flooded through him, and he calculated how long it would take to reach her, if he could get there before any blasted wolf or wild boar or Fraser appeared. He urged Loki faster.

She ran toward him through the grass, the kittens still wrapped in her arisaid. Her silky hair streamed behind her, and her cheeks shone wetly. "You left me! You promised ne'er to leave me!"

He circled and leaned down. "Hold the kittens tight." Then he scooped her into his arms. Never had a woman felt so good against him.

He felt her body heave as she sucked in a shaky breath. Guilt for leaving her and making her cry made his skin tighten. "I'll ne'er leave again. I promise. The kits will have a good home, as will you. Doona fash, sweetling. 'Tis all right."

Her breathing calmed with his soothing words, and her shudders reduced to the odd hiccup. They moved slowly toward the others, grouped at the edge of the glen. She waved, and they waved back.

"Darach."

"Aye."

"You ne'er really left, did you?"

"No. I ne'er really left."

She turned her head to the side and leaned her cheek against his chest. Her face tilted toward him and the need to kiss her lips beat like a winter storm within him.

"Verily, I'm glad. 'Twas something my father would do when I was a bairn. Leave me in hopes I would follow. Or maybe to teach me a lesson. In truth, I am a trial, I know it well."

Darach grunted. He tried to look away from her mouth, still wet from her tears, and failed.

"I knew you would come."

"Did you, now?"

"Oh, aye. You're my angel."

The kittens mewed, and she cooed to them, kissing their faces and letting them suck her fingers. Darach closed his eyes and listened. For the first time in a long time, he didn't see the faces of all the dead MacKenzies in his mind's eye—killed by Moire and Fraser, by him for being too blind to see their black hearts.

Maybe it would work out with Caitlin. She would be safe with him, and he would enjoy having a woman around to see to his comforts, to calm him at the end of the day.

He rested his chin atop her head.

"Darach?"

"Aye."

"I will name each kitten after one of the four cardinal virtues: Prudence, Justice, Fortitude, and Temperance. That way, whene'er you hear their names called, you'll be reminded on how to get into Heaven."

The peace inside him evaporated. The blasted cats were not welcome in his home.

"Darach?" she asked again.

"Aye." Wariness tinged the word.

"Have you mice in your keep? The kits are fair good at catching vermin."

⁓

"Just be thankful there weren't seven of them," Lachlan said, tossing a stone into the loch. "Elsewise she'd have named them after the seven deadly sins, and you'd be calling for Gluttony, Greed, Envy, and Sloth."

"Och, doona forget Pride and Wrath," said Oslow.

"Or Lust," Darach added roughly.

They were almost home and had stopped to water the horses. Darach had immediately entered the loch to cool his privates. It was a humiliating experience that, again, had Lachlan bowled over with laughter. Darach had no doubt his other foster brothers would soon hear of his ordeal.

Oslow had joined them afterward, and they were enjoying a peaceful rest on MacKenzie land in the late-afternoon sun. Caitlin, Brodie, and Gare were in a field a short distance away, playing with the kittens. Caitlin was trying to decide which kitten exhibited which virtue, to be so named. Darach had yet to tell her the kits were going to the miller.

"She's a bonny lass," Oslow said, picking up on Darach's previous statement, "but she's not for tupping, no matter the state of your loins. Unless you marry her, of course, then you can bed her whene'er you want. She'd give you fine sons, no doubt."

Darach did not want to think about tupping Caitlin. He'd just cooled his privates—although talk of marriage should keep his cock soft.

"I'll not be marrying the lass, Oslow, but if I did, she'd more than likely give me daughters. All of them looking like her, causing trouble. I'd be an old man in my grave before I was forty."

"Nay. She'd give you sons. Braw lads as strong-minded and fearless as her. But if you're not interested in the lass, I'll introduce her to my Angus. He needs a wife, and I'm sure he'd be as smitten with her as Gare and Brodie."

The blood heated in Darach's veins, flushing his face. He looked toward the field, trying to make out what Caitlin and the two younger men were doing. Naught of consequence. Just playing with the kittens.

Playing with the kittens—*like hell*. Brodie was a right rogue with the lasses, and Gare was such a pitiful lad, caught betwixt man and boy, she'd want to save him just like she'd saved the baby bird. Most likely he'd try to make himself look as pathetic as possible with the hopes of ensnaring her, the devil.

Darach stood abruptly and made his way across the rocky shore to the field. Lachlan's snort followed him. Sure enough, Gare and Brodie sat beside her, hanging on to every word. Scoundrels, both of them. He frowned, and they jumped to their feet. *Let Caitlin see who was master and laird here—the most dominant MacKenzie male.*

After sending them to Oslow, he sat on the grass beside her. She looked pleased to see him. Maybe now would be the time to tell her the kittens were going to the miller. He willed himself to begin, but one of the cats tumbled into his lap and mewed up at him. *Bloody fiend.*

"Och, would you look at that. He loves you, Darach. Maybe he will be called Justice, for he is drawn to you, and you are the most just man I know."

He puffed up and deflated at the same time. 'Twas a good decision to send the cats to the miller. Not only did it show Justice, but also Prudence, Fortitude, and Temperance. Surely she would see the right of it.

The kit ran up his body and batted his hair. Darach started in surprise. Grabbing it, he held the wee thing in front of him. The cat reached out and swatted his chin.

Caitlin fell sideways onto the grass, laughing. "You've ne'er had a cat before, have you?"

Darach grunted and brought the kitten closer. He had to admit it was sweet—big eyes and downy, soft fur. It suckled the stubble of his beard, and his heart turned over.

"They're starved, poor babies," she said. "He's trying to nurse. All we had was water. It helped, but their bellies are empty."

There would be lots of milk at the miller's.

"Caitlin, I doona think…"

She gazed at him, her eyes wide, trusting. A happy

glow surrounded her, and the words stuck in his throat. Maybe she could keep the kits until they were old enough to be on their own. House them in the kitchens and out of his sight and the sight of his dogs for a week or two. Then they could go to the miller.

"Aye, Darach?"

"'Tis naught, lass. We'll be home soon and they can have their meal."

Picking up a kitten, she held it close. "I think this little lass will be Temperance, for she's the only female and needs to have much restraint to live with three brothers. It must be a trial, doona you think?"

"I lived with four brothers, and aye, 'twas a trial."

A wistful look crossed her face. "I did so wish for a brother. Or a sister. But my parents were not blessed with bairns after me. Instead, I had lots of pets—cats, dogs, horses, and pigs."

"Pigs?"

"Aye, pigs are wonderful pets. Although I caused such a fankle when my father wanted to butcher the dear thing, I was ne'er allowed to bond with a pig again."

"And what happened to it?"

"I doona know. I lost more than just my parents the night of the fire. Verily, 'twas a torment. I longed for pets after that, but I feared to show favor to any creature, lest my uncle hurt the animal. I was verra careful when I fed Cloud apples. The guards who followed me knew, I'm sure, but one older guard in particular didn't mind." She turned to smile at the stallion tethered with the other horses. "I'm thankful you saved him too."

His stomach soured at the insight into her life after

her parents' death, at how afraid, alone, and sad she must have been. Yet she'd shown none of that to him or his men. And he knew she must have felt it—her heart was as big as the loch.

"I want you to have Cloud," he said suddenly. It was the least he could do.

Her eyes grew round. "Truly?"

"Aye. But wait to ride him until we return to the keep. I doona want him to spook and throw you out here. Let him get used to you in the stables first, aye?" Where he could have a healer on hand and spread out some hay to soften her fall.

With an excited holler, she threw her arms around his neck and almost knocked him backward. One arm settled around her waist, the other hovered just above her hair. The devil take him, he wanted to touch her, to hold her still for his kiss.

She pulled back, eyes alight, cheeks creased into identical dimples. "Oh, thank you, Darach. I'll take such good care of him, I promise."

"I know you will."

"He isna a mean horse. Just fearful. He had as bad a time of it as I did."

He reached for her hand. Held it gently. "Lass, we need to talk about that. Who took you from the fire? Was it your uncle?"

"Aye, he was there. He saved me, but he wouldnae let me go back to help my parents. I knew if he would just let me go, I could pull them free. 'Twas not true, of course, but at the time it seemed most cruel."

"How did you get from there to the keep? Was your uncle the stable master? I've met one or two grooms who treated their animals harshly." Maybe that was when the laird had seen her.

She looked away, intent on the kittens playing in the grass.

"Caitlin?"

With a sigh, she looked up. "I doona want to tell you."

"Why?"

"Well...what if I cause so much trouble you want to send me back?"

She still didn't trust him, and it sliced through him like a knife to his gut. Though to be fair, after he'd left her in the glen with the kittens, who could blame her?

"I'll not send you back, love. I promise. Just tell me who your uncle is."

"Och, you say that now, but you havnae seen the mischief I cause. I doona mean it, of course, but it happens all the same." She pulled her hand away, picked up the kitten that slept in her lap, and whispered, "Maybe you can be Prudence and teach me well, for I am sorely lacking in that virtue."

Darach leaned over and pet the last kitten to be named. "If he's Prudence, then this final one is Fortitude, and you have more of that than all my warriors combined." He placed his fingers beneath her chin. Her blue gaze, frightened and worried, locked with his. It hurt his heart to see her so distressed. What was she hiding?

"Please, lass, will you speak on your uncle? Is he the cruel stable master at the castle where you were housed?"

"Nay, Darach, he's not the stable master. My uncle is the cruel laird."

Four

CAITLIN GAWKED AT DARACH'S CASTLE. SHE'D NEVER seen such a grand structure. Built atop a hill, it overlooked a fair-sized village on the southern tip of Loch Maree. The stone walls around the bailey rose about three stories high—a bastion of strength. A portcullis guarded the entrance, and beyond that, the keep reached toward the sky.

"My father and grandfather built it in the Norman style," Darach said. "The stones are mortared and the walls ten feet thick. Naught will harm you here, lass."

Pride tinged his voice, and Caitlin smiled.

"God's truth, 'tis a magnificent sight. My uncle's fortress was wood."

"The keep was still wood when I was a bairn. 'Twas not as safe, but much warmer in the winter."

"Surely you have a hearth?"

"Aye, in every room, two in the great hall, but the stone holds the damp."

They made their way through the village as people called out to them in greeting. Caitlin garnered much attention sitting on the laird's stallion, and she smiled and waved as they rode by.

She noticed that the folk welcomed their laird formally, but none gave him a personal greeting. Even Lachlan shared a special smile with a woman. Darach seemed oblivious to the slight, but Caitlin was perplexed by it. Surely his people were happy to see him?

Deciding she must be mistaken, she let it go and soaked up the cheerful hustle and bustle around her. It reminded her of her parents' farm.

"That's Caitlin," she heard Gare tell a lad about his own age. "We saved her from the Frasers. She'd been knocked out and tied over a horse. Our laird is keeping her at the castle."

A thrill shot through her. 'Twas wonderful to think she would be staying at Darach's keep—at least until she could figure out how to get to Inverness and then across the sea to France. She did not know how long she'd have till Fraser or her uncle found her. And they would—Fraser's eyes had gleamed madly every time he'd visited her uncle's castle to bargain for her. She knew how relentlessly obsessed he was. He'd bring that madness here, hurt all these good people if she didn't leave soon.

But until then, she would have a room of her own and could go to the stables to feed Cloud whenever she wanted, nurse her kittens in the kitchen, even visit people in the village and make new friends—all without fear of repercussions.

Her throat tightened, and she swallowed to loosen it. She hadn't had a friend in three years. People in her uncle's keep were afraid of him and had kept their distance. She'd understood and never blamed them, but it had been a lonely, difficult time.

One best forgotten, for she was *not* going back.

She was going forward—with the MacKenzies for now, later to her mother's family, God willing.

At the moment, however, she needed to find the kitchen and tend to the kittens, then for a bath. A real one. In a tub filled with hot, soapy water. She'd done what she could to wash when they'd stopped to camp, but verily, her hair was knotted like mice had burrowed in it. None of the men had thought to bring a hairbrush. 'Twas not the Highland way, Oslow had said.

Leaning back against Darach, a longing rose to throw her arms around him and kiss the fierce scar that slashed through his eyebrow, to bite his strong, stubble-covered chin and lick his soft lips. Aye, she wanted to kiss those lips, have them pressed to her own. She wanted his hands to tunnel into her hair and hold her fast as he kissed her back.

An urge to move her hips overcame her, and she thrust her bottom against the hard mass behind her.

His arms wrapped around her body, holding her still. "By the love of God, lass, doona move. We're almost there."

His hoarse voice made her want to move some more, but he held her so tight she couldn't shift even one inch. Instead, she pressed her cheek to his chest and inhaled his scent—leather, fresh air, horses, and that uniquely musky scent of man.

Of Darach.

He shuddered against her, and an answering shudder

racked her body. He stilled. His breath came heavily against her ear, tickling her neck.

"Caitlin, are you all right?"

"Nay, I feel strange. Jittery and odd in my belly, and I canna catch my breath." She wrapped her arms around his and held tight. "Do you feel sick too?"

His legs pressed against her thighs and heat rushed through her, flooding her groin. Caitlin almost moaned, but she didn't want to worry him.

"Aye, I've felt sick e'er since I sat you on my horse, but you canna give in to it now, sweetling. We're almost there and you'll be free of me."

"I doona want to be free of you."

"Aye, you do," he said firmly. "Or you willna be a maid much longer."

She gasped. Surely he couldn't... He wouldn't... "What do you—"

"You know exactly what I mean, so quit squirming and not another word. You've almost done me in with your last ones."

He urged Loki into a trot and they passed under the portcullis. She pushed aside her disturbing thoughts and concentrated on her surroundings. The horses' hooves echoed loudly as they proceeded through a stone tunnel and into a large bailey. The keep, which she now counted at five stories high, stood at the far end. She could see other buildings as well—the stables, the barracks for his warriors, the kitchens, with a nearby well. Looking around for a chapel, she was surprised by its absence. The bailey was large enough for several of them.

In front of the barracks stood three poles. One

had what looked like a leather bag hanging from it. When he noticed her looking at them, he said, "'Tis for training my men. It's safer than sparring with each other if they're learning something new."

"Where's the chapel?" she asked. "God's truth, you have room enough for three."

"There isna one."

"Why e'er not?"

He shrugged. "A priest wanders in from time to time and gives mass in the hall at the village."

"But—"

"It works the way it is. A chapel will be built. Eventually."

She tried to hold her tongue and failed. "The state of your soul and the souls of your people should be your first priority."

"Nay, their continual safety is my priority. The state of their souls means little when a sword is driven through their bellies. And I know what you will say to that, but 'tis too late. We have arrived."

They came to a halt outside the keep. A gray-haired woman appeared at the top of the stairs that led down to the courtyard. Not one hair was out of place and every pleat in her arisaid was folded perfectly. She looked dour, and Caitlin bit her lip. Then the woman smiled, and her face creased into laugh lines.

"Greetings, Laird MacKenzie," she said with a formal curtsy. She eyed Caitlin, then turned to Oslow. "Husband, you look as if a mangy fox sits atop your head. Did you not use the hairbrush I packed in your bag?"

Caitlin gasped. "Nay. And when I asked for one, he said 'twas not the Highland way. These men think 'tis a badge of honor to carry the forest home with them. Verily, I have a clan of mice living in my hair."

Darach snorted. "To keep as pets, I wonder? Or to feed the kits *you* carry home from the forest?"

"Och, no. The kittens are too young for mice. I will feed them milk."

"Then you should go do so."

He grasped her waist, lifting her from the saddle, and leaned over to gently set her down. When her feet touched the ground, she leaned into the stallion's side and looked up at him. Without Darach's strong arms around she felt...bereft. "And you?" she asked.

"To the loch, to wash off the forest I carry with me."

"'Tis Darach's ritual," Lachlan said. "The water cools him down from hot thoughts."

"Hot thoughts?"

Darach gave Lachlan a dark look, then ignored her question and motioned to the gray-haired woman who'd descended the stairs. "Edina, this is Caitlin. She will be living with us. Put her in Lachlan's room and shift Lachlan to the top floor. 'Tis colder up there, but the extra steps will warm him, give him time to think before he speaks."

Lachlan grinned. "If it's colder, perhaps you should sleep up there, Brother. Less trips to the loch."

"Are you feverish, Darach?" Caitlin asked. "Maybe you should go straight to bed. I'll see to your needs."

Darach closed his eyes as if he were praying, which pleased her. Surely God wouldn't strike down a pious man.

Lachlan laughed and leaned over to kiss the top of her head. "By God, I am glad we found you. 'Tis a fortunate Scot who'll snare you as wife. Doona you agree, Darach?"

Darach gazed at her a moment, then nodded his head. "Go feed your kits, lass." As he wheeled Loki around, he said to Edina, "Take care of her."

Caitlin watched the men go, her heart pounding. "Darach!"

He turned to her. She was at a loss for what to say as she stared at him. Foolish tears would surely fall if she didn't speak, so she said the first thing that entered her mind. "You need a chapel. There is no more important time to be concerned about your soul than when the sword is in your belly."

❧

Edina led Caitlin across the bailey, toward the kitchen. The housekeeper had suggested she might want a bath before she did anything else, but Caitlin was adamant about feeding the kittens first.

"I'm surprised the laird let you keep them," Edina said. "He doesn't like cats."

"Aye, he pretended to leave me when I refused to abandon them, but deep down I knew he'd come back. He's such a softhearted man. Darach wouldnae leave me in danger after saving me from the Frasers, now would he? Especially o'er helping these wee ones."

She burrowed her face in the folds of her arsaid and kissed the kittens' heads.

When she looked up again, Edina's brow had furrowed. "You speak of Laird MacKenzie?"

"Aye, how many Darachs have you here? Is it a common name?"

"Nay, there's just the one. But softhearted?"

"Like your Oslow. A dear, sweet man."

Edina smiled. "That he is, but my Oslow wouldnae want anyone to know it. Nor would your Darach."

Her Darach. Caitlin liked how that sounded even though it could never be. It warmed her inside, which made her think of his fever. "I hope he'll be all right." When Edina looked at her quizzically, she continued. "The fever. Maybe he shouldnae be swimming if he's coming down sick."

"Ahh, well now…I doona think you need worry. Surely, Laird MacKay was teasing him."

"Teasing him?"

"Aye."

"So he's not sick?"

"Nay." Edina raised a brow. "How old are you, lass? You look long past the age of marriage, yet you seem younger. I was seventeen when I married Oslow. Eighteen when I had Angus."

"I'll be twenty next month. Not so old."

"Not so young, either. You should be married and having bairns. Where's your mother? Your father?"

"They died three years past. I've been alone e'er since, but I plan on finding my mother's family in France. Surely they will take me in."

"And how will you get there?" Edina asked, brows raised. "'Tis not a journey to make lightly. You doona want to be stuck in the Highlands without shelter o'er the winter."

"I have Cloud." At the housekeeper's confused

look, she said, "My horse. And surely if I leave in a few weeks I can make it to the mainland before snowfall. 'Tis not quite summer. Maybe I can ride with a merchant heading east?"

"Ah, lass, I fear you've not thought this through. 'Tis a dangerous journey, especially for a woman. Have you e'er met your mother's kin? Do you know if they're good people?"

"Well...nay, but my mother was a fine, hardworking woman, and she loved me well. Surely her family would do the same."

They reached the kitchen door, and Edina waylaid her with a hand on her arm. "You know naught of her circumstances before she met your da. Stay with us a wee while. See if you like it. The MacKenzies will take care of you. You willna be alone any longer."

Caitlin's chin wobbled with a sudden onslaught of emotions. "Thank you, Edina. It means much to hear you say so. But..."

"But what, lass?"

"My uncle and Laird Fraser, they'll find me." A tremor racked her body and she breathed deeply to quell her panic. "They willna stop. I've seen the madness in Fraser's eyes, the greed in my uncle's. I willna have that foulness unleashed on clan MacKenzie. Nor will I be taken back by the devils, locked up, and worse. Those men are not men at all. They're monsters."

"And the MacKenzies will strike them down. 'Tis what good people do."

Caitlin's heart squeezed. She held the kittens with one arm, then wrapped the other arm around Edina's slim shoulders. "Darach leads an honorable clan."

The other woman sighed and patted Caitlin's back. "'Tis not true of everyone. I must tell you there's a lad inside named Fergus, just seven years old. His father, a MacKenzie, beat his mother to death in front of him." Caitlin pulled back, horrified, as Edina continued. "It's been three months, and the boy's not said a word. He'll sleep only in the kitchen and refuses to take a bath, for his mother was bathing him when her husband struck her. We take turns at night watching him."

"Oh no. Poor laddie."

"You may not want to get too close, for he smells poorly," Edina continued. "We tried to force him to bathe, but Laird MacKenzie forbade it. He said the lad needed time to heal, and scrubbing him with soap and water was not the way to do it."

"Aye, he's right. Fergus must want to change for himself or it willna work, like a dog that's been abused. My mother taught me how to soothe such animals. Too much attention makes them nervous. They must be enticed into the world again."

They entered the kitchen and Caitlin's eyes adjusted to the darkened room. Along one wall hung several pots over a large hearth. The other wall housed two ovens. Wooden shutters opened to the afternoon light, keeping the room cool, and two large tables filled the center.

On a bench near the fire, an old woman was cleaning and scaling a basket full of fish. Caitlin smiled in greeting. The woman smiled back toothlessly.

"Caitlin, this is Aila," Edina said. "Aila helps our cook, Ness, who's at the village right now. I'm sure she'll be back soon. Word of your arrival will have reached her ears."

Caitlin was about to go over and make the old woman's acquaintance when she saw a bedraggled lad crouched on a pallet in the corner. She gasped softly. "God have mercy. The poor dear."

"Aye," Edina said, nodding.

His plaid and lèine were torn and soiled, his hair matted, his face, hands, and bare legs dirty. Maybe not so different from other lads his age, but this boy was filthy from lack of bathing, not from chasing pigs through sties or catching frogs in swampy waters— childhood pastimes Caitlin remembered fondly.

She hesitated a moment before heading toward the table nearest the lad. "Hello, Fergus," she said, then proceeded to ignore him. She opened her arisaid and laid the four kittens on the table so he could see them. They mewed for milk as they tumbled over one another and tried to climb up her dress. She laughed as she pulled sharp claws from the material.

"They're hungry. We must feed them before they tear up my arisaid. 'Tis the only one I have."

Edina lifted a wooden pail that sat in a hole in the ground near the wall and poured cold milk from it into two saucers. "Our laird will find you some more. His mother died ten years ago, and he still has her clothes. I'll help you alter them, if you like."

"Thanks, Edina, but I doona wish to be a problem."

"Och, 'tis no problem. It would be a joy to see our lady's arisaids put to good use."

She smiled as the housekeeper brought the milk over and laid down the saucers for the kittens. Their incessant mewing stopped as they gathered around and lapped up their meal.

Caitlin pet their silky heads. Their coats were brown, black, and gray, with dark, distinct stripes on their faces and bodies, and rings around their thick, blunt-ended tails. Fergus stood up and craned his neck to see them. She knew he wanted to come over and thought on how to involve him.

"Maybe they would like a place to sleep when their bellies are full. Would you mind sharing one of your blankets with them, Fergus? Their mother has died and canna share her warmth. When they're old enough, they can find a warm place to curl up in the castle."

She turned back to the kittens and continued stroking them. From the corner of her eye, she saw Fergus pick up a blanket. He came over slowly, eyes darting back and forth between the women and the kittens. When he was close enough, Caitlin smiled and held out her hand.

He gave her the blanket and stepped back.

After placing it on the table, she moved the kits and milk onto it. "Thank you, Fergus. The kittens appreciate your help. Edina, might I have a pail of hot water and a rag to wash my face and hands? Cats are verra clean creatures and doona like to be touched by dirty fingers."

"Oh, aye. 'Tis true. One must be clean to play with kittens. I'll wash my hands as well." Edina picked up a wooden pail.

"Maybe the larger one." Caitlin pointed to a pail big enough for the lad to stand in. Edina filled it with temperate water and set it in front of Caitlin with some clean linen rags and a bar of sweet-smelling soap. She almost moaned over the soap pressed with rose petals. She hadn't seen such items since her mother had died. Cleanliness was not valued by her uncle or his clan.

"Thank you."

Dipping her hands into the water, she scrubbed off the dirt, then soaked the rag and wiped it over her face, neck, and upper chest. *Glorious.*

Edina washed as well, then Caitlin cuddled the kittens who had finished their milk and now purred contentedly. Fergus took another step closer and reached for the little female. Voice low and calm, Caitlin said, "You must wash your hands first, Fergus. With soap." She continued to play with the kits, as did Edina, neither of them paying the lad much attention. Fergus hesitated, then dipped his hands, lathered them with soap, and dipped them again. It was not a very thorough job, but Caitlin didn't care. She could see by the tears in Edina's and Aila's eyes it was a breakthrough for the boy.

Caitlin held out a dry linen. "May I dry them for you, laddie?"

He caught her eye and this time held her gaze.

She smiled at him. "Truly, cats doona like water. They prefer a dry hand." He nodded slowly and held out his hands. Caitlin dried them, then lifted them to her mouth and kissed each one. She released him and turned to the cats.

"This sweetling is called Temperance. She is so named because she's the only lassie and needs to be patient with her brothers. This one is named Justice, after your laird, because he's such a good, just man. This one is named Fortitude because..."

Darach waded out of the loch naked. He'd stayed in longer than Lachlan, needing time to cleanse Caitlin's warmth from his skin and her words from his heart and mind.

"I feel strange. Jittery and odd in my belly, and I canna catch my breath."

To know she was drawn to him, wanted to be touched by him, was almost more than he could bear. How would he keep his distance with her living in his keep? Sleeping so close to him?

He must find her a husband. One who'd treat her well...or answer to him.

"I doona want to be free of you."

He shook his head. There was no room for a woman in his life. Certainly not one like Caitlin.

He'd desired a family once. Duty to his clan was his only priority now. Women made a man soft.

Pulling on his plaid, he secured it with his belt, then fastened his shoes and pushed back his wet hair. Lachlan had already dressed, and Darach saw Oslow, still looking travel-worn and waiting for them by the horses—impatient to give his final report, no doubt.

Upon reaching him, Darach took the reins in his hand and continued on foot toward the castle. The two men fell into step beside him.

"How much longer can you stay with us, Lachlan?" he asked.

"I would see this through. I'll not have you or the lass harmed because I left too early. You'll want all of us by your side when Fraser attacks. 'Twould be a waste of time to return home only to come right back again."

By "all of us," Darach knew Lachlan spoke of their foster brothers, Callum, Gavin, and Kerr, and their foster father, Gregor. They'd made a blood oath years ago to protect one another, and his brothers and Gregor would be much aggrieved if Darach did not call upon them in his hour of need.

He clasped Lachlan's shoulder. "It heartens me to have you by my side."

Lachlan returned the gesture. "Aye, Darach, as it does me, knowing you will stand by mine."

Lachlan was not meant to be laird of Clan MacKay, but when his older brother was murdered five years ago, he'd taken the helm, swearing to find his brother's killer—whom he was closer than ever to identifying. Darach looked forward to the day he could help Lachlan achieve justice for his clan.

They walked in silence, each lost in his own thoughts. Finally, Darach turned to Oslow. "Have our spies discover what they can about Caitlin from the Frasers. We must know what she's hiding—God willing, it's not as bad as she thinks—and the name of her clan. If they align with Fraser, I need to know their strength and their allies. Ask our people first. Her father, Wallace, was the brother of a laird, and he married a Frenchwoman named Claire. A love match, I suspect, that may have caused a breach between the brothers. Surely that is fodder for the gossip mill, and someone will remember."

"Willna she tell you herself?" Oslow asked.

"Nay, she's frightened and doesn't trust me. I erred when I pretended to leave her at the glen with those blasted cats."

Oslow harrumphed. "If you were to marry the lass—"

"Nay," Darach cut him off.

It did not help that everyone wanted him to marry Caitlin. God forbid she got the same idea. He'd seen how stubborn she was. It would make life most difficult, and right now, he needed a clear head more than ever.

"Have you increased the guard?" he asked.

"Aye, 'tis doubled within the castle, and the border patrol is tripled. Everyone is on alert, including the villagers. They know what was done to Caitlin and by whom. Gare and Brodie have told the story many times o'er."

Darach sighed. "Do you think the clan will leave it at that? Or will my keep be overrun by visitors tomorrow?"

Oslow smiled. "You'll be overrun. Everyone will want to meet her for themselves, express their outrage at her mistreatment. Maybe you should take her to the village in the morning and save them the trouble."

"I am laird, not a social convener. I have my people and my land to protect. I doona have time to squire her around."

"Doona worry," Lachlan said. "I'll take her, introduce her to all the brawny warriors and eligible young bachelors. You shouldnae be bothered with such trivial things as matchmaking."

Heat crawled up Darach's neck. One fist clenched

around the reins, the other by his side. Damnation. There was naught he could say now. He'd look a fool.

"You'll do no such thing."

Lachlan burst into laughter as Oslow coughed into his hand.

Darach marched toward the keep, refusing to look at them. After a moment, he stopped and sighed. "The Frasers will come. We must protect her."

Then he mounted Loki and raced toward the castle. To Caitlin.

Five

DARACH HANDED LOKI TO A LAD IN THE STABLE AND hurried up the hill toward the keep. He found himself breaking into a run and slowed down. Everything was in order.

About to mount the steps that led to the keep's heavy wooden door, he paused and wondered if Caitlin was still in the kitchen or in her room bathing. A vision of her naked in a tub of steamy water heated his chilled flesh. He sighed as the familiar ache filled his groin, all the time he'd spent in the icy water suddenly for naught.

Shaking his head, he glanced toward the kitchen and noticed a group of people milling around the building that stood separate from the keep.

The heat of desire turned to anger as he realized what they were doing.

His steward, Henson, a tall, thin, bald man, peeped through a closed shutter, while the stable master, Ronald, short and sturdy, stood behind on his tiptoes, trying to see past him. Others crowded around as well—some of the young women who helped in the keep and a few grooms. Darach's cook, Ness—a middling woman who had been lovely in her day and now was as round through the hips and breasts as one of the standing kettles in which she cooked her stews, peered through a crack in the door—perhaps as Caitlin soaked in the wooden tub in the kitchen.

He marched toward them, intent on bashing the heads of the men together. One of the lasses saw him coming and squeaked. After bobbing a quick curtsy, she hastened away. Others beat their own retreat, but Henson, Ronald, and Ness were too entranced to notice his arrival. Darach grabbed the men by the scruff of their necks and hauled them away from the window. They howled in surprise.

Ness rushed over. "Laird, 'tis not what you think!"

Darach stopped just short of braining them. Ronald and Henson cowered in his grip, petrified, but also guilt ridden. It was exactly as he'd thought.

"I believed they were spying on the lass as well and did give them a tongue lashing for it, but 'tis not true. She bathes the lad, and he stands there willingly. 'Tis a miracle."

When he looked over, tears trailed down her cheeks. Ness had five grown children of her own and had spent much time with Fergus in the kitchen, trying to mother him, to no avail.

He grunted and released the men, balling his hands into fists. "I willna abide any man spying on the lass. To do so is an insult to me, and I will act accordingly. She has the protection of the MacKenzies, and you will treat her with honor. Do I make myself clear?"

The men nodded. "Aye, Laird."

The message would spread like wildfire through the clan. Anyone who dared treat Caitlin with disrespect would be well warned. He walked to the kitchen door and pushed into the darkened room. His gaze found them immediately. Fergus stood naked in a pail of water, eyes wide. He held a squirming kitten in his hands as far away from his body as possible. Darach watched as Aila gave the lad a new kitten to hold and placed the other one on the table with its littermates. Caitlin washed the boy's body with a rag and soap, while Edina poured a pail of water over his hair, rinsing away the suds.

Darach wouldn't have said Fergus was willing, but as willing as any lad his age when put in a tub. It was a far cry from the last time Darach had come upon a similar scene—the lad struggling and screaming in fear as the women tried to wash him. Now, Fergus looked anxious and uncomfortable, but not deathly so. Till he saw his laird standing by the door.

At that moment, his face paled and he whimpered pitifully. Darach cursed his own stupidity. The poor lad had been in just such a position when his father had entered their cottage and attacked his mother. Darach had brought the boy's memories back unwittingly.

Caitlin looked up and met Darach's gaze. He turned to leave, but she stopped him.

"Nay, Darach, stay, but come forward slowly, so we can see more than just your shadow. Maybe sit on that stool." She pointed to a stool by the hearth. Darach hesitated, then moved toward it. The lad still whimpered. The sound crushed Darach's heart. He'd been unable to save the mother, but God willing, Caitlin could save the son.

"Look, Fergus," she said, "'tis your laird come to visit. You must show him your kitten, for Darach loves cats. He told me so himself when I found them in the forest."

Cheeky lass.

Darach sat and smiled at the lad. The squirming kitten distracted Fergus. He lost his pallor and turned to Aila, who handed him a third kitten, placing the second one on the table. Darach hid a grin. The poor kits, being used in such a fashion. He knew it was Caitlin's doing, none other would have had such imagination. She would win a place in the heart of every MacKenzie for this.

"Fergus, may Darach come closer to see the kitten?" she asked. "'Tis Justice you now hold, and he loves to crawl up your laird's chest to play with his hair. The kit may even suckle on his chin. 'Tis verra sweet."

She continued to wash the lad with soothing strokes, but she avoided staring at him, as if he were a dog she didn't want to aggravate. She'd mentioned her mother had been good with animals and had taught Caitlin how to tend them. Whatever she'd done had worked with Fergus too.

When the lad nodded, Darach moved the stool closer and sat on it. His knees were a hand's width away from Fergus, who eyed Darach for a moment, then sat Justice on his lap. Sure enough, the kitten ran straight up Darach's chest, making him wince as tiny claws found purchase in his clothes and skin. Justice batted the wet strands of hair hanging past Darach's ears.

The women laughed, and Fergus did something Darach hadn't seen him do in a long time. He smiled.

Thank you, Caitlin.

Ness had followed Darach into the kitchen and now held out a large linen to dry the boy. "Och, would you look at that? There's a wee lad behind all that dirt. Come and dry off, Fergus."

Fergus looked at Caitlin, and she nodded. "Once you're dry, you can have all four kittens at once."

Eyes round, the boy stepped gingerly from the pail and let himself be wrapped up by Ness. "I canna thank you enough, lass," she said, tears running down her face even though she smiled.

Caitlin smiled back, also teary. Lovely, too, with her flushed cheeks, damp hair, and wet clothes clinging to her curves. No wonder the men had been spying.

But underneath, Darach saw the exhaustion, her skin pale beneath red cheeks, eyes too bright. She needed a bath of her own, some food, and a bed.

He handed Justice to Aila, then stepped around the pail and took Caitlin's hand. "You look ready to drop. 'Tis time someone took care of you. Say good night to the lad."

"But I must tend the kittens, and Fergus needs my help."

"Nay, you've done enough. Fergus can tend the kittens now. Edina, Ness, and Aila will show him what needs to be done." He eyed the boy. "Isna that right, lad?"

Fergus nodded, looking lost in the folds of cloth.

"Are you sure, Fergus?" Caitlin asked. "The kits will need more milk and a pan of sand to use as a privy."

"Doona worry. I'll see to it," Edina said.

"But what about the dogs? I have yet to train them."

"They're out hunting with my men." Darach tugged her toward the door. "Say good night, Caitlin."

"But—"

"Say good night, Caitlin."

She huffed, then looked back at Fergus and stuck out her tongue. "Good night, Caitlin."

Fergus smiled again.

The sun was setting as Darach led her through the bailey. It was later than she'd thought, and other than a few men down by the stables, the big yard was empty. Maybe everyone had gone inside for the evening meal. When he reached the keep and mounted the steps to the second floor, she was suddenly self-conscious. What would his clan think of her? Especially knowing she'd been drugged and handed over to Laird Fraser like cattle.

They would speculate about her situation, of course—'twas only natural—but would they guess the truth? And if they did, would they consider her their enemy?

The hall was dark compared to outside, but her eyes soon adjusted, and she looked around the large, empty room. A grand hearth with a roaring fire took up the wall to her left. A smaller fire burned in a hearth in the opposite wall. Sweet-smelling rushes covered the floor.

She sighed in relief. Her uncle's keep had been dirty and the stink had made her gag.

Opposite them, stairs led to a balcony on the third floor that overlooked the room.

"Please stop. I want to see your home."

He changed direction and walked with her to the smaller hearth, which was flanked by several chairs with embroidered cushions and footstools. Heat from the flames poured over her.

A colorful tapestry depicting a hunt hung on the wall above the hearth. Darach followed her gaze. "My mother made it. And the one above the other hearth as well."

The detail in the design amazed Caitlin. She couldn't imagine the time and patience it must have taken to complete. "She was fair talented with a needle. 'Tis a skill I lack."

"You have other talents."

"Like what?"

"Like what you did for Fergus. We've been trying to soothe him for months. None thought to do what you did."

Caitlin shrugged, embarrassed and pleased at the same time. "'Twas not difficult. I just told him cats are verra clean creatures and doona like to be touched by dirty fingers. So he washed his hands. Then he wanted to kiss the kits, so he agreed to have his face washed."

"And the bath?" Darach asked.

"Well, he wanted to hold and cuddle the kits, now didn't he? So he agreed to a bath. Edina and Aila helped me. As did the kittens."

He gazed at her, dark eyes intent on her face. A blush rose in her cheeks and she looked away, overheated despite her damp clothes. The rest of the hall came into focus. Lit sconces and an array of finely crafted weapons covered the remaining walls.

High above, narrow, shuttered windows were built into the outside wall. For defense as well as light.

Toward the main hearth was a table on a dais, with wooden chairs on one side. Additional tables and benches were pushed back and stacked neatly in a corner. They would be set out when Darach's household and his men gathered for dinner.

"Isn't it time for your men to sup?"

"Most of them are on patrol. You will meet everyone soon enough. Maybe in the morning we'll go down to the village."

"I'd like that."

She shivered as a draft blew the heat from the fire away, and concern crossed Darach's face. "You'll catch your death of cold down here in those wet clothes, and you look weary enough to sleep where you stand." He reached down and scooped her up into his arms. She squeaked in surprise.

"Darach, put me down."

"Nay. You're exhausted."

She squirmed to get loose. "What if someone comes in? I doona want them to think me feeble. Put me down."

He snorted and his arms tightened around her as he carried her across the great hall. "If they do, I'm sure you'll disabuse them of the notion."

Caitlin didn't know whether to be pleased or miffed by his comment. For certain, she didn't want to seem weak, but it was the way he'd said it, like she was a harridan or something. She poked him in the chest for good measure. He smiled.

The door squeaked open and Lachlan entered. He

raised an eyebrow when he saw Darach carrying her. They slowed to speak to him.

Caitlin flushed. "He willna put me down."

"Are you chilled?" he asked.

She thought about it. The surge of heat from earlier had faded. "Aye."

"Then he should not. He should have you in a hot bath or a warm bed." His lips twitched. "Which would you prefer, Darach?"

Darach spun on his heel and marched up the stairs that led to the balcony and the third floor. "Both," he replied over his shoulder.

Caitlin frowned when Lachlan laughed. He did find much to laugh at. Too often she didn't know what had amused him. She couldn't imagine him leading his clan the way Darach did—with such power and control.

They were halfway up the stairs when she realized he'd misspoke. "You canna have me in both, Darach. In the tub, I'd be wet and naked. In the bed, I'd be warm and dry. They're opposite."

He stumbled and almost dropped her. When he spoke, his voice sounded strangled. "Aye, lass. Maybe we should speak on something else."

They reached the top of the stairs, and he walked down a shadowy corridor lit by sconces. He stopped in front of a door and pushed through. Caitlin cast an eager glance around the chamber, lit by a roaring fire in a grand hearth. A large, soft-looking bed with a canopy, a carved chest, and a stand with a washbasin and ewer filled the room. Beside the pitcher, sat a hairbrush.

She gasped and struggled to free herself from Darach's arms. For a moment, he held her tight. After he released her, she ran for the hairbrush and held it against her chest, then tried to look everywhere at once.

The soft quilts and pillows on the bed tempted her, but she couldn't fathom having a sleep just yet. In front of the hearth sat a chair with an embroidered cushion and a footstool. She hurried over and sat as close to the fire as possible, soaking up the warmth.

Darach crossed the room and unlatched the shutters over the window. "Come and look."

He pushed them open just as she rushed to his side. The gloaming was upon them, coloring the sky in soft purples and pinks. The view spread out over the castle wall, to the village and loch below.

"Oh, Darach. It's beautiful! What a gift. I shall treasure it always. If e'er I am uncertain or afraid, I shall close my eyes and picture myself here with you."

"What do you mean? Picture yourself here with me?"

"Well, I must go soon, mustn't I? If I leave it too late, the snow will be upon me before I reach France's shores."

He stilled, other than a tiny twitch below his eye. "To France? You seek your mother's family?"

She sighed with relief at his understanding. "Aye, 'tis what I must do. I'm glad you see the right of it."

He crossed his arms over his chest. "Nay, Caitlin. I doona see the right of it. I see only the wrong. We are in the Highlands. 'Tis a difficult trek to the coast, even in summer, and crossing the North Sea can be treacherous at any time of year. Who will show you the way? I canna leave to take you. We broke the peace—attacked the Fraser laird and stole from him. My clan is on the verge of war."

"But if I leave, Fraser and my uncle willna come. I canna bear to see anyone hurt because of me."

He grasped her arms. "'Tis not your burden. The Frasers are our enemy and a threat to all good people in the Highlands. We are prepared to fight."

"But maybe if I leave—"

"Nay! We will still fight. Laird Fraser is a rabid dog and needs to be put down. His clan culled of rot. What are you thinking, lass? Have you met your mother's family? Do you know where they live? What sort of people they are?"

"They live in Lyon, and they are the sort of people who raised my mother."

"They did live in Lyon. By now they may have moved or died. And even if you made it as far as the French coast, 'tis still a long trip inland. Do you think a lass like you with a horse like Cloud will even make it to Inverness without being accosted? You have no coin, no sword, no one to show you the way. 'Tis a fool's journey. For the love of God, stay here."

"I canna!"

"Why e'er not?"

The familiar panic that she tried so hard to tamp down pushed up from her belly and threatened to close her throat. "My uncle and Fraser—they'll find me. I willna go back! I'll be free of them in France."

"Nay, Caitlin, you'll be abused or raped or dead in France—if you even get there. You'll only be safe if you stay with the MacKenzies. 'Tis all right to be afraid, lass. You survived a horrendous ordeal. But you must think clearly. You canna go to France."

"Am I your prisoner, then?"

He reared back from her. "Nay, of course not."

"So if I wanted to ride Cloud through the gates tonight, I could?"

"You would die."

"But would you let me pass, if 'twas what I truly wanted?"

His eye twitched steadily, along with a muscle in his jaw. Finally he said, "I took an oath to keep you safe, lass, but aye, you could leave. You *can* leave. But not alone. I will send men with you who know the way and will keep the brigands at bay."

So he wouldnae control her, lock her away as her uncle had done.

The pressure inside her eased, and on a half sob, half laugh, she threw her arms around his shoulders, impulsively pressing her lips to his. They were as soft as she'd imagined. He stiffened for an instant, then wrapped her in his embrace, one hand sinking into her hair, the other sliding downward to anchor their hips together. A rumble sounded in his chest, and he angled his head, licking the seam of her lips. When she gasped in surprise, he slipped his tongue inside her mouth to rub against hers. Heat scorched her skin at the contact, and her breasts tightened—hard and aching. If he hadn't been holding her, she would have collapsed to the floor like a rag doll.

The brush fell from her fingers and crashed to the floor. He yanked his head back, lids heavy, breath harsh and quick. Her own breath rasped in her throat.

"You shouldnae have done that, Caitlin." His voice grated like he'd swallowed a handful of gravel.

A wave of remorse washed over her. "I'm sorry. I didn't mean to. I was just so happy. It willna happen again, I promise. Please, doona send me back."

He groaned and pulled her close, tucking her head beneath his chin. "I willna send you anywhere, sweetling. No matter what you do. 'Tis just...you are such an innocent. I doona think you understand..."

Caitlin waited for him to finish. His hand stroked her hair, and she melted into him. She wanted him to keep caressing down her spine to her bottom. "Understand what?"

He sighed. "My point exactly. Most women wouldnae have to ask. 'Tis troublesome."

"I'm sorry," she said again, wavering between self-pity and annoyance. "I did not know my gratitude was so unwelcome."

"That was not gratitude." Now he sounded annoyed. He tilted her chin up with his finger so she looked at him. "Have you ne'er been kissed before?"

Heat flooded her cheeks. She tried to turn away, but he held her tight. "'Tis not your business. I willna tell you."

"Aye, you will."

She stepped on his foot, so he'd release her, but instead he wrapped his leg around hers. Trapped and off balance, she clung to him.

"Caitlin," he prompted.

Her lips pressed together. It was mortifying that, at almost twenty, she'd only been kissed once—by an ogre who'd just told her not to do it again.

The ogre tipped her back farther.

"Hundreds of times," she said.

"I doona think so. I think your father kept a good eye on you, and then your uncle locked you up. You know naught of kissing or anything else."

"Fine. I have ne'er been kissed properly, but two did try. The first my father caught before the lad could do more than hold my hand. He was flung from the barn onto his backside. The second I kneed in his privates, a trick my father taught me after the first lad's failed attempt. In return for my actions, I received this." Caitlin pointed to her bruised temple.

"Fraser," Darach ground out, then yanked her into a hug so tight she could scarcely breathe.

For someone who did not want her touch, he held her very close. What was the difference between a hug and a kiss? Surely they were just as intimate. So much so that if her father had seen them, he'd have done much more than throw Darach out onto his backside.

"Did you get him good?" he asked.

"Aye. He fell to his knees, then rolled onto his side and curled up like a bairn. When he could finally stand, he hit my face and then my belly while his men held me. I fainted shortly after. I think maybe he kicked me too, for I have a large bruise on my hip and one on my thigh."

"I will kill him." He grasped her waist and gently moved her back to look down at her torso, as if to see the damage.

She moaned again, but this time from fear. "I doona want you hurt. Any of you."

"He dared lay hands upon you, Caitlin. For that alone, I will gut him. None hurt what is mine to protect."

Caitlin sighed as she lay back in the tub. The water felt almost as good as Darach's kiss—the heat, the melting sensation. Although when she thought about it, as she had endlessly, the kiss had not been nearly as relaxing. His touch had wound her up, created an urgency to... To what? To press closer, for sure. To touch and be touched.

Maybe that's what it was like to mate, for she knew the female took the male inside her body. She'd seen the animals on the farm in the act, the male mounting the female from behind, but they didn't look like they felt the way Caitlin had when Darach touched her. Like everything in the world had stopped and her body had gone crazy, melting and boneless yet energized at the same time.

She wondered how it would feel if Darach mounted her in a similar fashion.

The muscles in her belly clenched as she tried to picture it, but she couldn't grasp how they would come together. He had male parts different from hers, and she knew they fit inside a woman, but she wasn't sure how. She pictured them kissing again. This time, however, she imagined his hand sliding all the way down her back to squeeze her bottom, like she'd wanted him to earlier. Her center pulsed, and she pressed her knees together, causing the water to lap at her breasts.

The waves felt strange against her hot skin, almost painful, and she bit her lip. Her nipples were stiff, the twin mounds swollen. She ran her thumbs over the pink crests. A moan emitted unexpectedly from her throat as sweet sensations filled the tips and down between her legs. She quickly dropped her hands, but she couldn't stop picturing Darach's strong fingers doing what hers had just done. Closing her eyes, she tried to banish the hot thoughts, but they persisted.

Hot thoughts.

Her eyes popped open. Lachlan had said that of Darach. *The water cools him down from hot thoughts.* She'd assumed the words had meant fever, but Edina had implied something else. Had Darach experienced the same thoughts as her after their kiss? Had he envisioned touching her breasts in the way she'd just imagined? Stroking them with his thumbs?

She flushed as her body tingled and tightened. Then it occurred to her that Lachlan had teased Darach about it before he'd kissed her.

Maybe Lachlan referred to someone else? Someone Darach had met before her.

He was a big, braw man. Women would be drawn to him, maybe even love him, but surely he wouldn't touch a woman in such a way who was not his wife?

She sighed and shook her head. God's truth, she was simple. The specifics of tupping may have been a mystery to her, but she was fair certain men enjoyed it and tupped as often as possible. The maids had whispered about it at her uncle's castle. More than likely Darach had kissed many women before her, even had carnal knowledge of them.

Her throat tightened, and the bath no longer soothed her. She stepped from the tub, wrapped herself in a linen cloth, and moved to sit on the stool before the fire.

Something nagged her, but she couldn't put her finger on it. After blotting the water from her hair, she worked the brush through the long, thick strands. The bed tempted her, but she was loath to put her wet head on the beautiful feather pillow.

She leaned close to the fire to dry her tresses, and the elusive thought came to her. On his mount, as they'd ridden into the bailey, Darach had said if she didn't get free of him, she wouldn't be a maid much longer. That meant tupping.

A hot thought...about her.

⁂

Darach stood outside Caitlin's door and listened. All was quiet. Most likely she slept in the big bed, her body warm from the bath, her skin dewy.

He rested his brow against the wood and sighed. She was such an endearing mix of sweet and fiery. 'Twas obvious she knew naught of tupping, but he was fair certain she'd be an eager student.

Unfortunately, he could not be the man to teach her.

Still, he knocked softly on the wood. When she didn't respond, he tested the handle. It turned.

Foolish lass.

He peeked inside. The bed was empty and a jolt of alarm shot through him. He rushed forward only to see her sitting on the stool in front of the fire, asleep, her head pillowed on the seat of the chair.

He walked slowly toward her, wondering how he would have let her go if she had insisted on leaving tonight...or any other night.

Her hair hung like a swath of silk to the floor—the

same rich brown as a young doe. Wrapped in a large bathing cloth, she was completely covered except for one shoulder that peeped out the top. He'd seen her in less, but just knowing she was naked beneath the linen had him exhaling shakily.

A small smile curved her lips as if she were having pleasant dreams, and her cheeks were flushed a rosy pink. He wondered if the rest of her was flushed as well. He could find out. His hand reached down of its own accord before he stopped himself. The devil take him, he was a degenerate bastard. She was in his care. Where was his honor?

Completely lost if he couldn't move her to the quilts without the linen falling off. The keep turned cold at night, when the wood burned down. He added more logs to the fire, then readied her bed.

With a fortifying breath, he crossed to her, secured the drying cloth, and gently picked her up. She sighed and snuggled into him.

After depositing her between the covers, he pulled the quilts to her chin. She made a small sound of protest, and he thought perhaps she might waken—wanted her to waken—but she settled back to sleep. He walked quickly to the door.

"Darach?"

Turning slowly, he lost his breath. She sat in a mass of quilts, the firelight glinting off her hair as it tumbled around her shoulders. Her hand reached for him, but he dared not take it.

"Aye, Caitlin."

She sighed, then lay back down, and he realized she wasn't fully awake.

"Are you all right, lass?" he whispered.

She didn't answer. He thought she had returned to slumber and was about to leave when her voice came to him, soft and drowsy. Most of the words were incoherent, but what he did hear rooted him to the ground.

"...touch me...please...Darach." Then after a soft moan that made his blood pound, she added, "Show me..."

Darach strode from the room, through the keep, and out into the cold night air. He would sleep in the kitchen with the kittens and Fergus. Aye, he would sleep there every night till Caitlin left his castle.

Six

CAITLIN STOOD IN THE MIDDLE OF THE VILLAGE SQUARE surrounded by Darach's clan. Pleased to make her acquaintance was the blacksmith with his four brawny sons, the miller's wife with her three well-fed sons, and Oslow's handsome son, Angus, whom she'd spoken to for quite a while. The tanner and his family were there, the baker, the tinker, the weaver. Plus all the folks who farmed the land and fished the loch, as well as many of Darach's men.

Her cheeks ached from smiling. Everyone was so friendly, so thankful for what she'd done for Fergus and outraged at her treatment by Laird Fraser.

She'd been hugged, kissed, and pinched more times in the last two hours than she had her entire life. Everyone had opened their hearts to her like she was their daughter.

But how would they feel if they knew the truth about her and the evil laird? Would they still want her to stay? Would Darach? He had pledged to protect her, but it was a promise based on half-truths, and she couldn't consider it binding.

Her smile slipped. Maybe she should take Cloud and just go, even though Darach had been so adamantly against it last night. She didn't deserve the love and protection the MacKenzies offered.

Glancing over her shoulder, she found Darach standing behind her with his arms crossed over his chest. He'd barely said a word since locating her in the stables earlier.

She hadn't noticed his reticence at first; she'd been too excited to be back on Loki and in his arms as they headed toward the village. But when they'd come across a group of his warriors training with Oslow, his bad temper had shown itself. Not that he'd yelled or even raised his voice. Nay, his heavy silence was enough to make the men quake in their boots.

He made the villagers nervous as well, for they bowed or curtsied formally, then avoided his gaze.

She moved closer to him and murmured, "If you'd looked like that when you'd found me, I'd have thought you a devil rather than an angel. Verily, Darach, if I have displeased you, tell me, and I'll leave."

His frown deepened. "You willna be going anywhere but back to the castle, where I can keep the scoundrels away from you."

Caitlin stared at him, uncertain of his meaning. Surely he didn't mean his clan—they were lovely people. He must be worried for her safety, lest the Frasers attack. "Och, there's no need for such vigilance. Look how many braw young men surround me. The MacKenzies would ne'er let a Fraser through."

Darach snorted and rolled his eyes heavenward, mouthing a silent prayer. At least, that's what it looked

like to Caitlin. Another of his warriors approached with
Gare, and she smiled, the pain in her cheeks forgotten
as she greeted them.

"Caitlin, this is Nab," Gare said. "He's one of our best
fighters and will help keep you safe from the Frasers."

She nodded. "'Tis an honor, Nab. God's truth, I
appreciate your vigilance. I canna imagine anyone getting past you and the other strong MacKenzies."

Nab's chest swelled. "For sure, we'd fight to the
death for you, lass."

She heard Darach snort again.

Darach wanted to kill Gare for spending the last
two hours introducing every young man he knew
to Caitlin. One glance and they were as besotted
as every other lad in the village, young or old. The
women too, who couldn't get over Caitlin's success
with Fergus.

Brodie was also there, but he was more interested in
advancing his relationship with the lasses by introducing them to Caitlin. It was nearly three hours since
they'd been surrounded by Darach's clan. What more
could the MacKenzies have to say?

Christ almighty, there was work to be done, crops
and livestock to be tended, cottages to be cleaned.
He was laird; he should send them home to see to
their chores. They would thank him for it at the end
of the day.

"It seems to me your clan is either extremely brave
or extraordinarily stupid not to be scared away by your
frowning face," Lachlan said.

Darach glanced over his shoulder at his brother, who mimicked Darach's stance and forbidding countenance.

With a dismissive sound that every Scot learned at birth, he turned back to keep an eye on Caitlin. "You exaggerate."

Another young man came forward to meet her. Darach's frown darkened. The lad glanced up and blanched when he found himself the object of his laird's scrutiny. He gave Darach a nervous bow but did not retreat from Caitlin, as Darach desired.

"Like I said, extraordinarily stupid or extremely brave."

Darach stepped toward the lad, but Lachlan stopped him with a hand on his arm.

"Oslow's found someone with information on Caitlin's clan. I'm sure you'll want to talk to the man yourself."

Lachlan pointed to the edge of the village square, where Oslow stood beneath a leafy tree with a gnarled, old Scot named Sim MacDuff. His daughter had married a MacKenzie, and Sim had moved in with her three years ago, when his wife had died. Darach stepped toward him, then hesitated. He looked back at Caitlin.

"Oh, for Christ's sake," Lachlan said. "I'll watch o'er the lass. I promise to glower at any man who dares approach her."

"'Tis for her own protection. Some of them are right rogues. And doona let her hear you curse or you'll be in for another lecture."

Lachlan made the same dismissive sound Darach had made earlier, then positioned himself behind Caitlin. After watching for a moment to make sure

Lachlan kept the men in line, Darach headed through the crowd toward Oslow and Sim.

"Laird, this is Sim MacDuff," Oslow said when Darach reached them.

"Aye, I remember. How are you, Sim?"

"Me old bones do ache now and again, but I can still keep up with the latest bairn. A rough-and-tumble lad me granddaughter birthed last year."

Darach smiled, his first in what seemed like ages. "I've met the lad. Iver Keith MacKenzie. He'll do you proud."

"To be sure."

Darach braced his hand against the tree. "You have information for me about a husband and wife named Wallace and Claire, parents of the lass we rescued?" He looked toward Caitlin as he spoke. To his dismay, he saw Lachlan weaving his way through the crowd toward them. Brodie now stood guard behind Caitlin with a forbidding scowl on his face. Darach was surprised to see the man looked fiercer than Darach and Lachlan combined.

When Lachlan reached them, he raised a hand to gainsay Darach. "He'll do perfectly well. I promised to put a good word in with Murdoc MacKenzie. Brodie is sweet on Murdoc's daughter."

"He's sweet on all the daughters. He'll forget his task the moment one of them smiles at him."

"Nay, I've seen him with Laren. He behaves like an idiot around her. Forgets how to speak and trips o'er his own feet." Lachlan grinned slyly. "Glares at any man who looks her way. True love, I reckon."

Darach caught his meaning and shook his head.

He was not in love with Caitlin. "I promised to keep her safe. That's all." His fool of a foster brother kept grinning and unease shivered up his spine. He was not falling in love with the lass.

He turned back to Sim. "What can you tell us?"

Sim straightened, so he no longer leaned on his walking stick, proud to be the center of the lairds' and Oslow's attention. "I remember the tale because it happened the same summer me daughter married your kin. Una met Fletcher at the summer fair and I wouldnae abide the match until I'd met the lad's clan, seen where he lived."

The men nodded in agreement.

"On the journey west, we passed through MacInnes land. 'Tis Wallace MacInnes of whom you speak."

MacInnes.

The name made his stomach sour, and he realized he'd begun to think of Caitlin as a MacKenzie, the woman she'd become if she married one of the besotted, young men around her—became a wife, a lover, a mother.

Which would be better than her ill-thought-out plan to go to France. On the road. Alone. And for what? A family she'd never met?

Nay. She'd have to stay here and marry—and not into his clan. That would be torture. He glanced at Lachlan. A MacKay, perhaps. *Caitlin MacKay.* That name bothered him even more, and he glowered at his brother who caught the look and raised his brow.

"Wallace MacInnes was the eldest son of the laird," Sim continued. "He was betrothed to the daughter of a wealthy, lowland laird. I doona remember the clan."

"The eldest? Doona you mean the second son?" he asked.

"Nay, he was the eldest and would have been laird when the old laird died, but he met a French lass when he was on a mission for our king. Wallace brought her home intending to marry her. 'Twas said her beauty rivaled the sun and the moon put together."

Darach glanced at Caitlin. Aye, that he believed.

"The laird forbid the match, but Wallace was in love with the lass and married her anyway. He gave up the lairdship to his younger brother, a miscreant of a man by all accounts, and settled on some land that had passed to him from his mother. Me daughter did think it a grand story, but when I heard the old laird died a few months later, I thought the lad a fool. He could have been laird and married his French lass if he'd only waited a while longer."

A week ago, Darach would have agreed. Now he wasn't so sure. If he'd been Wallace and Claire had been anything like her daughter, would he have disobeyed his father and married her? Maybe Wallace had thought his father would come around and set things straight before he died.

He gazed toward Caitlin again to find her staring back at him. She smiled, and just like that, he was caught. His heart faltered for an instant, then started up with a fierce pounding. It was as if the world had ground to a halt.

"Laird?"

The village slowly came back into focus, and Darach found himself the object of the men's attention. Lachlan looked amused.

"What is it?" he asked, his raspy voice belying his calm demeanor.

Sim's brow puckered in confusion. "I asked if I may take my leave? 'Tis long past the noon meal, and I did promise me granddaughter I'd watch the bairn for her."

Darach nodded, still trying to collect himself. "Aye. You've been verra helpful. If you remember anything else, please tell me immediately."

Sim nodded and headed toward the village, leaning heavily on his cane.

Darach, Oslow, and Lachlan turned back toward Caitlin, falling silent as they watched the crowd, especially the young men who vied for her attention.

"Caitlin MacInnes," Lachlan said.

Darach bristled again at the name. He wanted to shout out, *Caitlin MacKenzie.*

"Bah, she's not a MacInnes," Oslow said, expressing Darach's outrage. "The MacKenzies have claimed her. One of our young men will snatch her up. If not our laird, then maybe my Angus. She did speak to him a long while."

"She does not plan to stay. She thinks to find her mother's family in France," Darach said.

Oslow and Lachlan whipped their heads toward him. "Has she even met them?" Oslow asked, appalled.

"Nay. She doesn't even know if they still reside in Lyon."

"That does not bode well," said Lachlan.

"Are you letting her go?" asked Oslow.

"She's not my prisoner. I canna stop her from leaving."

"Then delay her long enough that the snow is

upon us. By then she will have been wooed by some young MacKenzie."

Darach's fists clenched. Angus would rot in hell before he married Caitlin. They all would.

"Do you know Clan MacInnes?" he asked Oslow.

"Nay. But I've heard their laird is cruel. The people are in a bad way."

"Find out what was done to Caitlin after her parents died and if her uncle had anything to do with the fire that killed them. And if Clan MacInnes joins forces with the Frasers, I need to know their strength."

"Aye, Laird." Oslow retreated toward his horse.

"And, Oslow," Darach said, stopping him.

"Aye?"

"Tell Angus not to get his hopes up." He turned back to watch Caitlin as Oslow left, ignoring Lachlan, who had raised his brow.

"So, you'll marry her, then?" his brother asked.

"Nay, I'll send her away with you to find a decent husband."

Lachlan's jaw dropped. "She'll not go, Darach. She wants to be with you, even if she says she wants to go to France. Besides, she's the granddaughter of a laird, daughter of the man who should have been laird. We doona even know to whom she lawfully belongs, and you haven't said it, but that man may be Fraser."

Darach grunted, not wanting to acknowledge that fact. It made things more difficult, but in the end, it didn't matter. She was not going back to the Frasers or Clan MacInnes. Or to some unknown entity in France.

He'd promised to keep her safe.

⁓

Caitlin leaned back contentedly against Darach's chest as they rode along the path that led to the keep. The morning had been pleasant but exhausting, and she'd been relieved when Darach had swept her away on Loki. The strain of the last five days had caught up with her, and all she wanted to do was curl up on her bed for a long nap.

After that, she would consider all Darach had said last night. He was right: her plan was ill-conceived. She needed to make the decision to find her mother's family after she was rested and not so frightened Laird Fraser would find her. If she decided to go, she would need weeks to prepare. Now was not the time to be running anywhere.

"How did you sleep last night?" he asked after she stifled a yawn.

"Good. I doona even remember falling asleep. One moment I was drying my hair by the fire, the next I awakened on my bed. 'Tis a wonderful chamber, Darach. I canna thank you enough. And for the clothes as well. They're lovely." She smoothed her hands over the fine material of her skirt.

"There's no need for thanks. I'm glad they're to your liking." He maneuvered his steed around a rock in the trail, then wrapped his arm about her waist. "And your dreams? How were they?" His voiced had lowered, and the husky timbre caused a flutter in her belly.

"I doona recall. When I first awoke, I'm sure I remembered something, but they slipped away like water. 'Tis a shame. I think they were significant."

"How so?"

"I doona know. They just felt…different."

He exhaled heavily and his breath ruffled her hair. "I understand. More than you know."

"Why? Are your dreams significant too?"

"Aye, since I met you. And I remember every one of them."

"I'm sorry to be such trouble. You should have left me with the Frasers. I would have escaped eventually."

His fingers tightened on her waist. "Nothing in this world could have compelled me to leave you."

She twisted to look at him. "But MacKenzies may be killed."

"Aye, and the Frasers will be defeated. We've spent years preparing for this conflict. I've trained my men, strategized, made provisions for every outcome. We willna fail." He kissed the tip of her nose. "Besides, you had no choice in the matter. You were drugged when I stole you."

"Saved me," she said.

"What?"

"You didn't steal me. You saved me."

He brushed his fingers along her cheek. "Aye."

They passed beneath the portcullis and rode across the bailey, to the stables. When Darach helped her down from his mount, she crossed to Cloud, who whickered a greeting from his stall.

"How's my sweet lad?" she asked as he snuffled her hands for apples.

Darach handed Loki to the groom and joined her. Cloud checked Darach's hands for apples too. When none were forthcoming, he snorted, making her smile. She looked at Darach to see him grinning as well.

"It looks like I'm not the only one giving him treats. I reckon he'll get fat as a sow with all you softhearted men spoiling him."

Darach huffed in a similar fashion to Cloud. "There are no softhearted MacKenzies."

"Aye, that's why I saw Brodie giving him carrots earlier, and Edina told me Oslow had nicked some apples from the kitchen. All your hardened warriors are pussycats at heart, led by the biggest pussycat of all."

Darach stared at her, a strange look in his eye. "I'm no pussycat, Caitlin. Make no mistake." He leaned down, his breath caressing the sensitive skin of her neck as he whispered into her ear. "I am laird first, then a clansman with simple desires. Bar your door at night, sweetling. It costs a man much to walk away from a willing woman."

Seven

A THRILL OF ACCOMPLISHMENT BURST THROUGH Caitlin as she looked at the supplies she'd gathered over the last week and laid out on her bed: neatly folded clothes that had belonged to Darach's mother, including several arisaids, chemises, a warm cloak, hose, and sturdy shoes; a worn pack to go over Cloud that Ronald the stable master had found and Caitlin had mended; oats, apples, and some cheese Ness had pressed on her for helping Fergus; a cup, knife, and other necessities from Edina; and a map Oslow had dug out of a cupboard before showing her the route she would take through the mountains to Inverness. And Cloud, of course, down in the stables.

She even had a quill, paper, and ink Darach had given her two nights past—his face stony, that muscle jumping wildly in his jaw—after she said she needed to make a list to help her decide on her best course of action and to prepare for her trip, just in case. She'd felt very responsible and mature, and had beamed up at him despite his dour expression.

And for the first time in a long time, she'd felt in control of her own destiny.

Even if she didn't go to France, it was good to know she was prepared for any outcome.

The only thing she didn't have was money—a few coins she could use in a pinch. But money was hard to find in the Highlands. People tended to barter goods and services, not pay for them.

Besides, she wasn't comfortable taking hard-earned coin from any of the MacKenzies. She needed to get it from someone who had coin to spare—like Darach or Lachlan, although she doubted Darach would be so inclined.

That left Lachlan, but what on earth could she do for him that he'd pay for?

After carefully fitting everything into her pack, including the hairbrush Darach had gifted her, which she laid on top, she propped the bag in the corner, ready to go if the need arose.

Heading into the hallway, she was just in time to hear the door bang open below as Lachlan and Darach entered the keep. She hurried to the top of the stairs, and a smile broke free when she saw them walking toward the small hearth, their plaids swaying and swords banging against their legs. Both so big and brawny.

"Caitlin!" Lachlan hailed when he saw her. "Come join us for a cup of mead."

"Aye, I should like that. Thank you."

She ran down the stairs toward them. Darach pulled out a chair for her, then sat down with little more than a grunt.

"Is something bothering you, Darach?" she asked.

"Nay. I'm just...lost in thought."

"About what? Maybe I can help."

He grunted again, and when she opened her mouth to question him further, he said, "Leave off, Caitlin. I doona want to talk about it."

The sting of his rejection bit sharply, but she let it go with a silent sigh. He was preparing for war, for sending his warriors off to die. No doubt he had a lot on his mind.

She couldn't stop the guilt from rising, however, or the feeling that she was responsible. It made her shudder to think of all the MacKenzie lives that might be lost.

Darach read the emotions on her face and reached out his hand to give hers a squeeze. "'Tis not the coming war that bothers me, Caitlin. I relish the fight with the Frasers. I canna wait for it. The clan canna wait. My worry is for you and your ill-conceived plan to leave us."

"I'm not planning to leave you, Darach. Not yet. But you told me I must think clearly. 'Tis smart to be ready, aye? Like you are with Fraser."

He nodded reluctantly and leaned back. "Aye."

Edina bustled in with some cups and a pitcher of mead on a tray. "Shall I pour for you, Laird?" she asked.

On Darach's nod, she served them and retreated back to the kitchen.

Caitlin took several sips to ease the tightness in her throat. She liked working toward her goal and gathering her belongings, liked the feeling of being in control of her life after she'd been controlled for so long, but when she thought about leaving, she ended up with a knot in her chest and an ache in her stomach.

The longer she stayed, the harder it would be to leave. And if she left it too late, Fraser would be upon her. Unless she decided to do as Darach asked and stand with them against the Frasers instead of running. 'Twas a problem that left her head spinning and her heart in a tangled mess.

"Do you have everything you need then, lass?" Lachlan asked.

"Aye, other than money. 'Twould be good to have some coin just in case."

"There's no need for it here, but it would be useful in the larger towns."

"'Twas what I thought. But how do women who live there earn coins? Is it hard?" For the life of her, she couldn't remember her mother ever handling money.

Lachlan huffed out a laugh. "It can be—verra hard, depending how good the woman is."

When Darach snorted, she looked over at him. He would not meet her gaze.

Feeling like she was missing something, she asked Lachlan, "Well, how do *you* make money?"

"The last coin I earned was for besting my foster brother Kerr, which is difficult. He's built like a great, bloody rock, and he's fast. But he was certain of his success, and I had precut the wooden sword I tossed him."

Caitlin's eyes stretched so wide they felt like they might fall from her face. "You gambled and you cheated—oh, how wonderful! 'Twas all in fun, aye?"

"Nay. He should have been vigilant enough to discover my deceit, understand?"

She looked at Darach for clarification, but he was smiling and nodding too.

"So, 'tis all right to cheat, then?" she asked.

"Nay!" they said together.

"But, you just said—"

"'Twas all right for me to cheat with Kerr because 'twas a test, to see if he was paying attention. So the wager was that I could beat him in a fight, but the test was of his vigilance—and he failed."

Caitlin pursed her lips and thought on what the men had said. "So are you always testing someone's vigilance when you gamble?"

"Nay, just Gregor and our foster brothers. Otherwise, you make a wager believing in your skill," Darach said.

She sat up. "I have skills. I'm verra good with animals. I'll wager that I can bring your dogs to heel."

Lachlan had just taken a drink of mead and almost blew it through his nose at her statement. "Those bloody hounds are monsters, Caitlin. You havnae seen them. At least wait until they come back from the hunt before you commit."

"Nay, there's no need. I'll bet that I can train Darach's hounds without meeting them first."

He laughed again. "And what coin do you have to gamble?"

"I doona have any. But if I lose, I'll…mend some of your clothes."

"Accepted. What else do you want to wager?"

"Lachlan, I doona think—" Darach started to say.

"Nay, I want to wager," she told him. "I like winning."

A reluctant smile tilted Darach's lips, and she smiled back at him, warmth spreading outward from her chest like melting butter.

Lachlan snapped his fingers between them. "Pay attention. I like winning too. What else do you want to gamble?"

She thought on what else she was good at. "Well, I've read much of the Bible. 'Twas the only book at my uncle's keep. I'll wager I can recite a verse word for word."

"Nay, that's too easy."

"Well...how about that I can teach *you* to recite a verse word for word."

"Nay, that's too hard," Darach said. "He'd just refuse to learn and you would lose the wager."

Caitlin tapped her finger against her lips. Surely God would want her to teach Lachlan a story from the Bible, and He'd provide a moment when Lachlan would have to listen to her.

"I wager that God will make you sit still and listen as I read to you from the scripture."

"Divine intervention?"

"Aye."

Darach groaned as Lachlan shot out his hand. "I accept."

They shook on it, giving her an idea. She grabbed his hands and turned them over, palms facing down. "Hold your hands here." Then she sat opposite him and placed her hands beneath his with their palms touching. "I wager I can slap the top of your hands before you pull them away. Like this." Then she slowly moved her hands out to the side from beneath his and touched the tops of his hands. It was a game she'd played endlessly with her father, and then with some of the warriors and maids in her uncle's keep, although that never lasted long.

"That's it?" Lachlan asked.

"Aye. One coin that I can best you one time."

"You doona have any coins."

"I do. You just havnae given them to me yet."

Darach puffed out a laugh as Lachlan took a coin from his pouch and tossed it to her with a cocky grin. "Here's a free one, sweetling. Keep it out, though. I'll be winning it back shortly."

She smiled sweetly and tucked the coin into a fold in her arisaid, then held her hands out palms up, in front of Lachlan. Darach pulled his chair closer.

When Lachlan laid his palms over hers, she said, "Ready?"

He'd barely finished saying "Aye," when Caitlin whipped her palms out to the side and slapped the tops of his hands.

"I wasn't ready," he protested, a frown darkening his face.

"Then you shouldnae have said 'aye.'"

He looked at Darach to back him up, but Darach just shrugged, his eyes sparkling. Lachlan held his hands out. "Again."

Catlin placed her hands beneath his and waited. And waited. As soon as he looked up from his hands to her, she whipped her hands out and slapped him.

Lachlan pulled his hands back with a loud curse.

"Language, Laird McKay. 'Tis not the Lord's fault you failed to remain vigilant."

Darach practically hooted this time, and a puff of pride filled her. Aye, she was good at this game.

Lachlan dug in his sporran and tossed her another coin, which she slipped into her arisaid. "Maybe you would like to try again?"

He laid his hands out one at a time, arms tense, brow furrowed. This time she pretended to strike, but just jerked her hands, causing him to yank his hands back both times. As soon as he placed his palms against hers the third time, she struck for real and slapped him.

"Again!" he yelled as he tossed her another coin. They played the best of three next, and she won every game.

Finally he slumped back in his chair. "I'm done. I may as well just hand you my purse."

"'Tis difficult to lose, I'm sure," she soothed. "Perhaps you would like to change positions? Maybe you'll be better on the bottom than the top."

Lachlan muttered something about a bishop and a nun as he carefully held out his hands, palms up this time. She placed her palms slowly over his, then looked him in the eye. "Please, doona hurt me, Laird McKay. I bruise easily."

After that it was easy, and she received two more coins for a total of six. "The other bets still stand, aye?" she asked. "Half the amount wagered that I can train Darach's hounds; the other half wagered that you will stay still and listen as I teach you a passage from the Good Book."

"Nay. Half the amount wagered on Darach's hounds, the full amount wagered on reading to me from the Bible. But I have to be a captive audience—no tying me in place or telling it to me when I'm sleeping."

"Agreed. And, Laird MacKay, I would ne'er be in your room while you were sleeping!" Then she spun around, coins clinking together, skirts swishing, and swept toward the stairs.

❧

Darach watched her go, liking the fire in her eyes and the sparkle of her smile, the way her long hair swayed as she walked away from him and how she practically leaped up the stairs.

To count her money, no doubt.

When she disappeared, he glanced over at a bemused-looking Lachlan.

"What were you thinking?" he asked his brother irritably. "Now she's one step closer to leaving."

"Nay, she willna be able to train your dogs, and if by chance she does, no way in hell will I sit still for one of her lectures—and that wager is all or naught."

"Aye, you will. She'll figure something out."

Lachlan sighed. "Maybe, but by then she'll have been here long enough she'll not want to leave. You willna lose her, Darach."

He crossed his arms over his chest. "'Tis not for me I worry. 'Tis for her."

"Then doona be an idiot. Give the lass a reason to stay."

Eight

"HATI, STAY!"

Caitlin stood about twenty feet away from the huge dog and glared at him across the open expanse of the bailey, eyes wide, stare direct. She put as much authority into her voice as possible as she battled the big male for dominance. His brother, Skoll, lolled on the grass beside him. Skoll had submitted to Caitlin after the first day of training in return for treats and her approval. It had been three days, and while she had made good headway with Hati, he still did not obey her to the extent she wanted.

If Darach's dogs had been smaller or the kittens' safety not at stake, she might have accepted Hati's reluctant obedience and claimed her coin from Lachlan. But the hound gazed intently at the four kittens playing on a blanket with Fergus several feet away. Caitlin was fair certain, as soon as her back was turned, he would run after them—again.

The dogs were named after the wolves Hati and Skoll in Norse mythology, who'd chased the sun and the moon, trying to eat them. According to legend, when their quarry was caught, the world would come to an end. 'Twas no wonder Darach's dogs misbehaved, when they had such namesakes.

But Caitlin was stubborn, and Hati would submit as Skoll had—from sheer boredom if naught else.

A number of people loitered in the bailey, watching her progress, and a few warriors stood guard over the kittens should Hati test Caitlin's authority again. That niggled, but Darach had insisted, obviously not believing she could control the large dog. A few more days and she would prove him wrong.

"Such good lads," she crooned and approached to give them treats and pets, causing their tails to thump madly on the trodden-down grass before she retreated again. They had stayed in place for over an hour now, and she was about to release them when their bodies tensed with excitement. Skoll pushed himself into a sitting position, muscles quivering, while Hati whined eagerly at something behind her.

Or someone. Darach most likely. He was their alpha, and they obeyed him with complete devotion.

Her own excitement rose too, and her stomach dipped when she sensed him behind her. She wanted to turn around but was afraid to, lest the dogs disobeyed and ran to him. Instead, she widened her eyes and stared them down.

They stayed.

"I would ne'er have believed it—another wager won," Darach said into her ear. "You are to be commended. My beasts behaving and Fergus out here among his family, clean and happy, playing with the kittens. 'Tis true what they say. You are a miracle worker."

Her heart filled at the compliment. "'Tis only that they want to obey more than they want my displeasure. And Fergus wants to be where the kits are."

"Fergus wants to be where you are. As does half the clan."

A blush rose in her cheeks. She wanted to ask if he felt the same.

Probably not, if his absence the last three days was any indication. She'd seen him briefly during the day, at the evening meal, and maybe for a short time before bed. At night, she barred her door as he'd requested, but only because she didn't want to upset him when he'd asked her so nicely. It felt wrong to lock him out, and her heart protested every time she did so—but like Hati and Skoll, she also wanted to please him.

"Would you like to see them crawl?" she asked, excited to show off their latest trick.

"You've taught my beasts to grovel?"

"Aye, it took all morning. It keeps their joints limber."

She almost laughed at his pinched expression. By the look of him, one would think he took great pride in his dogs' unruliness. She could scarce wait to show him how they could bow, roll over, and beg too.

"Stand here and let us come to you."

She grasped a treat in each hand and walked between the dogs. "By my side," she commanded. Skoll obeyed immediately, but Hati looked back at Darach longingly before complying. Caitlin directed them into a down position facing Darach.

"Stay," she said and walked back to him.

She sat on her haunches and held the treats low to the ground. The dogs eyed them greedily.

"Crawl!"

They started toward her, bellies to the ground. When they reached her, she held up a hand for them to stop, then gave them their treats along with much love and praise. Darach crouched beside her and also praised them. The dogs shivered with excitement, looking as if they would burst through their skins, but they continued to hold their positions. Caitlin was well pleased.

She stood and called out, "Release!" They sprang forward, catching her by surprise and knocking her into Darach, who was still on his haunches. He stayed upright for a second, then lost his balance, and they fell backward onto the grass, Caitlin sprawled on top of him. The dogs hovered over them, barking and licking.

Darach's arms came around her protectively. "Back!"

His hounds obeyed but continued to jump around. Skoll began running in circles around them, faster and faster. Hati joined his brother, nipping at his flanks. Everyone was running now, coming to their assistance.

Caitlin looked over just in time to see one of the kittens make a dash for safety. Hati took to the chase like a demon to a sinner, knocking over a pile of wood and a basketful of laundry. A horse reared and stamped its hooves.

"The kittens!" she called out.

People dashed to restrain the dogs and scoop up Fergus and the kits, who were squirming to get free. The last little one, Fortitude, darted through the crowd with Hati on his heels. Caitlin's heart caught in her throat as Hati gained on the wee feline. They neared the well, and she saw Lachlan reaching for the kit just as it leaped onto the wooden trestle above. It scrambled to the top and settled down.

Lachlan tripped over Hati, who yelped in surprise. Both dog and laird went flying. Hati crashed to the ground. Lachlan toppled backward into the stone well, and he hung there, his arms and legs dangling over the edge, arse dipping down. Thank the saints he was too big to fall through the hole.

A quiet descended. Hati rose meekly to lick Lachlan's hand, then rested his head on the laird's arm, pleading forgiveness. Fortitude stared at them from his perch, tail swishing as he washed his face. Skoll flopped to the ground with a loud huff.

Caitlin still lay on Darach, who shook with anger. Her insides jostled as his body heaved. What right did he have to be angry? They were his dogs. She wasn't the one who'd let them run wild, named them after demons who wanted to destroy the world.

She sat up, kneeing and prodding him mercilessly as she straightened her skirts. He groaned, but it came out sounding strangled. Glaring at him, she was surprised to see a smile on his face. And not like any smile she'd seen before. This one stretched wide across his cheeks, dimpling his left one and crinkling the bridge of his nose and eyes.

And the sounds coming from his throat…first a snort, then a huffing sound that turned into great hoots of laughter. He pushed himself onto one elbow and surveyed the scene, especially Lachlan, who looked ridiculous lying over the well. The laird tried to get out but appeared to be stuck. Darach collapsed back onto the ground, stomach heaving.

Caitlin stared at him, entranced by the joy on his face. His clan stared as well, some laughing with him, others with their jaws dropped—all except Lachlan, who scowled.

Darach caught his eye. "Didn't your mother teach you not to run near the well?"

Lachlan scowled harder. "I wasn't running. I was leaping to save that bloody cat. Christ Almighty, it almost killed me."

Caitlin's smile vanished, and she frowned at Lachlan. "Laird MacKay, your language would make Lucifer cackle. 'Tis a good thing you did not die or you'd be explaining to God why you dare such blasphemy. Or worse, begging the devil for mercy! If our poor Savior—"

Darach's burst of laughter drowned her out.

Caitlin turned to him, annoyed. She was just getting warmed up. He picked up her hand and kissed her palm, causing her insides to melt. "Let's go help Lachlan, aye?" Then he led her through the crowd, toward his glaring friend. Skoll fell in beside them.

When they reached the well, Lachlan held out his arm for assistance, but Darach shook his head. "'Tis obvious you need more than just physical help, Brother. Caitlin will see to your soul. 'Tis lucky you have her to instruct you while you're stuck. It may take me a while to free you." He dropped her hand, then headed toward the keep with the dogs at his heels.

Brimming with pleasure, Caitlin patted Lachlan's knee. "Are you familiar with the story of Moses and the Ten Commandments, Laird MacKay? 'Tis one of my favorites from the Good Book."

Caitlin played with one of her newly won coins as she lounged on a blanket in the bailey with Fergus, the kittens, Ness, Edina, and two young women, named Rose and Heather, who worked in the keep. The dust had settled from the earlier excitement, and the dogs had been forgiven. They now lay a few feet away, snoozing in the afternoon sun.

To her amazement, Hati appeared to have given up all interest in the kittens. He paid them no mind as Fortitude stalked his tail and Temperance batted Skoll's ear. She assumed the collision with Lachlan had scared him into submission.

As she pet the huge hound, he thumped his tail, causing Fortitude to attack it. The dog lifted his head to watch the kitten for a moment, then flopped back down.

"'Tis a rough life you lead, Hati."

"Wonders will ne'er cease," Edina said. "First our laird laughing, then his devil dogs reduced to mere playthings for the kittens. It gives me hope. Maybe my Oslow will yet learn to use a hairbrush."

"I doona know," Caitlin said. "Oslow takes great pride in his mane."

"'Tis true. But you create miracles, Caitlin. Perhaps you could speak to my husband on his grooming habits."

Ness snorted. "Or lack thereof."

The women tittered with amusement, familiar with Oslow's wild hair and bushy eyebrows.

"None have e'er considered me a miracle worker," Caitlin mused. "'Tis chaos I create. My dear father often said so, and I'm sure Darach would agree." She thought back on Edina's words and furrowed her brow in confusion. "What do you mean about Darach not laughing? I find him to be exceedingly good humored."

Heather and Rose, sisters with bright-red hair and freckled complexions, gaped at her. "You are so brave," Heather said. "I canna do more than glance at him before my knees quake. He looks so fierce."

Caitlin couldn't fathom it. Darach was such a braw man—and laird too. She would think they'd be lined up trying to catch his attention. "Doona either of you find him handsome? He's fierce, aye, but only when he's protecting his clan. He took such good care of me when I was sick." She wrinkled her nose as she thought about it. "Except when he pretended to leave me with the kits, but deep down I knew he'd come back. His heart is verra soft."

Rose leaned in. "Are you sure? I hear he hunts down wild boar, kills them with his bare hands, and eats the raw flesh. For sure he's part beast."

Heather scooted closer. "And he swims the loch every night to battle the monster. What man can do that?"

Ness made a disparaging sound and rolled her eyes. "'Tis untrue. What silly girls you are to believe such nonsense about our laird. Many a night he spends in the kitchen watching Fergus, so the women can return to their families. Aye, he likes wild boar, but cooked with apples and honey." She paused, then dropped her voice to a whisper. "But I have heard he meets a faery woman during the full moon. She gives him speed and strength in return for sexual favors."

Caitlin gasped and looked, wide eyed, at Edina.

"I have ne'er heard the likes," the housekeeper said. "Ness MacKenzie, you should be ashamed of yourself for believing such nonsense. 'Tis understandable such stories coming from young lasses, but you are a woman grown."

"How do you know it's not true? He doesn't indulge with any of the women, and he must find release somewhere."

"Aye. Just not with a MacKenzie. Oslow tells me he has women in other clans, the same as Laird MacKay does here."

Caitlin's head spun. 'Twas good to know Darach was not under the spell of a faery, but the idea of him being in love with another women made her stomach roil.

"'Tis the way of unmarried men, sweetling," Edina said. "It doesn't mean he loves any of them."

Her chest loosened, and she breathed easier. 'Twas silly, of course. It's not like she could claim him as her own.

"Is there something wrong with the MacKenzie lasses that he willna choose one of us?" Ness asked.

"He wouldnae want to dishonor them," Caitlin said. "They are under his protection. If he engaged in carnal relations with a MacKenzie he would have to marry her." She sighed heavily. "And he says he ne'er wants a wife."

They fell silent. Skoll stretched out a hind leg to scratch his ear, and Temperance jumped back. Caitlin pocketed her coin and picked up the kitten to soothe the feline as well as herself. The thought of Darach childless and alone the rest of his life caused a cramping in her heart. He was a man with much love to give. He would be a wonderful husband and father.

"What about you?" Heather asked. "Maybe he'll marry you?"

She looked up to find all eyes on her and shook her head. It was impossible.

"Why not?" asked Rose. "He held your hand earlier and watches you closely. 'Tis said he'll make you his lady." She leaned forward. "Has he kissed you?"

"Not really. I kissed him once, but he pushed me away." When the women's eyes widened, she blushed. "'Twas not meant in that way. I was happy about my new home and threw my arms around him. 'Twas naught but gratitude."

The shame of his rejection swelled anew, and Edina patted her arm. "You're under his protection as well, Caitlin. He cares for your honor." She grinned. "But that doesn't mean he didn't like it."

Caitlin couldn't help the flare of hope that filled her breast...before she crushed it. Those sorts of dreams were for other women. Her chance for a happy marriage was gone—whether she decided to leave or stay.

"I would be afraid to marry him, no matter he was laird," Heather said with a shudder.

Caitlin's teeth clenched. Darach did naught but tend to his clan, and this foolish girl would disparage him? Not just her, her sister as well, and Ness with her silly story. But it went deeper than that. They expected everything of Darach and gave nothing in return. Not a warm welcome, or a shared jest, or even a thank-you for his care. They left him on his cold, lonely pedestal while they dwelled happily down below.

"Shame on you, Heather, for having such thoughts. If you were Darach's wife, he would treat you with naught but respect. He would protect you always and see to your happiness. And Rose, daring to call him a beast. Do you think he has no feelings? He gives all for his clan, and I have yet to see one of you extend a hand or a smile in heartfelt welcome. None have asked how he fares or thanked him for his care."

Her voice had risen and the dogs sat up, agitated. "What has he done to deserve such disrespect? Has he beaten or starved you? Has he wasted the clan's resources on his own greed and gluttony? Has he shamed the people into believing they have less value than the ox in the field?"

She looked at each woman as she spoke. "He has provided for you and kept you safe. You are blessed. I have seen the horrors of a laird who abuses his people, and 'tis a travesty. Fortunately for you, Darach would die before he'd allow that to happen."

Tears welled in Heather's eyes, and she squeezed her sister's hand, who'd turned as red as the devil's forked tongue. Ness stared at her arisaid, unable to meet Caitlin's eyes—none of them could.

The only one who did was Edina, who watched her with consideration. "Aye, you're right. He is an honorable man and a worthy laird. I too have seen the ravages of an uncaring laird. Thankfully, I met Oslow and became a MacKenzie. To be sure, Darach deserves our gratitude and respect."

"'Tis more than that, Edina. He deserves your love

and kinship. You should welcome him as you would a well-loved father or brother, not distance yourself through formality."

"Surely he would yell at us," said Rose.

"I have ne'er heard him yell at anyone. Well, except for me, but I do try the patience of a saint. He only yelled because I put myself and others in danger. Surely you wouldnae be so foolish."

Rose shook her head. Heather had stopped crying and looked at Caitlin earnestly. "What should we do?"

She clasped the girls' hands. "First, you must look him in the eye. Hold his gaze and smile—like you mean it. Ask him how he fares and thank him for being such a good laird." They nodded intently, but when she added, "Touch him often," they gasped, which made her laugh. Instructing the women was almost as enjoyable as teaching Lachlan the Ten Commandments.

"Doona touch him in a familiar way of course. Pat his arm or shoulder, like you would Hati." She cuddled Hati to demonstrate. The lasses still did not look convinced. "Or maybe bring him something nice—a sweet or a flower. Involve him in your day-to-day concerns. Ask for his opinion. Invite him into your homes for a cup of mead or a family dinner. Share your stories and jests. He is the head of your family—treat him so."

Heather and Rose hung on every word.

Even Ness nodded thoughtfully. "You have given us much to ponder, lass. It pains me to think I could be so inconsiderate."

Caitlin squeezed Ness's arm. "I'm sure it couldnae

have been easy. He is resistant to being nurtured. But 'tis our job to care for stubborn men."

The four of them nodded in agreement. They would spread the word, and Darach would become the center of his clan's attention. A man well loved and appreciated, rather than isolated in his grand castle.

Ness heaved herself up with a sigh. "'Tis well past time I checked on the evening meal. We may have an overcooked bird tonight. But our laird ne'er complains—no matter if the bread be burnt or the oats mushy." She headed to the kitchen, saying, "Aye, a good man."

Heather and Rose jumped up too. To Caitlin's surprise, they curtsied to her before rushing off, their heads together.

She set Temperance down beside a sleeping Fergus, who had gained some color in the sun. It filled her heart to see him looking so well. Clean too. He had agreed to have a bath every Sunday night to keep the kittens happy.

"I suppose I should work some more with Hati and Skoll, assure their good behavior."

Edina placed a hand on her arm. "Nay, stay awhile. I would speak with you privately."

Caitlin's stomach dropped. She admired Edina greatly and didn't want to offend her. "Truly, I meant no disrespect, but I canna take back what I said."

"Doona fash, lass. I thought you spoke wisely. 'Twas good for us to hear. I thought merely to tell you a story, tell you how it was the Frasers became our enemy. It will help you understand why Darach seems apart from us. 'Tis not just the clan's doing; 'tis a choice he made as well."

Caitlin scooted closer to Edina. "I would verra much like to know. Oslow told me he saved the clan when he was only twenty. If I did not know him, I would scarce believe it."

"Aye, he did save us, but only just. The Frasers were once allies of the MacKenzies, although I knew better than most they were rotten to the core. You see, before I became a MacKenzie I was a Fraser. 'Twas a difficult life, full of uncertainty and abuse. The old laird was as cruel as the current one."

Caitlin shuddered. The Fraser laird was a degenerate of the worst kind; she couldn't imagine there being two of them.

"Darach was just a lad when I came here with Oslow," Edina continued. "Maybe five years old. A rough-and-tumble boy, except when his father was near. Then he behaved impeccably. When he was eight, he was fostered to the MacLeods. That's where he learned to be a great laird."

"Aye, he mentioned Gregor MacLeod. I would like to meet him."

"I'm sure you will. Soon. There is trouble stirring, and he is our greatest ally."

Trouble she had caused. How many of the men here, men she'd supped with, would die in the conflict? How many women like Edina would lose their husbands and sons?

Edina frowned. "I see what you're thinking and 'tis not true. Eight years ago, the Frasers betrayed the MacKenzies in the worst way. Conflict between the clans is inevitable."

"What did they do?"

"Laird Fraser negotiated a marriage between his sister Moire and Darach, who was nineteen by then and verra much in love with his intended—or so he thought. Moire was older by seven years and had been married before. She was a bonny woman but as rotten as her brother. I had seen it firsthand when she was still a lass. My mother and I worked in the Fraser keep, much as I do now. Moire often lied to create trouble for us, which finally resulted in my mother's death. I scarce escaped with my life."

"Oh, Edina, I'm so sorry. What did Darach say when you told him his betrothed was a monster?"

She sighed. "I stayed quiet at first. I didn't know him verra well, for he'd only returned to the clan from the MacLeods a few years earlier. I didn't have his measure, and Moire had her hooks into him strong. By the time I said something, 'twas almost too late."

The sun had dropped in the sky and the air cooled, but Caitlin was too caught up in the story to care.

"They were intimate, see, and 'tis a hard thing for a lad to separate love and lust. Moire claimed him with her body and blinded him to everything else."

"Her brother knew this?"

"Aye, he was part of it. While Darach was losing himself in Moire, Fraser was arranging for the MacKenzies' demise. 'Twas a week after Darach's twentieth birthday, two weeks before the wedding. I still had friends at the Fraser keep, and I asked what preparations were taking place for the wedding. When the cook whispered naught had been done, I knew the worst was about to happen. You see, if the Frasers ambushed the wedding, it wouldnae only be the death of the MacKenzies, but also our allies—Darach's foster father and brothers. 'Twould be a great blow to all decent people in the Highlands."

Caitlin shook her head, dread tightening her stomach, even though she knew the Frasers had not succeeded in their treachery.

"I told Oslow, who told Darach's father. I was afraid to get the Fraser cook in trouble, so Oslow promised to be discreet. The next thing I knew, our laird, Darach's da, was killed in an unfortunate accident on Fraser land and Oslow seriously injured."

"You must have been so worried."

"Aye, and they said he was too sick to return to us, so by rights, they held him hostage. I didn't know whom to trust. Darach was devastated by his father's death and still being deceived by Moire. When they brought the laird back here for burial, Darach wanted to postpone the wedding, but Moire threw a fit. I heard them arguing. She said everything was prepared and if it did not go ahead, Darach would father a bastard."

"'Twas a lie?" Caitlin asked, feeling her eyes pop from her head.

"I canna know for sure, but I believe so. After that, Darach agreed to her demands. He was happy about the bairn and thought himself in love with Moire. I couldnae stand it anymore, and when she left, I told him everything."

"Did he believe you?"

"Not right away, but I could see it weighed on him. He went to see her the next night. 'Tis rumored there are hidden passageways into the Fraser keep, and he'd been meeting with Moire secretly for months. He returned the next day with Oslow, battered and bleeding, and called our men to arms. We were ill prepared for the onslaught, but Darach managed to get most of us safely into the castle. Many warriors on both sides were killed that day."

"What about Moire and the bairn?"

"She died a month later. 'Tis said she tumbled down the stairs and broke her neck. I heard through my kin she and her brother had been fighting. I came across the clan wisewoman a few years later and asked if she'd seen Moire's body. She said there were no signs of pregnancy."

Relief flooded Caitlin. She was glad Darach had not had the heartache of losing a bairn. Gladder still Moire was dead. 'Twas not very Christian of her, but the woman had caused such turmoil and would have continued to do so.

"We've been fighting with them e'er since," Edina continued. "Wee skirmishes here and there. We're stronger now than e'er before and would have attacked sooner, but the King interceded two years ago with a command for peace. Our laird broke that peace when he saved you."

Caitlin dropped her head in her hands and groaned. "I know you say 'tis not my fault, but I dread the spilling of any more MacKenzie blood."

"As do I."

Tears pricked her eyes. "That's why he doesn't want a wife or bairns, why he is separate from the clan. He blames himself for their deaths and doesn't believe he deserves their goodwill.

"Aye. He'll spend the rest of his days punishing himself for being a foolish lad in love."

Caitlin wiped her cheeks. "I willna allow it. I'll make that man happy if it's the last thing I do." She took Edina's hand. "Come. We have work to do."

Nine

DARACH TRIED NOT TO SIGH IMPATIENTLY AS A LASS named Heather told him a convoluted story about two MacKenzie lads and a pig named Zeus. If Lachlan had been there, he would have raised an eyebrow and said something indecent—to Darach's ears, at least. To the lass, it would have sounded perfectly respectable.

"So, who do you think I should choose?" she finally asked.

That's what the story had been about? Picking a lad to fancy? Why hadn't she just said so in the beginning? He knew both lads and would easily choose... Hmmm, who would he choose? Each boy was a bit of a scoundrel. He'd disciplined them both on occasion. And where had the pig fit in?

"Neither," he said, thinking the bizarre meeting was over.

But the lass pouted. "You canna say neither, Laird MacKenzie. You must choose."

Darach's eyes widened, amazed the lass had contradicted him. The same lass who three days ago could barely look him in the face. He couldn't stop the grin that creased his cheeks.

"'Tis verra poor manners to tell your laird what he can and canna do, Heather. Neither lad is grown enough to be a good choice. Either wait a year, or pick another lad."

She returned his smile shyly. "Aye, you're right. My mother said the same thing. 'Tis just that me sister, Rose, is seeing Tavis MacKenzie and she ne'er stops talking about him. 'Tis most aggravating. I would like to have me own stories to tell."

"You will, lass. You're a bonny girl. Doona fret."

He turned to leave, but she placed her hand on his arm and patted it awkwardly like she would a dog. "Maybe someone older, then?"

"Aye, that's a good choice."

"How much older?"

For the love of God, how much more of this could he take? She was the third woman to stop him this morning. Anice MacKenzie, the clan weaver, had brought him a beautiful new plaid. He'd been very touched, but the woman had spent a considerable amount of time regaling him with stories of her twelve grandchildren. Then Robina MacKenzie had waved at him from across the bailey and brought him a package of sweets. It was the fourth such package he'd received in two days.

And yesterday in the village, women had surrounded him, inquiring about his health and asking him in for a cup of mead. His meeting to discuss the repairs needed after the winter storms had to be rescheduled. Not to mention with all the mead in his belly, he'd scarcely been able to sit his horse on the ride back to the castle.

"Laird?" Heather prompted.

He glanced at her, trying not to let his exasperation show. "I doona know, lass. Maybe another woman could advise you best. I must see to my duties now."

She blushed but still smiled. "Certainly, Laird. I thank you for your time…and for your sacrifice, of course."

He hesitated. "Sacrifice?"

"Aye. As our laird. You take such good care of us. 'Tis much appreciated."

His chest tightened, cutting off his breath. For a moment, he could not speak. None other than Caitlin had ever said those words to him. 'Twas not necessary, for it was his duty, but the sentiment affected him greatly.

Heather did not notice. Instead, her eyes lit up and she giggled. "If you see my sister, ask her to tell you the story about the priest, the cow, and the Englishwoman. I laughed so hard I hurt my belly. After that, Rose would moo every time she saw me. Do you think it's possible to die from laughing?"

Darach had to clear his throat before speaking. "I doona think so, lass. And if you did die laughing, I'm sure the angels would take you straight to Heaven."

He smiled and headed for his solar, wanting to avoid any more encounters. Something was going on, and he was sure Caitlin was behind it. Who else would cause him such trouble?

His solar faced south and caught the morning sunlight through the two arched windows. It was his favorite room in the keep. A fire blazed in the hearth, creating a comfortable haven, and a wool rug covered the floor—an extravagance, for sure. On the wall behind his desk hung a tapestry depicting a Highland battle that had graced the wall in his room at the MacLeod keep when he was a lad. A farewell gift from his foster father, Gregor—he could not imagine the room without it.

Darach's steward had placed a report on his desk that needed attention. It sat atop a pile of other reports and unfinished business. He'd meant to go through them yesterday, but the time had slipped away—into the myriad discussions he'd had with the women, no doubt.

He had to admit their solicitude had pleased him at first. Although it had been so many years since they'd held his gaze, he'd been a little unnerved. Now he was just annoyed. Did he really need to know that wee Robbie MacKenzie had lost his supper all over Odara MacKenzie's skirts? Or that Tearlach MacKenzie had drunk so much he'd mistaken Coira MacKenzie for his wife and kissed her? Well, that one had been amusing, especially when Coira's husband had caught them and tossed Tearlach into the sludge pile behind the mill.

But the rest…

He sighed and sorted through the work on his desk. He would barely get through half of it before he had to go to Odar MacKenzie's cottage for dinner. The blacksmith's wife had sent him an invitation with her youngest son. Darach did not want to offend the family by refusing.

A knock sounded at the door. *Please God, not here too.* "Come in."

Oslow walked through the door, and Darach released the breath he'd been holding.

"Am I disturbing you, Laird?"

"Nay, I was just worried lest you were another well-intending woman. 'Tis one more reason not to have a wife. How does a man get any work done with the constant chatter?"

"Well now, not all women are the same. Especially the sweet ones like Caitlin. She wouldnae be a bother."

Darach snorted. "She's the worst of the lot. She blathered the entire trip here, and she's done something to make the women come after me."

"Come after you?" Oslow asked, trying not to smile.

"You know what I mean. They willna leave me alone. Tonight I go to Odar MacKenzie's for supper. Can you imagine?"

"A travesty, that. Maybe you would like me to lock him up?"

Darach's mouth twitched before he sighed. Aye, he could see the humor in it. It would most likely be an enjoyable evening. The blacksmith had four rowdy sons who told a good story, and the food was sure to be plentiful. "Maybe I'll take Lachlan with me. He is much at ease with people."

Oslow took a seat across from Darach and they discussed the latest news from their spy in the Fraser keep. He'd told them the Frasers were not officially allied with Caitlin's clan, but in the past year, the Fraser laird had gone there to visit three times. On the last trip, he'd taken a number of chests with him. It was rumored he'd be bringing home a great prize.

Darach scowled. Caitlin had been that prize.

Well, neither her uncle nor Fraser could control her now. She was safe with the MacKenzies, no matter how much trouble she caused—at least until she chose to go on her fool's journey to France.

"You willna be angry with her, will you?" Oslow asked.

"I would ne'er blame her for the acts of corrupt men." He couldn't believe Oslow had asked him that.

"Nay, I meant for telling the women you were lonely and needed to be nurtured."

For a second, Darach's jaw dropped. Then it snapped together so hard, he thought he might have broken some teeth. "She said what?"

Oslow's eyebrows rose in alarm. "Oh, well, those weren't her exact words. I most likely confused them with something else. Edina did blather on, and I was only half listening. As you said, women do chatter."

Darach rose from his chair and clenched the edges of the desk, turning his knuckles white. She'd told the women he needed to be nurtured? That he was lonely? For the love of Christ, he was their laird, not a bairn to be coddled.

Oslow rose too. "She said many other things as well. That you were a great laird and an honorable man, and the MacKenzies were lucky to have you. She felt we didn't appreciate you enough."

He would be the judge of that. Darach released the desk and marched around it. "Where is she?"

"Gone."

The word hit him like a punch in the gut and he

came to an abrupt halt. "What do you mean, gone? She's left already?"

"Not to France. Just to the loch with Cloud. She's been riding him most days. I have men guarding her every step."

Relief rushed through Darach. His knees weakened, and he leaned back against the desk to cover it up. It was one thing for him to send Caitlin away with Lachlan, another for her to just disappear across the ocean.

She would be the death of him, yet...unless he got his hands on her first.

❧

A loud banging startled Caitlin into wakefulness. She'd been alone, drowsing by the small hearth in the great hall, dreaming of Darach. She'd waited up to tell him that Fergus had finally agreed to move into the keep, with the kittens of course, and not to worry when he couldn't find the lad in the kitchen.

Peering around the back of the chair to see who'd entered the empty hall, she saw Hati and Skoll bounding toward her. She hugged each dog and closed her eyes as they licked her face. When she opened them, Darach towered over her, scowling.

"What's the matter?" she asked. "Didn't you have a good time?"

"Nay, 'twas verra pleasant. Odar's wife, Fia, is a good cook, and the lads told some amusing tales. Every one of them matched by Lachlan, who regaled them with embarrassing stories of our childhood. Now, not only do they think their laird is a pathetic, lonely man in need of nurturing, but also a right hooligan. It couldnae have been better."

Caitlin pushed the dogs away. They slunk into a corner and lay down, watching their master. She wanted to join them. He eyed her with an intensity that made her heart race. He was angry, aye, but also... Well, she didn't know what else.

She rose from the chair. "Where's Lachlan?"

"He took a detour on the way back to the keep. He'll be gone most of the evening."

"Where'd he go?"

Darach exhaled heavily and rolled his eyes. "Visiting."

"At this time of night?"

"'Tis what men do when they have willing women to...visit."

She gasped. "You mean he's tupping."

His eyebrows shot upward. "Christ Almighty, Caitlin, women doona say that word!" He pointed his finger at her. "And doona lecture me on my language."

"What word would you prefer me to use? Swiving?"

"I'd prefer you to say naught at all—about anything! Especially when it comes to me and how I choose to lead this clan!"

He stepped forward and the heat from his body engulfed her. They'd been much closer many times in the past, but tonight something lurked beneath his controlled visage—something that longed to devour her.

And God help her, she wanted to be devoured.

Retreating, she bumped into the chair. 'Twas a good thing it was there, for her knees suddenly gave out, and she dropped to the seat. He leaned down, hands locking on to the armrests.

Her breath caught—she was not just nervous, but excited too. A prickly heat rose along her chest and her breasts ached—they were too confined, too hot.

She wanted him to move away but also come closer. Her hands traveled up his arms to push him back, but they gripped the material of his lèine instead.

"You should be in bed, Caitlin. With the door barred."

She licked her bottom lip. His eyes narrowed on the movement, and the muscles beneath her hands tensed.

"I was waiting for you." It came out a whisper, but it throbbed with something else, something…carnal.

He heard it too, and his nostrils flared as if he could scent her. Grasping her waist, he lifted her against him, pelvis to pelvis, chest to chest, and slid a hand beneath her backside, so she was supported. Her feet dangled above the floor, and she wrapped her arms around his neck.

A burning heat filled her. Her hips rocked against him instinctively. He was so big, so hard. Everywhere.

His fingers dug into the soft flesh of her buttocks and held her tight. "If I'm so lonely, maybe you should comfort me. Even the strongest man needs comfort." He sounded ragged, but she sensed the anger, the pain beneath his words.

"I want to comfort you, Darach. Always. I ne'er want you to be alone or unhappy."

His arms wrapped tight around her, one still anchoring her hips to his, the other angled across her back. He dropped his head into the crook of her neck and shuddered. She held him with all her might.

She didn't know how long they stayed that way—it could have been minutes or hours—but suddenly he lifted his head, burrowed his hand in her hair, and against her lips said, "Then doona leave," before he dropped his mouth to hers.

He was not gentle. His lips did not tease or finesse. Rather he simply demanded entrance and she gave it.

She would have given him anything.

He plundered her mouth, and her fingers curled into his scalp, pressing him closer. She rubbed her tongue against his. A liquid heat spread in her belly, dipping low between her legs and out to the tips of her breasts.

She squirmed, but not to get away. Instead, she rubbed against the angles and planes of his torso. The hard muscles of his chest flattened her aching breasts. The ridge at his pelvis chafed the vee of her thighs.

Groaning, he shifted his hand from her hair to the back of her leg to pull it up and around his hip. She moved her other leg into the same position. The movement tangled her skirts, and he helped her 'til her ankles locked at the small of his back. Still his mouth ravaged hers. She moved with him now, her tongue following his as he advanced and retreated in her mouth, her hips finding a rhythm as he rocked his pelvis against hers.

Something built inside her, an urgency. For what, she wasn't sure. She just had to get closer, squeeze tighter, agitation rising alongside wonder. He turned and sat with her on the chair, his hand tucking her legs down either side of him, so they dangled through the armrests to the floor.

A small space opened between them and she cried out. An answering rumble echoed in his chest. His sporran was in the way, so he pushed it to the side and pulled her up hard against him. She shuddered.

"Caitlin. Look at me."

His voice was so raspy she could barely understand him. Didn't want to understand him. Her sluggish mind protested being drawn back from sheer bliss.

He grasped her upper arms and pushed her away, so she angled back over his legs. "Look at me."

Her lids were heavy. When she managed to open them, he groaned. One hand supported her shoulders. The other lifted to trail down her face.

"Ne'er in my life have I seen anyone as lovely as you."

He leaned forward and captured her lips again. Light kisses that nibbled, licked, and sucked. His tongue teased; his teeth gently scraped. The pressure built once more, and she rocked against him, moaning.

"Doona stop," he said.

She was beyond stopping. Beyond anything but the burgeoning ache between her legs that urged her onward. When his hand stroked down her throat and palmed her breast, she cried out, then clasped her hand over his and squeezed.

Something was happening to her. Her head dropped back and he kissed her throat as he kneaded her breast, his fingers flicking over her nipples.

He loosened her linen chemise and had just slipped his hand inside her dress when she heard it. A pleading whine by her right ear. It didn't make sense until she heard Darach say, "Hati, lie down." But his voice was weak, and the dog didn't listen.

Darach cleared his throat. This time he spoke with authority. "Lie down."

She turned her head to the side and saw Hati reluctantly lower himself to the floor, eyeing them anxiously. Paws padded across the rushes, and Skoll flopped down beside his brother. He barked once, then laid his head on Hati's back, also watching.

Darach sighed heavily, tightening his hand on her breast as if to memorize the feel of it before releasing her. He fastened her chemise and dropped his head to the crook of her neck, breathing deeply.

Awareness slowly crept back to Caitlin. The room came into focus, and she once again heard the crackle of the fire, felt the warmth of the flames on her back. Embarrassed heat rushed up her skin when she remembered what she'd done. She squirmed to get away, but Darach tightened his arms around her.

"Doona move." He sounded like he was in pain. More than likely she'd hurt him climbing all over his body. Rubbing against him like a…like a… She couldn't even find the words.

Darach pulled back to look at her, lids lowered as if to shield his thoughts.

"I'm sorry," she blurted out.

His brows shot up. "For what?"

"For what I just did. For kissing you and…and…" She couldn't say it—it was too dreadful. She lowered her voice. "'Twas most ungodly."

He laughed—a short, hard sound. "God is in all creation, Caitlin. Surely if He didn't want us making love, He wouldnae have made it so pleasurable." Darach's face turned bleak. "And 'twas my fault, not yours. I took advantage of you."

"You did?"

"Aye."

She didn't understand. She was the one who'd trapped him with her legs, climbed on top of him like the monkeys her father had told her about. A confused frown creased her brow. "I didn't hurt you?"

He dropped his head into the crook of her neck. His breath puffed against her skin as if he laughed, maybe sighed.

When he raised his head, he tilted her face up with his fingers. "You didn't hurt me. 'Tis what happens when a man makes love to a woman. Until he finds release, 'tis…uncomfortable."

Her dismay must have shown on her face, for he shook his head and said, "God help me, I'm making it worse."

He gripped her waist and tried to lift her, but her legs were trapped by her heavy skirts and the arms of the chair.

"Raise your arisaid, then your feet," he said. "I'll pull you free."

When they were untangled, he rose, placed her back in the chair, and moved toward the hearth. After a moment, he turned to her. She noticed his plaid bulged in front where his privates were located. He caught her staring and shifted his leather sporran over himself.

"I knew I hurt you with my indecent rubbing. Is that why it's swollen?" She couldn't take her eyes from it.

He rested his forehead against the mantel, rubbing the back of his neck. "Lord have mercy, I have ne'er met a lass so innocent. Do you know naught of intimate congress?"

Her mouth snapped shut. She'd seen animals in the act, aye, but always from a distance. When she'd asked her mother about it, she'd been told a man's parts fit into a woman's parts like a broomstick into a bucket. She'd said naught of the broomstick breaking.

"So...'tis not broken?"

"Nay." He looked over his shoulder toward the door and mumbled something under his breath about Edina. She thought he was going to leave, but instead he moved stiffly to the other chair and sat down. Color came and went in his cheeks. "Caitlin, what we did, the way we touched each other and how our bodies reacted, mine as well as yours, is all part of lovemaking. If we'd been married, I'd have...finished the act."

She scrunched her brow. "You mean, put your broomstick into my bucket?" She didn't think that had happened, but it would be good to know if she were still a maid.

He half laughed, half coughed at her question and nodded his head. "Aye, that's what I mean. Who told you that?"

"My mother." Caitlin had been about fourteen. She'd asked other questions too, but Claire had said she'd tell Caitlin when the time was right. That time had never come.

"What else did she say? Did she tell you that if we'd finished, we could have made a bairn?"

Caitlin rolled her eyes. "I know where bairns come from, Darach. I'm not a lass of five."

"Well, you're not a lass of nearly twenty, either."

She gasped at his jab, and he groaned. "I'm sorry.

I just meant you're verra innocent for a woman your age. I ne'er should have touched you. When I think what could have happened…"

She leaned toward him. "Tell me."

Startled eyes met hers. She watched, fascinated, as his pupils dilated. He sat back as far as he could and cleared his throat. "Go…to…bed."

"But how will I e'er—"

"Now!"

He'd yelled at her—for no good reason. And just after she'd told Heather and Rose their laird would never raise his voice.

She stood with a disdainful sniff and tossed her hair. "Maybe I'll ask Lachlan."

At his outraged look, she marched toward the stairs. At the bottom, she hesitated. She didn't want to ruin her grand exit, but she knew if she didn't ask the question, it would bother her all night. And it's not like she could ask Edina and admit to such shameful conduct.

She turned back to him. "Darach?"

"Aye." He sounded at his wit's end.

"You doona think… That is to say…I'm not possessed, am I? By a succubus or something? It's just…to behave so wantonly."

The air exploded from his lungs with an exasperated bellow. "For the love of all that's holy…no!"

She took the stairs two at a time and was almost at the top when he yelled, "And bar your bloody door!"

Ten

"GOOD MORNING, CAITLIN. YOU SLEPT LATE."

Caitlin jumped as Edina appeared from behind her, and she almost tumbled down the stairs she'd been quietly descending to the second floor.

Her words came out quickly, sounding guilty even to her own ears. "Aye, I waited up to tell Darach that Fergus had moved into the keep. I didn't want him to worry lest he went to the kitchen and found the lad gone."

"That was thoughtful of you."

Edina passed her with a basketful of laundry and Caitlin fell into step behind her. They crossed the great hall and exited into the bailey.

It was well past midmorning, yet the yard was unusually quiet, with only a few people milling about. She blinked in the bright sunlight. "Where is everyone?"

"Darach and Oslow took a number of men on patrol and many of the rest have been deployed in preparation for the conflict. We still have a strong guard at the castle and in the village, of course. Laird

MacKenzie would ne'er let any harm come to you or any of the others."

Caitlin stopped, her jaw dropping as Edina hurried down the outside stairs.

"They've gone?"

"Aye, early this morning."

When she reached the grass, Edina entered another door at the base of the stairs that led to the keep's supply room and disappeared inside.

Feeling a good cry coming on, Caitlin flopped down on the top step and put her head on her knees. How could Darach be gone? She needed to see him, speak to him...to touch him. She needed reassurance about last night.

Uncaring man.

But the tears wouldn't come. How long would he be gone? Would he even miss her? She jumped up and raced down the stairs, following Edina into the supply room. The housekeeper was in the corner, counting bags of oats. A lit candle burned in a sconce on the wall.

Caitlin hurried over. "When will they be back?"

"Oslow thought maybe a week."

"Are they in danger?"

"I doona think so. The Frasers are a tricky bunch but not as well prepared as our laird. He's been planning this conflict for years."

"But it isna the big one, right? He would have said goodbye to me before he went to war."

"Aye, Caitlin. Doona fash."

As Edina moved through the storeroom making notes, Caitlin hovered behind her, feeling lost and scared, having a hard time catching a full breath. Even if the clan weren't going to battle, Darach could still fall from his horse or tumble off a cliff. What if he banged his head and didn't remember her? She was proof it could happen.

Well, not really, but Oslow had said it sometimes happened.

And it was harder to contain the fear that rose over Fraser and her uncle finding her knowing that Darach was gone. What if they somehow got past the castle walls and spirited her away before he returned?

What if she never saw him again?

The pain that ripped through her at that thought pushed any fear for herself away. She leaned back against a bag of grain before she fell down and tried to calm her racing heart, to take deep breaths and loosen the stricture in her throat, the twisting in her guts.

The idea of going to France to find her mother's family now seemed like torture. She wouldn't get any farther than the village before she turned Cloud around and raced back to Darach.

"Did you see them off this morning?" she asked, her voice sounding weak.

"Aye. 'Twas not long after sunup."

"So they'd planned it ahead of time." He could have told her yesterday. He'd had plenty of time.

"I knew Oslow was going, but I didn't know Darach intended to go as well. Maybe 'twas something he and Laird MacKay decided at the last minute."

He'd taken Lachlan too, and most likely Gare and Brody.

Edina placed a bag of oats in her hands. "Quit pouting and make yourself useful."

"I'm not pouting."

"Aye, you are. He'll be back before you know it."

"'Tis just…well…" She shifted fretfully on her feet. "Did he say anything about me before he left?"

"Caitlin, 'twas verra busy. I did not stop to chat with the laird. I barely had time to say goodbye to my husband." She headed for the door carrying a second bag of oats.

Caitlin followed. "You're right, of course. 'Tis selfish of me. I'm sorry."

When they reached the stairs, Edina placed the bag down and took a seat. She patted the step next to her. "Come sit down and tell me what's bothering you."

Caitlin plopped down on the stair. She sniffed. "He didn't say goodbye."

"You'll see him soon enough. You can spend your time riding Cloud and teaching the dogs new tricks."

She shook her head. "I need to see him now. I have…questions."

"What kind of questions?"

Heat rushed up Caitlin's cheeks. Edina would surely think she was wicked if she knew about last night. "Oh, 'tis naught. Just…questions."

Edina harrumphed and took her hands. "You will tell me everything, Caitlin. Especially if this has aught to do with Darach MacKenzie kissing you."

Her heart sped up. How had Edina known? Caitlin was certain no one had seen them. "We did no such thing, I swear. Well, maybe a wee bit. But not what you think."

"And just what am I thinking?"

"That he, you know, put his broomstick in my bucket."

Edina raised a brow but said naught.

The pressure on Caitlin to say more increased. "We just kissed...a lot...and, um, rubbed. Then he put his hand under my chemise and touched...you know."

"Nay, I doona know. Where exactly did he touch you?"

Caitlin could barely get the words out she was so mortified. "My breast."

"And that's all? Not between your legs?"

The idea horrified her. "Nay! I swear. I would ne'er let that happen."

"Aye, you will, but you must promise me not till you're married. 'Tis verra important you stay a maid, do you understand?"

Caitlin nodded. She could scarce meet Edina's eyes. Her stomach twisted so tightly she thought it would never loosen. "Were you a maid when you married Oslow?"

Edina hesitated. "I was a maid when I met Oslow, aye. I ran away from the Fraser keep to ensure I remained a maid. Your virginity is a wonderful gift to be given only to your husband on your wedding night." She lifted Caitlin's chin. "Can you make me that promise?"

Caitlin repressed a shudder lest she give too much away. She would *never* give her husband her virginity. If it was impossible to marry Darach, she would remain a maid forever.

Her heart clenched at the thought. She would never know what it was like to "finish the act" or sleep in his arms. She would never have a child or a proper home.

The futility of her situation sank deep. Why must she remain a maid? Surely Darach wouldn't do anything to hurt her. Or put her in danger. It was most unfair that men could take a lover but women could not.

"I doona like the look in your eye," Edina said. "You must promise me you willna let Darach bed you until you're married. The first time you make love should be special. It signifies the joining of two people and seals the wedding vows."

"What do you mean, seals the wedding vows?"

"Intimate congress validates the legal and spiritual union a man and woman make when they marry."

Caitlin stilled. The words echoed in her head. "So if a wedding takes place, but the husband and wife doona make love?"

"It can be annulled."

Her heart beat so fast she couldn't catch her breath.

Edina's brow puckered with worry, and she placed a hand on Caitlin's neck. "Put your head down, lass, and take deep breaths. That wouldnae be a problem, believe me. If our laird married you, he wouldnae forsake his wedding night."

She could still have the life she wanted—married to Darach, sleeping in his bed, nursing his children. She'd never worry him again or cause trouble. And they could "finish the act" again and again.

He'd asked her to stand beside him and fight the Frasers, and she would—despite her fear of capture, of being locked up and controlled again. Or worse.

He said he would keep her safe.

"Do you think Laird MacKenzie would be happy with me?" she asked.

"Happier than he's e'er been."

"Even though he says he ne'er wants to marry?"

"Aye, lass. Men doona always know what's best for them."

Well, maybe she just had to show Darach that *she* was best for him. Caitlin smiled as the sun moved from behind a cloud and filled the bailey with light. She could marry Darach. She *would* marry Darach. As soon as she'd fixed her wee problem.

"We'll need a priest," she said.

Edina gave her an assessing look, then nodded. "He's on his way. Oslow told me Father Lundie is at some of the outlying farms and should arrive in a day or two. He gives mass in the village when he's here."

"That's good, but I doona understand why there isna a chapel at the castle."

"It hasn't been a priority. Our laird's been busy preparing for battle. 'Twould be nice to have a holy man living here. Too many MacKenzies have missed last rites because the priest didn't arrive in time, and Father Lundie is getting old. 'Tis hard for him to travel from place to place."

Surely Darach would like a chapel in his yard. Maybe between the barracks and the keep. Or farther down, by the stable.

"Is the father a good man?" she asked.

"Aye, and a good priest—always concerned for the people, and he doesn't judge harshly."

It sounded like he would be an asset to the clan. Poor Darach just had too much to do and no one to help him. Wouldn't it be nice if someone else took on the responsibility? Shouldered some of the weight?

Caitlin jumped to her feet, her earlier despair forgotten. She had a new purpose, a new plan. "I look forward to meeting Father Lundie. I have so many questions for him and innumerable sins to confess."

"Innumerable?"

"Aye. Do you think he'll approve of the union?"

"I think he'll be more than happy to marry you to our laird."

She spun in a happy circle. It was wonderful to be able to hope again. To dream. "I pray 'tis so, for I would like naught better than to be Darach's lady."

❧

Darach refused to marry the lass, no matter how badly he wanted to tup her. Which meant he couldn't tup her. Which meant he couldn't eat or sleep or think of anything else but tupping her.

This was exactly why he'd decided not to marry or have bairns in the first place. Women were a distraction. Nay, not all women. *Caitlin* was a distraction. When he should be concentrated on protecting his clan and defeating their enemies, she tugged him around by the heart and the cock in the same manner as Moire. He was the biggest kind of fool.

A low-hanging branch clipped his head, and he cursed his own stupidity. He wasn't fit to lead. This was the MacKenzies' greatest hour of need and their laird couldn't even walk through the forest without banging into a tree.

With a disgusted sigh, he lowered himself onto a boulder and rubbed his brow. The ache in his head didn't even begin to drown out the ache in his groin.

If he'd thought his need was bad before he'd touched Caitlin, now it consumed him. And it didn't matter how many times he swam in the icy loch—the need came back.

He dropped his head to his hands only to be assailed with images of her as they'd kissed last night: bright eyes, swollen lips, flushed cheeks. And the way she'd felt... God almighty, he'd never touched anything so soft. The worst of it was she'd wanted him too. She'd moved against him as he had her. Both of them seeking the other.

"You look like hell," Lachlan said.

He didn't glance up. "Go away."

"Why put yourself through this anguish? Marry the lass and be done with it. You can go back right now, handfast her, and take her to bed. Tonight. Tup her till you canna move, then focus on the job at hand—defeating the Frasers. Kill the man who betrayed your clan, killed your father, and abused your *wife*. You know you want to. You're just too stubborn to change your mind."

Darach tried to ignore Lachlan, but his heart had picked up and his ears were straining to catch every word. Everything within him wanted to grab on to the idea and run with it. Straight back to Caitlin.

"She's going to leave. She doesn't think I can keep her safe. What kind of wife doesn't trust her husband?"

"The frightened kind. She's running around like a headless chicken with her so-called plan. Take her in hand, Darach. She needs you."

He snorted derisively and rubbed his head. "She needs a man who doesn't run into branches."

"You'll ne'er be the man you were before you met her. 'Tis impossible. She's wormed her way under your skin and will ne'er get out. Even if she left, you'd be thinking of her, worrying about her. At least if she's in your home, your bed, you'll know she's safe and happy. And you willna have to walk around half-cocked every moment of the day."

"I wish," Darach growled.

Lachlan laughed. "Full-cocked then, day and night." He settled on the rock beside Darach, jostling him. "Handfast her and plant your seed, for Christ's sake. Then put her to the back of your mind. 'Tis the smartest thing to do."

Darach sighed and looked at his foster brother. "What if this...feeling...ne'er goes away? What if it keeps growing and...and..."

"Makes you happy? She's a fine lass to love, Darach. You should be thankful."

He stared unseeing into the forest, trying not to picture the life that his brother's words had conjured. A life with Caitlin, their children, laughing together, growing old together. It unsettled him. It was the life he thought he'd once have with Moire. But that was a life based on treachery and deceit.

"I have to do what's best for my clan," he said, almost desperately.

"Then marry her. They doona want to lose her, either."

Darach pressed the heels of his hands into his eyes. It was true. The clan had taken to Caitlin like a bear to honey. They wouldn't begrudge him marrying her, having bairns. Well, maybe some of the besotted young men, but they'd get over it. And the women seemed to want his happiness, as Caitlin did. What had she said? She never wanted him to be alone or unhappy.

She'd been holding him tight when she'd said it, smelling sweet, like honeysuckle.

The desire surged again and he shuddered. His eyes popped open to focus fiercely on anything but the images in his head. He saw a torn leaf beside a snapped twig. Two paces farther on, a rock was scuffed.

It took him a moment to realize what he was looking at. He stiffened, instantly on alert. Lachlan followed his gaze.

"One of yours?" he asked, as Darach crouched beside the trampled foliage.

"Not bloody likely. Call Oslow. The tracks are only a few hours old. We might be able to catch whoever made them."

"And then?"

Darach's heart stilled. It felt like the threads of his life had just tightened into place. "I'll go back and marry Caitlin."

They'd been riding hard the last three hours to beat the approaching storm. Twilight was darkened by heavy, thick clouds, while an angry wind tore at the men's plaids and twisted their hair into knots.

Relief poured through Darach when the castle came into view. After five days of being away from Caitlin, his emotions were as turbulent as the coming storm, leaving him battered both inside and out. He wanted to marry her, bind her to him, wanted to give her a home and family, so she didn't feel the need to find her mother's family, yet at the same time, he was furious with himself for needing to do so. As much as he wanted her safe in his keep, in his bed, he also wanted to rage at her for driving him crazy, for making him weak. He was laird; he couldn't afford to be vulnerable.

He urged Loki faster. He would marry her and bed her tonight. He needed to be sharp to defeat Fraser, not muddled by worry and desire. She would be his for the taking, wherever and whenever he wanted, till he could bloody well think again.

But he realized it wasn't just sexual need that crippled him. He also needed to know she was happy, that she willingly gave him not only her body, but also her loyalty and love.

Even though it shocked him to realize how much he wanted that, he could see it made sense. It was right for a wife to love her husband and look to him to satisfy her needs. Emotionally as well as physically.

Women were sensitive creatures. They needed to love someone, and Darach was determined Caitlin would love him—for no other reason than it would make for a stronger marriage, which would make for a stronger clan. An undefeated clan.

As he raced up the hill toward the castle, he couldn't help but think of all the things he was going to do to her. How he would touch her and kiss her. Enter her body gently, so as not to cause her pain when he breached her maidenhead. Bring her to the brink of climax repeatedly before tipping her over the edge.

He had never bedded a virgin before. The idea of it hardened him beneath his plaid at the same time it churned his gut with worry. What if he lost control and pushed too hard? Hurt her despite his good intentions?

She was such a wee thing.

He tried to banish his thoughts as he led the riders under the portcullis. The first few drops of rain had started to fall, and he was almost at the keep when something caught his attention. In the fading light he saw a hole in the ground between the keep and the barracks. Several holes. Dirt was piled up beside them, and with this rain, it would make a terrible mess of his yard. Who the hell would do such a thing? And why?

Lachlan pulled up beside him. "I doona think you'll want to wait that long to marry her."

Darach couldn't wrench his gaze from the scarred earth. "What do you mean?"

"'Tis a foundation, is it not? For a chapel?"

All the anger, frustration, and uncertainty he'd felt since meeting Caitlin finally exploded.

"Bloody hell. Caitlin!"

The increasing wind and rain swallowed his bellow, but Darach knew where she was, and this time he would make her understand he was not to be trifled with. He swung off Loki and marched toward the keep, leaving his mount for one of the men to stable. His feet pounded up the stairs and he pushed open the heavy door with a bang. Lachlan and Oslow followed behind.

The dogs ran toward him, barking ferociously at first, then jumping for joy upon seeing their master. Darach ignored them and headed for the tables that were grouped intimately for the evening meal. Ten of his warriors supped there, as well as Edina, Fergus, two serving girls, Father Lundie, and Caitlin.

His angry glare found her immediately. Her eyes lit up when she saw him, then grew worried.

"Darach, you're back. It gladdens my heart to—"

"There are holes in my bailey." His voice crackled with barely repressed fury.

Silence reigned, then the sound of benches pushing back and people scrambling out of the way echoed through the hall. Soon, only Caitlin, Darach, and a few others remained. Fergus clung to Caitlin's skirts.

"Hold off," Lachlan said softly. "You're scaring the lad."

Darach forced a stiff smile onto his face and crouched down to Fergus's level. His voice trembled with the effort to keep it light. "Doona worry, lad. I'm just going to talk to Caitlin for a moment. She will tell me why she has torn up my bailey without my permission, and I will tell her why she's ne'er to do it again. Same as I did with you last week when you knocked the stool into the fire."

"But, Darach, this wasn't an accident. 'Twas to be…"

He seared Caitlin with a glance and she stopped talking, eyes round in her pale face. He could see the pulse beating frantically in her throat. Good, he wanted her scared, to know she could not run roughshod over his wishes, no matter what she desired. He'd put up with it for too long.

"Oslow, take Edina and Fergus to see the kittens."

"But—" Edina said, as Oslow hustled her and Fergus toward the stairs. She glanced back at Caitlin worriedly. Fergus gave her a commiserating look.

Father Lundie, white-haired and stooped, came forward. "Now, Laird, the lass was only trying to help.

'Twas my fault. Me old bones are tired, and I was pleased at the idea of residing permanently with the MacKenzies. I'm afraid I encouraged her in her plans to build you a chapel."

"I'm verra familiar with Caitlin's kind of helping, Father, and believe me, she didn't need any encouragement. Allow Lachlan to find you a place to sleep in the barracks, please." His words were clipped, his tone heavy.

Lachlan put his hand on the priest's arm, but the man pulled free and moved toward Darach. "She's such a kind lass. Truly, she meant no harm. Your lady was only thinking of you."

"My lady?" Darach glanced at the priest, then back to Caitlin. Her pale cheeks flushed a bright pink. It made her look even lovelier. His anger surged for noticing such a thing, and his brows pulled together. "I didn't know we were betrothed."

He was vaguely aware of Lachlan harrumphing in the background, but he ignored him. It mattered not that he intended to marry the lass; Caitlin didn't know that.

"Please, Laird. I beseech you, doona hurt her."

The priest's notion that he would abuse the lass added insult to injury, and he turned on Father Lundie, who looked ready to go down on his knees and beg. "I am not in the habit of harming women, Father. Lachlan will see you out!"

Lachlan took a firm grip on the priest and dragged him toward the door. "Doona worry, Father. Darach would ne'er harm her. Come tomorrow this will all be set right."

They exited and Darach slowly turned back to Caitlin. She looked like a young doe caught in a snare. So vulnerable and lovely it made his heart ache. He hardened the traitorous organ and glowered at her.

She edged toward the end of the table. He moved with her on the opposite side. About halfway, she appeared to realize she was trapped and stopped.

He could see her mind working, trying to come up with an excuse. Finally, she pointed a finger at him. "You left without saying goodbye."

His eyebrows shot up. "That's why you dug up my bailey?"

"Nay...but you should have said goodbye. Maybe if you had, you would have told me not to do so."

"Why on earth would I tell you such a thing when no sane person would e'er consider doing it?"

"Lots of people would consider it. Your clan wants a chapel, Darach, and a priest here permanently to see to their needs. You have been derelict in your duty."

His anger boiled hotter. "Doona speak to me of duty. I know my duty. And who are these people that think such things? The same ones who believe we are to marry?"

She flushed again, this time looking guilty. "I ne'er told anyone we were betrothed. Maybe someone saw you kissing me and assumed you'd ne'er do such a thing without marriage in mind. Do you kiss all the women you doona intend to marry?"

"Some of them, aye, and much more. Except they aren't aggravating, troublemaking lasses who take it upon themselves to ruin my bailey!"

Caitlin's chin wobbled, and she tightened her lips.

"I did it for you. I thought you would be pleased to have one less thing to worry about."

"I wasn't worrying about it. But now, 'tis all I'll be able to think about when the mud streaks o'er the grass and the holes fill with water." He slammed his palm onto the table between them and she jumped. "I didn't build a chapel because I didn't want one. I doona want the priest here, sticking his nose in clan business. 'Twas preferable the way it was."

"But I thought—"

"Nay, you didn't. You ne'er think, Caitlin. That's the problem. You just do whate'er you like with nary a thought to the consequences! What I doona understand is how you got the others to go along with it."

Caitlin twisted her hands in her arisaid. "Edina thought 'twas a good idea, and the other wives agreed. And Father Lundie said he would be grateful to stay." She hiccupped and tears spilled down her cheeks. "I'm sorry. 'Twas supposed to be a happy surprise for you."

He could see she meant it. Some of his anger eased, replaced by resignation. In all likelihood, she would create trouble like this their entire lives. He'd have to watch her like a hawk. Their children too, if they took after her. Did he really want to saddle himself with a lifetime of surprises?

Aye. But tomorrow would be soon enough. He'd let her dwell on her folly tonight.

"Well, I certainly was surprised." He stepped back, still on the brink. "Go to bed, Caitlin. We'll fix it tomorrow."

She hovered in front of him like she wanted to say something. Her hand lifted, her wet lips trembled.

Lust rose sharply at the sight, and he turned away. She cried out; then he heard her run from the hall and up the stairs.

Sighing in frustration, he stalked toward the small hearth at the other end of the hall. Caitlin's image danced sinuously in the flames, fanning his desire, and he considered calling her and the priest back to get the wedding over with.

No. He'd lasted this long. He could survive one more night.

Eleven

CAITLIN FELL ONTO THE BED, HER BODY RACKED BY sobs. Her heart squeezed painfully in her chest and her stomach twisted into knots. She'd caused so much turmoil—again—that Darach had turned away from her, couldn't even look at her. She'd thought he would be pleased by her efforts, but she'd only made him despise her.

A troublemaking lass. That's what he'd called her—yelled it at her. Any hopes of being his wife, of having a proper home and family here, had withered under his fury.

A fresh wave of agony washed over her, and she curled into a ball, her breath rasping in and out of her lungs. Turning her head into the pillow, she wept for everything she'd lost—a home, a clan, a family.

Darach.

Finally, she fell asleep. When she woke, her room was dark and cold, the shutters shaking in the storm. How long had it been? An hour? Two? She had no way of knowing and didn't care. All she knew was she had to leave. Now. Never again would she look into

Darach's eyes and see his disdain for her. Or worse, his indifference.

She had a plan; she could resurrect it—travel to Inverness and then cross the sea to France. She had the means to get there and she had a map. Staying longer only put the MacKenzies and herself in more danger from her uncle and Fraser. She'd never be out of harm's way as long as they could still reach her.

She would take Cloud and ride as far as possible tonight. Darach had made her a promise to keep her safe and he would only try to stop her if he knew. But in truth, it would be a relief for him—she caused trouble where'er she went.

Her pack laid under the window, ready to go, as if deep down she'd always known it would be impossible to stay. She dressed warmly, a strange roaring in her ears.

Opening her chamber door, she almost tripped over Fergus, who slept on the floor. He lay shivering, tucked up on his side. Caitlin crouched beside him and rubbed his hair. She would miss more than just Darach.

After lifting the lad and lying him on the bed, she covered him with quilts. He would be well loved when she was gone and quickly forget he'd ever known her—as would everyone else, including Darach. Soon she would be naught but a fuzzy memory.

Before she broke down again, she ran from the room and down the stairs. The hall was empty as she hurried toward the door. When she unbarred it, the wind pushed it open with a bang.

Despite the rain, she raced into the night, barely able to see through the downpour. The storm tore at her clothes and tried to push her back.

She could never go back.

The dogs brushed past her, making her jump. "Hati, Skoll, go home." She pointed toward the keep, but they dashed ahead, disappearing into the darkness.

The stable doors loomed, and she heaved them open. Inside, the horses whickered nervously. She moved blindly toward Cloud's stall and collapsed against his neck. He snuffled her cheek as if to tell her to pull herself together, she could make it on her own without Darach.

After attaching the bridle and securing the pack across his back, she led the stallion into the storm. He protested at first, but it was as if he sensed her desperation, and he settled down, ears pressed flat against his head in the driving rain. She used a rail around the corral to help her onto his back and then urged him toward the portcullis, where a flickering torch burned.

The gate was down.

Her jaw sagged. Why was it closed? It had never been closed before. She had gone in and out of the castle on a daily basis and it had always been open. Of course, she'd never tried to leave in the middle of the night before.

"Milady?"

She jumped. Some of the clan had started calling her by that title. Darach's lady. She'd protested at first, but inside she'd been thrilled. Now she was being punished for her conceit. She couldn't be a lady without a laird.

"Why is the gate closed?" she asked, barely able to push the words past her aching throat.

The lad gaped at her. He was around Gare's age and easily flustered.

"'Tis late. Someone could sneak in."

"Well, I need to leave. Now."

"But the storm—"

"'Tis an emergency. Open it!" Her voice broke on the last words and the lad looked at her with dismay.

"Is there trouble in the village? Does the laird know?"

"He said I can leave. You must let me out. Please."

It was her desperate plea that did it. The young guard hurried to a pulley and slowly raised the portcullis. He looked back at the keep. "If you wait one moment, I'll find someone to escort you to the village. 'Tis too dangerous for you on your own."

But Caitlin urged Cloud forward as soon as the gate was high enough. She raced from the castle, wind whipping her hair and clothes, rain pounding her body. It was both a punishment and a blessing. She welcomed it. It stopped her from thinking, stopped her from feeling the pain that crushed her heart.

Clutching the reins, she leaned forward and grasped Cloud's neck, letting him take the lead. He found the familiar path they'd taken to the water every day and followed the trail as it wound alongside the loch and into the forest. The loch turned into a river, and it raged beside them, hidden by the dark and the trees.

In the distance, she heard a dog bark, but she was too numb from cold and grief to do anything but pray Hati and Skoll were safe.

Thunder rumbled overhead, and Cloud flinched, almost dislodging her. She sat up and tried to soothe him, for the first time comprehending the precariousness of her situation. She looked over her shoulder, wondering if she should return and take shelter in the village. Surely it wasn't too far away— she could just follow the trail back.

Before she could turn around, lightning streaked the sky with a deafening crack, causing Cloud to rear up. She screamed and fought to stay seated, holding tight as he dashed into the trees. Branches whipped her head, almost knocking her from the stallion.

When he burst onto the muddy riverbank, she pulled hard on the reins to stop him, but his front legs slid over the edge and pitched her forward into the fast-moving water.

The cold hit her like a hammer as she was dunked beneath the surface. Struggling to resurface, she gasped for air as she broke through only to be dragged under again. She scrambled out of her cloak, but still she was too heavy, and she tore at the brooch on her arisaid. The need to breathe beat at her. Just when she thought her lungs would burst, the brooch opened and her arisaid drifted free. She pushed upward and breached the surface, drawing in great gulps of air as the current swept her downriver.

She grabbed on to the floating debris that passed by, but none of it held her up. Then a branch snagged her chemise and stopped her forward momentum. She grasped the felled tree, but her shaking fingers kept slipping, and when she tried to pull herself up, the raging water pushed her back. It sapped her strength and the will to hold on.

Maybe if she had someone to hold on for.

Good Lord, she was pathetic. After all she'd been

through, she would not die like this. She was stronger than that. She would survive.

With renewed strength, she grabbed another bough, but it snapped off, and she was dipped under the water again. She flailed to the surface but could barely keep her head above water as wave after wave swamped her. When her other hand slipped from the tree, the river greedily took hold.

For the first time, she lost hope. Limbs leaden, lungs burning, she slowly slipped under, praying Darach wouldn't find her torn, bloated body—that he'd remember her as she'd lived, not as she'd died.

Then, by the grace of God, she was grabbed by the hair and dragged upward. Her head cleared the water and she breathed air into starving lungs.

Something had her in its jaws. A small island loomed ahead and the animal steered toward it. Pain tore through her when she bashed into the rocks, but it was miniscule compared to the exhilaration and renewed hope rising through her. She struggled to hold on as she was dragged from the river.

The jaws released her, and a wet, hairy muzzle pushed into her cheek, whining and licking. Her arms encircled a strong neck, and her fingers squeezed floppy ears.

Hati.

She'd never been so happy for the smell of wet dog as he licked the tears from her face.

Darach's demon dog had become her savior.

❦

"Remind me ne'er to ask you for advice on wooing women."

Lachlan had entered Darach's solar uninvited and now leaned against the doorjamb, his words as irksome as his presence.

Darach frowned. "I wasn't trying to woo her."

His brother snorted derisively and sat in the chair across from him. "'Twas obvious when you shouted at her and called her names. A most inspired marriage proposal, that."

He ground his teeth, needing no reminder of his fight with Caitlin. He'd contemplated finding her and apologizing a hundred times during the last few hours, but he was still angry and didn't trust himself not to lose control of his temper—again. Besides, it wouldn't hurt her to ponder her actions for a while, to suffer a little.

Hasn't she suffered enough?

The thought gutted him and he clenched his fists. Aye, she'd suffered, but she'd also acted without thought for the consequences and deserved his reprimand. She wasn't a child; she was a grown woman about to become his wife. She needed to know there were boundaries she couldn't cross.

Building a chapel without his permission was one of them.

"I'll speak to her tomorrow and set things right. She willna suffer long."

"You're sure of that?"

Darach wrinkled his brow. "What do you mean?"

"You yelled at her and made her cry. What makes you think she'll marry you now?"

Surely women weren't so fickle. He'd been fair certain she would marry him when he rode toward the castle. Would she refuse him now because of a little fight?

Lachlan shook his head and Darach realized he must have spoken aloud.

"'Twas not a wee fight, Brother. You broke her heart. She'll not marry a man who considers her a nuisance."

"She's not a nuisance. 'Tis only her lack of foresight which is annoying. Do you think she was right to dig up my bailey?"

"Nay, but I think she was right about your clan wanting a chapel. From her perspective, she acted in the clan's and your best interest. Would it be so terrible to have a priest living here and a place for your people to worship?"

Darach gritted his teeth, jaw stubbornly clenched. "'Twasn't part of my plan. Not yet."

"Well, neither was Caitlin. If you want her in your life, you have to make room for her. She needs to create a place for herself, to feel she's necessary to someone, preferably you."

A knock sounded at the door and Darach's spirits rose. Maybe it was Caitlin come to apologize, unable to sleep either, knowing he was angry with her. He would be gentle, as Lachlan had suggested. Forgive her and tell her he cared a great deal for her. Then suggest they marry. He would promise her his fidelity and protection, and she would promise to love and obey him in return.

The door opened and Fergus stepped through. Darach's spirits dropped. It would not be so easy after all. Then he noticed the panic in the lad's eyes and his guts tightened.

He strode around the desk and crouched in front of the boy. "What troubles you, lad?"

Fergus hadn't said a word since his father had killed his mother, and Darach could see the strain in the boy's face. With Caitlin's help, he'd come a long way toward recovery, but not far enough.

Darach wanted to yell at him to hurry, but instead, he said, "Take your time, Fergus. Did something happen to Caitlin?"

The lad nodded, then shook his head. Darach gritted his teeth and took a calming breath. Fergus was making strange noises like he was trying to speak. Then he clearly said, "Gone."

Fear blew like an icy wind up Darach's spine. "Are you certain?"

"Aye. I slept outside her room. When I woke, I was in her bed, alone. She's gone, Laird." The words tumbled out of his mouth. Some of them were slurred, but Darach understood.

Caitlin wouldn't just leave. He pulled the lad into a tight hug, then hurried from the solar, Lachlan on his heels. "Check upstairs. Maybe she's with Edina."

Lachlan nodded and bounded up the stairs.

Hastening down the hallway, he came to Caitlin's chamber. The door stood ajar and the fire was almost out. Taking a candle from the passageway, he entered the room. Empty. Her personal items were scattered around, but when he searched for her boots and cloak, they were missing. As was her pack. Surely she wouldn't have gone out in this storm?

Maybe she was in the great hall. He strode down the corridor to the stairs, scanning the dimly lit hall as he descended toward it. "Caitlin," he called out. Then he saw the open door and felt the cold air pouring in. His heart stopped.

"Caitlin!" he shouted, panic rising as he ran across the room.

"She's not upstairs," Lachlan said from the upper level. Edina, Oslow, and Fergus trailed behind him.

"Check the kitchen, then start a search. I'm going to the stables."

Darach raced into the storm. Lightning lit the sky at the same time thunder cracked overhead. He prayed he would find her curled up with Cloud, warm and safe, but deep down he knew the worst had happened.

She had left him.

He pumped his legs faster, trying to outrun his panic. He'd done this. He'd driven her out in the middle of the night and into a dangerous storm. She'd gone to escape his anger, his disapproval. She'd gone because he'd turned her sanctuary into another hell, just like her uncle, like Fraser.

The stable door was open when he reached it, confirming his worst fears. "Ronald!" he yelled as he ran to Cloud's empty stall, hoping the stable master had seen Caitlin leave.

He mounted his nearly extinguished candle in a sconce on the wall, then quickly haltered his steed and sealed some rope and extra blankets in a leather bag. What else would he need?

Ronald appeared bleary eyed from his sleeping chamber. He wore a long lèine and leather boots. "Laird?"

"Caitlin and her horse are missing. Did you see them leave?"

"Nay. Why would the lass go out on a night like this? Is she daft?"

Darach clenched his jaw and ignored the question. She wasn't daft, just impulsive. The complete opposite of Darach, who thought everything through and strategized all possible outcomes. But how on earth could he have planned for this?

"'Tis obvious now," he said to himself. "I should have known she'd leave."

"Laird?"

He shook his head and mounted his steed, urging Loki toward the exit. "Prepare the horses. Laird MacKay is organizing a search." He hesitated at the door. "Have you seen the dogs?" Maybe they were with Caitlin.

"Not since the evening meal before you...well, before you arrived."

Ronald's tone disapproved, and Darach knew what he'd meant to say. *Before you yelled at Caitlin and drove her away.*

He spurred Loki from the stable, into the rainy night. It was too dark to see clearly, so he let the stallion have his head, trusting the animal's senses. The wind and rain pounded them, but Darach ignored it and concentrated on Caitlin.

A last ray of hope burned that she might be huddled under the stone at the portcullis, pleading with the guard to let her out. Surely his men wouldn't be so stupid as to let her leave on a night like this?

Aye, they would. They wanted to please her like everyone else, and she could be very persuasive. When he arrived, he saw the guard was just a lad, and

Darach's hopes fell. There was no way the young man would have stood up to her.

"Open the gate."

The lad ran over to haul on the pulley. The portcullis heaved upward.

"What's the emergency, Laird? Milady was verra upset when she left too."

Darach wanted to jump from Loki and throttle the lad. Instead, he asked, "How long ago was that?"

"Maybe an hour. I asked her to wait until I found someone to accompany her, but she insisted on leaving immediately."

"Did she tell you her destination?"

"To the village, I think."

She could be anywhere by now. Cold and wet. At the mercy of the elements and the wild animals. What if she somehow got through the MacKenzie border and was captured by Fraser? Or was thrown from her horse and broke her neck? He could pass right by her in the dark, hurt, on the ground. The notion chilled him far more than the rain and wind, and he pushed Loki faster down the trail.

At the water's edge, the path split, leading to the village on one side and alongside the loch, then into the forest on the other. If she'd gone to the village, Lachlan would find her. If, however, she'd followed the path into the woods, the path that led to Inverness, she would need him.

Darach turned the stallion toward the forest and cantered forward. He called Caitlin's name as he went, but the storm swallowed his words. Near the forest, he heard a dog bark.

His hounds would have followed Caitlin. They could lead him to her.

"Hati! Skoll!"

Lightning struck the sky, and for a moment, he saw Skoll bounding toward him from the woods before it turned dark again.

Aye, he was going in the right direction. He would find her. He just prayed he found her in time.

"Good lad, Skoll."

The dog turned and ran ahead of him, barking urgently. The trail weaved into the woods, and they followed it for another fifteen minutes or so. Then Skoll darted into the forest, toward the river.

Darach's stomach dropped. *Please God, not the river.*

The hound came back before disappearing into the trees again, obviously wanting Darach to follow him.

He slowed Loki and moved carefully off the trail. The riverbank was dangerous this time of year— slippery and unstable. He stopped his stallion and dismounted. Skoll pressed his muzzle into Darach's hand. He stroked the dog's head.

"Where is she, Skoll? Doona tell me she fell in the water." His chest was so tight he could barely speak.

Skoll licked his fingers, then turned to the river and barked again. Darach's dread mounted. She wouldn't survive long in the water. The river was high, fast, and cold from the spring runoff. If she hadn't drowned, she would soon freeze to death.

From out in the water, another dog barked urgently. Darach strained his eyes, trying to see. It had to be Hati. Maybe he was with Caitlin.

"Hati! Where are you?" he yelled.

More barking.

Darach didn't know his exact location, but he guessed he was near the bend in the river just before the rapids. A wee island was situated halfway across.

Heart racing, he returned to his mount and grabbed the rope he'd brought with him. He firmly tied one end to a tree, the other around his wrist. Then he shed his plaid and walked carefully along the bank in his lèine and boots, his belt looped around his waist.

When he was far enough upstream, he lowered himself into the river, barely feeling the cold. A felled tree provided a handhold to stop the current from taking him downstream as he made his way into the water. It deepened quickly, the current strong.

He reached the end of the tree and held on for a moment to orient himself. "Caitlin! Hati!" he called out. The dog barked again as lightning illuminated the night sky. Hati stood on the island. Darach thought he saw something else before the light disappeared—a shape on the ground at the dog's feet. He prayed it was Caitlin and she was alive.

Letting go of the tree, he swam strongly against the current as it tried to sweep him past the island. He would lose valuable time and energy if he didn't make it the first time.

He was almost there when a log struck his head and shoulder. The blow stunned him, causing him to sink quickly and suck water into his lungs. He struggled to resurface but couldn't tell which way was up.

He couldn't let her die out here alone. Then his feet struck bottom. With every ounce of his strength, he pushed upward, knowing this was his last chance. He broke free of the water, coughing and gasping for air.

Hati barked frantically nearby, and Darach saw he was almost past the island. Gathering the excess rope, he threw it as far as possible toward the boulders. It snagged and pulled taut, stopping his forward motion.

Hand over hand, he pulled himself along the rope toward the island. Finally his fingers groped some rocks, which he clung to with all his might. He dragged himself free of the river, body shaking and retching water from his lungs. His head and shoulder burned, but he ignored them.

Hati stood over him, barking and licking his face. "Good lad. Where is she?"

The dog darted over the rocks. Darach followed as fast as he could, gathering up the rope as he went. He circled the island and at last saw her curled up on the ground. Relief followed by fear washed through him as he raced to her side.

He'd found her, but what if he was too late?

Pulling her into his arms, he squeezed tight. She shivered violently, and he said a fervent prayer of thanks she was alive.

His throat and chest tightened as he pressed kisses from her forehead down to her mouth. "Caitlin. Sweetling, can you hear me?" He chafed a hand against her cheek, trying to warm her. Her breath was shallow and her skin tinged blue. She may be alive now, but if he didn't find shelter soon, she would die in his arms.

"Caitlin, answer me."

She moaned softly. Dropping his head, he spoke firmly into her ear. "I made a vow, Caitlin, and you willna make me break it. As God is my witness, you will live to see another day, so I can sit you down and tell you why you'll ne'er run from me again!"

One of her hands lay between their chests and when her fingers moved in acknowledgment, the dam broke.

"Please, dearling. Live for me." Then he kissed her forehead and set her down.

She moaned again. The sound gutted him, but if she was in pain, that meant she could feel the cold. If she felt the cold, she was alive.

"Hati, come." He motioned the dog to lie next to her. She curled into him, seeking his warmth. "Good lad. Stay."

Darach loosened the rope from his wrist and pulled it taut across the river. He found a heavy boulder and tied the line around it, testing it several times. Then he undid his belt and picked up Caitlin.

"'Tis good you're such a wee lass."

He laid her head on his shoulder, then belted them together, securing her legs around his waist, and her arms around his neck. It was frightening to think that if he went under she'd go with him, but he needed both arms to get them across the river. If he waited for help to arrive, she'd be dead.

He was about to step into the water when he turned back to curl his hand around Hati's ear, knowing the dog would follow him and also be at risk. "Good luck, lad. Swim hard and fast. The rapids are close." Hati leaned into him, then licked Caitlin's leg, as if urging

Darach on. "Aye, I'll get her home. She'd be dead by now if not for you. Thank you."

Hati barked and Darach strode into the river, holding the line. When the water touched Caitlin's leg, she jumped.

"Darach!"

"I've got you, love. We're crossing the river now. There are blankets on the other side. I willna let anything happen to you."

Her arms squeezed his neck. "I'm…sorry. I shouldnae…have…run."

"You have naught to be sorry for. I'm the one who's sorry. I shouldnae have yelled at you."

As the current swept his feet out from under him, Darach held the line. He flipped onto his back to keep Caitlin's head above water as best he could, then kicked his legs and pulled with his arms toward shore. His stomach tied into knots, fearing another log would hit him and loosen his grip.

He pulled faster.

The dogs barked, and then he heard a splash. Hati had jumped in. Darach said a brief prayer for him and for himself and Caitlin.

They were almost at the other side when the rope went slack in his hands and the current pulled them under.

Twelve

DARACH DESPERATELY REACHED FOR THE BANK. His fingertips slipped along mud and rocks before tangling in tree roots. He seized them and pulled himself upward, breaking the surface. As he gasped for air, he heard Caitlin do the same. Then she coughed and retched up water. Her teeth chattered so violently he was afraid she would bite through her tongue.

"We're almost there, Caitlin. Hold on."

Above him, Skoll barked. Darach considered untying Caitlin and pushing her up, but he was afraid of losing his grip and the current stealing her away. Instead, he searched along the bank for an easier place to exit, but it was too dark to see. Resigning himself to scrambling out where they were, he felt with his feet for a toehold and found a submerged boulder to his left. He grabbed another root farther along and climbed onto the rock. The river dropped to his waist.

When he searched for another handhold higher up, he found only mud, but then Skoll's strong jaws clamped onto his wrist and tugged. Darach dug his toes into the bank and climbed as the dog pulled from above.

They ended up halfway over the edge. The slippery mud was unstable and they slid back a few inches. The dog tugged again, and the bank began to crumble.

"Skoll, release!"

He let go, whining anxiously. Darach barely breathed, afraid the mud would disintegrate underneath them and sweep them back into the river. He had to move before Caitlin was crushed or they froze to death, but their position was precarious. Stretching his arms out as far as he could, he swung his leg to the side and over the edge. It caught and held.

"Come here, lad. Help me now."

Skoll grasped his arm again, and this time when he pulled, Darach used his leg to lever himself and Caitlin up and onto his back. The large dog dragged them clear of the edge just as the bank gave way. Darach quickly crawled a few feet into the forest, just to be safe, then leaned against a tree to catch his breath. Caitlin trembled in his arms. He rubbed her gently to warm her, afraid to press too hard, lest she was bruised or broken.

"Darach," she murmured.

"Aye, lass."

"Take me home."

He covered her ears, then whistled sharply for Loki, hoping the stallion would hear him above the storm. If not, he would carry her back.

When the horse whinnied nearby a minute later, he had never been so happy.

The journey back seemed to take forever. Darach

wrapped Caitlin in his extra blanket and held her close, but her shivering never stopped.

"Forgive me," she repeated over and over, and called out deliriously for his dogs and Cloud.

About halfway there, Hati appeared. Darach assured Caitlin her canine savior was alive and well. Unfortunately, he could not say the same for the white stallion—there was no sign of Cloud.

The portcullis was raised when they arrived at the castle. He slowed just long enough to tell the guard to call off the search. The light and warmth of the keep beckoned and he spurred Loki the rest of the way. Sliding from the stallion with Caitlin in his arms, he ran up the steps and inside. Both hearths were blazing with fire, heating the air.

When he saw Caitlin clearly for the first time, his heart stuttered. Mud caked her hair, and her lips and skin were tinged blue. She appeared to have lost consciousness.

Edina raced down the stairs, hair standing out in untidy tufts. "You found her!"

"Aye, but she's frozen. I need a fire and bath in my chambers."

"The fire's lit and the water heated. I'll have it brought to you right away."

As he moved past her toward the stairs, Edina stopped him.

The relief in her eyes turned to fear as she gazed at Caitlin. "She looks dead."

Darach scowled. "She's not."

"Och, of course not. Thank God."

He sprinted up the stairs to his room, where the fire blazed. Dropping down in front of it, he shed her wet arisaid and tore the soaked chemise from her body, horrified to see blue gooseflesh and countless scrapes and bruises on her skin.

Her eyes opened. They blazed into his, and she had a moment of clarity. "You canna see me naked. 'Tis not decent."

He almost laughed. Even in such a state, she would lecture him. He pressed his mouth to hers, then crossed the room and grabbed a quilt from his bed, wrapping her tight. "There. Now you're covered."

Her eyes closed again, and when she breathed a heavy sigh, he did the same, the band around his chest loosening.

Edina and several others maids came in with steaming water and filled a tub in front of the fire. When everyone but Edina had left, she turned to him, hands on her hips. "I'll bathe her now, Laird. You can leave."

Darach met her gaze. He had no intention of letting Caitlin out of his sight. "Nay, I'll bathe her. You can leave."

Her mouth dropped open. "I'll do no such thing."

"Well, neither will I."

Unwrapping Caitlin, he eased her into the steaming tub. She cried out as the hot water touched her skin.

"Hush, sweetling. You need the heat," he said. "It'll feel better in a moment."

She struggled weakly, trying to climb out, but Darach held her in the tub. He allowed her to keep her hands and feet hanging over the edge, and after a moment, she settled back, exhausted.

"Is that better, love?"

"Aye." Her voice was barely above a whisper, and Darach suspected she would fall asleep as the heat stole through her body.

Edina placed a linen cloth in the water to cover her torso. "'Tis a violation," she said. "If you stay any longer, you'll have to marry her. I'll insist upon it, as will the priest and the rest of the clan."

Darach gave her a wan smile. "Aye, Edina. I'll marry her. Tomorrow if she's well enough."

"Verily?"

He nodded and gently tipped Caitlin's head back to rinse the mud from her hair. A shallow cut sliced across her forehead, missing her eye by inches. "She fell in the river. God only knows how she survived."

Edina said a quick prayer and crossed herself. "How did she fall in the river?"

"I doona know, but the dogs saved her." He grabbed a bar of soap with lavender petals in it and rubbed it through her hair.

"And you, Laird. You look as sick as her."

"I'm all right." His shoulder and head ached where the log had hit him, and his lungs felt heavy from the water he'd inhaled. He needed tending, but he didn't want a gaggle of women hovering over him.

"There's blood on your shoulder."

Darach shrugged, keeping his face neutral as pain shot into his skull. "I had to go in after her. 'Tis naught to worry about." He massaged Caitlin's right hand to increase the blood flow. "Where's the healer?"

Edina crouched at the other side of the tub and massaged Caitlin's left hand. "She'll be a while. Mairi MacKenzie is in labor." The water had turned cloudy, and Edina removed the cloth that covered Caitlin's body. She caught Darach's eye. "The marriage need not be tomorrow. A few days will allow us to prepare a feast and sew a proper wedding dress."

Darach sighed. He just wanted to marry Caitlin and be done with it. He needed to know she was safe in his arms, especially after tonight. "Two days, no more."

"Three. I'm the closest person she has to a mother, and I insist."

He could see it was important to Edina, so he nodded in agreement.

The bath cooled quickly and they brought in another tub and filled it with steaming water to rinse her off. When that cooled, Darach dried and dressed her in the fresh chemise Edina provided. After untangling her hair and wrapping it in a linen, he lay her under the quilts and sent Edina to bed.

Finally, he eased himself out of his lèine. The blood-encrusted material pulled away from his wound and it bled again. He sat in the cool water, feeling wobbly, and rinsed the dirt away. A wave of nausea hit him, but he held it back.

When he finished, he dried himself, dressed in a clean lèine and plaid, then drew up a chair beside Caitlin. He tried to keep his eyes open, still worried lest she sicken further, but a black force pulled him under, and he slumped forward onto the blankets.

❧

Caitlin's eyes dragged open, her sight blurry. She blinked, and the room slowly came into focus. Quilts enveloped her on a warm, dry bed. It wasn't her room, but the stone wall lit by the dawn was similar to the one she'd stared at every morning in her own chamber.

She was home. And she never wanted to leave again. Darach had asked her to stay—aye, he'd yelled at her, but she'd deserved it. Then he'd come after her and saved her—again.

She would trust him to keep her safe from Fraser—and trust that he wanted her with him even if marriage between them wasn't possible. She would support him the way he'd supported her.

Rolling onto her back, she moaned, every muscle aching. Gently, she turned her head to the side and saw Darach.

Her chest constricted.

He sat in a chair with his upper body across the bed, fast asleep. Against all odds, he'd found her. She couldn't remember everything, but she knew he'd been desperate with fear when he'd pulled her into his arms. She'd heard it in his voice, despite the paralyzing cold that had fogged her brain.

Maybe he did care for her in a special way.

She reached out to stroke his head. Her fingers tangled in sweat-soaked hair as heat from his scalp scorched her hand. She pushed the quilts away and sat up in alarm.

"Darach!" Her hands touched his face to find him burning with fever. His color was high and his breathing labored. A tremor passed through his eyelids like he was trying to lift them but failed.

He never failed at anything.

"Open your eyes," she said, voice shaking.

Nothing.

She struggled from the bed. His hand squeezed weakly on her arm, but his eyes remained closed. She leaned down and kissed the corner of his mouth. "I'll be right back."

After staggering across the room, she yanked open the door. "Lachlan!" Her head spun, and she grabbed the wall for support, then made her way toward the stairs. "Lachlan!"

He appeared from behind her, hair rumpled, and scooped her into his arms. "Why are you out of bed? Where's Darach?"

"He's sick. He willna open his eyes." Fear crawled like ants through her body.

Striding back to the chamber, Lachlan placed her atop the quilts and crouched beside him. "He's feverish." He pulled back Darach's plaid, and Caitlin gasped when she saw blood on his lèine, over his left shoulder. His hair was matted with it.

He'd been hurt saving her.

Edina appeared at the door, sleepy eyed. "Is the lass all right?"

"I'm g-good," Caitlin croaked. Blinking back tears, she peered at Edina from behind Lachlan. "But Darach's in a b-bad way."

Edina hurried forward, placing her hand on her chest when she saw her laird. "The devil take me. I thought he seemed ill, but he said otherwise."

"'Tis my fault. He ne'er woke when I came in to check on them earlier. I should have known," Lachlan said, then turned to Edina. "Have you a salve we can put on the wound?"

She nodded and ran from the bedchamber. Lachlan

cut through Darach's lèine with a knife he found tucked down beside the bed. The wound, red and puffy, bled again as the linen was pried away. Lachlan pressed his knife against it and Darach shuddered.

Caitlin gripped his hand. "You're hurting him."

"Aye. 'Tis necessary."

He pushed harder this time and pus oozed out. "We must reopen the wound. Clean it properly." Then his brow furrowed. "I still doona understand why he's unconscious."

"There's blood in his hair. Do you think he's concussed?"

"'Tis likely. What happened last night?"

"I doona remember all of it, but he crossed the river to save me. Twice."

Lachlan shook his head, then leaned forward and kissed her brow. "You're both fortunate to be alive."

Her stomach twisted so tight she thought she might be sick. "Will he live?"

"Aye, Caitlin. Doona blame yourself. I've seen him take worse blows than this."

But she heard the underlying worry in his voice and knew he placated her.

Darach could die.

The healer arrived a short time later. She dressed his wounds, listened to his chest, and looked into his eyes. "The gash is infected and causing the fever. And his lungs are verra congested from the water he inhaled." She peered at the cut on his scalp. "But this is what troubles me. Head wounds are always perilous. If all goes well, he'll wake tomorrow."

"And if not?" Lachlan asked.

"Maybe the next day, or the next. Or maybe he'll ne'er wake at all."

Caitlin moaned. Lachlan wrapped an arm around her shoulders. He should be screaming at her, *Your fault! You did this!* She may have killed his foster brother with her selfish actions, and yet he consoled her. Once again she'd acted without thought to the consequences and someone else had paid for it. Someone she loved.

Aye, loved with her whole heart.

The realization made her tears start to spill. Of course she loved him; she'd loved him from the moment she'd opened her eyes and thought he was an angel. She loved him the way her mother had loved her father, the way Edina loved Oslow. Deeply, abidingly.

A forever kind of love.

The healer gave them a sympathetic smile. "I'll brew some herbs that will help. Pour as much into him as you can."

She examined Caitlin next, against her wishes, and told her to eat, drink, and rest.

After she left, Caitlin sat beside Darach, holding his hand and praying for his recovery. Eventually, fatigue overtook her and she fell asleep.

When she next awoke, she was in her own bed. Lachlan leaned over her. "He's calling for you. I'm hoping you can settle him." He helped her to the door and across the hall to Darach's chamber.

"'Tis good he's talking, isna it?"

"Aye. I believe so. Doona fash, love. He just needs time."

Darach lay on his back, eyes closed and skin pale. He tossed his head and clenched the blankets. "Caitlin."

She crawled up beside him and soothed his brow. He sighed as she snuggled closer.

Lachlan covered her with a blanket. "You should rest too."

Wrapping her hand around Darach's, she fought to keep her eyes open. Her head felt leaden, and she rested it on the pillow next to his. "Are you sure 'tis all right to lie with him? I wouldnae want the MacKenzies to think I'd compromised their laird."

Lachlan's mouth quirked as he tucked the blanket around her shoulders. "I promise you they'll think no such thing, but I'll tell Darach you were concerned for his honor."

When next she awoke, it was dark. She lay on her side facing the door with Darach curled up behind her, his arm around her waist. He no longer burned with fever, and the movement of his bare chest against her back was deep and even. She sighed with relief and laced her fingers through his.

"Caitlin," he whispered.

She twisted around with a gasp, which turned into a moan as her battered body protested.

"Are you all right?" he asked, rising on his elbow to loom over her.

"Am I all right? You're the one who's been hovering at Heaven's gate."

"Doona fash. I just needed a wee rest. Didn't I say you'd be the death of me?"

He was teasing, but the words curdled her stomach. She wrapped her arms around his chest and squeezed. "I thought I'd killed you."

"Nay, not yet. Though, to be sure, you took a few

years off my life." He hooked his finger beneath her chin and raised it so he looked into her eyes. "You will ne'er leave me again, do you understand?"

She nodded, unable to speak.

"Even if I yell at you, which I'm sure to do on occasion, you aren't allowed to leave. You may yell back, stomp out of the room, and maybe even hit me if the need arises, but doona e'er leave without telling me. Then I'll have time to send some men with you or lock you in your room." The teasing light in his eyes turned to dismay as he realized what he'd said. "Och, sweetling, I'm sorry. I'm such a fool." He leaned in and kissed her forehead. "I would ne'er lock you up like your uncle did. I promise. 'Twas meant in jest."

She snuggled against him, tucking her head beneath his chin. His words didn't affect her like they might have a few weeks ago. Before she'd realized she loved him and wanted to stay. "'Tis all right. I'm always saying things I shouldnae. It can be verra annoying. Someday you may *want* me to leave."

He kissed her lips this time, soft and tender. She felt it all the way down to her toes.

"Nay. I ne'er want you to leave."

"Aye, but, Darach, there are things you doona know about me. I—"

He kissed her again. "Hush. We'll talk about it later."

She sighed. They had too many secrets between them. Too many things she hadn't expressed. She could at least tell him this: "I'm sorry I was so determined to leave you, to find my mother's family in France."

"'Tis natural, lass. They were the only family you had left."

"Aye, but I acted out of fear. I thought if I could get far enough from my uncle, from Fraser, they would forget about me, and I'd be safe. When my parents died—"

Her voice thickened as the memories of those awful days bore down on her, and she swallowed to clear the lump from her throat. He pulled her closer, enveloping her with warmth.

"You doona have to talk about it, sweetling."

She took a deep breath and blew the air from her lungs. "I know. I just wanted you to understand why I left despite the way you cared for me and your assurances of my safety. Laird Fraser and my uncle controlled me, Darach. They would have used me. I was paraded like oxen in front of Fraser and others just like him. My fear that I would be trapped again pushed me down a dangerous path when I ran from you, and you ended up hurt because of it. I'm sorry."

He squeezed her tight for a minute, his big hand on the back of her head, her face pressed to his throat. Then he rolled her onto her back and captured her mouth with his. She wanted to be as close to him as possible, feel his skin against hers, but his quilt and her blanket had bunched up between them. Hooking a leg over his covered thigh, she trailed her hands down his spine. When she reached the quilt that covered his backside, she slipped her hands beneath it and squeezed the firm flesh. He moaned at the contact and thrust into her mouth, tangling their tongues for just a second, before he pulled back, breath rasping from his lungs.

She wanted him to keep going, and when he

rolled onto his back and circled his arm around her shoulders, she exhaled a frustrated breath. He laughed, a small puff of air teasing her ear.

"Is that it, then?" she asked.

"For now. You need your rest, Caitlin. As do I."

It occurred to her that for propriety's sake, she should sleep elsewhere, but she couldn't make herself get up. Her room would be cold and lonely, and what if he slipped back into that endless sleep?

"Darach!"

His eyes popped open. "Aye?"

"Are you all right?"

"I was. Now my heart is racing like a rabbit's. What's wrong?"

"'Tis naught. I just wanted to make sure you were well."

He squeezed her reassuringly, then closed his eyes. "I promise to wake with you tomorrow, Caitlin." He pressed her head to his chest. "Close your eyes."

She did, but they crept open again. Raising her head, she watched him. He was such a handsome man, even drained from his illness. Her heart filled to overflowing with gratitude that he'd found her—both times. If he died tomorrow, she wanted him to know how she felt.

"Darach." She tapped his chest.

He sighed. "Aye, Caitlin." He caught her hand in his.

She contemplated the perfect way to phrase it, but in the end, it was simple. "I love you."

He stilled. When his chest failed to expand with air after an appropriate amount of time, she became alarmed.

Then he breathed deeply and squeezed her again. "I'm…
glad. Sleep now, lass. We'll talk in the morning."

Sleep was the furthest thing from her mind now.
Maybe he hadn't heard her correctly. "Darach."

"Aye?"

"Do you love me?"

His arm curled up and he stroked her hair. "I…care
about you a great deal. Now close your eyes."

She tried. She truly did. "Darach."

He made an exasperated sound. "What?"

"When you say you care about me, does that mean—"

"Caitlin. Go. To. Sleep."

❧

For two days now, Darach had been confined to his
chamber with a trail of women coming in and out,
coddling him like a bairn. If he had to spend one
more minute in bed, someone would either have to
join him—that someone being Caitlin—or he would
have to strangle someone—that someone also being
Caitlin. She'd sent the clanswomen to his chamber to
watch over him in an attempt to keep him in bed and
entertained, but the only time he'd been entertained
was when Caitlin had sat on him moments ago, her
soft ass perched on his loins, her hands pressed into his
shoulders to keep him prone.

He pulled her leg over his pelvis so she rode him.
It proved everything was back in working order. Aye,
getting up was not a problem.

Her blue eyes widened. "Darach!"

He grinned. She looked shocked at what he'd done,
but also intrigued. She would enjoy their wedding

night. And if ever she let him out of bed, he would have that talk with her, clear the air of secrets, and ask her to marry him. He had no doubt she'd agree. She loved him.

He grinned again.

She squirmed to get off him. He grasped her waist firmly, holding her close. "Mmmmm. That feels good. Shift your hips forward, Caitlin, then back. If you want to keep me in bed, I swear 'tis the only thing that'll work."

Her jaw dropped open and he saw a sliver of pink tongue. He longed to suck on it.

"You mean like we did before?"

The blood in his groin surged at the reminder, and he groaned. "Just like that."

"Laird MacKenzie!"

Darach jumped at the icy, disapproving voice. Edina stood at the door looking like an avenging Fury, holding a pile of folded linens and a bar of soap in her arms.

Caitlin squeaked and wriggled off of him, jabbing his privates as she did so. Pain lanced through him and he rolled to his side, groaning. Through bleary eyes, he saw her rush toward Edina.

"I swear, Edina, naught happened. I was just holding him down so he'd stay in bed and then…well, I doona know exactly, but he ne'er touched me…you know…there."

Edina grasped her arm. "You are not to be alone with him till the…till the time is right. Do you understand?"

Caitlin nodded, then looked over her shoulder at him longingly. Despite the sharp ache in his lower half, he grinned at her. She returned his smile. He swore his heart danced a jig.

Edina scowled again. "Caitlin!"

Her head whipped back around.

"Go check on the bath for our laird. Make sure the lads doona spill any water on the way."

He almost laughed when Caitlin sighed and dragged her feet to the door. She lingered at the opening. "Is Oslow back? I want to know if anyone's seen Cloud today."

She'd been devastated to learn Cloud had disappeared after her spill into the river. Then yesterday, he'd been spotted in a distant field looking healthy and feisty. The men had tried to tempt him with apples, but he wouldn't come near them. Caitlin swore she would go to him as soon as Darach was well. Which was another reason he'd stayed in bed.

"I doona think so," Edina said, "but I heard Laird MacKay in the bailey. Maybe he's seen your horse."

"Maybe." Still, she lingered.

"Oh for heaven's sake, lass. Shoo!"

Caitlin jumped and scurried away. Edina followed to make sure she had left, then partially closed the door.

Darach raised a brow. "I ne'er heard Lachlan arrive."

His chamber was situated directly above the bailey. If his foster brother had returned, Darach would have known it. Lachlan always called out a cheerful greeting.

Edina shrugged, then moved toward him, her eyes boring into his. "You are not to take advantage of the lass until you marry her. I want your word on it."

Darach scowled. He didn't need to be lectured by his housekeeper. He understood his duty. The door opened and several lads entered just as he formed a retort befitting his status as laird. They carried buckets of water for a bath. Darach's mouth snapped shut.

When the tub was full, Edina turned her back and he rose naked from the bed and lowered himself into the water. It felt good to wash away the sweat of the last two days. His shoulder was still sore and Edina helped him soap his hair after he covered himself with a cloth. He sighed as her fingers massaged his scalp and then rinsed the suds away.

"You ne'er gave me your word," she said after a moment.

"I doona need to. I willna tup the lass before I marry her."

She scoffed. "You say that now, but you'll be unable to stop yourself when you're close enough to feel her heat."

An image of him pressing his hand against Caitlin's womanhood through her chemise seared into his brain. His body responded and he crossed his arms over his groin, then frowned.

"That willna happen."

"Most likely, but make sure of it by marrying her first."

He sighed, unused to being opposed. But ever since Caitlin had arrived, Edina and several others had begun expressing their opinions, even if they differed from his. "I give you my word the lass will be a virgin on her wedding night. I'll speak to her in my solar this afternoon. We'll marry three days hence."

"You may speak to her in the hall," she said primly, "and I need at least a week."

He threw his hands up. "Bloody hell, Edina. We agreed to three days."

"Aye, but you'll only marry her once, and she deserves everything to be perfect."

They stared at each other. He slanted her a look that had intimidated many of his warriors. She crossed her arms over her chest and lifted her chin.

Damnation.

A heavy, fast tread sounded in the passageway, and he quickly rose from the bath and grabbed a towel. The door pushed open after a brief knock, and Lachlan strode inside. He looked like he'd been riding hard. Their eyes met.

"Fraser is here with a representative of the King and Caitlin's uncle."

Thirteen

"WHERE'S CAITLIN?"

Panic fought with Darach's innate self-discipline. On the one hand, a precise plan had formed the moment Lachlan had said Fraser was here; on the other hand, he just wanted to grab Caitlin and lock her in her room despite how she might feel.

"She's downstairs with Fergus," Lachlan said. "Doona worry. The portcullis is locked and Oslow has Fraser, MacInnes, and their men under guard. I rode ahead. They should arrive shortly."

Caitlin's laughing voice drifted up from the bailey, and he moved to the window to look out. The dogs trailed her, and she had Fergus, who carried a kitten, by the hand as she headed toward the kitchen. Two more of the kittens darted in front of them; a third sat atop the well.

Darach couldn't help smiling. The Lady's Guard.

He quickly dressed and went to his solar, sitting behind his desk. Lachlan followed and sat in the chair across from him.

"Will you write the lads and Gregor—ask them to come?" he asked.

"Aye." Darach pulled out his quill to request aid from his foster father and Darach's three remaining foster brothers, Kerr, Gavin, and Callum. They would support him in this conflict.

"I think Kerr is at Gavin's, trying to woo Isobel," Lachlan said, grinning. "She's running him a merry chase. And Gregor is visiting Callum, helping him ferret out the traitor in Callum's clan. 'Tis fortunate they can travel in pairs."

Darach finished the first letter and sprinkled it with sand to set the ink. "What was the name of the King's man with Fraser?"

"Birk Anderson. A Lowlander."

"How does he know Fraser?"

"According to your man inside, he was on business for the King and took shelter with them during the storm."

Darach tapped the quill against his lip. On the surface, the men were here for Caitlin. The uncle's involvement was a testament to that. No way in hell would they get her. The question was: Why had Fraser involved the King? Was it simply to force Darach's hand, or was it more complicated than that?

"And we doona know the man's business in the Highlands?"

"Nay."

He returned his attention to the letters but listened for any screams from the bailey. He'd just finished the third letter when he heard feet running up the stairs and down the corridor. The door burst open, and Caitlin stood there, hair streaming down her back, cheeks flushed. She was so beautiful his heart hurt.

"Why are you out of bed?" she asked.

Darach paused. Should he tell her Fraser would soon arrive with her uncle? Nay. Not yet. She'd most likely do something foolish. "Doona fash, Caitlin. I'm well."

Moving forward, she felt his brow. He wrapped his arm around her hips, and his anxiety lessened.

She removed her hand, apparently satisfied he wasn't feverish, and smiled at Lachlan. "Edina said you may have seen Cloud. I want to fetch him."

"Nay!" Lachlan and Darach said together. Darach tightened his arm around her as if she would be kidnapped at any moment.

She stiffened. "But he willna come for anyone else. 'Tis my fault he's out there alone. I need to bring him home."

"Not now," Darach said. "'Tis best you stay in the keep."

"Why?"

"Must I give you a reason? Canna you do as I ask just this once?" he snapped, instantly regretting his tone.

Her eyes widened with hurt, and he felt that familiar twisting in his gut. "I'm sorry. It's just…" He searched for some excuse to give her.

Lachlan sighed. "Tell her. She's bound to find out soon enough."

"Tell me what?" Then the color drained from her face. "Has Cloud died?"

Darach squeezed her waist. "Nay. By all accounts he's alive and well."

"Then, I'd like to see him. 'Tis a beautiful day. Let's all go together."

Lachlan rose from the chair and stood behind it. "I

would love to, but Darach needs to speak to you first. Come sit down."

She hesitated, glancing at them warily, then sat in Lachlan's seat and folded her hands in her lap. A strange expression crossed her face—sad but, at the same time, resolved. "Are you sending me back, then?"

Darach's brow rose. She still didn't trust him. How many times did he have to tell her he would protect her before she believed him? It was an insult she thought so little of his vow and his feelings for her. He may not have professed his love, but he'd said he cared for her. Did that mean naught?

"You. Are. Not. Going. Back." He had to grind his teeth to remain calm.

Her gaze met his before she stared down at her hands, where she'd twisted her fingers together. "You doona have all the facts, Darach. You made a vow to me based on half-truths. If you break that vow, I'll understand."

Half-truths? She sounded so serious his heart began to race. Suddenly he dreaded what she was going to say. The Caitlin he knew was innocent of any wrongdoing...other than digging up his bailey, of course. And running away in the middle of a storm. And approaching Cloud when he'd told her not to. Well, she may not be innocent, but her heart was pure.

When she sat up, shoulders back and chin raised, a shiver ran down his spine.

"I ne'er had amnesia," she blurted out. "I lied because...because...if you knew the truth, you might return me to my clan, and I doona e'er want to go back. You see, my uncle used me to...to—"

A knock at the door interrupted her. The quill snapped in Darach's hand as his breath caught. Truth be told, a part of him didn't want to know Caitlin's secret, and the intrusion was welcome.

"Enter," he said.

The door opened to reveal Oslow, his eyes fierce. "They're here."

Caitlin glanced at him then back to Darach. "Who's here?"

When he failed to answer, she asked again, voice shaking. "Darach, please tell me, who's here?"

He stared at her, and every feature of her face burned into his mind—big, blue eyes, fair skin, rosy lips. His nerves settled, and the panic faded away. He needn't worry. She was safe with him in his castle. His clan supported him, his foster father and brothers supported him, and the King would support him once he knew the truth.

If not, they would go to war. Caitlin belonged to him.

"Fraser, your uncle, and a representative of the King. They want you back. We will disabuse them of that notion."

❧

For what seemed like the hundredth time in the last hour, Caitlin paced from her window to the door, then back again. In the eyes of the law, she was a commodity that had been stolen. Fraser and her uncle were here to claim her like a disputed pig, and Darach would have no choice but to return her.

What would they do to her if they got her back?

Her knees weakened, and she grabbed the shutter

for support. First, they'd lock her up, after she'd sworn never to be so confined again.

And it would mean physical and emotional harm and degradation. But worse, it would mean a lifetime without Darach or the rest of the MacKenzies. No cherished home or husband. No beloved friends or pets. How could she live, knowing happiness was only a few days' ride away? Surely God wasn't so cruel.

Nay, He was not. He'd sent her an angel. A human savior who'd vowed to protect her. Darach was a strong laird of a powerful clan. He cared about her, had come after her when she'd fallen into the river, and claimed she would never go back to her uncle or Fraser. She'd have to trust him to keep his word.

Aye, of course he'd keep his word if he could, but he didn't know the whole story. She hadn't had time to tell him the facts before they'd been interrupted and a mountain of fear and panic had consumed her.

Darach had taken one look at her and strode around the desk to squeeze her tight. "I'd no more give you to Fraser than I would my own mother."

Then he'd passed her to Oslow with instructions to lock her in her bedchamber—if she agreed—and place a strong guard in front of the door. When she'd peered over her shoulder, he was busy with Lachlan at his desk, focused and remote. He'd forgotten her already. No teary goodbye, no passionate kiss, no heartfelt declaration of his intentions. He'd soon be faced with the facts of her situation and see it was impossible to keep her.

She went to the bedchamber door again and tried the handle. Locked. Oslow had instructed her to bar the door from the inside, then proceeded to lock it from the outside with her consent. She supposed it was for her own safety, but she'd spent three years at her uncle's keep under guard, and it brought back bad memories.

Why hadn't she told Darach earlier? She'd been with the MacKenzies for nearly a month. Why hadn't she told him everything when he'd first asked? Now he was faced with discovering her secret from his enemy, who was sure to twist everything. Maybe even claim things that weren't true. Darach would be ambushed and humiliated in front of his clan because she hadn't trusted him.

She groaned and fell face-first onto the bed. There was no way she could get out of this one. If Darach couldn't save her, no one could.

Darach sat in a large, intricately carved chair on the dais where the high table usually stood, waiting for Fraser and the others to arrive. The tables and benches were stacked neatly in a corner and both hearths roared with fire. He had a moment of pride as he took in his surroundings. The keep was clean, bright, and fresh smelling, the surrounding castle a modern-day bastion of strength. Bright tapestries and jeweled weapons adorned the walls.

He seldom noticed the family treasures, but for today's meeting, they were an important indication of the clan's prosperity. As was the fine-smelling liquor in a golden, bejeweled goblet that sat on a table beside him. He wanted to impress Caitlin's uncle and the

King's man with the MacKenzies' physical strength and wealth. At the same time, he wanted to impress upon Fraser that the MacKenzies were undefeatable.

His warriors lined the walls of the hall and Lachlan and Oslow stood on the dais to either side of him. On the floor to his left, Hati and Skoll sat with their ears forward and eyes alert. Every once in a while, one of them would bark or growl low in his throat.

He noticed Lachlan eyeing the prized whisky made of malted barley and raised a brow, saying, "Maybe you should keep your mind on the task at hand rather than the *uisge-beatha*."

"'Tis not my mind I want on the drink but my tongue and lips. God's truth, that smells incredible. Where have you been hiding it?"

"In a place I knew you wouldnae look. The library."

Lachlan snorted. "'Tis no wonder you enjoy reading so much."

Darach smiled, then sighed. "'Twas my father's, and his father's before that. I intended to unseal it with my brothers-in-arms on the day of Fraser's defeat. Now I wield it as a weapon for Caitlin."

Lachlan shuddered. "'Tis regretful such a prize will be wasted on filth."

"Aye." Darach picked up the goblet and inhaled the rich aroma. His mouth watered. He took a sip, then passed it to Lachlan and Oslow for a taste. When it returned to Darach, he lifted it into the air. "To Fraser's head on a stake, and Caitlin's everlasting happiness."

"Hear ye," Lachlan and Oslow murmured together.

The door banged open and bright sunshine streamed in before several bodies blocked it. Two armed

MacKenzies entered followed by Fraser—a dirty, mean-looking devil with beady eyes and greasy hair. With him were an older man who looked like a bloated pig and a tall, wind-swept man with clean, ginger-colored hair and a trimmed beard. He appeared to be Darach's age, with bright eyes and a firm jaw.

Lachlan leaned toward Darach. "The last is the Lowlander, Birk Anderson. He sits his horse well and keeps a small but noticeable distance from the other two. The second man is obviously Caitlin's uncle, Laird MacInnes. I doona see any resemblance, do you?"

Darach eyed the group. Sure enough, Anderson kept a space between himself and Fraser and MacInnes. The Lowlander stood well balanced on his feet as he discreetly scanned the room and the Mackenzies. Darach guessed he'd be good with a sword, but none of the men had been allowed to enter with a weapon.

Fraser watched Darach with a sneer on his face. He did naught but stare back stonily, hiding his fury toward Caitlin's abuser. It disgusted him to have the rabid dog in his home. He'd become hunched, gray, and pitted in the eight years since Darach had hid in the secret passageway that led to Moire's bedchamber and listened to her and Fraser talk freely about the treachery they had planned for the MacKenzies. He'd wanted to slice them open right there but had forced himself to think of Oslow, who'd been a wounded prisoner in the Fraser keep at the time.

By God's grace, he'd managed to save Oslow and warn his clan of the impending Fraser attack. A month later, Moire had been dead by her brother's hand. Most likely burning in Hell for her sins.

Soon, Darach would send Fraser to join her.

Turning to watch Laird MacInnes, Darach repressed the urge to pummel the man. Caitlin's uncle gaped everywhere at once, jaw slack, eyes greedy. Darach tried to see past his revulsion and note any similarities between MacInnes and Caitlin, but there were none. The uncle was large, with dark features. His nose curved, hawk-like in his face, and his chin square. As well, his manner couldn't have been further from that of his niece. Darach didn't think Caitlin had ever noticed the jewels embedded in some of the weapons mounted on the walls. She'd been too concerned over the dogs, the kittens, and Fergus.

MacInnes was the biggest threat to her. Legally, he controlled her and had every right to demand her return. Morally, he was a degenerate bastard who Darach wanted to gut for hurting her and possibly killing her parents. Unfortunately, he needed the uncle on his side. If sleeping with the devil was the only way to keep Caitlin safe, he would do so. But maybe there was another way. MacInnes's cruelty to his niece should not be rewarded.

Darach wondered again at the lack of familial resemblance between them. She'd said she took after her mother, but surely something of her father's family would appear in her features.

When the group drew close enough to smell the liquor, he lifted the goblet, swirled the whisky, and took a sip. MacInnes eyed the *uisge-beatha* and licked his lips.

"I would offer you a drink and a meal, Laird MacInnes, and you, Master Anderson, but you enter my home with my enemy."

"Well now, we're just here to clear up a wee misunderstanding," the uncle said, smiling as he gestured with open hands.

Darach forced himself to nod; it almost killed him to do so. Fraser wore a look of scorn that Darach wanted to knock off his face. Hard.

"My companions doona want your hospitality, MacKenzie. We came for that which you stole from me and for breaking the King's peace. My man Anderson is here for that."

"*Your* man?" Darach asked, allowing amusement to tinge his words. "Are you King now, Fraser?"

MacInnes guffawed and Darach wanted to turn his tongue and sword on him too. Instead, he shook his head. "The King said naught of allowing lasses to be beaten and drugged, of tying them belly-down over a horse like a sack of oats. Or maybe Miss MacInnes's uncle knows naught of how you treated his niece? The lass nearly died from her injuries."

MacInnes glanced sideways at Fraser, brow furrowed in false concern, then stepped away. It was obvious he wanted to disassociate himself from Fraser and ally with the MacKenzies after seeing their wealth.

"'Tis not your business how I treat my property," Fraser said. "The lass disobeyed me. And I ne'er drugged her. 'Twas her uncle who did that."

MacInnes looked startled and turned pleading eyes on Darach. "'Tis not how it seems. She was anxious, that's all. The herb was meant to soothe her. Maybe I erred and gave her too much. It breaks my heart to think my dear Caitlin was so abused. I'm grateful you saved her."

Fraser's eyes bulged with fury. "He did not save her. He stole her. Took her off my land, along with the white stallion, and attacked me and my warriors."

"We doona have the stallion," Darach said calmly. "But if he's caught on MacKenzie land, I will gladly keep him. For good."

"You have no right. The stallion belongs to me. Caitlin MacInnes belongs to me."

"'Tis a pity, then, that I have her." Darach's gaze shifted to Anderson. "Is it not right to help a damsel in distress? If you had seen her bruised face and held her feverish body as she fought for her life, you wouldnae condemn me. 'Tis what good men do."

"Aye," the Lowlander said, "but you shouldnae have been on Fraser's land in the first place."

"Then we wouldnae be here today, for Caitlin would be dead." Darach picked up the bejeweled goblet, drank the *uisge-beatha*, then tossed the goblet at Fraser's feet. "I will pay a fine for being caught on your land, but no more. Take it and leave. But be warned, 'tis the last time you will e'er leave MacKenzie soil alive."

Fraser lunged at Darach. Anderson moved quickly and held him back.

"Nay, you will give her to me now," the laird said. "By King and Christ, I demand my wife back!"

Fourteen

A COLLECTIVE GASP ROSE FROM THE MACKENZIES AS Fraser's words echoed throughout the hall. Everything inside Darach turned to ice. His blood. His breath. His heart.

"Aye," Fraser sneered. "She's mine. Bound to me by King and the holy church. Witnessed by her uncle. You will return her as my rightful property or face sanctions from the Crown and the church."

A burning rage rose within Darach, melting the ice inside—his Caitlin, forced to marry this loathsome creature by a man who should have protected her. "That is how Frasers treat their new brides? By beating them and tying them o'er a horse? Tell me, do you force them to the marriage bed too? Or just rape them on the cold forest floor!"

He wanted to leap from his chair and smash his fists into Fraser, MacInnes too, but a strong hand settled on his shoulder. Lachlan. Darach breathed deeply, forced down his fury.

Caitlin was not going back. No matter what had happened or who claimed her, she was his. He would send Fraser and MacInnes home, follow with his army, and kill them in a fair battle. The King's man too, if he stood in his way.

"She's my wife. It willna be rape," Fraser said.

Bile rose in Darach's throat at the notion of any woman having to endure such abuse. Then Fraser's meaning sank in. He'd said "willna."

He closed his eyes as relief rose like bubbles in his veins. There hadn't been time for Fraser to touch Caitlin before Darach had saved her—she had said as much. The marriage vows had not been sealed. Still, he needed to tread carefully.

The King's man, Anderson, looked at Fraser. "Is she a maid, then?"

Fraser bristled and raised his chin. "'Tis not your concern."

"You made it my concern when you involved me in this dispute. Is she a maid?"

Fraser scowled. "Not for long."

The Lowlander's brow crinkled and he looked at Darach, then back to Fraser. "I doona think Laird MacKenzie will release her to you long enough to complete the act. Your marriage is in jeopardy of being annulled, Laird Fraser."

"I have signed contracts. I paid for her in salt and gold." He nodded to MacInnes. "Show them."

MacInnes glanced apologetically at Darach, then looked through his sporran, dithering first with the clasp, then the contents. After a moment, Fraser snatched the leather pouch from him and lifted sheets of parchment into the air.

"By law, she belongs to me!"

Darach signaled to Oslow, who stepped off the dais and reached for the marriage contract.

Fraser held it to his chest. "You canna have it."

Darach rolled his eyes. "Then give it to the King's man. Or doona you trust him either?"

Fraser passed it to Anderson. As he read it, his eyebrows lifted. "She must be a winsome lass. 'Tis much to give for a wife with little in return." He glanced at Darach. "Maybe I could meet her? She can tell me in her own words what happened."

"Nay!" Fraser and MacInnes said together.

"The lass is a bit addled and can be disagreeable," MacInnes added. "She's bonny, but she canna keep a thought straight in her head."

"On the contrary," Lachlan said, "I find her exceedingly bright. As for being bonny, 'tis true, once the bruises faded and the poison left her body."

The MacKenzies around the great hall voiced their agreement.

Anderson looked curiously at Lachlan. "Your name, sir?"

"Lachlan MacKay, laird of Clan MacKay."

"My foster brother. We were raised together by Laird MacLeod. Mayhap you've heard of him? Or my other foster brothers, the lairds MacLean, MacKinnon, and MacAlister?" Darach gazed at the three men before him. "You shall meet them soon enough."

Anderson nodded. "I look forward to it."

"You think to flaunt your alliances here?" Fraser asked scornfully. "Know that I have the backing of the King and the church. None are more powerful than them. Caitlin is by law a Fraser and will bear me a son." He grabbed the parchment from Anderson and shook it at Darach. "'Tis contracted."

"Then we shall break the contract. Goods may have been exchanged, but you havnae bedded your bride, Fraser. The contract is incomplete and the marriage invalid."

"That isna for you to decide. 'Tis for her uncle to decide, and I doona think MacInnes will want to return the goods I gave him."

All eyes turned to Caitlin's uncle. He wrung his hands and shifted his feet. "Well now, 'tis my duty to protect my clan, and my people were in need. The gold and salt from Fraser has already been used."

Darach schooled his features and showed just the right amount of compassion. Underneath, he felt naught but disgust. The treasure was most likely locked in MacInnes's keep. His clan would never see any of it.

By rights, it should have been the bride's family that paid a *tocher* to the groom. For Fraser to pay for his bride was unusual and, in Darach's mind, immoral. "So you canna return the...payment."

"Nay, but maybe something can be worked out. I see you care for the lass, but I canna allow you to keep her without benefit of marriage and a wee boon to Clan MacInnes. Of course, if I'm wrong..." MacInnes glanced significantly at Fraser.

"She's already married, you traitorous blackguard! We were joined by a priest. I have completed my side of the bargain, and by law, you must complete yours. Give me your niece!"

MacInnes snarled back, "I doona have her. Stay calm, Fraser."

"There's naught to work out! You will demand her return and hand her over to me. Elsewise, you breach the contract."

Anderson stepped forward. "Aye, he's right. Caitlin rightfully belongs to Fraser. Lest the wedding ceremony was invalid—then, MacInnes must return the goods, terminating the contract, and Caitlin reverts to her uncle." He gazed at Darach. "'Tis time. Please bring the lass. I must speak to her."

❧

Caitlin sat on the middle of her bed, knees pulled up to her chest, hands dug into her hair. It had been at least an hour. She'd spent a third of that time pacing, another third trying to convince the guards at the door to let her out—to no avail, as Oslow had the key and wasn't there—and the last third raging at her circumstances until she was spent.

Now she watched the door, waiting to hear the verdict.

If she'd been braver, she'd have fashioned a rope from the bedsheets and climbed out the window, but it was a long drop down and she'd never been good with heights. Besides, she'd promised Darach she would never again leave without telling him.

A knock sounded, and Lachlan called her name. She rushed over and removed the bar to open the door.

Lachlan's smile faded when he saw her. "What have you been doing to yourself, lass?"

Caitlin wiped her hand across her cheeks and down her hair. It felt a tangled mess. "What do you mean?"

"You look like a madwoman. We want you to look safe and happy, not like you've been locked in a dungeon." He took her elbow and led her into the bedchamber. "Do you have a brush?"

Caitlin picked it up from her washstand, her hand trembling. He took the brush and worked the bristles through the tangles in her hair. "You have naught to worry about, love. Darach will refuse to let you go, and your uncle will return to his clan satisfied. He's already received Fraser's gold."

"What about Fraser?" she asked.

"What about him? The MacKenzies and the Frasers have been at war for eight years. Naught will change." He put the brush down, then wet a linen cloth in a basin of water and gently wiped her face. "Doona let them see how frightened you are. They doona deserve your tears."

"I doona cry for them. I cry for Darach, for you, for Fergus—all the MacKenzies. For the kittens, Cloud, and the dogs. I ne'er want to lose any of you."

Lachlan put the linen down and pulled her to his chest. "They couldnae separate you from Darach with a whole herd of horses. Or me, for that matter."

"Or us, lass."

Caitlin looked up to see her guards standing in the doorway. She knew all three, had supped, ridden, and laughed with them. Dredging up a smile, she said, "Thank you, but I fear I've put you all in terrible danger."

"From Fraser?" one of them asked with a snort. "He's a wee ablach, that one. He couldnae find his arse with his sword."

Laughter bubbled up from her throat despite the severity of her situation. "And my uncle?"

"That one would have no trouble finding his arse, lass. 'Tis the size of the pink sow. I'm glad you doona take after him."

"Och, but I do. My bottom is soft as churned butter." Four pairs of eyes dropped to her backside. Blood scorched her cheeks, and she cursed her tongue for speaking so inanely.

Lachlan grinned. "That's better. Now you resemble a sweet, young woman, rather than a loon. When you're downstairs, faced with Fraser and your uncle, think not on their wicked words but their misshapen backsides. 'Tis the last thing you will see of them before Darach kicks them off his land."

Giggling, she took his arm, and they walked to the door. "I doona think Darach would be happy to know I think on Fraser's bottom."

"For certain. I can scarce wait to tell him."

Caitlin laughed, but she quickly sobered as they approached the top of the stairs. Slowing, she bit her lip. "Does he know?"

"That you're married to Fraser? Of course."

"'Twas not a real marriage. I didn't want it, and it was ne'er consummated."

"Aye, he knows. We'll get you out of it, lass. We just have to prove the ceremony was invalid."

When they reached the hall, everyone but Darach turned toward her. She hesitated, stomach roiling. Lachlan tightened his grip on her elbow and ushered her toward the dais.

Hati and Skoll stayed intent on the enemy before them.

"Caitlin," her uncle bellowed. "Come down here."

"Nay," Darach said. "She stays where she is. She is an honored guest in my keep."

Lachlan positioned her next to Darach. She would have been glad to see him except for his stony expression—what she could see of it, anyway. He must be furious with her. Why hadn't she explained the situation to him when she had the chance?

"Darach," she whispered.

"Not now, lass."

Aye, he was mad. There was an edge to his voice that was only there when he was trying to stay calm. She'd come to recognize it during the weeks she'd been with him.

Swallowing past the lump in her throat, she looked at the men before her. Fraser and her uncle frowned, while a third man with ginger-colored hair appraised her curiously. It made her want to stick out her tongue.

Instead, she smiled.

He inhaled audibly, and his eyes widened. Beside her, Lachlan snorted. Darach drummed his fingers on the arm of his chair.

"Caitlin, this is Birk Anderson, a representative of the King. He has some questions for you."

"Tell them we are married, wife." Fraser looked even more repellent than she remembered, and she couldn't help shuddering.

"'Tis untrue. The marriage was not consummated, and it can be annulled. Father Lundie and Edina said so."

Darach turned to her. "You spoke to the priest and Edina about this but not to me?"

Despite his glare, she was relieved he'd finally looked at her—but also a wee bit flummoxed. "Well,

I had to confess, now, didn't I? It's been years since I reconciled my sins. And Edina only mentioned it when she…when she… Well, 'twas a private conversation." Heat bloomed in her cheeks as she remembered Edina chastising her for being intimate with Darach.

He stared at her a moment, nostrils flaring, then returned his gaze to Fraser. Caitlin felt dismissed, and her ire rose. She was the one who'd been drugged, beaten, and forced to marry a demon of a man. And now they haggled over her like a bag of oats.

"I willna go back. You canna make me. Father Lundie says I am a free person and can make my own choice on whom to marry."

"Caitlin, hush…please," Darach said, raising his hand to gently squeeze her forearm.

Her uncle glowered at her. "Aye, she'll hush, or I'll pull her tongue from her mouth."

The warriors lining the walls bristled, some shouted out in harsh tones. Lachlan stepped forward angrily.

With deadly calm, Darach drew a vicious-looking dirk from within his sleeve. Sunlight from high above danced along the metal as he slowly played with the blade. "My goodwill only goes so far, MacInnes. Doona speak to her in such a manner. You are her uncle. You should shield her from harm, not cause it."

Caitlin's throat tightened with emotion. No one had ever defended her from her uncle before. All those years in his keep, he'd controlled her with threats and deprivation, and his clan had allowed it.

But not here. The MacKenzies protected her. Darach and Lachlan protected her.

With sudden clarity, she knew she was safe—surrounded

by a clan who had claimed her, who were willing to shed blood for her.

She felt humbled, and a wave of thankfulness surged through her. She looked at her tormentors—her disgusting, feeble uncle and her pathetic, revolting "husband" who had to buy a wife. Then she gazed at Darach, his brawny shoulders, arms, and chest a testament to his strength, his shrewd gaze gleaming with intelligence, his posture one of power and control.

Relief and happiness bloomed in her chest, and she suddenly wanted to stick out her tongue again. This time at her uncle and Fraser. Instead, she just smiled.

Fraser watched her, his eyes gleaming like a rabid wolf's. The madness there made her smile fade. He would use trickery to kill the people she loved.

"Caitlin, tell Master Anderson how you came to live with your uncle," Darach said. "How he…saved you from the fire that killed your parents. 'Tis a story that deserves telling."

She saw a glance pass between him and the King's man. Why would they want to know about the fire? It had naught to do with her marriage.

"'Tis not necessary," her uncle protested.

"On the contrary. She wouldnae be here if not for you. For that, you have my thanks."

The gratitude toward her uncle grated, even if it was for saving her life. The only reason he'd even fed her was so she'd be healthy enough to wed a man of his choosing. Fraser hadn't been the first prospective groom to look her over, but he'd certainly been the worst.

She sifted through her memories, trying to contain

the grief that always rose when she thought about her parents' death. "I ne'er met my uncle 'til I was sixteen. I grew up on a farm with my mother and da west of MacInnes land and didn't know my father had given up the lairdship to marry my mother. The night my uncle arrived, a terrible fire broke out in our cottage as we slept. My parents were killed in the flames. I would have died too, but my uncle saved me. Afterward, he took me to his keep. 'Twas a terrible time."

Anderson turned to MacInnes. "Do you know how the fire started?"

Her uncle shifted his stance and clasped his hands around his belly. "Maybe an untended candle or a spark from the hearth. The lass was verra excited and could have knocked something o'er."

Caitlin gasped. "Doona say such a thing unless you know it's true. I couldnae have killed my parents."

Darach took her hand and rubbed her palm with his thumb. "Do you remember anything else? Any of the men behaving oddly or loitering in places they shouldn't?"

"Are you implying my men started the fire?" MacInnes asked. "I assure you they had naught to do with it. They were the first to notice the flames and report it to me. I ran into the blaze to save the lass at great risk to myself."

Darach let go of her. He looked relaxed, but Caitlin had the sense of a great, hunting cat readying itself to pounce. "How did you reach her? It must have been hard going—the heat, the smoke."

"I knew where she slept. She's a wee lass. I carried her out."

"You thought to save her before your brother?"

"I called out to him but he didn't respond. Afterward, I took the lass back with me and gave her a home."

"You locked me in at night and put a guard on me during the day," Caitlin said.

"I fed and clothed you."

"One worn arisaid and two chemises. The food was even worse."

"I tried to find her a decent husband, but as you can see, she's verra disagreeable."

She pointed at Fraser. "You call that decent?"

Fraser's lips curled up in a snarl. "You'll come to regret those words, wife."

Darach flicked a finger, and Hati and Skoll lunged toward the men, hackles up.

With burning eyes, Fraser lunged back at them. Caitlin knew she witnessed madness.

Anderson kept one eye on the hounds, the other on her. "Had you met Fraser before the ceremony?"

"Twice. And twice I said I wouldnae marry him, or anyone else of my uncle's choosing, but he made me do things by hurting one of the maids and some of the animals I cared for. I ran away, but they caught me. I was locked in my room after that."

"The lass hasn't a coherent thought in her head," MacInnes said. "'Twas done for her own safety. And 'tis my right to discipline my servants and livestock."

"Caitlin too?" Darach asked, eyes hooded.

"Aye, she is my property."

A heavy silence fell, filled by her uncle's wheezing and the dogs' low growls. Shame flooded Caitlin, and she cast her gaze down. She knew the feeling was misplaced, but it wouldn't leave her.

"Father Lundie," Darach called out.

She glanced up to see the priest making his way toward the dais.

"It must be determined whether the ceremony between Caitlin and Fraser was valid in God's eyes."

"Of course it was valid!" said Fraser.

"Not if she was forced," said Lachlan.

"I ne'er touched the lass," MacInnes protested. "Ask the priest, Father MacIntyre. She was unmarred."

Father Lundie stood with the other men now, and shook his head. "Father MacIntyre is strong in heart and mind, but he's blind as a bat and nearly deaf. He shouldnae be performing a wedding ceremony."

"Fraser hit me, I remember that," Caitlin said. "Kicked me too."

"'Twas after the ceremony, not before. She hadn't been touched when she said her vows." Fraser gave her that ugly, possessive stare.

Anderson's brow crinkled. "What do you mean, lass? About remembering?"

"Well, some of it is blurry, but I remember being given a dress to change into and throwing it out the window. I was kept in my room and then... I doona rightly know. Naught is clear 'til I met the MacKenzies."

"The herbs," Darach said. "MacInnes admitted he gave Caitlin calming herbs. To...soothe her. She was not in her right mind when she stood before the priest."

"'Twas not meant to harm her, only to make things easier," her uncle said. "Now I know better. It willna happen again, especially if you marry the lass."

Her mouth dropped open. Marry the lass? Is that what this was all about? Aye, she could see it. The

MacKenzie land and wealth would have called to her uncle like a siren to a sailor.

Panic rose again and this time she couldn't stop it. If Darach was forced to marry her, he would never forgive her, and then she had no hope of…well… marrying him.

She closed her eyes, knowing her logic made no sense. Then he answered, and her panic abated.

"You get ahead of yourself, MacInnes. We must settle the matter of Caitlin's marriage to Fraser first."

'Twas a game of words he played. Darach would never let himself be trapped in matrimony. He would make her uncle admit he drugged her and have the wedding to Fraser invalidated.

Her shoulders sagged in relief.

"The matter of the herbs is troubling," Father Lundie said. "The vows are void if she knew not what she pledged."

"I agree." Anderson turned to Fraser and her uncle. "The contract is hereby negated. All goods paid to MacInnes must be returned, and, Fraser, your marriage to Caitlin MacInnes is annulled."

"Over my dead body," the Fraser laird spat out. His hands curled like claws.

Darach smiled. "That can be arranged."

Fifteen

THE PORTCULLIS RATTLED AND SQUEAKED AS THE heavy iron grill opened in front of Laird Fraser. Ten armed and angry MacKenzies guarded him. In the distance, across the clearing, Fraser's men gathered on their horses in a small group.

Darach stood three paces to the laird's right, fists clenched and jaw tight, with Anderson and Oslow behind him. Hati and Skoll growled softly nearby, ready to rip apart their master's enemy.

Darach's control was slipping the longer Fraser was in his home, and he'd had to stop himself several times from pulling his sword and gutting the degenerate bastard.

"You look ready to kill me, MacKenzie," Fraser said, eyes gleaming. "Will you forego your honor and put an arrow in my back as I walk away? Or slay me where I stand, unarmed and defenseless?"

Darach took a moment to unclench his fists. "Nay. I promise free passage through MacKenzie territory for you and your men. You have my word."

Fraser nodded, then stepped closer. Darach's men also stepped closer.

"Then now's a good time to say this: I plan to kill you, MacKenzie. And the woman will watch. Then I'll take her to wife and spread those thighs. Before the year is out, she'll have borne me a son and all who bear your name will be dead. You have *my* word."

The MacKenzies around him growled in outrage, the ringing of their drawn swords filling the air. Darach wanted to growl too, wanted to snarl like his hounds and use his bare hands to pummel Fraser into the ground. Instead, he inhaled deeply and held up his hand to calm his men.

"And I say this, Fraser. You leave my land living for the last time. When next we meet, I will cleave your body in two and feed your guts to the pigs. Your clan will be cleansed of filth and depravity and left to honest men and women. You will ne'er threaten me and mine again. With the King's man as witness, our truce is broken. Leave while you still can." He drew his sword and pointed it at Fraser's throat. "Or I'll take your head, honor be damned."

Fraser's lips drew back in what might be called a smile—one as bestial as Hati's and Skoll's—then he slunk under the portcullis like a rabid dog.

Darach signaled a number of his warriors. "Follow them to the border."

He stood watching, sword out, until every last Fraser disappeared into the forest; then he turned to Anderson. "You may inform the King that the MacKenzies and the Frasers are at war."

❧

Caitlin sucked in a breath and stood up from the steps leading to the keep as the group of warriors in the distance split apart and Darach appeared, marching toward her, Oslow and Anderson on his heels, the dogs racing ahead of him. She couldn't make out his features, but she'd recognize that stride, the way he held himself, anywhere.

"Lachlan!" she called out.

After a moment, Lachlan appeared at the open door to the keep and looked across the bailey toward Darach. "It is done," he said.

"What's done? What do you mean?" But he'd already turned away and reentered the keep.

She hovered on the bottom step, frightened and unsure. When the dogs reached her, she wrapped her arms around them.

If Darach or the clan should come to harm because of her, she would never forgive herself. And why hadn't her uncle left with Fraser? Why was he still here?

Darach was close enough for her to see him clearly now, and she swallowed nervously at his stony expression. What had he done? Killed Fraser? Declared war? Agreed to send her back?

When he held out his hand to her, she sobbed and ran to his side. He pulled her tight under his arm and kept walking. "You've told me everything, aye? You've left naught out?" he asked.

"You know everything. Maybe even more than I do."

He nodded and pressed a kiss to her temple. "I'm sorry they put you through that, sweetling. You will ne'er be hurt or abused in such a way again."

They reached the steps and the dogs bounded up ahead of them. Caitlin lifted her skirts and ran to keep up as Darach took the stairs two at a time. At the top, he stopped abruptly and turned to her. He looked so serious that her heart stuttered. Then he stroked a hand down her cheek, and she melted.

"Caitlin—"

Lachlan stepped out of the doorway and frowned at them. "'Tis only half-done. For heaven's sake, you can ask her later. And doona let her uncle know your intentions right away, although 'tis not hard to guess with that look on your face."

Darach grunted and released her, then followed Lachlan into the darkened keep.

"Ask me what?" Caitlin asked as she trailed after them. "And what's half-done? What are you talking about?"

But neither man responded.

When her eyes adjusted to the dim light after the brightness outside, she saw the dais had been removed and a large table with a bench on each side had been laid with food and drink. Her uncle sat facing her, at the edge on one side, eating and drinking like a starving hog. Father Lundie sat beside him with an empty plate, sipping slowly from his cup, looking like he was trying not to breathe through his nose.

The door banged shut, and she turned to see that Oslow and Anderson had followed them in. Other than Gare and Brodie standing guard at the door, everyone else had left the great hall.

"Master Anderson, will you sup with us?" Darach asked. He indicated the seat beside Father Lundie.

Caitlin slowed. She did not want to eat with her uncle, but then Darach called her name too. "Caitlin, sit next to me, please."

He stood beside the bench waiting for her. She

dragged her feet to the table after she caught his pointed stare and sat down opposite Anderson. Darach sat beside her, between her and Lachlan, with Lachlan opposite her uncle.

Oslow took up position behind Darach while Edina served the meal, then bustled back to the great hearth, where warming dishes were laid out.

When her uncle spat the bones from the partridge onto the rushes that covered the floor, Caitlin pushed her trencher of greens and fowl away. Her stomach would only revolt at the food.

"You have much to thank me for, Niece," MacInnes said after he finished his ale in great gulps, the drink spilling over the sides of his cup into his beard.

Darach's hand squeezed her leg gently under the table, but she found it hard to hold her tongue, as he so obviously wanted her to do.

"Is that so?" she said.

"Aye. You were naught more than a farm girl when I found you. Now you will be lady of a great castle."

She looked from her uncle to Darach, searching his eyes, then back to her uncle. "I was far more than just a farm girl, Uncle. I was happy and well loved. I would rather have people who love me in my life and live on a farm, than be unhappy and unloved living in a great castle. And I think you are mistaken about Laird MacKenzie's intentions toward me."

Her uncle made a loud, dismissive sound, making Caitlin's pulse pound with anger.

"He wouldnae go to such lengths to separate you from Laird Fraser unless he wanted to keep you for himself, and I doona intend to let him keep you for free."

Fury burned within her, and she opened her mouth to say that Darach would do for any lass what he'd done for her—and that she was not a cow to be bartered—but Darach again squeezed her leg. She turned to him, waiting for him to cut down her uncle for suggesting such a thing.

Instead, he took a sip of the whisky from the bejeweled, golden goblet, swirled the liquor, then took another sip before placing it down. MacInnes watched, his eyes shining with greed.

"You already have the gold from Fraser," Darach said. "I will kill him before the year is out and you willna have to return the payment."

"You will do so anyway. And I wouldnae count so easily on killing him." MacInnes steepled his hands in front of his chin like he was thinking. "Maybe I should bring my niece home with me. 'Tis not safe for her here if you are at war."

Darach stabbed his knife into a juicy piece of meat on his trencher and handed it to Caitlin. She took it with her fingers and put it in her mouth because to do otherwise would be rude, but she could barely swallow it.

"She is in my castle, MacInnes, surrounded by my men. None can get to her here...or get her out," he said.

"Aye, but as her only living relative, it is my duty to see to her safety. As I see fit. Isn't that right, Master Anderson?"

The King's man looked down at his plate, obviously weighing his words. "I think you both would do well to strike a deal that is mutually beneficial rather than involving the King in this dispute. You may not like the outcome."

"I agree," her uncle said, looking back to Darach, who nodded and also said, "Aye."

Caitlin gasped, feeling like she'd been struck. They were going to deal for her? As she just sat there watching, saying nothing? Her outrage turned to panic, a trapped feeling overwhelming her. "Wait!" she cried out.

The breath rushed in and out of her lungs as she met their stares. Her uncle did not deserve to prosper for his ill treatment of her, and Darach would be forced into a marriage he didn't want, honor bound to take her to wife. He'd hate her for it.

"I do not merit this transaction. Truly, I'm a worthless woman. I am disobedient and careless. I have no skills, no attractive qualities. I would make a terrible wife."

MacInnes frowned at her. "It takes no skill to bed your husband, to have his bairns. Your maiden blood is all that's required."

Her eyebrows shot up. "Well then…I am not a maid!"

MacInnes's face turned a deep reddish purple before he yelled, "You lie!"

"Nay. I swear. I'm a harlot of the worst kind. I'm not good enough to be anyone's wife. Ride away and count yourself fortunate to be rid of me, Uncle."

All eyes had turned to her—Lachlan, Darach, and Oslow all looking exasperated; Father Lundie looking concerned; Anderson looking confused. She didn't spin around to see what Brodie and Gare looked like, but she'd surely heard Brodie snort.

Her uncle's jowls quivered with outrage. "She was a maid when she left my keep, I made sure of it. 'Tis someone here who's ruined her. I had other men lined up if Fraser fell through. Now who will want her?"

"MacInnes," Darach said, "I'm sure Caitlin isna a—"

"I am," she said, cutting him off in her haste. If she had no value to her uncle, maybe he would leave too. "None will want me now. My bastard children will roam the halls wherever I live. They'll overrun your keep, Uncle. More mouths to feed and bodies to clothe. You best leave me to my sinful ways."

"You *besom*," he said. "I had plans for you."

Caitlin winced. It was one thing to name herself promiscuous, another to hear it from someone else. But if her uncle washed his hands of her, it was worth soiling her reputation.

By the scowl on his face, Darach didn't agree. "You willna insult your niece in my presence, MacInnes. Caitlin is obviously—"

"A *besom*," she interjected. "Oh, aye, I'm a horrible, degenerate woman. I canna help myself." She warmed to her story and let her imagination run wild. "I'm a present-day Jezebel who will lead your clan to debauchery and shame, Uncle. 'Twill cost you much gold."

Her uncle blanched and looked accusingly at Darach. "Who is responsible for this? What man has dared sully my niece?"

"Aye, Caitlin," Darach said, turning to her. That muscle ticked in his jaw again. "Tell me, who would be so bold?"

"'Tis not important," she said, folding her arms across her waist and trying to look unperturbed.

"I think it is. I will beat him black and blue for daring to touch a lass under my protection. Then I'll decide whether to hang him for his impudence."

"Nay," she gasped, her serenity vanishing.

"Aye," he said.

She glanced wildly around the table. Father Lundie reddened under her appraisal. She quickly averted her gaze and looked over Darach's shoulder at Oslow. He scowled at her. Gulping, she lowered her gaze before peering around Darach at Lachlan. But Lachlan raised his brow in such a manner, she knew he would deny her.

Please, she mouthed, but he shook his head, then nodded toward Darach. She sat back slowly, biting her lip.

"Well?" Darach asked.

There was none else she could name. Once her uncle left, Darach could refute her allegation. "'Twas you," she whispered.

"Louder, please."

"'Twas you!"

His eyebrows rose mockingly. "If you say 'tis so, it must be true, for I know you would ne'er make up a story."

Caitlin glanced at her uncle, hoping he would throw his hands up in disgust and leave. Instead, he smiled and licked his lips. Unease trickled up her spine.

"Since you have violated my niece in the vilest way, Laird MacKenzie, I must insist you marry her. For a price, of course. 'Tis a long journey I undertook to find my niece so dishonored."

Darach's eyes bore into her. "Aye. I'll marry her."

"Nay, you canna," she said.

But he reached for his goblet and pushed it across the table toward her uncle, whose fingers closed around it. "We are agreed," Darach said.

She clapped her hands to her head. "But 'tis not his fault. 'Tis my fault. Doona make him marry me. Darach was the innocent victim of my lewd advances!"

Lachlan choked, then broke into a fit of coughing. A part of her wanted to aid him, but Darach's freedom was more important.

"He was sick. He ne'er knew what I did. 'Twas not my intent to trick him into marriage."

"'Tis too late," her uncle yelled, tucking the goblet into his plaid. "We have agreed."

"But he just lay there, feeble. I am to blame!"

Darach rounded on her, nostrils flaring. "Caitlin. Stop. Talking." He took her arm and stood, pulling her up beside him. Lachlan had placed his elbows on the table and head in his hands. His body still heaved and Caitlin would have slapped him on the back if Darach hadn't been in her way.

"If you can contain yourself for a moment, Laird MacKay, please take Caitlin back to her room. She is to stay there for the rest of the day. None but me go in or out."

Lachlan straightened and she saw with surprise his cheeks were wet. She thought maybe he'd been crying, but his eyes danced merrily. "Aye, Brother. I just need a moment. I feel so…feeble."

Caitlin's cheeks flushed. They didn't believe her. She opened her mouth in one last attempt to explain, but Darach squashed her to his chest and drove his lips onto hers. The kiss was forceful, dominant, and it chased the thoughts from her head. Her knees buckled, but he held her up. When her arms twined around his neck, he grasped her waist and pushed her away. She blinked up at him.

"Get her out of here before she ruins everything," he whispered to Lachlan, who'd moved beside them.

Lachlan grinned from ear to ear. "Aye. Come on, love." Then he cupped her elbow and led her away.

With a thud, Darach lowered his prized bottle of *uisge-beatha* onto the round table that sat between the chairs in front of the small hearth in the great hall. He'd filled MacInnes's cup with the golden whisky—for the fifth time—and the man slumped sideways in the chair Darach had come to think of as Caitlin's.

It felt like a violation.

The liquor was as strong and smooth as a well-trained stallion and had caused the man's eyes and face to shine brightly in the firelight. He slurred his words but was still coherent enough to make sense.

It was a fine line, plying MacInnes with enough liquor to loosen his tongue but not enough to make him keel over—all in the hopes of discovering some way to extricate Caitlin from his guardianship before Darach married her. It's not that he didn't want to wed the lass, but the idea of rewarding her uncle for his immoral behavior went against everything Darach believed.

He'd asked Father Lundie, Lachlan, and Birk Anderson to join them. They sipped their drinks carefully, understanding the need for clear heads. All had agreed earlier, when MacInnes was indisposed, that it was likely he had started the fire that had killed Caitlin's parents in order to control his niece.

The murderer should not profit from his crime.

Gulping back a hefty slug of whisky, MacInnes slammed down his cup. The amber liquid sloshed over the rim, making Darach wince. The heathen hadn't even tasted it.

"God's truth, that's the finest whisky I've e'er had." MacInnes ran the words together. He wiped a dirty sleeve across his mouth and smirked at Darach. "Maybe I'll add a few bottles to the marriage contract. What say you, MacKenzie? Is she worth it? Does the wee slut burn up the bed linen?"

The blood boiled in Darach's veins. He clenched his jaw and tucked his hands beneath his arms to keep from squeezing the life out of the man. "She's a lovely lass. I'm happy to take her to wife."

"Aye, my brother was the same. It mattered not that the Frenchwoman carried another man's brat in her belly; he had to marry her. I told him to just swive her on the side, but he was in love with the tart. 'Twas all right with me. Worked in my favor, now didn't it?"

Darach's breath caught in his throat. Wallace MacInnes wasn't Caitlin's natural father? What would that mean for guardianship, if there was no blood tie to her uncle? Was it still valid? He didn't know the legalities, but if naught else, he could contest guardianship until he had solid proof of MacInnes's involvement in the fire.

His eyes darted to Birk Anderson. When the man smiled and nodded, hope flared in Darach's chest.

Still, he needed to pin MacInnes down. "Maybe Caitlin was conceived after your brother and Claire were married. The first bairn may have died."

MacInnes took another swig. He squinted as if in thought, then shook his head. "Nay, the timing is right. Besides, he ne'er had a child with his first wife before she died, and God knows I should have fathered a few dozen bastards by now. 'Tis sad to say, but our seed is weak. Our line dies with me." He didn't sound sad as he held out his cup for a refill. "Means there's none to come after me who'll want my gold."

Darach filled the cup halfway. He didn't want the man passing out just when he'd become talkative. If Darach could prove MacInnes had caused the fire, it would mean more than just freedom for Caitlin; it would mean justice for Wallace and Claire. The need for it burned in his heart. Her parents had loved Caitlin dearly and turned her into a sweet, caring lass—something her uncle's treachery had not undone.

Darach would make him pay for his misdeeds. "Did you speak to your brother after he left with Claire?"

"Nay, not for many years. We had naught to say to each other."

"He didn't want to know clan business? How you handled things?"

"I was laird. It had naught to do with him, no matter what some might have said."

So there had been dissension within the clan after Wallace had left. Maybe certain people had wanted him back, and he'd become a threat to MacInnes? But why wait so many years to kill him?

Darach nodded in agreement. "'Tis necessary to

rule with a strong hand. But sometimes 'tis helpful to hear what others think."

"Bah, they were young men and old fools. I took care of them."

"And Wallace. Did you take care of him too?"

MacInnes shrugged. "He was far away. Ne'er came back. 'Twas not necessary."

"So why visit after all those years?"

"I'd been to a wedding nearby. 'Twas the brotherly thing to do."

MacInnes rested his head on the heel of his hand and closed his eyes, swaying in his seat. Darach knew he was losing the blackguard and ground his teeth in frustration. A drunken confession wouldn't be enough to convict MacInnes, but if added to the information Darach's men were gathering, it might suffice.

Darach nudged him to wakefulness. "You said you went to a wedding and stopped in to see Wallace."

"Aye. He lived in a cottage smaller than my hall and fed slop to pigs. Can you imagine?" He laughed and shook his head. "Claire didn't like having me there, kept Caitlin away. But finally I saw her, and she was even more bonny than her mother. 'Twas a moment I'll ne'er forget."

"Why? What was so important about Caitlin, MacInnes?"

The beast smiled. "What else? To men like Fraser, she was worth her weight in gold."

⁂

The candle sputtered on Darach's desk. It was late. MacInnes had passed out hours ago after saying little else. They had dumped him in the barracks, then reconvened in Darach's solar. Each man had written an account of what MacInnes had said, then Anderson had sealed the parchments with the King's stamp. They were now safely tucked away for later.

Next, Darach had worked with Father Lundie and Anderson on the wedding contract. If the King decided MacInnes was lawfully Caitlin's guardian despite the lack of blood between them, MacInnes would receive from Darach the equivalent of what Fraser had given him, plus the bejeweled goblet, a steady supply of whisky, and Darach's alliance and protection. However, if it was proven MacInnes had gained guardianship of Caitlin by murdering her parents, the contract was void and MacInnes would face execution.

Either way, it bound Caitlin to Darach in marriage without him immediately having to fulfill his end of the contract to MacInnes. Now they just had to get him to sign. Darach didn't think that would be a problem. Anderson had worded the document with great skill. It was clear and murky at the same time.

After blowing out the candle, he made his way down the corridor. Gare and another guard stood outside Caitlin's door. When Gare saw Darach, he looked down, but not before Darach saw the indignation in his eyes.

"She's still a maid, lad. I havnae dishonored her. She told the lie so her uncle would leave her alone. As usual, she got more than she bargained for."

Gare sighed with relief. "Will you marry her, then?"

"Aye. Tomorrow she'll be my virgin bride, I promise you that."

"And I promise I'll always protect her, Laird."

Darach nodded and clapped his hand on Gare's shoulder. It was good Caitlin had their loyalty.

"Has she barred the door?"

"Nay, I doona think so."

Darach wasn't comfortable that Caitlin slept with the door unlocked, no matter how many guards protected her. But he needed to see her, touch her. Know she was safe. He pushed open the door and caught the look of misgiving on the lad's face. "I said virgin, Gare. I doona make promises I canna keep."

Inside, the fire burned low, leaving just enough light for Darach to see clearly as he slid the bar into place and walked across the room. Caitlin lay under the covers, facing him. Her hair fanned across the pillow and her lips had parted. As the blood rushed to his loins and stiffened his cock, he groaned. For the first time ever, he wondered whether he'd be able to keep his word. Maybe he should leave; one more night sleeping without the lass wouldn't kill him.

He looked to the door but couldn't make his feet move. Stifling a curse, he leaned his sword against the wall, shed his plaid, wool socks, and shoes, and crawled into bed beside her. She curled into him without waking. He wrapped both arms around her and squeezed. The tension in his gut slowly lessened.

He closed his eyes, tried to sleep. She was so soft, so warm.

Hell, it wasn't enough. He wanted to feel her against him skin to skin, whether it killed him or not. He pulled his arms away and tugged his lèine over his head, so he was naked. When he looked down, his breath caught in his throat. The covers were pulled back and she wore a light linen chemise with a low, round neck. The tops of her breasts were exposed. He trailed his fingers across the mounds, and she sighed in her sleep.

He found the bottom of her chemise and gripped it, tempted as he'd never been tempted before to strip her, then he let go. He was a fool. There was no way he'd be able to keep his word if she was naked too. The linen was a weak barrier, but it was better than naught. And was it not a violation to take such liberties while she slept? She wasn't his wife yet.

With a sigh, he rolled onto his back and tucked her into the crook of his elbow. Her head rested on his chest and her arm wrapped around his waist. His arousal throbbed painfully, but at the same time, he felt the rightness of the moment, a sense of peace. She was in her proper place by his side and he would keep her there always.

Satisfaction beat like a steady drum within him. Caitlin was his, but he knew with a certainty he was also hers.

He could last the night. Dawn was only a few hours away.

Sixteen

CAITLIN FLOATED IN A SEA OF WARMTH. THE MOST
enticing smell enveloped her—musky, male, with
a dash of *uisge-beatha*. She breathed deeply, and the
muscles contracted in her belly. Eyes drifting open, she
stared at tanned skin over a muscular chest.

Darach.

Her heartbeat surged and suddenly she was wide
awake. They lay nestled together on their sides, facing
each other, her head tucked beneath his chin. Morning
light crept past the shutter and she heard people calling
to each other from the bailey. She peered up. Darach's
eyes were closed, his face peaceful. Beneath her hand,
his chest rose and fell evenly.

Even after all the trouble she'd caused, he'd held
her through the dark hours 'til dawn. Protected her.

Smiling, she reached up to kiss his chin. The
coarse morning stubble scraped her lips. She liked it.
Restlessness pulsed through her and she squirmed in
his arms, only to stop in shock as she encountered bare
skin—all the way down.

She exhaled shakily, stirring the crisp hairs on his

chest. Where were his clothes? Surely they hadn't—nay, he would ne'er have touched her without her consent. She would know, wouldn't she?

The idea should have frightened her, but instead, she felt thrilled and snuggled closer. His chest hair tickled her nose. She rubbed her fingers through the crisp fleece, enjoying the rough texture. Finding a nipple, she circled the small, flat nub. He inhaled and moved his leg over hers. Her chemise had ridden to midthigh during the night, and the direct contact of skin on skin sent shivers of excitement along her nerves. Heat pooled between her thighs, and she trembled.

He was so big, so warm. She palmed his chest, then pressed her hands outward to the tips of his shoulders. The muscles bunched beneath her fingers. She squeezed, amazed at his power, the feel of iron beneath silk. His arms tightened around her, and before she knew what she was doing, she licked him.

He tasted like he smelled—delicious with a trace of salt. She nibbled into the hollow at the base of his neck, then along his collarbone. A groan rumbled in his chest. Her hands slipped downward to his stomach, where the skin smoothed over several ridges of muscle. They contracted at her touch, and he rolled on top of her, his weight pushing her into the bed.

Crushing, but also exciting.

His legs locked on either side of hers while a ridge at his pelvis pressed into her center. She closed her eyes and moved her hips against him. Her breath caught at the sensation, and she moved again, then circled her arms around his waist to splay her palms on either side of his spine.

"Caitlin," he mumbled. His hand moved heavily over her, squeezing her breast, then sliding down to her waist. Through her light linen chemise, her skin tingled. He thrust forward with his hips and she lifted to meet him. Sparks exploded behind her closed eyelids, and she moaned. She wanted to spread her thighs, but his legs held hers together.

He buried his hand in her hair and lifted his head. "Caitlin?" he asked, louder this time.

She opened her eyes. He had a flushed, sleepy expression, but his eyes glittered in a way she'd seen before—the night he'd kissed her in the hall and on his bed. It made her heart race, the blood pound through her veins. Her lips and breasts felt tight and hot. Her center ached.

He dropped his head to the crook of her neck, shuddered. "Doona move if you know what's good for you."

Without thinking, she bit his shoulder.

He snapped his head back. "What in God's name are you doing?"

She had no idea, but she had to do it again. Stretching up, she bit his other shoulder. He rolled away from her, but her arms were wrapped around his back and she went with him. Free of restraint, her legs splayed over his hips. She pressed into him. His hands dropped to her backside, held her still.

"Doona move!"

But she didn't listen and kissed his chest until she reached his nipple. Her lips surrounded it, sucked gently. With a grunt, he arched upward and raised his knees behind her. Then his hands slipped under her chemise, and curved around the twin globes of her bottom.

"Darach," she said, panting. "Darach, I need..." She didn't know what she needed, just that she had to have it.

"Aye, love, I know. I'll take care of you." His voice was rough, and it stirred something low in her belly.

Rolling her again to her back, he moved down her body so they were eye to eye. He was heavy between her legs, but it wasn't enough. She wrapped them around his waist and clasped tight.

He laughed and groaned at the same time. "I knew you'd like this."

"Like what?"

"Tupping."

"Is that what we're doing?"

"Not quite. I promised to keep you chaste."

Then he captured her lips, took over. The kiss was hot, wet, and she welcomed the invasion. He dominated her mouth, surging in and out in a rhythm that drove her wild. When she tried to snare his tongue, he sucked hers into his mouth and wouldn't let go.

Finally, he released her to trail his lips down her neck. The teasing kisses made her writhe beneath him. She cried out for more and raised her hands to his shoulders, digging in.

Darach pushed her chemise down to capture her breast. He cupped it in his palm and sighed. "So beautiful." Then he took her nipple in his mouth and teased it. Caitlin nearly came off the bed. The warm, wet heat of his tongue shot straight from her breast to that aching spot between her legs. Gasping, she plowed her hands into his hair.

He kissed across her chest to her other nipple, flicked it with his tongue, then bit down. The breath shuddered from her lungs. She cried out from the pleasure, head twisting on the pillow, pressure building inside. She was too hot, too needy.

He moved back and knelt between her legs. Her chemise was bunched around her hips, exposing the tops of her thighs. His hands caressed her calves and knees, then grasped the linen chemise. When he hesitated, she saw the conflict in his eyes. Longing battled with duty and honor, desire with restraint. The air huffed from his chest and he dropped his head, shook it.

"I canna. You deserve to know I'm your husband when I look on you like this."

He crawled away to sit on the side of the bed with his back to her. The breath rushed in and out of his lungs. Caitlin couldn't think, couldn't move. She lay gasping for air while the heat poured off of her. Her body ached, and she felt...unfulfilled.

She gripped her thighs together to assuage the need that pulsed between them. It was a poor substitute for Darach's body. Sitting up, she pulled her chemise into place and hugged her knees.

"Darach, you canna marry me. I willna allow it."

He frowned at her over his shoulder. "Aye, you will."

"But you doona want to marry. Ever. You'd be unhappy. Maybe if I knew you loved me." She held her breath, hoping he'd declare his feelings.

Instead, he exhaled and leaned forward, head in his hands, elbows on his knees. "Caitlin, this afternoon I will wed you, and tonight, I will bed you. I canna wait any longer."

Her brow wrinkled in confusion. He could have bedded her now, but he'd chosen not to. She supposed that was honorable, but she didn't want his honor; she wanted his love. Sniffing, she raised her chin. As God was her witness, he would love her before she married him.

He glanced back again and sighed. "Give me your hand."

She hesitated, then placed her palm in his. Pulling her forward, he wrapped her arm around his chest until she leaned against his back, chin on his shoulder. He turned his head so their lips were almost touching. "You doona want me unhappy, do you?"

She gasped. "Of course not."

"Then you'll marry me." He flattened her hand to his chest and guided it downward through the crisp, brown hairs, then across his belly, before wrapping it around his manhood.

The skin was soft and warm over a large, pulsing shaft. She tried to pull away, but he wouldn't let go. Instead, he moved her hand slowly up and down his length. A flush heated her cheeks. She glanced at his lap, fascinated by the sight of their clasped hands stroking his rigid flesh.

"You will marry me this afternoon or your uncle will take you back and I'll surely die from wanting you. Is that your desire?"

"Nay," she whispered, voice shaking with the same hunger that marked his face. She moved her hand on her own now, and he released it to grasp the back of her head.

"Then promise you'll marry me."

She looked into his eyes and saw his need. Unable to deny him, she said, "I promise."

He captured her lips and stroked his tongue against hers. She explored his mouth with the same rhythm as her hand down below. Up and down. In and out. He groaned, then rose from the bed, chest heaving. Her hand fell to her lap and she stared at the naked length of him—long, strong legs; curved buttocks; muscular back; and broad shoulders. Reaching out, she cupped his backside.

He leaped forward with a throaty growl and snatched his plaid from the floor, wrapping it around his body. Caitlin couldn't stop the smile that crossed her face.

Gathering the rest of his clothes and sword, he leaned down for a hard kiss. "You'll pay for that later." Then he headed for the door. When he opened it, he said over his shoulder, "I'll send Edina to help you get ready," before shutting it behind him.

Her smile faded. Edina would be displeased if she knew Darach had touched her. Although, he hadn't stroked between her legs, the act Edina had been most adamant about. But what would she say if she knew Caitlin had stroked him?

Excitement coursed through her again as she pictured her hand touching his flesh. The throbbing in her core renewed. She fell sideways onto the bed and curled into a ball. Running her palms down her body, she squeezed them between her thighs. Tonight, she would make love with her husband. In just a few hours, he would touch her everywhere.

Especially down there.

Evening couldn't arrive fast enough.

"Throw me the soap," Darach yelled at Lachlan, who stood shivering a few feet away in the water. By the time Lachlan had arrived for his morning wash, Darach had already swum to the rocky island in the middle of the bay and back. Now he barely felt the cold.

Lachlan grabbed the soap and pitched it at Darach's head. When he ducked, it splashed in the water nearby.

"You'll smell like roses," Lachlan said, "but maybe Caitlin willna mind. 'Tis better than your usual stink."

"My wife will love me howe'er I smell. 'Twill be a verra agreeable marriage."

"Once you learn to do as she asks."

Darach considered a sharp reply, but when he thought on Caitlin's lovemaking this morning, he knew it was true. She'd been very demanding. Never before had he resisted such temptation.

A satisfied grin crossed his face. Aye, he'd do exactly as she asked. Starting tonight.

Lachlan groaned. "I can see what you're thinking, and I doona want to know. As long as she's still a maid on her wedding night."

"She is. In truth, I should be nominated for sainthood. My betrothed is verra curious."

Lachlan rolled his eyes, then dived under the waves and rinsed away the soap. He hurried to the shore as Darach washed himself more leisurely.

"Lachlan."

"Aye."

"You'll stand up with me?"

Lachlan lowered the drying cloth from his hair. "I'd be honored. I canna think of a more worthy bride."

"Thank you, Brother."

"The groom, howe'er…"

Darach hurled the soap back at him.

They made their way to the keep slowly, anticipating the day's events and the arrival of Gregor and their foster brothers following that. It was disappointing the rest of the family couldn't be here for the wedding, but they would have their own celebration afterward.

Following a late breakfast, Darach and Lachlan strode across the bailey, toward the barracks where Caitlin's uncle had slept the morning away. Darach wore his best plaid, linen lèine, hose, shoes, and sporran. He also had a blue velvet jacket to wear during the ceremony. *Wedding finery*, Lachlan had called it, also dressed in his best.

The courtyard was a hive of activity as Darach's clan readied for the nuptials. Everyone was welcome at the celebration, and his hall and bailey would be full of revelers until the wee hours. The ceremony would take place on the steps of the keep, in front of his people. Time was too short to announce the banns, but Darach cared naught for that. He knew all of Caitlin's secrets—he hoped.

It amazed him to think they'd be married in a few hours. The idea made his heart lift and his stomach twist at the same time. He frowned at his conflicting emotions and concentrated on the task ahead—convincing Caitlin's uncle to sign the wedding contract.

Darach carried the papers in one hand, and the last bottle of his father's *uisge-beatha* in the other. It hurt something fierce to waste the prized drink on MacInnes, but Darach didn't want the man at his wedding. Better MacInnes lay passed out in the barracks than attend Darach's nuptials and ruin Caitlin's day. And if it helped with the signing, all the better.

Father Lundie and Birk Anderson waited for them at the barracks' door.

"Is he awake?" Darach asked.

Anderson shook his head. "Still out like the dead. I placed a bucket of water inside to rouse him."

"Laird MacKenzie, I fear the contract willna be to Laird MacInnes's liking. What if he refuses to sign?" Father Lundie wrung his hands. "I canna deceive him as to what is written."

"I doona ask you to. All I ask is you read every paragraph to him but no more. If he asks for clarification, Anderson will give it. The contracts are fair, Father. MacInnes only loses if he isna Caitlin's legal guardian or he is found guilty of a hideous crime."

Father MacInnes crossed himself. "I pray 'tis not true. It would be most upsetting for the lass to know her parents were murdered."

"Aye," Darach agreed. "But better she know the truth than be deceived by the devil. Come. We tarry." Darach pushed open the door and stepped inside. The others followed. On a pallet in the corner, MacInnes lay rumpled and wheezing. Darach nudged him with his foot.

"Go away."

Darach pulled up a chair and sat by the man's head.

He stank like a dead dog, forcing Darach to breathe through his mouth.

"You must rise and sign the wedding contract, MacInnes, else you'll lose your prize. There's a drink in it for you."

MacInnes opened one bloodshot eye. "Canna we do it later?"

"Nay. The marriage takes place immediately. You doona want her wed before you've sealed the deal, do you?"

MacInnes heaved himself upright. He looked like he might vomit. Darach pushed a chamber pot toward him with his foot. "If you lose your guts, do so in there. Then come to the table." He rose and headed to the far end of the room. Behind him, he heard MacInnes retching. Father Lundie stayed back to help. Darach and Lachlan made themselves comfortable on the bench, while Anderson opened the shutters to air the room.

A few minutes later, the priest led MacInnes to the table. He sat opposite Darach, who placed cups on the table and poured five drams of whisky. MacInnes eyed them greedily and reached for one. Darach stopped him. "After we've signed."

MacInnes scowled but nodded. He winced at the movement and dropped his head into his hands. Darach didn't feel the least bit sorry for him. He'd abused Caitlin for years and deserved more than just an aching head and sick stomach. If all went well, he'd be convicted of his crimes and punished to the full extent of the law.

"The King's man and Father Lundie crafted the

contract according to our discussion last night. If the wording is agreeable, we'll seal our bargain with a drink. What say you?" Darach asked.

MacInnes inclined his head slowly. "Aye."

Darach hid a grin. If MacInnes was in pain now, wait until Father Lundie was done with him. The priest's heart was in the right place, but when he preached, his voice took on a piercing quality that would drive a nun to drink.

"I've asked Father Lundie to read it to you."

The holy man cleared his throat and spread the parchment in front of him. He pronounced every word precisely, his speech loud and deliberate. The sound grated annoyingly on Darach, which cheered him. If it was difficult for him to listen to, it must have been hell for MacInnes, who sank lower and lower, toward the table, as the reading progressed.

Finally, MacInnes grabbed the parchment from the priest's hands. "Enough. I'll read it myself."

Darach almost laughed aloud, for he was certain MacInnes was unlettered. He did not have the discipline to learn to read and write. Sure enough, he scanned the parchment randomly, moving too quickly through the sheets to understand the words. When he arrived at the end, he held out his hand for the quill.

"Wait," Darach said. "Are you sure you understand what's written? 'Tis no shame in being untutored in letters. Father Lundie would be happy to continue his oration."

MacInnes blanched and snatched the quill from Anderson. "I understand." He quickly scrawled his mark on the parchment, then passed it to Darach, who signed his name and gave it to the other men to witness. Darach didn't need everyone to sign, but he would take no chances with Caitlin's safety.

When it was done, he distributed the *uisge-beatha* and they raised their glasses together.

"To Caitlin," Lachlan said. "The sweetest bride in all the Highlands."

MacInnes scoffed. "Bah, she's a nasty one, she is."

Darach clenched his jaw and breathed deeply. It took all his strength to stay on his side of the table. He raised his glass higher. "To justice. May deserving souls be rewarded and liars be hanged."

❦

"By the saints!" Caitlin screeched as Edina poked her with yet another pin. "I swear, if you do that one more time, I'll…I'll…"

Edina cocked her head, her mouth full of pins. "You'll what?"

"I doona know, but I promise you willna like it."

She rubbed at her hip, where the pin had pricked her. Darach would wonder at all the bruises on her body. The older woman shrugged and went back to work.

Caitlin stood on a stool in the middle of her chamber, surrounded by clan women adding the last touches to her wedding dress. Ever since Darach had left this morning, she'd been pinched, poked, bathed, primped, and fed. Now, hours later, her hair was curled and tied with ribbons, and the dress was almost complete. From outside, smells of roast fowl and suckling pig wafted from the kitchen.

"I doona know how you organized everything so

quickly. Darach only offered to marry me yesterday, and I didn't agree until this morning."

"Nell and I started planning three days ago as soon, as Laird MacKenzie informed me of his intentions. I used the measurements we took when you first arrived to begin your dress."

Her brow furrowed. "What do you mean, his intentions?"

"To marry you, of course. We had to keep it verra quiet. He didn't declare for you formally till yesterday."

Edina went back to work. When she poked Caitlin with another pin, she barely felt it. Darach had decided to marry her three days ago? "'Tis impossible. He was concussed."

"Aye, which is why we waited, but 'twas actually before that, when he brought you back after your fall in the river. Although Oslow says Laird MacKenzie had decided to marry you when they were on patrol. He heard Darach and Laird MacKay talking about it."

A lump formed in Caitlin's throat. She couldn't believe it. Darach had wanted to marry her before she'd been in danger. Maybe he did love her after all. It wasn't simply for duty's sake. "Did he say anything else?"

"About what?"

"About…I doona know… How he felt."

Edina and the other women laughed. "Caitlin, men doona sit around talking about their feelings like women do. If they care for a lass, they show her."

Caitlin scrunched her brow. What had Darach shown her? Certainly he'd protected her, risked his life and defied the King for her. He'd honored her enough to wait until they were married to claim her, and he'd forgiven her for digging up his bailey. That, more than anything, meant something.

"Do you think he cares for me?" she asked.

The women laughed again. Edina cut the last thread, knotted it, and lowered her hands. "He's marrying you, isna he?" She stepped back and walked around Caitlin, tucking here and fluffing there. When she reached the front, she adjusted the amber brooch on Caitlin's right shoulder. It matched the necklace between her breasts—two entwined silver hearts with amber in the middle. Gifts from Darach.

Edina arranged a ribbon in Caitlin's hair, then nudged her under the chin and smiled. "And now, you're ready to marry him."

The women left shortly afterward with instructions for her to sit still and not touch her hair or dress. It was an impossible request, of course, and she walked to the window to see what was going on outside. A warm breeze caressed her skin as she leaned out. Vast numbers of people in colorful plaids and ribbons rushed around, preparing for the wedding. They called cheerfully to each other over the noise.

When Oslow arrived a few minutes later, nervous excitement surged through her. She took his arm in a tight grip at the door of her chamber. Pipes played below. She fidgeted in time to the music, enjoying the feel of the fine wool skirt against her legs. Never before had she worn such lovely garments. The blues and greens of the material accentuated her eyes, and her hair was actually curled.

'Twas a miracle.

She pulled a lock over her shoulder to admire it.

Surely Darach would think she looked bonny—it had taken long to dress, but the results were well worth the pinpricks and pulled hair. She wanted to laugh but knew it might well turn into a fit.

She was marrying Darach. Today.

The sound of running feet came toward them, and Fergus barreled around the corner. He stopped abruptly when he saw Caitlin. "You look like a faery queen."

The compliment pleased her, but to hear the little boy speak and see the light in his face was the real reward. He was such a dear and looked so sweet in his pressed lèine and plaid. A small sporran circled his waist and his hair lay neatly against his head.

"If I look like a queen, you must be my gallant knight." Her voice broke, and she blinked, causing a tear to roll down her cheek.

"Och, doona start crying, lass." Oslow quickly wiped the wetness away with a kerchief. "If your eyes are red and your cheeks blotchy, I'll ne'er hear the end of it. Edina gave me strict instructions to keep you smiling."

Caitlin giggled at the thought of Edina wagging her finger at Oslow. The MacKenzie men were tough on the outside but soft and sweet, like pudding, beneath—and she was about to marry one.

"I'm to tell you to come now. Everything's ready." Fergus danced around, unable to keep still. Caitlin understood how he felt, but her feet were suddenly glued to the floor, as her doubts about Darach's willingness rose again.

Oslow tugged at her arm and somehow she followed him down the stairs and across the hall. When the door opened, she was momentarily blinded by sunlight. Then she saw Darach standing outside, on the top of the steps that led to the bailey. He was so big and handsome in his fine clothes, hair glinting red brown in the afternoon sun.

A smile creased his face as he looked her over from head to toe. "You're a vision, lass." Taking her free hand, he kissed it. "I'm a fortunate man."

"Are you sure, because—"

"I'm sure. I've ne'er been more certain of anything in my life."

"And you've forgiven me for digging up the bailey?" For some reason it was important to hear the words.

"Aye, Caitlin. Doona fash. I only wish the chapel was ready, so we could marry in a proper church."

"All the world is God's church," Father Lundie said. "'Tis an honor to join you before your people."

For the first time, she noticed the priest waiting on the step below them and the clan spread out in the bailey. Edina beamed up at her from the first row. Next to Darach, Lachlan grinned and winked at her.

After kissing her cheek, Oslow descended toward Edina and wrapped his arm around her shoulder. They looked like proud parents. Caitlin's chest tightened.

Darach squeezed her hand, pulled her close. She leaned into his side and gazed up at him. He brushed a kiss across her lips, causing the clan to cheer. Father Lundie cleared his throat, then began speaking in a solemn voice.

The ceremony washed over her in a blur. When Darach grasped both her hands to give her his vow, the tears broke free, streaming down her face as he pledged to love, comfort, honor, and keep her. His eyes held hers as he said the words, a tremor running through his voice. Her vows were similar, but she stumbled over her pledge to obey, praying God would forgive her ahead of time, for it was an impossible promise to keep. It's not that she didn't want to obey Darach, but surely God didn't mean all the time.

Darach raised an eyebrow as if he could read her mind, and she flushed. Already she was proving to be a terrible wife.

Before she knew it, Lachlan had given Darach the wedding rings. Father Lundie blessed them, and Darach placed one upon her finger. A satisfied smile crossed his face. When it was Caitlin's turn, her hand shook so much she kept missing. Darach steadied her with his other hand, and she finally pushed the ring onto his finger.

They knelt, and the last prayers and blessings were said. Then Darach helped her up, pulled her close, and kissed her. Not briefly, like before, but a long, drugging kiss. One hand sank into her hair and the other wrapped around her waist. Caitlin's knees weakened and her arms circled his neck. The blood pounded so loudly in her ears it drowned out the cheering crowd and rousing pipes.

"Darach?" she asked when he finally released her.

"Aye?"

"Will you look on me naked, now you're my husband?"

The air gushed from his lungs. "'Tis a certainty, lass."

"Then I shall look on you naked too." She gently bit his ear. "The sooner the better."

He laughed and scooped her up to carry her over the threshold into his keep.

The reception lasted several hours. Caitlin's cheeks hurt from smiling, her stomach from laughing, and her feet from dancing. The food had been delicious, but she'd been too wound up to appreciate it, even though Darach had fed her the choicest morsels of pickled eel, smoked mutton, and suckling pig. Afterward, the floor had been cleared and they'd danced the first reel of the night. Since then, she'd barely sat down, going from partner to partner, until Darach had claimed her again and positioned her beside him at the table.

She reached for her mead and drank deeply. The fermented drink quenched her thirst and sweetened her tongue. When it was empty, she lowered the mug.

He wiped the moisture from her lips, then licked his thumb. "Mmmmm."

She kissed him. "I canna believe you're my husband."

"Not quite."

"What?"

"Husbands take their wives to bed. I havnae done that yet." He leaned down and whispered in her ear, "Or have I, you wee *besom*?"

A blush rose along her cheeks. Should she tell him the truth, or did he already know she'd told a falsehood? And what exactly had happened last night while she'd slept?

He kissed her neck and took her earlobe in his mouth. The sucking sensation drove every thought from her head. She shivered and tilted her chin to give him better access.

He nibbled along her collarbone. "I've been

thinking upon our night together—the first time we made love, when I was ill. Since I doona remember, I'd verra much like you to tell me about it."

Her eyes popped open and she scooted away from him. "What?"

"You heard me. 'Tis unfair for you to have such sweet memories while my mind is blank. I would like every detail."

"But…'tis not decent."

"Aye, it is. I'm your husband now. You can tell me anything."

"Well…it was, it was…much the same as last night."

"Last night?"

She lowered her voice and added, "When you were naked in my bed."

Darach's eyes widened. Then he snorted and dropped his head in his hands. His shoulders shook. Was he laughing, or had she upset him? She bit her lip, wondering what to do. Maybe he teased her, like her father had teased her mother.

When he raised his face, however, it was grave. "How was it the same as last night, sweetling?"

He didn't look like he was jesting, so she tried to come up with a reasonable response. "Um, you were naked."

"Aye, we've established that."

"And you, well, you kissed me."

His arm circled her hips and dragged her along the bench until she was snug against him. He leaned closer. "Where?"

"On my lips."

He smiled against her cheek. "Anywhere else?"

It was as if a drug had entered her blood and compelled her to answer. "Maybe my breasts, like you did this morning."

"Did you like that?" His thumb traced lazy patterns on her hip.

"Aye. Will you do it again?"

"Aye." His other hand caressed her thigh. A tight, heavy feeling filled her center and her knees relaxed opened. His fingers moved higher along her leg under the table. "Close your eyes, Caitlin, and tell me where else I kissed you."

The laughter, yells, and cheerful piping faded into the background. Her lids drifted shut as she thought about where else Darach might bestow a kiss. "My hand."

"And?"

"My arm."

The fingers on her hip brushed her belly. "How about your stomach? Would you like me to kiss you there? Or maybe your thigh?" His other hand squeezed close to the core of her womanhood. It felt hot and swollen, and she wanted to spread her legs all the way. "Tell me what else we did. How we made love."

She imagined them on the bed linens, bodies entwined. "We lay together and you touched me all over. Then we coupled."

"How? What did it look like?" His voice was rough and heavy, making the heat spread in her womb. A picture formed in her mind of the male entering the female. She'd seen the animals mating on the farm.

"Well, you were behind me and we joined."

His breath, which had been loud and jagged in her ear moments ago, stopped. "From behind?"

She hesitated. Maybe that was wrong. "Aye?"

He groaned. "Christ Almighty."

Her eyes popped open at the curse. "Darach!"

"Were you naked?" he asked, dragging her onto his lap.

"What?"

"When you imagined us making love, were you naked?"

Many of the clan were drunk, but some had noticed Darach's amorous behavior and cheered him on. She was suddenly embarrassed. He held her too intimately in front of everyone.

He grasped her chin and made her look at him. "Caitlin, answer me." His eyes had that wild, fervent look she loved, and she relented.

"Of course we were. Doona you know anything about coupling?"

A strangled laugh exploded from his throat. "More than you, and now I'm imagining you naked, on your knees, in the middle of our bed. You have no idea what you've done," he growled.

"What do you mean?"

"I need to be in control tonight."

"Why?"

He looped his arms around her and rose from the bench. "Because I doona want to hurt you when I take your innocence."

Seventeen

"EVERYBODY OUT!" DARACH GLARED AT THE MEMBERS of his clan crowding into his bedchamber. He tightened his arms around Caitlin for fear they'd start undressing her. It may be tradition, but it wasn't going to happen to his wife—he'd be the only man seeing her naked.

Drunks, all of them.

Lachlan leaned against the wall by the window with his arm around his leman. Usually the lovers were more circumspect, but like everyone else tonight, they'd imbibed too much. She was an attractive, older woman whose husband had died and children were grown. No one thought ill of her; it was the way of the world. Darach had women he visited in his foster brothers' clans as well.

Used to visit, he corrected. He was married now, and would have no need of other women. If he could get his wife alone.

He caught Lachlan's eye. "You could bloody well help."

Lachlan grinned. "I would ne'er presume to tell your clan what to do."

Darach could barely hear him over the din, but he knew Lachlan was enjoying this too much to lend a hand.

Edina tugged on his sleeve. "Laird, I should speak to Caitlin alone before…well, you know."

"Nay. She doesn't need your counsel. I'll tell her everything she needs to know."

Caitlin frowned and pinched his arm. "Doona be rude. If Edina wishes to speak to me, I'm happy to do so."

His brow rose. "So she can tell you about lovemaking?"

Caitlin's eyes widened and a flush covered her cheeks. She leaned toward Edina. "I must do as Darach says. He's my husband. Maybe we can talk tomorrow."

"But, Caitlin—"

"Would you have me disobey him?"

"Well, nay, but—"

"She'll be all right," Darach said with a finality that made Edina's mouth flatten.

Caitlin cast him a grateful look. His frustration rose another notch. He wanted her grateful for more than just that. He wanted appreciation in her eyes after he'd touched her all over and she'd come apart in his arms. He wanted her cuddled against him, naked in the bed, before they fell asleep. He wanted her beside him in the morning when he woke.

Damn it, he wanted it all. Right now.

She let out a surprised squeak as he tossed her on the middle of the bed and leaped onto the foot of it. His head almost touched the ceiling. "Get out now, or I'll throw the nearest person out the window!" He looked pointedly at Lachlan, who laughed. The rest of his clan, however, took his command seriously and backed toward the door.

Edina hovered nearby with her hands clasped. "I thought my husband might have a word with you, Laird. Explain about young women." Oslow stood behind her, looking horrified.

"There are things you can do to—" She stopped abruptly when Darach jumped off the bed and marched toward her. Oslow grabbed her arm and pulled her from the room.

Darach slammed the door behind them, then turned to Lachlan and his leman. The woman clutched Lachlan's waist in a death grip.

"Get out before I kill you," Darach said. She squeaked and ran to the door. He opened it just far enough for her to pass through.

Lachlan grinned and sauntered toward Caitlin, who sat primly on the bed. "Are you all right, love? He didn't hurt you tossing you about like that, did he?"

"Nay, I'm fine. Do you want a cup of ale before you go?"

Darach fisted his hands. What in God's name was she doing?

"Aye, that would be much appreciated." Lachlan's eyes danced merrily.

Caitlin hopped off the bed and reached for the pitcher of ale someone had placed on a side table. When her back was turned, Darach lunged at Lachlan, but the bugger darted behind a chair.

She swung back with three mugs of ale on a tray. "I thought we could talk about the woman you were with, Lachlan. She seems lovely, but 'tis most disrespectful not to marry her."

Lachlan's grin faded. It transferred to Darach, who

almost laughed aloud. This would get the trouble-maker out of the room. "I agree. There's no reason to be afraid, Brother. Marriage is a wonderful thing. Surely you want to make your lass happy?"

Most likely, the woman had even less desire to marry than Lachlan. The last thing she wanted was another man to care for. Caitlin, however, didn't know that.

Excitement lit her face as she handed out the drinks. "We could have the wedding before you leave. I'll tell Edina to keep everything in place and you can be married tomorrow afternoon, aye?"

Lachlan stared at her, face blank, then tipped the mug back and drank the entire contents. When he was done, he retreated to the door. "I'm not going home just yet, lass. You doona need to rush things."

Darach followed, tempted to block Lachlan's escape in order to see him flail beneath Caitlin's eager gaze.

"I shall have to speak to her about your cursing, of course. 'Tis a wife's duty to help her husband get into Heaven. I'm sure if she's vigilant, she'll break you of that unfortunate habit in no time."

Lachlan paled and reached behind him for the latch. Darach leaned his shoulder against the door. Their eyes met.

"You're sure you doona want to stay for another drink?" he asked.

"Nay, I wouldnae want to disturb your wedding night."

The silence lengthened.

Caitlin reached for the pitcher. "There's more."

Lachlan yanked open the door and ran out. Darach

slammed it shut behind him. After sliding the bar into place, he turned to his wife.

She had a mischievous smile on her face. "I thought he'd ne'er leave."

Darach's jaw dropped. "You did that on purpose?"

"Well, I couldnae kick him out, now, could I? That would be rude."

He threw back his head and laughed. So much for being innocent. Caitlin laughed too, and twirled in a circle. His heart swelled as he watched her. So lovely, so devious.

Lady MacKenzie.

"Come here, Wife." He had a hard time speaking around the lump in his throat, and his voice sounded rough.

She glanced down, then peeped at him through her lashes.

His blood thickened. He couldn't get the image of her naked, on the bed, out of his head. Didn't want it out of his head. "Caitlin, come here." He could barely form the words.

She walked toward him, stopping a few feet away.

"Closer."

Eyes lowered, she inched forward till their toes touched. His heart pounded as he waited for her to look up. When she did, he traced his fingers along her brow and down her cheek, then rubbed his thumb across her lips. "My beautiful lass."

Smiling, she placed her hands on his chest. "Do you like my curls?"

He lifted a lock of hair from her shoulder and wrapped it around his finger—soft as lamb's wool. Kissing the strands, he said, "I like everything about you."

"Even when I—"

He pressed his finger to her lips. "Everything."

Her pupils dilated, cheeks flushed. A tremor ran through her and a warm puff of air caressed his finger as she exhaled.

Looping his arms around her waist, he dropped his head to her ear and traced the whorls inside with his lips. "Do you have any questions?"

She shivered. "About what?"

"Making love, sweetling. I doona want you frightened."

"I'm not." Another tremor raced through her. "Well, maybe a wee bit nervous."

Darach understood; he was nervous as well. Which didn't make sense. He'd had his first woman when he was sixteen, and many others since then. He'd even been betrothed for a while.

But he'd never made love to a woman like Caitlin. Innocent, untutored.

His wife.

No wonder he was nervous. Her pleasure, or lack thereof, in the act would set the stage for years to come. He'd heard of men, his foster brother Gavin, for one, whose wives wanted naught to do with intimate congress. Their marriage had been a disaster.

Nay, Darach wanted Caitlin to enjoy making love, but how could she when she was a virgin? Maybe he should have had that talk with Oslow after all.

"Darach?"

"Aye?"

"Are you planning to kiss me anytime soon?"

He smiled. "I will when you're out of these clothes and ribbons." He pulled her toward the bed, picked up the brush from the washstand, and sat down with her. She leaned back against him. He gently released the ribbons adorning her hair, then pulled the brush through the strands until they shone like silk. She sighed with pleasure.

"Face me, love."

She turned toward him, and he swept her hair behind her shoulders. The ends curled and tendrils framed her face. So beautiful.

His hands dropped to the silver-and-amber necklace between her breasts. "This belonged to my mother. The brooch as well. They were a gift from my father when they married. Maybe someday our son will give it to his wife."

She nodded, a film of tears covering her eyes.

He wiped them away.

"Do you want bairns, then?" she asked.

"Aye, every one of them looking like you."

Her brows rose. "But you're so bonny. Your hair glints red in the sun."

"So you said when we first met—in front of my men." The corners of his mouth lifted. "Poor Gare was aghast."

"I doona remember, only that you were there and I was safe."

He pressed his lips to her forehead. "May that always be so." His fingers found the clasp at the back of her neck and released the necklace. Next, he undid the brooch, causing the fine, woolen material of her arisaid to fall away. Her chemise was a soft, embroidered linen and covered her almost completely. He trailed his hand down her sleeve and linked his fingers with hers.

"Shall I get under the covers now?" she asked.

"Not unless you want to wear your shoes to bed."

She giggled. Her blue eyes shone brightly in the candlelight. Unable to resist, he kissed her. Their lips clung. When he pulled back, she went with him. Her arms wrapped around his neck, and he anchored her against his body. Finally, they separated, gasping for air.

"Your shoes."

She nodded dazedly. He lifted her and sat her across his lap, one arm circling behind her, the other unlacing her slippers. Her hip nudged his groin, and he had to grit his teeth to contain his desire. The need to lay her on the quilt, spread her legs, and push inside was strong, but if he did, it would be over in seconds. She'd never want to be intimate again. Nay, he had to take it slow, bestow pleasure before he broke through her maidenhead. Give her a taste of everything love-making could be.

He just had to stay in control.

She played with the front of his collar and slipped her hand inside his lèine. Fingers ruffled through chest hair, brushed a nipple. His control wavered. With a jagged exhale, he grasped her hand, brought it to his mouth, and kissed her palm. "You canna touch me just yet."

"Why not?"

"Because when you do, I stop thinking. 'Tis verra pleasurable, and I get caught up." He placed her arm around his neck. "We have to take it slow."

"Why?"

"Because we do." She was so innocent and didn't understand their joining would hurt. Maybe that was good, for he didn't want her anticipating pain when she should be craving his touch.

Her hose were still on and he moved his hand under her chemise, to her knee. Untying the ribbon, he slid the material down, trying to ignore the silky, smooth feel of her skin. Moving to the other leg, he worked the second band loose. Their eyes met. Her lids were partially closed, her lips parted. He groaned and leaned in to kiss her. She welcomed him—hot, eager. Her hands clenched his hair. When she pulled her knees up and dropped them open, he lost it. His palm pressed urgently up her inner thigh, toward her center.

She rocked her hips, seeking his touch. "Darach!"

He paused. Her muscles quivered beneath his hand.

Never before had he seen anything as arousing as Caitlin in the throes of passion, back arched over his arm, eyes closed, knees spread. Her chemise rose upward, and he pushed it above her waist, exposing dark, glistening curls above soft pink folds of skin. The air rushed from his chest as he saw the evidence of her desire.

Wet, swollen. Waiting for him.

He could barely catch his breath. His cock throbbed almost painfully, so tight and full he thought he might explode. Just a few more minutes. She was ready for him, but he wanted her to peak once before they joined. By the look of her—chest and cheeks flushed, panting—it wouldn't take long.

He cupped her mound, and she groaned, rubbing the slippery surface against his hand. Leaning down, he kissed the hollow at the base of her throat, then traced upward to her chin and found her mouth. His tongue thrust inside. Down below, he stroked her flesh, circling her nub, then down to her entrance and back up again.

She whimpered into his mouth, thrust her hips harder. He deepened the kiss and moved his fingers faster, with more pressure. Her grip on his hair was almost painful, but he welcomed the sign of her arousal. Slowing, he circled her opening, then carefully pushed inside. She was tight, like a wet, silk glove, and moaned at the invasion. Rotating his hand, he tested how much she could take. Not enough.

Maybe he could stretch her. He slid his middle finger in too, while his thumb stroked the tight nub beneath her curls.

Her hips found the rhythm, jerking faster every time until she bucked beneath him and cried out, "Darach! Darach, I… Oh God." Her body tensed as her inner muscles clamped his fingers again and again, till finally she pressed her knees together. He stopped, held her tight, then gently removed his hand.

She shuddered, curving her body into his. He stroked her back and hair, pressed soothing kisses to her flushed face.

"Did that feel good?" His voice was so rough he barely recognized it.

She caught her breath. "I…I think so."

"What does that mean, you think so?"

When she bit her lip, his fear intensified. She hadn't liked it. "Was it supposed to be like that? I just wanted more and more. Did I do something wrong?"

His muscles unclenched, and he hugged her tight.

"Nay, Caitlin. You were perfect. I didn't want to stop either."

"'Twas the same for you?"

"Not quite. But it will be before we're done."

Her eyes widened. "There's more?"

He smiled at the look on her face. "We've barely started." Lifting her from his lap, he stood her between his knees. She clasped his shoulders for support as he raised her chemise over her head.

The breath caught in his throat as he finally looked upon his wife naked—happy and flushed with desire.

She was a wee lass but had curves in all the right places: hips, waist, rosy-tipped breasts. His hands slid up her thighs, thumbs caressing the hollow at the curve of her hip, the slight swell of her belly. His palms dipped into her waist, then curved over her ribs before cupping her breasts. She gasped as his fingers trailed over pebbled nipples.

His throat tightened suddenly, and he wrapped his arms around her, resting his head on her chest. In all his life, he'd never been this aroused by a woman, yet he found himself just wanting to hold her. He closed his eyes and inhaled the warm, fresh, flowery scent of her mixed with the muskiness of their arousal.

She held his shoulders and rested her cheek on his head.

"Darach?"

"Aye?"

"I'm glad you're my husband."

"I'm glad you're my wife. I promise to keep you safe and happy, lass. Always."

"I know."

It pleased him she had no doubt he could protect her, provide for her.

Caitlin was his—to comfort, to pleasure. He slid his hands down her spine, to the jut of her backside that had caused so much trouble sitting in front of him on Loki, rubbing innocently against him. He kneaded the soft flesh and she swayed forward.

He grinned. She liked that. Finding her nipple, he suckled her breast. She moaned and dug her hands into his hair. She liked that too.

He wanted her so aroused she barely noticed the pain of his entry, so needy she couldn't resist. Patience was a virtue, and if it meant Caitlin enjoying herself, he had plenty of it.

Her knees buckled and a primal pleasure filled him, knowing his touch did that to her. He rose from the bed, pulled back the quilts, and laid her upon the linen sheets. She stared at him, her breath heavy, eyes bright. Trailing his fingers down her body, he watched with fascination as she undulated beneath his touch.

"Spread your legs," he said hoarsely.

She did, even raised a knee so her foot was flat on the bed. One hand lifted above her head, her lips parted. Candlelight played over her skin, caressing curves and dipping into hollows.

With a groan, he tore off his clothes and tossed them to the floor.

"Wait," she said, sitting up onto her knees and tucking her feet beneath her backside. "I want to look on you too."

The air huffed from his lungs. He didn't want his size to frighten her. Never before had he felt so engorged, so desperate to be inside a woman. Her eyes trailed over his shoulders and chest, then down his stomach. They widened when they took in his cock. Darach cursed silently and slid onto the bed, rolling her beneath him.

Worried eyes met his. "Will you fit?"

"Aye. It'll be tight, but only the first time." Her thighs cushioned his shaft and he inhaled through his nose and out his mouth to gain control. If he wasn't careful, he would lose his seed before he even entered her. "I need to lay between your legs, Caitlin."

The heat of her core welcomed him as she opened her thighs, and he positioned himself over her. His hand cupped her breast, gently pinched her nipple. She arched and groaned into his mouth. Raising her knees, she rubbed against his shaft.

Mindlessly, he thrust forward, the tip of his cock pushing at her entrance but not yet breaching it. She rocked against him, bit his shoulder. Darach growled, wanting to push all the way in. Instead, he slipped his hand beneath her hips and lifted her into a better position.

"Wrap your legs around my waist," he said.

She did, heels digging into the small of his back, teeth nibbling along his neck. He took her mouth with his, then slowly pushed inside. Hot, silky flesh enveloped him, sent shivers of excitement through his body. He shook with the effort to restrain himself as he pressed through her maidenhead.

Heaven.

Then she wrenched her mouth from his and tried to wriggle free with a small moan. "It hurts."

Hell.

He paused. Only his tip was past her entrance. Holding her still, he dropped his face into the crook of her neck. It took all his strength not to thrust the rest of the way. Maybe that would be best, just to finish it, but she had tensed her muscles against him.

He raised his head, jaw so tight it was difficult to speak. "Caitlin, look at me."

Her eyes were frantic, glancing everywhere but at him. "You must be doing something wrong. Why does it hurt? It didn't hurt before."

He wedged a hand behind her head. "Look. At. Me." She did, and he held her gaze. "I'm not doing anything wrong. Once we're joined, it'll stop hurting."

"But—"

He kissed her firmly. "Trust me."

She hesitated, then nodded.

"Good. Now take a deep breath." Her rib cage expanded as she inhaled, then let go. The tension in her body lessened. "Another." The second breath relaxed her further. "Does it still hurt?"

She shook her head. He kissed away the tears on her lashes. "This is just the beginning, lass." Then he thrust forward.

She cried out, but the pleasure that rushed through his body blinded him momentarily to her distress. She was so hot, so wet, enveloping his shaft in a velvet tunnel. His stones tightened, and he knew he was about to lose his seed. A few strokes and he'd be done.

He gripped her shoulders, so she couldn't move. The tears were back in her eyes, and she'd bitten her lip. Concern fought with the need to seek his own release. Damn it, he would see to her pleasure first.

"I'm in now, sweetling. It willna hurt anymore." He could barely get the words out.

She nodded.

He loosened one hand from her shoulder to wipe the tears from her cheeks, then kissed her. Long and slow. By the time he pulled back, she breathed heavily. Her gaze had that aroused, hooded look he loved. Trailing his hand down to play with her breast, he watched for signs of excitement. She closed her eyes, arched her back.

The movement shifted her hips. Her silky flesh rubbed along his length, and he thrust forward before he could stop himself, so he was pressed to the hilt again. Her eyes popped open.

He expected to see pain there, but instead he saw desire.

"Do that again."

His breath caught and he had to clench his muscles to stay still. "I canna, not yet."

The witch had turned him into a lad again. Wedging his hand between their bodies, he found her nub, circled it, and prayed she responded quickly.

She grabbed his head and dragged it down for a kiss. He fisted his hand in her hair as she writhed beneath him. When her heels dug into his backside, his control snapped. He withdrew and pushed forward. Everything swelled, tightened, and he did it again. Harder this time.

Breaking the kiss, she whimpered as she bucked her hips. His weight bore down on her, his brain turned off. They found a rhythm, thrusting mindlessly until she screamed, and her inner walls contracted around him in waves.

He shouted as his body stiffened, and his seed released. With a final grunt, he collapsed on top of her. Unable to move or think, he lay there, gasping for air.

Slowly, he came back to his senses. Caitlin's chest heaved beneath him.

"Canna. Breathe." She pushed against his shoulders.

He rose onto his elbows. "Sorry."

His arms felt weak, his head heavy. He pulled out of her with a groan and rolled onto his back, staring at the ceiling. Never before had he lost himself in a woman so completely, been so overcome.

His control had vanished.

Anxiety niggled in his gut and he closed his eyes. Even with Moire, he hadn't felt such all-consuming passion. And look where that had ended.

He turned his head toward her. She looked as dazed as he felt, and he trailed his fingers down her cheek.

Making love to his wife had been the most incredible, most terrifying experience of his life.

"Caitlin."

"Aye." Her voice was barely above a whisper.

"Doona lie to me again. Ever."

She bit her lip. "I didn't mean to. It just came out."

"I know. But I'll protect you. Always. You doona have to make up stories to stay safe."

She nodded, then rolled over and climbed on top of him, her head on his chest. His arms surrounded her, and the anxiety eased from his belly, replaced by a profound sense of peace.

"Darach? Do you love me yet…just a wee bit?" Her voice sounded sleepy as she drifted toward slumber.

He glanced down to see her eyes closed, her breath coming slow and even through parted lips.

Did he love her? He knew without a doubt he would die for her, would leave his clan, his brothers, for her, just as her father had done for her mother. Was that love? Darach had thought he'd loved Moire, but when she'd betrayed him, his pain had been more about his foolishness than her deceit. He'd grieved the child she'd lied about more than he'd grieved her.

But if something ever happened to Caitlin…

His stomach clenched, and he refused to think about it. She was safe, warm, sleeping in his arms, surrounded by his clan, his castle. And his bairn could be growing in her belly. That frightened him as much as it pleased him.

Aye, maybe he loved her.

He kissed the top of her sleeping head. "Just a wee bit."

Eighteen

"GIVE THEM TO ME."

Edina tugged the bed linens from Caitlin, who let go reluctantly. An embarrassed flush heated her cheeks. "I only thought to wash them. I bled last night." She whispered even though no one else was in the chamber.

Bundling the sheets, Edina nodded. "Of course you did. 'Tis your maiden blood, a sign of your virtue. Our laird will be pleased."

A lump formed in Caitlin's throat at the mention of her husband, and she blinked back the tears that had threatened to fall ever since she'd woken this morning in their marriage bed—alone. She knew she was being foolish, but she couldn't help it.

"Did you see him earlier?" she asked.

"Aye, he and Laird MacKay went to the loch hours ago. Now come and have your bath before the water cools."

Caitlin seldom slept late, but when she'd first stirred and found him gone, all her doubts had resurfaced, and she'd pulled up the covers, hoping he'd come find her. Reassure her.

He hadn't.

What if she'd done something wrong, offended him with her lusty behavior?

Well...if she had, it was his fault. Maybe if he'd instructed her on what to expect, she mightn't have been so...so...mindless. Aye, he was negligent in his duty as her husband.

Feeling better, she wound up her hair, dropped her chemise, and stepped into the lavender-scented water. It stung at first, but the heat soon worked its magic. With a sigh, she lay back and closed her eyes. The lapping of the water reminded her of his hands stroking her skin. Her breasts tightened, grew heavy. His weight on her had been exciting too, and she clasped her hands against her belly, where he'd pressed her down.

"I'll return to help you dress as soon as I've served the laird his noon meal. I willna be long."

Caitlin sat forward with a squeak, sloshing water over the tub's edge. She'd forgotten Edina was here.

Her gaze fell on the door swinging shut behind the housekeeper, and she almost ran to lock it...although perhaps it would be better if she threw it open and yelled for Darach to come find her, comfort her.

Preferably in bed with his arms around her.

Groaning, she dropped her head in her hands. Maybe she should crawl back under the covers for the rest of the day.

Nay. She was a lady now; she had to act like one. She thought about waiting for Edina, but an urge to see Darach beat at her and she rose from the water. After drying herself with the towel, she donned her best gown, brushed her hair, and walked in a dignified manner out the door. At the end of the corridor, however, she lost her courage and peeped around the corner to see if she could spot Darach in the hall below.

"Are we spying on someone?"

The words were whispered in her ear and she shrieked and spun around. Darach pulled her close, so she didn't tumble down the stairs. "Are you well, lass? Maybe we should go back to bed. The corridor is drafty. I'll warm you in no time." His hands slid down her back to cup her bottom.

"To comfort me?"

"Aye. I'll make you verra comfortable."

"Darach! Get down here," Lachlan bellowed at them from below.

With a muttered curse, Darach glanced past her shoulder. "Why must you yell like a bloody fishwife?"

"Because otherwise you'll be heading back to bed, and I'll be left to deal with MacInnes on my own." He smiled at Caitlin, who'd turned to face him. "Morning, lass. Did you sleep well?"

Images of last night flooded her mind as Darach took her hand and led her down the stairs. He glanced back when she didn't answer. Noticing her embarrassment, he grinned, then stopped for a kiss. "Aye, she slept well, splayed over me like a bairn."

"I did no such thing," she said, but the memory of her crawling on top of him took the force out of her protest. Lachlan would think her wanton. "Take it back." She poked Darach in the ribs.

"Why? You're my wife. You can sleep any way you like with me."

They reached the bottom, and Lachlan also kissed her. "Your uncle is coming. Maybe you should stay upstairs. I'm afraid 'twill be unpleasant."

"But I just came down. Edina has a meal prepared."

"Aye, but he'll most likely upset you when he doesn't get his way. We can send you up a plate."

"'Tis best, sweetling." Darach patted her backside dismissively. "Eat your meal, then have a nap. I'll come up afterward."

"Nay."

"Nay?"

"He's my uncle. 'Tis my right to know what's happening."

Darach planted his hands on his hips. "I doona think you understand the wedding vows, Wife. You are to obey your husband."

She rolled her eyes. "God only meant some of the time, Husband."

"Some of the time?"

"Aye."

"And did He tell you which times?"

"Nay, if God spoke to me, I'd be a saint, and a saint surely wouldnae do as we did last night." Caitlin crossed herself for good measure.

Lachlan laughed as Darach sighed. Taking her hand, he led her to the high table. Edina arrived with a steaming trencher of mutton and greens. Darach used his knife to cut the juiciest morsel and fed it to her. Caitlin didn't care for mutton, but she smiled as she ate it because he was being so sweet.

Lachlan sat on her other side. Breaking off a piece of bread and piling some meat on it, he glanced at

Darach over Caitlin's head. "You should tell her before MacInnes gets here."

Darach grunted in response.

She looked at him, but he stared across the room, lost in thought. The food in her stomach hardened, and her heart began to pound. Surely he couldn't… He wouldn't… "Tell me what?"

Darach saw her expression and cursed. She would have rebuked him, but her throat had closed shut.

"I'm not sending you back, Caitlin. You're my wife, for God's sake. Even if you weren't, I wouldnae give you to him. How could you think such a thing?"

She released the breath she'd been holding in a gush of air. "Well, you weren't there, were you? You abandoned me."

"What?"

"This morning. I needed you, and you'd gone for a swim with Lachlan. You were derelict in your duty as my husband." She sniffed and eyed him accusingly.

"You were sleeping."

"I needed comfort."

"I held you all night."

"You did?"

"Aye."

"You see? That's comforting to know. If you were there this morning, you could have told me that."

He stared at her for a minute. "So I'm to lie in bed till you awaken?"

"Well, nay, but maybe you could kiss me before you rise. Wish me a good morning."

"Even if you sleep?"

"Aye."

A slow grin crossed his face. "If you insist. I'll wake you every morning with a kiss."

"And praise."

"Praise?"

"Well, I need to know, doona I?" She leaned toward him and whispered, "Did I please you last night?"

Darach's eyes darkened, and he dragged her against his side to whisper back, "Aye, you pleased me."

"I did everything all right?" Her hand gripped his lèine uncertainly.

"You were perfect."

"But I was so…wild."

"I liked it. I want you that way every time, aye? Moaning and squirming beneath me, pulling my hair, digging your heels into my back. We have a lifetime of loving ahead of us, Caitlin, and I couldnae be more pleased that you respond to my touch." His voice roughened and his fingers gripped her hip. "Maybe we should have that nap, now."

The last was said loudly and Lachlan threw his hands in the air. "MacInnes is coming. You have to finish it."

"Finish what?" she asked.

Lachlan looked significantly at Darach, who sighed. He cut another piece of meat and fed it to her. "Your uncle will want his due for giving you to me in marriage. What he doesn't realize is there are conditions in the contract that must be met first."

"What conditions?"

"Well, first, the King must decide if MacInnes's claim to you is valid."

She crinkled her brow in confusion. "What do you

mean? He's my only living relative. I doona know my mother's family."

"I'm your family now. Husband and father of your bairns, if we are so blessed. The MacKenzies are your clan."

Lachlan reached over and squeezed her hand. "And you're my sister, Caitlin. A beloved member of my family too."

A lump formed in her throat. "Thank you, both of you, but I spoke of my father's family. Heaven knows I wouldnae choose him, but MacInnes *is* my uncle."

Darach sighed and pressed her head to his chest. Caitlin didn't now what was going on, but she knew she had to see his face. She pushed back. His eyes were troubled.

"Husband, you will tell me what's on your mind, else I'll assume the worst and maybe run away again." It was a lie, but Caitlin thought the threat would loosen his tongue.

"You'll do no such thing. You gave me your word."

She raised a brow and waited, heart tripping.

He sighed again, hand caressing her hair. "It has come to light your mother was pregnant with you when...when—"

The door opened and Oslow strode toward them, claiming Darach's attention. Caitlin squashed her frustration. What had he been about to say?

A contingent of warriors entered and took up position in the hall. The men who were eating joined them, while the serving girls scurried to clear the tables and put them away.

Oslow stopped in front of Darach. "MacInnes is on

his way. Birk Anderson and Father Lundie are with him. Each has a copy of the contract."

Darach nodded and returned his gaze to Caitlin. She waited for him to finish what he'd been saying about her mother. Instead, he cupped her face and kissed her. "Your father loved you verra much, Caitlin—as his own. Naught can take that away from you." Then he straightened and faced forward, arm around her waist.

"Be strong," he whispered as MacInnes entered the keep.

Caitlin shuddered when she saw her uncle. He was even filthier than two days ago, red-faced with dark, sunken eyes. Worse was his stench, which wafted toward her as he approached. If Caitlin hadn't known the evil in his heart, she would have thought him a wretch and felt sorry for him. As it was, she had a hard time not gagging.

He curled his lip in disdain at the sight of her. "Niece, you are well provided for because of me. You ought to be on your knees in gratitude."

"I'll ne'er be grateful to you, Uncle. But I'll gladly go to my knees for my husband and thank him every day."

Darach's arm tightened around her as Lachlan made a strange, choking sound. When Oslow's face reddened, she knew she'd somehow misspoken.

"Hush," Darach said. "I will speak to your uncle."

"Nay. Let the *besom* continue," her uncle sneered. "'Tis amusing to hear what else the slut will do."

Darach tensed, and as if he'd ordered it, Oslow struck MacInnes across the face. She gasped as her uncle stumbled backward. When he straightened, blood

dripped from his lip. His eyes darted fearfully around
the room. Every MacKenzie looked ready to kill him.

Rising to lean over the table, Darach glowered at
him. "Count yourself fortunate, MacInnes. If it had been
me, you'd be dead. Your time here has ended. Leave."

"Not before I get my due. The contract hasn't been
filled. I want my gold."

"You shall have it, if the King rules in your favor."

"What do you mean?"

"First, it must be decided if you're Caitlin's true
guardian."

"I'm her uncle."

"Not by blood."

The silence that fell was deafening. MacInnes stared
at them, eye twitching. Caitlin slowly stood beside
Darach. Moments ago, he'd been trying to tell her
something about her mother...and father. Something
that had troubled him.

"He's not my da's brother?" she asked, voice trembling.

Darach's arm came around her in support. He held
her gaze. "He is."

"Then how...?"

"Your mother was pregnant with you when she
met your father, Caitlin. He loved you as his own,
but you did not come from his seed. Your uncle told
us so last night."

The words echoed loudly in her head, and she
gripped Darach's lèine. "'Tis untrue. He lied."

"Nay. 'Tis to his detriment, he had no reason to lie."

Her uncle started arguing, but Darach's eyes never
left her face. He stroked her head, then slipped his hand
beneath her hair and rubbed her nape. "Caitlin—"

"I'm all right," she said, sinking to the bench.

Be strong.

Now she understood his words. Forcing a deep breath, she fought back the heartache. She would not let her uncle see her weep.

"I will see you off my land, MacInnes. Ne'er cross it again." He nodded to Birk Anderson, who stepped forward. "Master Anderson has agreed to present our dispute to the King. If he judges in your favor, I'll deliver your gold. If not, our acquaintance is over."

"This is treachery!"

"Nay, 'tis what we agreed. You read the contract. If you disagreed, you shouldnae have signed your name to it."

MacInnes sputtered incoherently, hands fisted. "It matters not who her father is. My brother claimed her as his own, which makes me her guardian upon his death."

"Maybe, but we'll let the King decide. In the meantime, I would think back on the night your brother and his wife died. The King may have some questions about the fire."

The color drained from MacInnes's face. "Questions?"

"Surely you want your King to know the truth? I do, for my wife's sake, as well as my own. Which is why I've begun looking into the matter."

"You'll find naught. The fire was an accident."

"I hope so."

Caitlin looked from one to the other, her head swimming. Not only was her father not really her father, but her uncle also might have set the fire that killed her parents? Darach hadn't actually said so, but surely that's what he meant. She started to rise again, but his hand on her shoulder held her down. Lachlan smiled at her reassuringly. They wanted her to hush.

She bit her lip and tasted blood. Why on earth would her uncle murder her parents? It didn't make sense. Her hands hurt, and she realized she'd clenched them so hard her nails had scored her skin. She unclenched them, flattening her palms on her dress.

MacInnes turned to her, eyes filled with hatred. "If you hadn't spread your legs, you would have stayed married to Fraser. You're just like your mother—she was a whore too."

Darach shoved the table out of his way, and it crashed over, clay pots smashing to pieces on the floor. Caitlin shot to her feet as he leaped toward MacInnes. Lachlan caught him from behind just as Anderson and Oslow stepped in front of her uncle.

"Darach, nay!" she cried.

"Calm yourself, Brother," Lachlan said softly. "He'll get his in the end. Remember our plan."

Darach struggled for a moment, then stopped. He shook off Lachlan and caught his breath. She rushed forward to wrap her arms around his waist. Anger trembled through him.

Behind them, a flapping noise filled the room, drawing everyone's attention. She turned to see Edina on the balcony above the great hall, shaking out the unlaundered bed linen. Caitlin gasped in horror as the housekeeper hung the bloodstained sheet from Caitlin's bed over the railing for everyone to see before glaring at MacInnes.

Closing her eyes, Caitlin prayed she'd been

imagining things. Surely Edina wouldn't humiliate her in such a way. She peeped upward and moaned at the mortifying sight. Darach's arm held her tight as her knees sagged. His anger had abated, and he was back in control. Kissing the top of her head, he whispered, "'Tis a sign of your virtue, lass. None can question you now."

He spun them back to face her uncle, who also stared at the sheet, shaking with fury. Darach held her in front of him, arms looped around her waist. "My wife was a maid, MacInnes. If you'd spent any time with her, you'd have known she was innocent, forced to lie in a desperate attempt to free herself from your tyranny. You made her life a living hell—one you'll become acquainted with before I'm through. You will be held accountable for your crimes."

MacInnes paled and stepped backward. "We shall see what the King says. I will return to my clan to await the verdict." He nodded sharply, then turned and left the hall. Oslow and the other warriors, as well as Lachlan and Anderson, followed behind him.

Caitlin let out a sigh of relief, suddenly exhausted, her battered mind and heart reeling. "I ne'er thought my uncle would give in so easily."

Darach traced his fingers over her cheeks. "He hasn't. I'll see him to the border of MacKenzie land, and he'll pretend to go home."

"Pretend?"

"He'll ride to Fraser instead, aye? Then Fraser will either kill him or join with him against us. Either way, it works in our favor to have the two scoundrels together."

"Why?"

"'Tis easier to keep track of them. Your uncle isna a clever man. He'll do as Fraser says. I have spies in Fraser's keep, so we'll be informed."

She closed her eyes and rested her head against her husband's chest. She wanted to keep asking questions— about Fraser, her father, the fire—but at the same time, she knew if she did, she'd break down, so she pushed them away. For now, she'd live in blissful ignorance and let Darach take care of her, just as she'd take care of him.

Starting today, she'd create as peaceful a life for him as possible. It helped calm her to focus on other things, and she began making a list in her head of tasks to accomplish: a cleaner keep, his favorite foods, organize his solar, spend time with his men and show them how much she cared. They could teach her about weaponry. Darach would be pleased to know she'd learned to swing a sword.

"I'll work on the chapel while you're gone. When will you be back?" she asked.

"Soon...wait for me to return, and we'll start it together, aye?"

"If it pleases you. But what else can I do? The dogs are trained, and I canna work with Cloud. Has anyone seen him today?"

"I doona know, but I promise to look for him while I'm gone. And you can kiss me to start." He nuzzled behind her ear and down her neck playfully, but his hands were gentle on her back.

She giggled, sounding half-mad.

His arms wrapped tightly around her.

"I can do better than a kiss."

"I doona have time to love you properly, lass, and I can only imagine you must be sore." His voice thickened. "I willna cause you more pain."

"That's not what I meant." She knelt down in front of him, the rushes cushioning her knees, and placed her hands on his legs. His eyes widened as a flush crept up his cheeks. She watched, fascinated, never having seen him so perturbed. He glanced around the now empty room before looking back at her, swallowing hard. His hand brushed her hair away from her face.

"Caitlin, as much as I appreciate the gesture, I doona—"

"'Tis your turn to hush. My uncle was right about one thing...I should give thanks. If not for you, I would be dead—or certainly praying for death. I couldnae have been given a better savior. Or husband. Thank you, Darach MacKenzie. With all my heart."

The breath exhaled from his lungs, and he reached down to pull her back into his arms, looking pleased, relieved, and disappointed all at the same time. He laughed shakily into her hair. "'Tis I who should be giving thanks, and you will ne'er kneel before me again. Well, only if you want to during...um, certain times—and not to give thanks."

"What do you mean?"

"I canna talk about it now. 'Tis hard enough to leave you as it is."

When she crinkled her brow in confusion, he kissed her palm, then pressed it to his groin. His erection pulsed beneath her hand. "Oh," she said, fingers curling around his wool-covered shaft.

"Aye, oh," he said roughly. "My innocent temptress."

Then he kissed her, deeply, one hand cupping her behind, the other holding her head.

Sweet oblivion.

She melted into him, wanting more, but he pulled back. His thumb caressed her lips. "I'll return as soon as I can."

Nineteen

CAITLIN SAT IN HER CHAIR IN FRONT OF THE SMALL hearth in the great hall. She didn't remember walking there after Darach had left, but the glow of his kiss had faded, and now she felt drained.

Wallace MacInnes wasn't her real father.

Tucking her feet beneath her, she wrapped her arms around her legs and dropped her head to her knees. It was all too much. Everything that had happened in the last three days—the last three years—came crashing down and threatened to smother her.

Her mother had been pregnant when she'd met Caitlin's father—nay, not father. When she'd met Wallace. Did Caitlin's real father die? Had her mother loved him?

Who was he?

She choked back a sob and closed her eyes. A piece of her had been torn away today. The piece that knew she was the beloved daughter of Claire and Wallace MacInnes, part French, part Scot, orphaned by an accidental fire. Now none of it was true. Not only was Wallace not her father, but also, his brother had killed him and her mother for reasons Caitlin couldn't fathom. Didn't want to fathom.

The evil of it appalled her, and she shuddered.

Something cold and wet touched her brow. She raised her head to see Fergus standing in front of her between Hati and Skoll, whose snout had roused her.

The lad looked at her gravely, then leaned forward and wrapped his skinny arms around her neck. "When I feel sad, Edina and Nell, even our laird, tell me 'tis all right to cry."

She bit her lip, trying to contain herself, then lowered her feet to the floor and pulled him closer. "I know."

"I doona always want to, but when I do, I feel better, aye?"

Nodding, she kissed his hair. He sounded just like Darach, and a lump formed in her throat. Most likely her husband had said those exact words to the lad. Pressure built in her chest and a tear leaked from the corner of her eye.

"You can cry too, Caitlin. I'll comfort you." He climbed onto her lap and tucked himself beneath her chin. She curled around him, resting her cheek on his head.

When Hati lowered his jaw to her knee and looked at her with his soulful, brown gaze, her heart squeezed. She tried to muffle the sobs, but they kept coming, one after the other. Her father had been so dear to her. She'd been his little lass, his piglet.

No longer.

A fresh wave of sorrow hit her and she covered her face. "I'm sorry. I shouldnae be carrying on like this."

"Nay, you should." Fergus pried her hands away so he could wipe her cheeks. "Our laird told me to take care of you since he canna be here. 'Tis what family does for each other, aye?"

"Aye."

"Then 'tis all right. I'm not your son, and I doona think I can be your husband since you already have one, but I'll be your brother. I always wanted a sister."

Caitlin half sobbed, half laughed. "And I always wanted a brother." She kissed his brow. "But you must know I'll also love you as a son."

The lad smiled and laid his head on her chest. "'Tis all right if it makes you feel better. I'm glad to have a mother again, even though I miss my ma. She made the best oatcakes and would let me take my frogs to bed."

A memory rose of Caitlin wanting to take her pet mouse to bed when she was just a wee thing. Her mother had demanded her father get rid of it when she'd discovered Mousey in Caitlin's pocket. Caitlin had cried her eyes out when he did, but in the morning, she'd awakened with one of the kittens from the barn sleeping in her arms. Her father—aye, her father—had winked at her from his spot at the table before heading out to do his chores.

She smiled at the memory and felt the warmth of his love fill her. He'd often told her stories of watching her mother's belly get big as Caitlin grew inside before popping out like a little piglet. She'd laugh as he described how he almost dropped her because she was slick as a fish from the loch.

Aye, he'd loved her. And she'd loved him. If anyone were to tell her she couldn't love Fergus because he wasn't really her son, she'd laugh. If Fergus were to say it, she'd be devastated. To believe her father incapable of such love did naught but dishonor him and her.

Kissing the lad's head once again, she wiped her tears and rose, dislodging him from her lap. The dogs danced around her, pleased her mood had lightened.

Then she spotted the horrid bed linen displayed on the rail above the hall. Growling with displeasure, she marched up the stairs and snatched it down. When Edina appeared, Caitlin stalked toward her, the bloody sheet balled up in her hands.

"'Tis what I would have done for my own daughter, so quit frowning and burn the bloody thing if you wish," Edina said.

"I will. I'll throw it in the fire!"

"You're lady of this castle. You can do as you like."

Caitlin hesitated. It would be wasteful to destroy a good linen.

Edina held out her hand.

Caitlin passed it over meekly. "Please, doona show it to anyone else."

"There's no need, Lady MacKenzie. All know what a fine woman you are."

~∞~

Darach sat atop Loki, surrounded by his warriors and Lachlan, watching MacInnes and his men disappear into the forest. It burned Darach to let the devil go after what he'd done to Caitlin and her parents, but it was also a relief. Never again would the filth be close enough to his wife to upset her in any way. From now on, her life would be full of love and laughter.

Tears were henceforth forbidden. He'd damn well make sure of it.

"He'll turn north at the second ridge and ride to Fraser," Lachlan said.

They'd brought MacInnes to this spot on the edge of MacKenzie land so it would be simple for him to make the detour to Fraser's home. Best to keep the rabid dogs in the same den for an easy kill—unless they turned on each other first. Either way worked for Darach, though it would please him to dispense justice personally.

The sun was setting behind the trees when he turned, and he let out a frustrated sigh. He'd wanted to sleep with Caitlin tonight, hold her and ease her distress over her father, but even at his fastest, the castle was still a five-hour ride away. It wasn't worth the injury to the horses or his men to push on through a moonless night for his own selfish desire.

"She'll be all right," Lachlan said, guessing Darach's thoughts. "She's a strong lass and will see the right of it soon enough. She'll not wallow in heartache for long."

Darach agreed, but his guts twisted thinking of her alone at such a time.

They were approaching the clearing where they would make camp, when Lachlan came to an abrupt halt. Darach, lost in thoughts of Caitlin, kept going. Then an arrow whistled past his head and landed in the tree next to him with a resounding thud. He drew his sword as Loki reared, realizing he'd led his men into an ambush.

"God's blood," a familiar voice rang out with

disapproval. "You ne'er even looked up. Didn't I always teach you to scan ahead?"

Darach settled Loki, heart still pounding from the sudden attack. He was now sharp-eyed and clear-witted—seconds too late. That's what came from having a woman at home.

Sighing, he sheathed his sword, which calmed the other MacKenzies. The huge, redheaded Scot with gray streaks, who glowered at him from atop a black horse was a welcome sight.

Darach glowered back. "You're on my land, you old bugger. I trust my men to keep my borders safe."

"Your men are like wee lasses, concerned with getting their beauty sleep and not messing up their plaids. I could have marched a herd of *elefaunts* through your borders and your lads would still be snoring in their quilts."

Darach heard his men mutter beneath their breath. He hid a smile. "Hah! *You* are the *elefaunt*—thick-skinned, fat, and wrinkled. And so loud you make my ears ache."

Gregor MacLeod sat up straight on his horse and patted his firm belly. "I'm as fit as I was when I first laid eyes on you—a wee, snot-nosed lad, crying for his mother."

"I cried, all right. I'd ne'er seen an *elefaunt* before."

Gregor threw back his head and laughed, then rode forward to greet Darach.

"Where's Lachlan?" he asked, crushing Darach in his arms after they dismounted.

"Right behind you, with my sword at your back. Did no one teach you to cover your arse?" Lachlan asked, having circled behind Gregor.

He spun around, grinning, and knocked Lachlan's sword away. "Aye. What makes you think I'm not protected?"

Darach smiled as he saw his foster brothers Callum, Gavin, and Kerr appear from the trees—all big, strong men, with answering smiles on their faces.

Callum, laird of Clan MacLean, reached Darach first. He was the leanest of the brothers, with sculpted muscles and hawk-like, green eyes. His hair was short and straight, and as dark a brown as it could be without being black. Additional lines marred his face from the last time Darach had seen him, etched there since Callum had taken control of his clan after his father's suicide. A suicide Callum believed to be murder. If anyone had the shrewdness to unravel the sinister plot, it was him.

"'Tis good to see you, Brother," Darach said. They embraced, pounding each other on the back.

"And you, Darach. Your lovely lass face, as Kerr would say, has been sorely missed."

Kerr, laird of Clan MacAlister, shoved his way between them and wrapped Darach in a bear hug. He was the biggest, the oldest, and without a doubt the loudest of the brothers. The man even topped Gregor in height, muscle, and the unending ability to bellow. Of course, it was when Kerr went quiet that a man needed to worry.

Now was not one of those times.

"I ne'er said lovely lass face, you daft bastard. I said ugly-ass face." Kerr nodded toward Darach's last foster brother, Gavin, laird of Clan MacKinnon, who punched Lachlan's shoulder in greeting. "Our Gavin is the only one who's bonny as a lass. Spends enough time grooming himself in Isobel's mirror to make sure of it."

Gavin scowled. "Blasted thing. If you would just marry my sister and take her home with you, I'd be rid of it. She uses it in the sun to blind unwary folk." Then he smacked his head as if he'd just made an embarrassing blunder. "I forgot. She doesn't want a dim-witted donkey like you for a mate."

Kerr grunted. "She doesn't know what she wants. Why in God's name your mother made you promise to let Isobel choose her own husband is beyond me. She'll stay a maid her whole life just to spite me."

Gavin sighed and nodded, obviously in complete agreement.

He was indeed a bonny man who made the lasses swoon. As fair and tall as his Norse ancestors, with blue-green eyes and long, blond hair, he was the complete opposite of Kerr, who was as dark as the devil himself. But there was a shadow in Gavin now. He'd changed after his disastrous marriage, after losing his son. Turned from the laughing young lad Darach remembered to a bitter and sometimes callous man.

The transformation weighed heavily on Darach's heart—on all their hearts—and he prayed for a miracle every day. Maybe this time together could lighten Gavin's spirit and bring back the fun-loving boy of Darach's youth. God willing, Caitlin could work her magic on him too.

They made their way into the clearing and set up camp. With the fire roaring, they settled down on their plaids for fried oatcakes, roasted rabbit, and much ale. Darach knew the night would be long and looked forward to it, even though he missed having Caitlin by his side.

"I canna believe you let Gregor get so close," Gavin said as he gnawed on a haunch of meat. "You used to be able to sniff out an ambush a mile away."

Darach frowned, feeling the heat rise up his neck. No one could see it in the dark, but it irked him all the same. He never should have been so careless, and before he met Caitlin, he wouldn't have been. Which didn't make sense, because now that she was in his life, he needed to be even more vigilant.

"It's to be expected," Lachlan said. "His mind's elsewhere nowadays. 'Tis surprising he can even feed himself or mount a horse. All he can think about is Caitlin."

Four curious sets of eyes turned toward him. Gregor's stare sharpened, his fresh-off-the-griddle oatcake forgotten. "Who is Caitlin?"

Darach sighed. They would question him like a bunch of old women far into the night now. "My wife."

As one, their jaws dropped, making Lachlan laugh. Kerr was the first to recover. "I canna believe you waited this long to tell us."

"And how was I supposed to get a word in? The only one who knows how to hold his tongue around here is Callum."

"That's because he's thick as a bloody brick," Kerr said. "He doesn't have an intelligent thought in his head."

Callum picked up a stone and flicked it at Kerr, hitting him in the middle of his brow. Kerr slapped his hand over the injury and rolled backward. "God damn it, you wee shite. That hurt."

The other men fell over laughing. Callum turned to Darach with a grin. "The stone shattered upon his head, I'll wager. The man's a bloody, great rock. He'll crush poor Isobel the first time he touches her."

Gavin sat up abruptly. "Och! I'll hear no more of that. There'll be no talk of crushing or touching my sister. She's an angel."

They'd all met Isobel, and though she was a beauty, there was no doubt she was more devil than angel. She'd run Kerr a merry chase over the years and would continue to do so as long as he allowed it. The problem was he was trying to woo her. Subtlety was not his strong point. He was a man of action, and it would not surprise Darach to one day hear that Kerr had given up and kidnapped her like the men of old.

Gavin, Darach was fair certain, would be relieved.

"I ne'er thought you'd be the one to marry," Gavin said. "Callum, aye, if Maggie will still have him after all these years. Or Kerr, if Isobel e'er relents—"

"She'll relent. I have a plan."

The men all groaned. Kerr's plans usually began and ended with him using brute strength. No doubt it would not go over well with his future bride.

"I ne'er expected to marry either," Darach said. "But Caitlin…" He couldn't continue, unable to describe what she'd done to him, how she'd somehow found her way into his heart, become as necessary to him as breathing.

He didn't need to, because Lachlan took over.

"She's lovely. A sweet, funny lass. Mind you,

she doesn't mean to be funny. I doona know when I've laughed so much as watching Darach trying to control her over the past few weeks. Her intentions are good, but she's trouble. It follows her around like a faithful hound."

"Why would you marry a troublesome lass?" Gavin asked.

"Because he loves her," Lachlan replied, startling Darach. "We all do, even when she's executing some harebrained plan you know will cause more problems than the ones she's trying to solve."

Warmth spread in Darach's chest at Lachlan's amused tone. Aye, Caitlin was lovable. Darach would adore her till the end of his days. Tuck her next to his heart and keep her there. Not that she needed to know that. She'd most likely take full advantage of his feelings and have him build three chapels in his bailey instead of one.

Gavin snorted. Venom filled his words when he spoke. "I thought Christel was lovable when I married her. We were going to live in wedded bliss with our bairns for the rest of our lives. Women lie."

Darach's ire rose. His eyes hardened and met Gavin's bitter gaze. "If you think to disparage my wife by comparing her to Christel, Brother, have your sword ready. Your wife was vain and selfish, on par with my Moire. They poisoned both our lives, causing death and heartache. I know not the pain of losing a bairn as you do, just the notion of it through Moire's lies, but I did lose many of my clan, including my father, through her treachery. Caitlin is the antidote to that poison. A lass full of joy and goodwill despite her own hardship and sorrow. You will treat her as a beloved sister when you meet her, or you will leave my land."

Silence fell. It was as if everyone, including the horses and creatures of the forest, waited with bated breath for Gavin's answer. His mouth was carved in a straight, hard line while pain and anger ravaged his handsome face. Darach could see his brother wanted to fight, wanted to release his grief in killing blows and bloodshed. Then his expression crumpled with regret.

"Forgive me," he whispered.

The night breathed once again. Darach held out his hand.

Gavin clasped it in a bruising grip. "I've let her taint every part of me. I am pleased for you, Brother. Caitlin sounds like a wonderful lass."

"She is...when she's not digging up my bailey or drowning in the river."

"God's blood," Gregor exclaimed, eyes wide. "You will recount everything."

They did, Lachlan telling most of it while Darach added to or protested Lachlan's debatable remembrances. His brothers laughed themselves hoarse over Darach's numerous trips to the loch, Lachlan losing all his coin, and Caitlin branding herself a *besom*, then claiming Darach was an innocent victim of her lewd advances. They listened with quiet dread as he related saving her from the river and the subsequent ill health that befell them both. They erupted in anger upon the telling of her parents' murder and Caitlin's treatment by Fraser and her uncle. Then they sighed like women when Darach finally made her his bride.

"I'm so happy for you, lad," Gregor said, his voice rough as he wiped a tear from his eye. "I think you've found your Kellie."

Darach's heart skipped a beat, then raced to catch up. Kellie MacLeod, Gregor's beloved wife, who'd died years before during childbirth, taking her triplet babes with her. Kellie, whom he'd never stopped grieving, never thought to replace. The woman who'd inspired him to create peace in the Highlands by bringing the brothers together.

She'd been Gregor's life. His love. His happiness.

Fear settled in Darach's heart at the thought of losing Caitlin in such a way. He caught the eye of Kerr and Callum and knew they were thinking of Isobel and Maggie. Not their wives yet, but surely meant to be. And maybe meant to die bringing their bairns into the world.

It was a heartrending thought and Darach pushed it from his mind, determined more than ever to protect Caitlin and see to her happiness.

He raised his cup, a slight tremor in his voice as he spoke. "To Gregor and Kellie MacLeod—a great man and an even better woman. May we all be destined for a love just as true."

Twenty

"LAIRD MACKENZIE."

Darach rolled over with a groan and tried to block out Gare's annoying voice. Aye, the sun was up, but Darach had only gone to sleep a few hours ago—after Gregor had brought out the *uisge-beatha*.

"Laird MacKenzie, there's someone here to see you. A woman."

That got his attention, and he cracked open an eye to look into Gare's worried face. His brothers and Gregor slept scattered around him on the dewy ground.

"She says she knows you well."

Darach frowned, rubbing the sleep from his eyes. Who on earth could it be? The nearest farm was at least an hour's ride away.

He sighed, head pounding, and squinted toward the woman. Too far away to see clearly, he pushed back his plaid, stood, and walked gingerly toward her. For sure, his hair stuck out in all directions, but he was too tired to care.

His warriors backed away as he neared, and his eyes widened. Wynda MacIntyre.

What in hell is she doing here?

The aging, buxom redhead lived in the neighboring clan to the west and Darach had...visited her upon occasion. Four times to be exact, which had been three times too many. She'd been happy to have him in her bed, but Darach was ashamed to say, after he'd tupped her, he couldn't leave fast enough. There was something about her he didn't trust, and he should never have returned—not the second time, the third, or the fourth time.

"Good morning to you, Wynda," he said, stopping several feet away. "Is there trouble that brings you so far from home? Your clan and Laird MacIntyre are well?"

She moved closer, and Darach had to stop himself from backing up. "They're all right, Laird MacKenzie. I only thought to share your company if you are returning home. I shall be visiting my cousin, Firth MacKenzie, at your village for the summer. 'Twill be good to see more of you." She laid her hand on Darach's arm and stroked her fingers through the rough, springy hair that covered it.

He quickly stepped back. Her blue eyes hardened as her arm dropped back down.

"I am recently married, Wynda. 'Tis not a personal offense, I assure you." He gentled his voice in order to spare her feelings. "You are welcome to ride with us, of course, and I wish you a happy visit with your cousin, but...I willna seek you out. You understand."

After a moment, she looked up. "Aye, Laird, I understand. I understand that men stray, and when you do, you'll know where to find me."

The thought repulsed him, and he squared his

shoulders. "Some men behave so, as I'm sure you know, but I would ne'er disrespect my wife or my vows in such a manner. Doona expect to see me after today." He inclined his head, then turned back toward camp.

Her voice drifted over his shoulder. "We'll see."

Caitlin was not responsible for the mess in the kitchen. She'd been in there trying to re-create some of her mother's favorite dishes for Darach, dealing with not only her own faulty memory—for it had been over three years since she'd helped her mother cook—but also the grunts of disapproval coming from Nell every time Caitlin did something different. And apparently there was a big difference between Scottish and French cuisine, at which her mother had excelled.

Her father had always praised Claire's cooking, and now Caitlin knew why. When she'd arrived at her uncle's keep three years ago and finally come out of her depression, the tasteless food she'd been given had been a shock. She'd thought it would be better at the MacKenzies, and it was, but still nothing compared to her mother's cooking. She could re-create it if only she could remember what her mother had done.

Unfortunately, Nell had blamed Caitlin for the fire in the bread ovens. She'd had naught to do with it, but had still been chased out of the kitchen along with her "daft foreign ideas" before her dishes were done. 'Twas most unfair.

She sat, disgruntled, on the steps in the bailey leading up to the keep. What else could she do? She'd wanted something to show for herself when

Darach came home. Her mother had always kept busy making special dishes for Caitlin's father, helping with the farming, and keeping their cottage spotless. She'd also cared for the animals, of course, a skill she'd taught Caitlin.

But until Cloud was found, the creatures at Clan MacKenzie were not in need of her services, so she wandered into the keep and through the great hall, looking for something to clean. Unfortunately, Edina had everything dust free and smelling fresh. Maybe Caitlin could find something to do in their private rooms. After taking the stairs two at a time, she wandered down the corridor, peering into each bedchamber and looking for disorder.

It wasn't till she came to Darach's solar that her heart picked up. It was a cluttered mess. Parchment lay in jumbled piles on his desk, books littered the floor, and hardened wax was dribbled everywhere. The only thing that seemed clean was the beautiful wool rug on the floor. She'd seen Edina beating it in the bailey to shake off the dust numerous times, along with the tapestry on the wall. Why would she have left Darach's desk in disarray?

Striding toward it, Caitlin sat in his well-worn pine chair. Fortunately, her father had taught her to read, so she would have no trouble organizing Darach's correspondence and putting his books in order by topic and author. To start, she swept the excess sand that he used to dry the ink into her hand and tossed it out the window, then she placed all the writing implements in one, easily accessible spot. Next, she gathered up the books and placed them on a chair to be sorted later.

She'd just begun on the mounds of parchment when Edina came into the room and shrieked, making Caitlin knock one of the piles to the floor.

"Lord in Heaven, lass. What are you doing?"

Gathering together the scattered letters, Caitlin placed them back on the desk. Edina hovered nearby, a horrified look on her face.

"I'm helping my husband. I doona know how he finds anything; his desk is a mess."

Edina groaned and caught the back of the other chair for support. "You will get out from behind there now, and ne'er touch anything in here again."

"'Tis all right, Edina. I can read. I willna throw away important letters."

"You willna throw anything away. Get out now before you cause any more damage and he kills us both!"

She came around the desk with a shooing motion and Caitlin hurried to the door. "You doona understand. Darach will be happy for my help."

Edina did naught but glare at her and slam the door shut behind them. Caitlin was sure if Edina had carried a key, she would have locked it.

Tears of frustration burned her eyes. She blinked them back and strode down the corridor, hoping her stiff spine and angry gait would express her full displeasure. She was lady here; there had to be something she could do that would please her husband.

In the bailey, the clashing of swords rang out in the fresh, warm air. If her mother could help her father with the farming, maybe Caitlin could help Darach to defend the castle.

She spotted Oslow instructing the young warriors

at the far end of the bailey and ran toward him. He saw her coming at the last minute and pulled her aside just as a practice arrow whizzed past her head. Caitlin looked at the archer, who'd fallen to his knees and become a ghastly shade of white.

"Forgive me," she said. "I didn't mean to get in your way."

The lad nodded weakly and croaked an incomprehensible answer.

She turned back to Oslow, who scowled at her, fingers biting into her arm. "Would you have your husband come home and find you dead, then?"

"Nay, doona be silly. I just wanted to speak with you. I've decided to learn how to wield a sword. Darach would be happy if I knew how to defend myself, maybe fight alongside him one day."

Eyes wide, Oslow stared at her for a moment, then threw back his head and laughed. Then laughed some more. When it looked as if he would never stop, Caitlin marched back to the keep. She'd find her own sword and teach herself how to fight.

On the walls of the great hall hung a multitude of magnificent weapons. She eyed the biggest, a great battle-ax, and yanked on the handle. It didn't budge. Grasping it with both hands, she pulled again with all her might. Suddenly it came free of its moorings and the heavy, sharp blade swung downward. A tanned arm shot out just in time and grabbed the ax, stopping its fall inches above Caitlin's foot.

Her heart stopped at the mishap, then started to pound as she looked up into Darach's furious face. She'd never seen him so angry, even when she'd dug up the bailey. The ax must have been very important to him.

"Christ Almighty!" he bellowed, placing the weapon back with one hand and wrapping the other around her waist. His body shook, his eyes black with fury. Caitlin promptly burst into tears—great, gulping, shoulder-heaving tears.

It had been a difficult day.

She planted her face on his chest, which rose and fell with deep, agitated breaths. His heart beat so fast, so hard, she could feel it against her cheek. His other arm came around her, squeezing to the point of pain. "Shh. Doona cry."

Nodding her head, she cried even harder. He lifted her into his arms and headed for their bedchamber. He shut the door and sat with her in one of the big chairs before the hearth. She tucked up beneath his chin and let the tears run their course.

When her sobs had been reduced to the odd hiccup, she sighed and clasped his hand. He was still tense and the occasional shudder racked his body. Caitlin stroked his palm soothingly.

"What in God's name were you doing?" he asked, voice cracking.

Her mind wandered back through the events of her day, every one of them ending in disaster. All she'd wanted was to please her husband, but she'd just been a bother. To Nell, to Edina, to Oslow—and to Darach. She thought about telling him everything, but it occurred to her he might not be sympathetic.

"Nothing," she said, for lack of a better response. She prayed he would accept her answer and move on.

He didn't. Grasping her chin, he forced her head up, so she looked at him. Narrowed eyes clashed with hers.

"Caitlin," he prompted.

"Aye?" She tried a halfhearted smile.

A frustrated sound burst from his lips and he frowned. "What did I tell you on our wedding night?"

Their wedding night? Surely he didn't want to talk about that now. Heat rushed up her cheeks as images of their bodies entwined on the bed, the same bed that was behind them, played across her mind. She shrugged, heart pounding, and tried to look away.

"I will hear you say the words, wife."

She gasped. God in Heaven. How could he ask such a thing? She'd endured enough over the last few days without this additional embarrassment. She tried to get off his lap, but he held her in place. Everything inside her quickened—her breathing, her temperature, the ache between her legs.

She searched for something decent to say. "You said you were glad I was your wife." Maybe if she reminded him of those words, he'd cease this torment.

His arms tightened around her. "Aye, and I meant it. But after that, what did I say?"

She closed her eyes, only to be bombarded with more lusty images. The heat on her skin was so hot she wanted to strip off her clothes. "You told me to spread my legs."

It came out a whisper, and he stilled. His hand gripped her waist.

"What—what did you say?"

"Spread. Your. Legs. Those were your words."

Her voice was thick and heavy, same as her body, and when she opened her eyes, his face had been transformed. That intent, feral expression that gave her such a thrill had replaced anger and frustration. His hand stroked up her stomach and stopped just below her breast.

He swallowed, blew out a heavy breath. "I remember. But...but after that. What did I say to you after that?"

"You told me to wrap my legs around your waist."

He dropped his head to her neck and groaned. It vibrated through her body, setting everything aflame.

"Caitlin, you're killing me." His teeth nipped her throat. "I want to know about after the loving. What did I say when we were done?"

"God's truth, I canna remember. But I think I'd like you to kiss me now, aye?" Her hands fisted in his hair and tugged upward.

"Aye," he agreed, then locked his lips to hers.

Mouth hot and greedy, she opened it immediately. He plunged inside, stroking the sensitive flesh, capturing her tongue and sucking it into his mouth. She felt wild, out of control, and pressed her body to his, rubbed her breasts against his chest.

He growled into her mouth, then released her lips and kissed down her neck. The warm puffs of breath on her skin were like an arrow straight to her core and filled her with the desire to spread her knees and lift her hips. She arched upward—an offering. Wanting more. Wanting everything.

"Darach!"

He pressed his big hand to her breast. She

shuddered. The need to be possessed by him pulsed through her body.

"I canna wait. Please."

He captured her mouth in a hard, possessive kiss, then stood with her in his arms and strode to the bed. By the time he laid her on the quilts, he'd already released her brooch, the one he'd gifted her on their wedding day, and her arisaid fell open, leaving her in her linen chemise. With no time wasted, he stripped off her shoes and hose, then grasped the bottom of her chemise and pulled it over her head.

Her hair tumbled around her bare shoulders, and she giggled. Looking up, her laughter faded. He watched her intently, eyes stroking her naked body, then caressing her face and hair as he would a precious gift. Her heart swelled with love, and she reached toward him. He gently took her hand, sat on the edge of the bed, and kissed it, loving every finger, her palm, the back of her wrist.

"You are a miracle, lass. My miracle."

Tears filled her eyes—happy tears. "I love you, Darach MacKenzie."

He smiled, kissed the wetness from her cheeks. "I love you too, Caitlin MacKenzie."

She gasped, pulled back to see his face. "You do?"

"Aye, of course I do. I wouldnae have married you elsewise. Only true love could have tempted me to the altar."

With a squeal of joy, she threw her arms around his neck, laughing and kissing wherever she could reach—his ear, his head, his brow.

"Say it again," she demanded.

"Nay." His hands stroked her back, curved around her bottom. "'Tis not something a warrior says easily. In fact, I may ne'er say it again."

"Aye, you will, every night, or I'll ne'er leave you alone."

"I doona want you to leave me alone."

Their eyes met and the intensity between them changed, deepened. She stroked her fingers across his lips.

"Take off your clothes, Husband."

In a matter of seconds, he stood naked beside the bed and stared down at her. She reached out to stroke his thigh, his strength a marvel to her. Her hand caressed higher through the rough hair and she ran her fingers along the crease where his leg met his body. The muscles quivered beneath her touch, and she smiled.

Darach MacKenzie loved her.

She made him tremble.

"Touch me," he said, voice rough, hands fisted by his sides. Her own excitement rose to know he fought to control himself.

Her hand surged upward, exploring his rigid shaft with her fingertips. Lightly, then harder, circling the crest and over the moist tip. The trembling increased, as did his breathing, and his flesh pulsed. It fascinated her. So primitive, so exciting. She remembered how he'd filled her between her legs, and she squeezed her thighs together to contain the sudden, hot ache.

"Enough," he said with a shaky breath, and moved over top of her.

She lay back against the soft quilts, loving the feel of his body weighing her down, wedged between her legs. Loved the pressure in that exact spot. First it soothed her, then it made her squirm. Her arms wrapped around his shoulders, and she rubbed her feet against the back of his calves.

"Tell me again you love me," she said, nibbling his neck, inhaling the wild scent of him—pine, fresh air, horses. He smelled like her man.

"Well now, I doona know for sure, but I can say with nary a doubt that I love this spot right here." He kissed the tip of her nose. "This spot too, and this one." He kissed the corner of her mouth and her chin, making her sigh.

Then he kissed his way down her neck to her nipple, laved it with his tongue. Her breath caught. "I definitely love it right here." He took her breast in his mouth and sucked. Hard. She groaned and arched her back. His hand stroked upward to squeeze her other nipple, and she jerked, hips rocking against him, knees opening wider.

"Darach, for the love of God."

"You wanted me to tell you I loved you. I'm not finished yet."

She whimpered as he moved farther down her body. Each kiss given with love driving her closer to madness. Every nerve ending screaming that he mount her, take her.

When he reached the crease where her thigh and body met, she realized he wasn't going to stop. A wanting for this last, intimate kiss filled her. At the same time, she was horrified. She tried to sit up, but his hand pressed her back onto the bed, held her down. His other hand pressed her knee wider.

She raised her head. Their eyes met. "Darach, nay."

A treacherous smile curved his lips. "Caitlin, aye."

Then he lowered his head and licked her womanhood from bottom to top in one slow sweep. Everything exploded and she squealed. Her hips bucked against him, her muscles clenched. Gripping her pelvis, he found her nub and sucked. Another wave of bliss crashed over her. He moved up her body before it was over and entered in one quick thrust. She clamped around him, her pleasure deepened, intensified. He drove into her, hard and fast.

It was almost too much. She sobbed for him to stop, to not stop, to slow down, to speed up. Then something broke, her body tensed at the same time as his, and she tumbled over the edge. He shuddered above her with his own release, his mouth covering hers in a carnal kiss.

This must be what Heaven's like.

❧

She had no idea how long they had lain there, boneless. She didn't even remember him rolling over with her.

"Am I too heavy for you?" she asked.

"Nay, love. I like having you on top of me."

She rubbed her hand over his muscular shoulder. Her mind and body were mush. The things he did to her.

"I must say, I love tupping. I canna imagine anything more pleasurable than what you just did to me."

"What we did to each other. And we doona tup, Wife; we make love."

She smiled against his chest, loving his domineering tone. "Aye, Husband."

They rested together for a while, hands idly caressing, lips kissing. Brisk air wafted in from the open window and blew over their naked bodies. It made her shiver, and he covered them with the quilt.

"Do you want to talk about your father?" he asked. "I doona like it when you cry, but if it makes you feel better, I'll listen."

Propping her chin on her hands, she looked at him, one eyebrow raised. "Well, thank you for that, my laird and master."

A flush crept up his neck. "All I meant was…it kills me to see you upset."

She smiled and kissed him. "I understand. Men are weak."

His outraged expression made her laugh. He smacked her lightly on the behind and she shrieked, startled and thrilled at the same time.

"You'll be getting more of that if you're not careful, lass."

He looked like her laird and master now. The urge to sit up overwhelmed her, and she straddled his pelvis. It surprised her to feel him harden between her legs. Her hips rocked against him. "More of what precisely?" It came out a whisper.

The breath gusted from his lungs and he pulled her back to his chest. "More of me, a lot more, but not yet. I want to talk about your father. You must be sad about it."

She sighed. "Aye, I was verra sad yesterday, but then I realized I was being daft. It mattered not if I came from his seed. He loved me as his own. For me to think otherwise dishonored him."

Darach tightened his arms around her. "You have the right of it, lass."

Her mind wandered for a moment, and she played with the rough hairs on his chest. "I did wonder about my mother, though. Do you know how she came to be pregnant with me?"

"Nay, lass. I'm sorry. If you want, I can make inquiries."

Was that what she wanted? It would satisfy her curiosity, aye, but it wouldn't make her any happier. "'Tis not necessary. My life is here with you and the MacKenzies. A long and happy one with bairns and grandbairns, if we are so blessed."

He nodded and squeezed her tight. "You deserve every happiness, lass, after what you went through. 'Tis a miracle you weren't changed by the ordeal. You have a light within you that warms even the darkest soul."

"'Twas hard at times. But my uncle had taken so much away from me, I wouldnae let him take my spirit too. 'Twas the one thing I had left from my parents. They had loved me well, shaped me into the woman I am today. I couldnae let my uncle destroy that. So I made a choice to give thanks for everything I had—a beautiful sunset from the window at my uncle's keep, a wee bird landing on the sill, an apple fallen from a basket that I could sneak to Cloud. And eventually God brought me the greatest gift of all—you—for which I am eternally grateful."

He delved his hands into her hair and raised her head for his kiss—hard, yet soft at the same time. His lips worshipping hers, his tongue a gentle caress. Then he laid her head back down on his chest, one hand stroking her hair, the other curved possessively around her bottom.

Aye, she was happy. She couldn't be more so. But there was one thing she did want to know. "What was it you asked me about earlier, the thing on our wedding night I couldnae remember?"

He tensed beneath her and she glanced up to see him frown.

"What I told you was ne'er lie to me again, yet when I asked what you were doing with the ax you said, 'Nothing.' That was a blatant lie. If naught else, you were attempting to chop off your foot. Only by the Grace of God did I get there in time."

She groaned silently. Why had she brought that up? She really was a daft bat.

"Well?" he asked.

"Well what?"

"Why did you lie to me, and what in God's name were you doing with the ax?"

"I didn't lie...exactly. I just avoided the question. I doona always want to tell you everything. And the reason I had the ax was because Nell kicked me out of the kitchen when I was trying to make one of my mother's dishes. She blamed me for the fire in the ovens, but it wasn't my fault."

"So...you were going to kill Nell with the ax?"

"Of course not. Are you mad? I'd ne'er kill anyone."

"Then why did you have the ax?"

"Because Edina shooed me out of your solar. She was most rude about it. I just wanted to help you organize a wee bit."

He stilled beneath her. "You were in my solar?"

"Aye."

"Organizing?"

"Well, not verra much. 'Tis an awful mess, but she shrieked at me to get out."

Caitlin lay there, waiting for him to respond. When he didn't, she looked at him. He stared at the ceiling, a muscle ticking in his jaw.

"Darach?"

His chest rose and fell slowly beneath her hands. "Doona go in my solar without me again. Please." He closed his eyes briefly. "So you wanted the ax to kill Edina, then?"

She giggled, a bit nervous about telling him the rest. "You're a daft man. No wonder God made women."

"Aye, because everything you've said so far makes perfect sense."

"I had the ax because of Oslow."

"Oslow? What did he do?"

"He laughed at me. In front of your men. 'Twas most hurtful." She tried to sound wounded to gain his sympathy.

"I'm sure he didn't mean it, but I'll speak to him."

She pushed onto her elbows, horrified. "Nay, doona do that. Really, 'twas my fault."

"Why? What did you do?"

She bit her lip, wondering how to tell him. Looking back, it may not have been a good idea, but at the time it made sense. After all, this was the fifteenth century. "My mother used to help my father with the farming."

He frowned again. "Aye?"

"Well, you doona farm. You're a warrior, so I

thought I could be like my mother and help you... with the fighting."

His jaw dropped, much like Oslow's had. It wasn't a good sign, and the heat stole up her cheeks. Darach closed his mouth, then opened it to say something, then closed it again and shook his head.

"That was why you had the ax? To fight?"

"Aye, if Oslow wouldnae teach me, I would teach myself."

He gripped her arms and sat up with her. "God in Heaven, Caitlin. I am your husband. I fight to protect you!"

"But what if you weren't here? Wouldnae it be better if I knew how to wield a sword?"

"Nay! You willna touch a sword, a spear, or that bloody ax again. You almost cut off your foot."

"'Twas because the ax was so heavy. Next time I will know how to handle it properly."

"There willna be a next time! Christ Almighty, woman, if you died, it would be the end of me."

That mollified her, but his anger was like a palpable force, and she dropped her gaze. His chest rose and fell in quick, sharp breaths. She should never have told him.

He huffed out a lungful of air. "This is about you finding your place."

"What?"

"My purpose is to protect those I care about, most importantly, you. Nell's purpose is to cook for the clan. Edina's purpose is to clean the keep. Except for my solar. No one cleans my solar but me."

She opened her mouth to protest, but he silenced her by placing a finger over her lips.

"You take care of people, and you tried to do that today, didn't you?"

Aye, she'd tried to do something nice for her husband, to make him happy like her mother had made her father happy. "You'd like my cooking."

"I'm sure I would. And maybe if you speak to Nell you can find a time to cook when it doesn't conflict with her. But the best way you can help me is by caring for the clan. You have a wonderful way with people. Make sure they're all right, that they feel cared for. Go see them, talk to them. Help them with their animals, take them some of your cooking if you want, ask for advice, share advice. Know their birthdays. Then you can tell me anything important I need to know. Does that sound like a good idea? One that doesn't involve sharpened metal?"

She answered by throwing her arms around his neck. "Aye, that sounds like a wonderful idea." Already she imagined all the things she could do in the village, how she could help the clan and Darach. Take care of the little things he would miss.

They held one another, and after a minute, his hands slid lower to massage the soft curves of her bottom. Her heart sped up. Maybe he would make love to her again. Like this. She shifted closer.

"Darach?"

"Aye?" He moved against her, harder now, sending that hot, heavy feeling to her groin.

"Do I have to be on my back when we make love?"

He raised his knees behind her, and she was wedged against him. If she lifted upward and then down, he would be inside her body. Lord in Heaven, how she wanted to do that. She rocked her core against his shaft, almost to the tip. He surged in response.

"Nay, you can be in any position you like." His voice shook, and he nipped along her collarbone to her shoulder.

"And if I like this position?" She rocked again, stroking him a little higher this time, nails digging into his back, breasts rubbing his chest.

"Then I like it too."

On the third stroke, he lifted her at the end and slid inside. They groaned and held each other tight. Darach tangled his hands in her hair and gave her a hard kiss, then surged inside again.

"I suppose now's not the best time to tell you my brothers and Gregor are waiting downstairs."

Her eyes popped open in horror. Then he hit a sweet spot inside and the protest in her throat turned into a lusty moan.

Twenty-one

"Pray forgive me. Darach ne'er told me you were here."

Darach looked down at his wife and his heart swelled. She was so lovely, all flushed and bright-eyed from their lovemaking, hair a little mussed even though she'd brushed it. His brothers and Gregor stood in front of the hearth in the great hall, staring at her with grins on their faces. They knew what had taken place upstairs and took no offense at being left to amuse themselves for a few hours. A man had his priorities—making love to his bride was at the top of the list.

She'd protested when he'd first told her about their visitors, but he'd quickly brought her attention back to the task at hand. Afterward, she'd scolded him the entire time she washed and dressed, saying, "They'll think I'm wanton." By the time they were ready to meet their guests, she was like a flustered hen. Darach braced for anything to spew out of her mouth.

"We were praying," she said. "As you know, my husband is a verra pious man."

His brothers and Gregor raised their eyebrows, except Lachlan, who coughed into his hand. Darach gave him a stern look, which Lachlan ignored. He moved forward to greet Caitlin with a kiss. "Aye, lass, for sure we heard him exclaiming to the Lord a few times."

She nodded earnestly. "He was lost to the pleasure of prayer."

Gregor took her hands in his. "I'm Gregor, lass. I too believe 'tis important to pray. My Kellie led me to the altar every night before bed and sometimes again in the morning before she died."

Darach sighed silently and rolled his eyes. The bastards were going to play this for all it was worth. Thank God Caitlin was oblivious, and his brothers knew not to laugh. If they did, he would have to kill them. He would not have her feelings hurt.

Kerr came forward next, shoving Gregor out of the way. "Congratulations on your nuptials, Caitlin. I'm Kerr. It would please me to introduce you to my Isobel. Maybe you can instruct her on the need to pray with her man."

"Oh, aye. I would be happy to," she said, looking a wee bit guilty.

Darach squeezed her fingers to let her know she had his support, even though she'd lied yet again. He supposed it was all right as long as no one was hurt. It wasn't as if anyone believed her—you just had to look at her face to know the truth.

Callum pushed between Gregor and Kerr. "I'm Callum, lass. My Maggie is more likely to wield a dagger than the holy book. Maybe you could give me some advice on how to instruct her?"

Caitlin looked at him seriously. "Well, 'tis always best to get on your knees. Maybe with another person, in a church or a bedchamber. And you can use candles or beads to enhance your prayer. Some of the best prayer I've had was with Darach when we used a candle. Of course, he was sick at the time—'tis important to know how to pray by oneself as well."

His brothers and Gregor looked at Caitlin with varying expressions of amusement and disbelief on their faces. Silence reigned a moment before Gavin turned to Darach and said, "You're one fortunate bastard. A bonny woman who has nary a bone of deceit in her body and likes to pray. Unbelievable." He walked forward and kneeled in front of Caitlin. "You are sister to us all now, Caitlin. I'm Gavin, and it fills me with joy to make your acquaintance."

She blushed prettily, and Darach wrapped his arm around her. He kissed the top of her head. Aye, he was fortunate, married to the sweetest, purest, most amusing woman in all the Highlands. He prayed—a real prayer this time—that she would retain her innocence for all their years together.

Apparently God wasn't listening, for she bit her lip and looked at each one of them. "We're not talking about prayer, are we?"

The men burst into laughter, but they swamped Caitlin with so much love and affection she forgave them, saying it was her fault for telling a falsehood. In truth, she and Darach had been napping.

The day progressed amid much rolling of eyes and backslapping. Caitlin cried with Gregor over the loss of his wife, Kellie, and with Gavin over the loss of his son.

She gave advice to Kerr on how to woo Isobel and to Callum on why he should marry Maggie immediately, despite the problems in his clan. Lastly, she reprimanded them all numerous times about their language.

It was a wonderful day.

When supper finished, they all indulged in a wee shot of Gregor's *uisge-beatha*. Caitlin tried some too, and made such a face while saying it was wonderful the men almost fell off their chairs. She tried valiantly to take another sip, but Darach took pity on her and finished it himself.

He was lost in his own thoughts, Caitlin curled up in his lap, when he heard her ask the men the dates of their birth. It made him smile, knowing she would remember each one and send them good wishes on their special day. She was asked the question in return, and Darach brought his attention back to the group. He would write the date down and spend months planning a celebration for her.

"'Tis the day after tomorrow," she said.

"What?"

"Aye, the fifth of June. I'll be twenty. The same age as you when you first saved the MacKenzies from the Frasers." She lowered her voice so only he could hear. "My great laird and master."

He smiled and kissed her, but his head whirled. Two days. What could he give her in two days that would even begin to match what she'd given him? He tried to think of anything she'd asked for over the last few weeks. She wanted a chapel, aye, but that couldn't be built in two days. She wanted to cook, but it didn't seem right that she do so on her own birthday. She wanted to clean his solar, but…well…no one cleaned his solar but him.

What else did she want?

He squeezed his eyes shut, trying to block out the noise around him, and instead heard Gregor, who had a love of horses, say, "Tell me, Caitlin, did you really ride the wild stallion?"

Darach crooned to Cloud in the sweetest, singsong voice he could muster, suppressing his aggravation and frustration in order to entice the bloody stallion. "Come here, Cloud, you good-for-naught, goddamn donkey, before I cut your stones off and feed them to my hounds. Then you willna be so proud." He held out a handful of apple slices and tried to tempt the skittish horse toward him from across the sunlit glen. Darach was into his third hour of persuasion, and the unnatural groveling was taking its toll.

He'd dragged himself out of bed at the crack of dawn, after giving his wife her too-brief morning kiss, and roused his brothers and Gregor for a day spent in the hot sun pleading with a moody, overgrown mule. All so he could give Caitlin the best present possible on her birthday.

If only Cloud would cooperate.

The latest sighting that morning had placed the stallion an hour's ride from the castle. It took another two to find him higher up the mountain, before beginning the fruitless endeavor of catching him. The others had helped at first, but that had only pushed Cloud farther away, so they decided it would be best if Gregor, who prided himself on being an expert on horses, helped Darach while his brothers lounged in the shade, drinking ale. But soon Gregor gave up too, and it was left to Darach to reason with the bloody stallion. He wanted to charge over there and force Cloud to submit, but that would only destroy whatever headway Darach had made.

He tossed an apple slice toward Cloud, who came forward cautiously to eat it, then retreated. Darach sighed. He was hot, tired, and fed up. He leaned forward, hands on his knees, muttering to himself. After a moment, he looked up to see Cloud standing only four feet away. Darach caught his breath. He wanted to lunge for the horse but knew it would only send the stallion running. Instead, he held out a piece of apple in one hand and the bridle in the other. "Come to me now, lad, and I'll take you to see Caitlin. It's her birthday tomorrow, and the thing she wants most in the world is to see you. It's my job as her husband to give her everything she wants, to make her happy. That's what you want too, aye?" Cloud came forward a step, then another. He huffed and tossed his head, then came even closer.

Darach turned his back on the horse and waited. Before long, Cloud snuffled over his shoulder in search of treats. It was easy to slip the bridle over the stallion's head.

"You daft bastard," Darach crooned. "Our sweet lass will be so pleased to see you."

❧

"Lady MacKenzie."

Caitlin looked up from the wee lass she bounced on her knee in the middle of the village square to see an attractive redheaded woman standing in front of her. The same woman who earlier had been talking to the men safeguarding Caitlin and passing out ale to quench their thirst. They'd enjoyed the refreshing drink almost as much as looking down the poor woman's dress. She was well endowed and maybe hadn't realized the men took advantage.

"I'm Wynda McIntyre, cousin of Firth MacKenzie. I have a message for you about the wild stallion."

Caitlin rose excitedly, lifting the lass and perching her on her hip. Maybe the men had found Cloud. "Aye, Wynda. 'Tis a pleasure to make your acquaintance. What have you heard?"

"Laird MacKenzie has spotted the horse but canna get near him. He needs your help."

Caitlin squealed with delight and jumped in the air. The little girl laughed. "Naught would make me happier. Did you see Cloud?"

Wynda frowned in confusion, bringing to light the lines on her aging face. She was still a bonny woman, although her mouth was hard and her eyes dissatisfied. Maybe she'd had a disappointing life.

"Cloud?" Wynda asked.

"'Tis the stallion's name—for his white coat."

Wynda shook her head. "Nay, I did not see him. A warrior approached me, asked me to give you the message. The horse is to the west. He said to follow the deer track to the summer fields." She pointed toward the mountain. "Shouldnae take long. Maybe I could go with you. I would love to see the stallion."

"Aye. It will give us time to get to know one another. You weren't at the wedding."

Wynda's mouth flattened. "Nay, Lady MacKenzie. I only arrived yesterday."

Spotting the lass's mother on her way back from her errand, Caitlin put the child down so she could run to meet her ma. The girl's hair and dress flew out behind her. Caitlin smiled. Maybe she and Darach would have a bairn of their own soon. They were certainly trying hard enough. Last night she'd woken in the middle of the night, gasping, with Darach pressed tight against her bottom, hands stroking the front of her body. By the time he'd entered her from behind, she'd been desperate for his possession. It still amazed her there were so many ways to make love.

She walked with Wynda toward the four guards. Caitlin grinned at them. All except one, who looked a little peaked, grinned back.

"Are you well, Comyn?" she asked.

The young warrior rubbed his stomach. "I drank too much, too quickly, I think."

Frowning with concern, she said, "Maybe you should go home and lie down. Surely three of you are enough to protect me from mishap?"

Comyn shook his head. "Doona worry, Lady MacKenzie. The malady eases already."

Caitlin bit her lip. He still looked pale, but she suspected he would carry on no matter what she said. Best to find her husband and Cloud, so the young man could be relieved of duty as soon as possible.

"We're going on a ride to the summer field. Laird MacKenzie has asked me to come. He's found Cloud and needs my help. Maybe the exercise will ease your pain."

Comyn nodded, but the oldest guard, Dearg, ran his hand through his grizzled beard. "Who told you this? I was not informed of such a journey."

"Wynda did. She heard it from another warrior. 'Tis all right. The summer field isna far. Just to the west, up the deer trail."

"I know where it is, lass, but I wasn't told to take you there."

Caitlin's eyes widened. "Has my husband restricted my wandering? I thought I could go anywhere on MacKenzie land as long as you were with me? 'Tis a lovely day for a ride."

Dearg nodded slowly. "You're not restricted as such, but—"

"Gare told me this morning the lairds were going to look for the white stallion. I thought they'd headed north, but they could have turned west," Eilig, the second-oldest of the guards, told him.

Ross, the last guard nodded his head. "Aye, 'tis what I heard as well."

Dearg tapped his finger to his lips. He turned to Wynda. "Who was the warrior?"

She shrugged. "Some skinny lad with a face full of pimples. I doona know his name. I was out for a walk toward the west, getting my bearings, and he came down the game trail. When I told him I was heading back to the village, he asked me if I might pass the message to Lady MacKenzie. He wanted to return. The men were wagering how long it would take the laird to capture the stallion—or concede defeat."

The guards laughed, and Dearg said, "All right. But if the laird isna in the summer field, we'll come home. I doona want to go on a pointless chase through the woods."

Wynda lowered her eyes. "I would ne'er subject Lady MacKenzie to such an ordeal."

"Please, call me Caitlin. I've only been married a few days. Lady MacKenzie is such a mouthful." She'd made the request of all the clan, but they'd simply patted her hand or pinched her cheek and continued to call her Lady MacKenzie.

So when Wynda shrugged and said, "As you wish," Caitlin was surprised.

'Twas a sign of things to come.

Pine needles crunched beneath the horses' hooves as they rode through the forest. She tried to make conversation, but after nearly an hour of Wynda's sly comments and hidden insults, Caitlin lost her smile. God's truth, the woman was a trial.

Catching her frown, a smug expression flashed through Wynda's eyes. She adjusted her dress, pulling it taut across her ample breasts. "'Twas a shock to discover the laird was married. When last I saw him, he was not betrothed. Or maybe he just didn't tell me during his visit."

During his visit? How well did her husband know this…this…viper?

Wynda reached out and patted Caitlin's arm. Her hand felt like a claw. "Doona fash, lassie. You're verra young. You doona know the ways of men. You havnae even grown into your woman's body."

Caitlin's jaw sagged, confounded and embarrassed all at once. "I'm twenty. My birthday's tomorrow."

She couldn't help herself and glanced at her

modest-sized breasts, then over to Wynda, who barely
kept hers contained. Had Darach tupped this woman?
Did he like her big bosom?

The question must have shown on her face, for
Wynda smirked.

She breathed deeply, eyes closed. Maybe Darach
had known the woman before, but he certainly
wouldn't have been intimate with her since he'd married. He was a good man. An honorable man. And it
did not matter what the woman thought of Caitlin's
breasts; her husband hadn't complained. He could
barely keep his hands off them.

She lifted her chin. "I doona believe what you're
suggesting. In no way would Darach sully our vows.
He loves me, and I love him." Her brow creased
with anger. "And from now on, you will call me
Lady MacKenzie."

Caitlin rode ahead, lost in fury. The gall of the
woman, coming into Caitlin's clan and suggesting
such a thing about her husband. Honor was important
to the MacKenzies, and Darach led by example.

Her guard must have been just as upset to hear
Wynda's lies. She glanced up to see how they were
taking it. Dearg was ahead of her, hunched awkwardly
in his saddle. For the first time she noticed their speed
had slowed.

"Dearg?" she called out.

He turned slowly and she gasped, urging her horse
toward him. His face was as white as Cloud and sweat
poured down his brow. "Sorry, Lady MacKenzie.
Maybe one of the others should take the lead. 'Tis my
bowel acting up."

Looking past her shoulder, he cursed and reached for his sword, barely able to pull it from its sheath. Caitlin followed his gaze and a horrified gasp escaped her lips upon seeing Ross laying on the trail farther back, his horse standing beside him with the reins down. Eilig was off to the side, looking ready to vomit into the trees. Comyn was nowhere to be seen. Caitlin assumed he was somewhere around the last bend.

How could she not have noticed? She'd been so busy trying to please Wynda she'd not even known the men were sick, possibly dying.

"You," Dearg said, pointing weakly at the redhead. "'Twas poison in the drink. I'll run you through before you do more harm." He lifted his sword but the weight of it tipped him over the side of his horse, and he crashed to the ground, shouting, "Ride, Lady MacKenzie. To the castle."

Caitlin screamed. She tried to dismount and help him, but Wynda grabbed her arm and smacked the horses to get them moving. Caitlin pulled on the reins only to have them torn from her grasp.

"I'll slaughter them all if you doona come with me." Wynda's face had transformed into a hate-filled grimace. She kicked her horse into a gallop and pulled Caitlin's horse behind her.

Before she could get her wits about her, the summer field came into view. With horrified certainty, she knew men waited there—Fraser's men.

Caitlin grabbed for the reins but couldn't reach them. Every second brought the field closer. She would have to jump; it was her only hope. The ground rushed up at her as she leaped from the back of her horse. Pain exploded in her body upon landing.

When she stopped rolling, she lay facedown in the dirt for a second before spitting out leaves and pine needles and crawling for the trees. Everything hurt, especially her ankle when she pushed down on her foot.

She'd just reached the edge when someone yelled. Caitlin dove into the bush. She peeked back through the leaves and saw Wynda at the end of the trail pointing in Caitlin's direction. A man came into view, then another. Big, mean-looking men. One whom she recognized as Fraser's man.

She turned and ran as fast as possible, limping on her injured leg. Branches whipped her face and tore at her hair and clothing. Behind her, she could hear the men crashing through the woods, shouting directions to each other.

They seemed to be all around her, almost on top of her. The breath tore through her lungs as panic and fear raced through her body. She fell, tried to get up, and fell again, so she crawled through the muck on hands and knees.

A large tree loomed ahead with a hole in its trunk. If she could make it inside, she'd cover the opening with a branch. Hide 'til they'd gone. Wait for Darach to find her. Then he'd take his revenge, and the Frasers would be slaughtered like the devils they were.

She was almost there when she was grabbed from behind. Caitlin screamed and kicked out with her good foot, making contact. The man grunted, and she was released, only to be caught a second time and pinned to the ground.

"Shut up, bitch. You'll have more than enough to scream about later." A rag was stuffed in her mouth and a hood thrown over her head. "Laird Fraser has plans for you."

Twenty-two

THE WOMAN'S SCREAM SOUNDED EERILY IN THE distance. Darach reined in his mount and looked southwest, across the glen the men rode through on their way back to the castle. Unease crawled up his spine. Cloud sensed it and snorted beside Darach. He laid a calming hand on the stallion's nose and listened, hoping to get a fix on the woman's location.

The other lairds had heard it as well and unsheathed their swords as they spread into a defensive position. Lachlan was closest to Darach. "That couldnae be more than a mile away. Maybe by the summer field. Do you have cattle up there?"

"Not yet." Darach spurred Loki, and the others followed. They had to proceed with caution. Darach knew it could be a trap, but his gut told him to ride like hell. What if...? Nay, Caitlin was back at the village. Safe.

He urged the stallion faster.

The field wasn't that far away as the crow flew, but they had to traverse a mountain river that was still high and swift with the spring runoff. Finding a place to cross would add another twenty minutes to their journey. The woman, whomever it was, might be dead by then.

Not. Caitlin.

When they finally reached the summer field, a good forty minutes had passed. Darach's stomach was cramped with worry and his lèine drenched in sweat. He couldn't stop picturing Caitlin in the grass, her head bashed in or an arrow through her heart—horrible images that he knew weren't true. Couldn't be true.

They approached the field cautiously on foot, from the north, spreading out amid the trees to minimize their vulnerability should there be an attack. It would be a boon for his enemies to kill all six lairds at once—especially one as powerful as Gregor. But if there was an attack, Darach couldn't have asked for better fighters by his side. Gregor had taught them well.

Scanning the field from his concealed position, Darach saw a woman lying on the ground near the trail that wound up from the east. Sunlight glinted off long, red hair, and the relief that rushed through him was so intense he was almost ashamed of himself. A MacKenzie woman lay injured, possibly dead, and he was overjoyed it wasn't his wife.

He composed himself and strode quickly along the tree line toward her. She lay facedown on the blood-soaked ground. He turned her over and frowned.

"That's the woman from yesterday. She rode in with us," Gregor said from behind him.

"Aye. Wynda MacIntyre. Her throat's been cut." He reached down and closed her wide, lifeless eyes. She'd died within minutes. Even if he'd been here sooner, he couldn't have saved her. Maybe she'd stumbled upon some of Fraser's men who'd managed to get through the MacKenzies' defenses.

He'd known they would come; he just hadn't thought it would be so quick. What else hadn't he thought of?

"Darach!" Lachlan shouted at him from down the trail.

His heart pounded in response. He could tell by Lachlan's voice it was bad, and the fear for Caitlin rose again. His feet couldn't move fast enough as he ran toward his foster brother. Lachlan was at the bend in the path about two hundred paces away. He held someone up.

Hope soared for an instant before crashing with heart-stopping anguish as Darach recognized Dearg, the head of Caitlin's guard. He was hunched over, grimacing with pain, but his eyes were filled with regret as he looked at his laird.

"I'm sorry," he said.

Darach threw back his head and howled.

Darach raced on a sleek, dappled mare along mountain streams and game trails in the moonlit night. Branches scraped his skin, but he never felt it. Beside him, Lachlan rode with twenty other MacKenzies who'd been waiting at the border with fresh horses and supplies. They'd been alerted the attack on the Frasers had begun when Darach had blown his battle horn a few hours earlier.

His first instinct had been to race after Caitlin and abandon the plan he'd set in motion years ago, the plan that would end the Frasers' cruelty in the Highlands for good, but Gregor had made Darach see past his fear and think clearly. They couldn't catch the Frasers before they reached their keep and locked Caitlin inside. All the MacKenzies could do was mobilize a force, led by Gregor, to hound the blackguards the entire way, so they never had time to hurt her—anymore than she'd already been hurt.

Now, troops of the six lairds were in strategic positions across the land, bracing themselves for the onslaught Fraser would unleash against Castle MacKenzie, while Darach prepared to infiltrate and conquer Castle Fraser.

As Gregor attacked from the outside, Darach would take a smaller force into the keep through a secret passageway Moire had shown him years ago. A dangerous route to get in and out, for sure, but one to which Fraser was oblivious...they hoped.

The passage led to Moire's old bedchamber, which was on the third floor. He prayed Caitlin would be nearby. After she was taken to safety, the MacKenzies would overrun the keep from the inside, disable as many of Fraser's war machines as possible, and lower the gate, letting in Gregor's attacking army. Afterward, Darach intended to burn the entire castle.

He would show no mercy to any fighting man.

The group approached their position outside of Castle Fraser and slowed. They'd arrived before Gregor and his forces, and Darach yearned to forge ahead, but it would do Caitlin no good if they were discovered and killed. Instead, he dismounted and watched the unfolding drama from his vantage point behind the trees.

Most likely Caitlin was already inside. The gate was

raised, and men ran with haste along the top of the battlements, in preparation for war. They would be scared but certain of victory—which worked in the MacKenzies' favor. The Frasers would never expect the second attack from the inside.

Lachlan stretched out silently on the ground beside him. Moonlight illuminated his blue-painted face and braids, an homage to his Pictish ancestors that all the brothers wore during battle—had done since childhood— giving him a frighteningly grim visage. His eyes were cold and hard yet burned with ferocity. A warrior's face.

A reflection of Darach's own face.

"I will see my sister home," Lachlan said.

A lump formed in Darach's throat, but he forced it down and calmed his thoughts. He looked up at the moon. Clouds drifted toward it like leaves on the water. He had no doubt Gregor also watched the sky, waiting for the right moment to signal Darach.

When the clouds covered the moon, an owl hooted twice, then once again—a sign from Gregor that he was in position, ready to attack from the outside and draw attention away from Darach's smaller force as they snuck into the castle.

Darach motioned to his men. He looked at Lachlan, grasped his arm. "If I die tonight—"

"You willna die."

"Aye, but if I do…"

They stared at each other. Brothers. Friends. Warriors. Lachlan clasped Darach's arm. "My promise to you stands. I'll protect her always. As sister…and as wife. But it willna come to that. You will come back to us, Brother."

❦

"Your husband will hang in the morning. By his own choice."

Caitlin peeked through the tangled knots of her hair and across the musty, cold bedchamber at Fraser. As usual, he was filthy. Maybe as filthy as her, for she was covered in dirt, blood, and bruises. Her uncle hovered in the background, a smile on his bloated face.

The journey here had been agony—tied and gagged, with a hood over her head, riding hard for hours on end with rough men handling her. But she'd take those circumstances any day over staring into Fraser's soulless eyes.

"What do you mean?" she asked, voice barely above a whisper. She couldn't quite catch her breath and her knees felt like they might fail her at any moment. To stay upright, she grasped the bedpost beside her.

Fraser tossed a piece of parchment in her direction. It landed on the dirty wooden floor. She picked it up with trembling fingers. He probably thought she couldn't read and had given her a letter full of nonsense, but Darach's broken seal was attached to the outside. Spreading the note, her throat tightened at seeing his familiar handwriting.

> *Me for her—but only if she remains untouched. I will hang at sunrise to see my wife safe.*
>
> *Laird Darach Alasdair MacKenzie*

Alasdair, defender of men. Caitlin sank onto the ragged quilts on the bed. He would save her again. This time with his life. The agony that ripped through her body pushed her forward over her knees. Her mind shut off, unable to take the pain, and she howled in anguish. A hand grabbed her hair and yanked upward. Her uncle sneered down at her.

"Not so high and mighty now, are you, lass? Just the daughter of a whore. That's what you'll be too, before we're through. I'll get my money for you one way or another."

Hatred so intense filled her that she thought she might burst. She leaped at her uncle, kicking and biting and scratching like a wild animal. He screamed and tried to fight her off. Finally, he hit her with a heavy hand and sent her flying against the bedpost. She crumpled to the floor as Fraser laughed behind them.

A devil of a man, if ever there was one.

Her uncle stepped toward her, fist raised, but Fraser held him back.

"Nay, MacKenzie wants her untouched. She'll remain so. For now."

Outside, the sounds of battle erupted, and her stomach clenched. Was Darach with them?

Fraser's fiendish eyes caught hers, and she shivered, making him smile. "Your clan and allies will soon be dead. Your husband, your friends, sacrifice themselves for nothing. We can withstand their onslaught for months."

He lifted Darach's letter. "But your husband willna wait that long."

He laughed again, amused by her anguished sob,

and walked toward the door. Her uncle followed. She saw guards in the dark corridor before the door shut and a bar scraped into place with an irrevocable bang. Her breath echoed frantically in the cold, neglected chamber.

They'd left a candle burning on the table. It shed enough light for her to see a window with one broken wooden shutter, a chair in front of the cold hearth, and a faded tapestry on the wall. Maybe the chamber had once belonged to someone special.

A daughter. A wife. Just like her.

Caitlin dropped her head to her knees and gripped her hair. She'd had to stand by and watch her parents die; she couldn't do the same for her husband. She loved him too much, needed him to live, to protect the MacKenzies and keep his part of the Highlands safe, along with his brothers and Gregor.

A demon like Fraser could not triumph.

Her gaze traveled the room again and fell on the window. It was small, but she might fit. She rose slowly and limped toward it, heart pounding.

Pushing the shutter back, she looked out. A sharp wind carried the sounds of men at war. Shouts, horses screaming, a volley of arrows.

Returning to the bed, she ripped the linens from the mattress and fashioned a rope as best she could. Her hands shook as she knotted the covers together, tied the line to the bedpost, and tossed it out the window.

Closing her eyes, she made the sign of the cross and said a prayer, asking for strength and courage. When she finished, she dragged the chair over from the hearth, stepped onto it, and put her head and arms through the window. The ground was terrifyingly far away, but she ignored her fear and grabbed the rope, thinking to slide or climb down once she was through.

Behind her, she heard a scratching noise. Blood rushed through her veins and pulsed in her ears, blocking out further sound. She squeezed one shoulder out the window, then the other, uncaring that her clothes ripped and her hair pulled. Looking down, the ground seemed even farther away. She closed her eyes, continuing to wriggle forward past her ribs to her waist. Her hips caught and she pushed with her arms against the outside of the castle wall. One last shove, and she would be free.

Just as her hips gave, however, hands clasped her legs and pulled her back. She screamed. Darach couldn't die tomorrow because of her. She fought fiercely, kicking and writhing, but she was dragged in past her hips and waist. An arm came underneath her and hooked around her shoulder, twisting her until she was all the way through.

Then she was squeezed against a broad chest, a pounding heart. She still couldn't hear, but the man crushing her felt right. Like Heaven and Earth rolled into one.

Like Darach.

Maybe she'd fallen and didn't know it. This was the afterlife.

Her arms wrapped around him. Slowly her hearing came back, and she could make out soft, frantic words.

"You will ne'er do that again. Do you hear me? You will ne'er go near a window or an ax or a river again. You will ne'er be taken from me or leave the castle again. I'll lock you in our room if I have to. If you damn well die on me, Caitlin MacKenzie, I will ne'er forgive you."

She sagged against him and let his words wash over her. Others moved around them, whispering to each other, but she paid them no heed, too intent on the feel, sound, and smell of her husband. Finally she tilted her chin and looked into a fierce, blue-painted devil of a face. A scream erupted from her throat before she could stop it. His calloused palm clamped over her mouth.

He shook his head, then removed his hand and pressed his lips to hers. Hard. It hurt against her bruised mouth, but she welcomed the pain. She was alive. Darach was alive. Everything would be all right.

He pulled back, her fierce, mighty warrior, looking like the Picts of old: bright-blue paint on half his face and body. His eyes had a frightening intensity she hadn't seen before.

"Are you hurt?" he asked quietly, eyes and hands running over her.

She shook her head, but then winced as he squeezed her shoulder.

His gaze narrowed. "You will tell me what hurts," he commanded, the whispered words sharp as daggers.

"My ankle. That's the worst."

He crouched down in front of her to examine her leg. When he wiggled her toes and rolled her foot, she bit her lip to stop from crying out.

"'Tis unbroken." He checked her other foot. "Anywhere else?"

"My hip and shoulder, but bruises and scrapes mostly from jumping off my horse."

He moved up her body, making sure for himself, then held her head and stared at her. "Did they touch you?"

Her heart expanded at the pain beneath his clipped words. "Nay. Your note dissuaded them."

He pulled her into his embrace. Hands weaved through her hair, and his body trembled.

A tangle of emotions rose within her—fear, relief, pain, worry. She blinked hard to hold back tears and tried to breathe through her rising panic.

He rubbed his hand up and down her back. "I'm here, Caitlin. Everything will be all right. Take a deep breath now. Doona cry. Be brave, sweetling."

He gazed down at her for a moment, making sure she was all right, then turned her to face the room. For the first time, she noticed it was filled to the brim with MacKenzies, all as fierce-looking as Darach. Where had they come from? And Lachlan too, though she scarcely recognized him as the lighthearted brother she loved.

"Fraser told me you were going to trade yourself for me in the morning?"

"That was only if I couldnae get to you first, aye?"

Her gaze shifted to the window through which she'd tried to climb.

His eyes darkened. "We'll talk about that later."

Lachlan stepped forward and Darach passed him her hand. The brothers' eyes met. "Remember your promise."

Slipping an arm around her waist, Lachlan nodded, then led her toward a chest near the wall she hadn't noticed before. She looked back, but Darach had turned away from her.

"Lachlan," she protested.

He crouched down and directed her into a dark, narrow tunnel. "Hush, Caitlin. The battle has just begun."

❧

Darach knocked on the door. The guards on the other side didn't respond. He waited a moment, then knocked again. This time he could hear them talking in the corridor. How many were there—maybe three? He knocked a third time.

One of the guards yelled, "Quit your bangin', slut, or I'll come in there and bang you back."

Darach's blood surged, and he clenched his jaw. They were animals. He would slaughter every one of them for even thinking of laying their hands on his wife. He knocked a fourth time. His men were ready in the darkened room, hidden in the shadows and behind the bed. Stealth was necessary for the plan to work; otherwise, they would have to retreat.

"Please," he whispered in as high a tone as possible. "I'll do anything."

The voices murmured outside. A second later, the bar grated as it slid back. Darach stepped into the shadows, dirk at the ready. The smallest of his men sat on the bed, half-hidden by the post, covered in a quilt, with his hair down, pretending to be Caitlin. He would take much teasing from his clansmen after the battle.

For now, everyone concentrated on the task at hand: exit the room undetected, overtake the battlements, and raise the portcullis. With only twenty-one men.

Darach needed to behead the snake so it wouldn't

rise again, and that meant killing Fraser and destroying his nest for good. No one in the Highlands would be safe otherwise, especially Caitlin.

The door opened and a man entered. Another came in behind him. A killing rage rose within Darach at the thought of what would have happened to Caitlin had he not been here.

The first man dropped his sword and twisted his sporran to the side as he approached the bed. "Turn over, ye wee slut." The second man stopped about halfway into the room to watch and wait his turn. The third man appeared in the doorway, looking nervously up and down the corridor.

Their deaths happened at once, like a well-timed Highland reel. An arrow to the head killed the guard at the door, Darach slit the second guard's throat from behind, and the third man got a surprise when he tried to turn over the "lass" on the bed. Not a sound was heard by any but the devil, who was surely waiting to lead the men to Hell.

The MacKenzies then exited in pairs, quickly moving to the end of each passageway as Darach led them to the battlements. It had been over eight years since he'd been in the castle, walked the walls with Moire on a starry night, tupped with youthful enthusiasm in her bed. Eight years since he'd crouched, hidden, and listened to her betrayal, then raced to find Oslow sick and injured, and brought him home.

Darach had become a man that night, recognized evil for the first time. It had eaten at him from the inside until Caitlin had healed him, showed him how to love again. He would do everything in his power to return to her, but if not, he would die knowing she was safe with Lachlan, maybe able to be happy with him one day.

Reaching the door at the top of the stairs that led to the battlements, Darach opened it slowly and peered out. Warriors manned the walls, but not many. Most were on the other side of the castle, where Gregor's forces had amassed. Darach exited with seven men and moved behind the Frasers. They died quickly and quietly.

The rest of the MacKenzies joined Darach and the others in the cool night. The moon had stayed covered, so only the stars in the sky and torches every hundred paces lit the darkness.

"Lock the door," he said.

Someone found a heavy bar leaning against the wall and slid it through the iron loops, stopping any Frasers from coming up behind them. Then they piled the dead bodies against it for good measure.

His men gathered around. Darach looked each one in the eye. "God's strength and courage to you all."

The men quietly responded, then spread out, ten led by Darach in one direction, around the battlement; ten in the other. They were all smart, strong fighters and knew what to do. The Frasers were caught unaware each time and went down easily. Any weapons of war the MacKenzies came across were disabled: burning sand and pitch tossed safely over the side, the boulders intended to crush the invaders used to seal additional entrances to the battlement.

When they neared the front of the castle, the enemy multiplied. Stealth and surprise were keys to the MacKenzies' success. The unexpected attack of an invading force from inside the keep confused the Frasers as Darach's men moved with deadly skill toward the portcullis. All would be for naught if the iron grill wasn't raised and Gregor's army allowed inside.

Covered now in blood and sweat, Darach knifed an archer who peered through an arrow slit, weapon at the ready. A Fraser killed meant one more of Gregor's men alive.

They were in the thick of it now, and when one of his men went to his knees after a heavy blow, Darach tossed his dirk into the man's attacker.

From behind, a sword whistled past his ear. He rolled just in time, so the blade glanced off his shoulder. He swept out his foot with a grunt, knocking the enemy to the ground and stabbing him in the side. A second man kicked Darach in the stomach. He rolled against the far wall, losing his sword. The Fraser came at him but stopped suddenly and fell to the ground.

The MacKenzie warrior Darach had just saved pulled Darach's dirk from the dead man's back. He tossed it to his laird with a grin. "Couldnae let the bastard scar your bonny face now, could I?"

Darach caught the dirk and grinned back. "My wife will thank you for it later."

"Aye, women do like a pretty lad."

The exchange invigorated Darach, and he fought fiercely toward the stairs that led to the portcullis. Behind him, his men were using the Frasers' own weapons against them, hurling rocks and heated pitch and sand down through the murder holes. Screams rose up to greet him.

Gregor's men began to climb over the unmanned walls using rope and grappling hooks, adding to Darach's force one by one. The battle was in their favor, but if they couldn't raise the portcullis, they would be trapped as the Frasers eventually forced their way onto the wall through one of the blocked entrances. The MacKenzies had to move quickly, while they still had the advantage.

Fighting his way down the stairs, he yelled a warning and raised his shield just in time as a volley of arrows shot upward from below. Both MacKenzies and Frasers were hit, and Darach wondered at the stupidity of the archers. Waiting with his dirk raised for another archer to show himself, Darach hurled it at the unprotected man when he did. The archer fell without loosing his weapon, but more bowmen appeared behind him. As a battle tactic, it was disastrous for the Frasers. They had their backs to the archers and didn't know when to get out of the way, acting as shields for the MacKenzies.

When the bowmen retreated to string their weapons, the MacKenzies pushed forward again, moving quickly this time as the Frasers still standing ran back down the stairs to get out of the archers' range, trampling the bowmen as they tried to reposition themselves.

The MacKenzies reached the bottom, and full-scale fighting broke out, swords clashing, bones crunching. The archway leading to the pulley that raised the portcullis was just ahead. Darach pushed forward, and the Fraser line fell back. His other men, the ten who had gone the opposite way along the battlements, appeared on the other side of the Frasers, who were now trapped. Darach let out his clan's battle cry—answered by his men. Seconds later, they overcame the last Fraser, and Darach raised the portcullis, jamming it open with a fallen sword.

Gregor's army poured through the entrance, flowing over the shocked and scattered Frasers. Hands on his knees, Darach took a moment to catch his breath and relish the victory. The Frasers would cease to be a threat to all good people in the Highlands.

Straightening, he strode toward the castle. It was time to behead the snake.

Darach pushed carefully inside the dark passageway that led to the Frasers' great hall, sword in one hand, dirk in the other, shield hanging from his belt. The fighting still raged in pockets near the curtain wall, but it would soon be over.

After eight years, the Frasers were defeated.

Clenching the hilt of his sword, Darach flexed each finger, noting they were stiff. His entire arm hurt, most likely from the blow he'd taken earlier to his shoulder. He considered switching the weapon to fight with his other hand, a skill Gregor had taught them all as lads, but then Darach heard raised voices, and he stilled.

Fraser and MacInnes. The vipers were in the nest, and they were arguing. The yelling stopped and a scream rang out. Darach snuck forward. Peering around the corner, he saw MacInnes leaning against the mantel in front of the great hearth with a dagger protruding from his belly, his filthy lèine soaked in blood. Fraser was nowhere to be seen.

Darach advanced slowly, the only source of light a few candles and a low-burning fire. The room was much as he remembered, dirty rushes on the floor, a central hearth with two chairs in front of it, benches and tables scattered around.

Fraser could be hiding anywhere, or he could have fled. If a secret passageway existed into Moire's bedchamber, most likely others existed in the keep as well. *Damnation.* If Fraser survived tonight, he might still come after Caitlin. Darach would have to track him down like a rat in a maze.

Shifting his gaze back to MacInnes, he saw the man had dropped to his knees in front of the fire. Blood dripped from his mouth. It would have pleased Darach to hang the bastard in front of witnesses for what he'd done to Caitlin and her parents, but this would have to do. Their eyes met, and MacInnes held out a bloody hand.

"Please."

Darach moved forward, his gaze scanning the room and up the stairwell. "Please what? Please help me? Please forgive me for killing my brother and abusing my niece?"

MacInnes whimpered. "You doona understand."

"What's to understand? You're a murderer. You sold a woman for gold into a lifetime of abuse and degradation. You are beyond forgiveness."

Darach was within reach now and drew the dagger from the man's belly. Blood gushed out and MacInnes sagged forward. Dropping the knife, Darach stepped away.

"Look into the fire, MacInnes. The devil awaits you."

MacInnes stared at the flames, his eyes wide and horror-filled. He moaned, then slumped back on his haunches, blood pooling around his knees. He opened his mouth as if to scream, but the only sound emitted was a final puff of air escaping his lungs.

Darach could only imagine that justice was being served—in Hell—by Lucifer himself. A fitting end to MacInnes's vile life.

Retreating to the other side of the room, he searched for any sign of Laird Fraser.

A mewing noise at his feet caught his attention. He glanced down and was shocked to see a tiny, white kitten with blue eyes the same intense shade as Caitlin's. He bent over to retrieve the animal just as an arrow lodged in the wall behind him, missing his head by inches.

Cursing, Darach dove behind one of the tables and flipped it over just as another arrow thudded into the wood. The kitten mewed again, more frantic this time, and he saw he still held it in his hand. Heart pounding, he tucked it into his sporran for safekeeping.

Peering through a hole in the wood, he calmed his breath and searched for his attacker. Judging from the direction of the assault, it had come from somewhere near the hearth. A lone warrior? Or maybe it was Fraser.

A man stepped out from behind a tapestry hanging on the wall, bow and arrow at the ready, then disappeared into the shadows before Darach could attack. The wall hanging had been flat a moment ago, so Darach assumed there must be a passageway behind it—which meant the man was most likely Fraser.

"Come back to see your clan and castle destroyed,

have you?" Darach asked, wanting to goad the man into revealing himself.

It worked, and Fraser moved into the light. He'd been an excellent shot in the past, and Darach knew he was fortunate to have survived the attack. The wee kitten in his sporran had saved him—just like Caitlin.

"My castle may burn, but not before I kill you," Fraser said, hate thick in his voice. "That wee slut of yours will mourn you like she did her parents, and I'll still be there, waiting to see if she's with bairn, waiting to take your child."

Darach inhaled sharply, but he refused to let fear and rage overwhelm him. It was what Fraser wanted. He needed Darach to show himself too.

Looking through the wood again, he assessed the situation. What were his advantages? Speed, strength, surprise. Fraser wouldn't dare get close enough to battle Darach with a sword, so he'd have to take the fight to his enemy. But even if he could close the distance unharmed, Fraser would escape down the passageway.

Aye, the passageway. That was the key. Somehow Darach had to block it before he advanced on Fraser, who had retreated into the shadows again.

His vile, disembodied voice floated across the room "Maybe I willna wait. Maybe I'll take your wife and cut the bairn from her. Give her to my men to use while she dies."

Darach ground his teeth, refusing to be provoked. He grabbed the edges of the table and set it on end, so he could stand. An arrow pierced the wood inches from his fingers. He snatched his hands back.

Fraser had moved in front of the hearth, trying

to get a better angle. Darach turned the table to stay covered and hefted his dirk. If the man ever lowered his weapon, Darach could use him for target practice. Suddenly Fraser dropped his bow and ducked behind one of the chairs. Darach hurled his dirk an instant later, but it landed in the mantel.

Retreating behind the table again, he cursed at the wasted move. Fraser laughed before throwing a burning log over Darach's head. It landed among the benches and tables behind him. The rushes caught fire immediately, burning like kindling. Another burning log landed closer to him. The bastard was trying to smoke Darach out, but Fraser had just given Darach exactly what he needed.

He cleared the rushes from around him and dragged the burning log closer. Fraser stood in the open, waiting for Darach to move. He did, tossing the log back toward Fraser. It landed at the base of the tapestry, which quickly went up in flames, blocking the secret passageway. Before Fraser could decide what to do, Darach used his great strength to pick up the table like a shield and charge ahead. Two arrows embedded in the wood before Fraser turned and ran. Darach heaved the table forward and it crashed into Fraser's legs, knocking him to the floor.

Jumping over the table, he landed on Fraser's back with a primal roar, pinning his enemy. The warrior in him raged with victory, and he grabbed Fraser's hair, pulled back his head. The husband in him seethed with fury and he readied his sword. The son in him wept with sorrow and he pressed it to Fraser's gullet, heart beating fiercely, body trembling.

Flames crackled behind them. Smoke and heat filled the air.

"You killed my father. You killed my clansmen. But you will ne'er touch my wife, my bairns, or any living thing again."

Then he slit Fraser's throat.

Twenty-three

"CAITLIN!"

Caitlin's head whipped up from the wound she'd rebandaged on one of Darach's men, and she scanned the MacKenzie bailey, her heart racing. People chatted, rested, or were busy doing chores. She couldn't see her husband, even though she was sure he'd been the one to call her name. Then the crowd cleared.

There he was, by the stables, looking so big and bonny atop Loki, a wide smile creasing his face and touching her heart.

"Darach!"

It had been four days since she'd last seen him in Fraser's castle, since he'd pulled her back through the window and into his arms. She'd known by the second day he was alive and well, and the Frasers had been defeated with only a few losses to the MacKenzies. They'd taken time to help the innocent victims of war as best they could—releasing prisoners from Fraser's dungeon and freeing the animals from the stables as the keep went up in flames, helping the peaceful members of Clan Fraser who were in need, burning the dead to prevent disease. Then it had been a slow journey back home to accommodate the injured.

She lifted her skirts and ran toward her husband, joy bursting through her body, the pain in her ankle forgotten. After just a few steps, however, she was scooped up from behind and caught in Lachlan's arms. She struggled to free herself, but he tightened his hold.

"You'll damn well sprain it all over again, you daft bat," he said.

"Let me go. It's Darach!"

"I know who it is, but until I pass you over, you're still in my care, and I willna let you run around the bailey like a headless loon."

Caitlin glared at him. He glared back and carried her down the hill toward her husband. She looked over at him, his beloved faced crinkled in amusement as he watched them.

"Trouble, Lachlan?" he asked.

"Hah! Is water wet? She's bloody impossible. And to think you wanted to saddle me with her for good. She willna sleep. She willna rest her foot, so I made her a crutch, and she let your hounds chew it. I made her another one, and it floated away in the loch. The loch! What in bloody hell was she doing in the loch?"

Caitlin was sure Lachlan had deliberately slowed his pace just to torture her. Or maybe so he could draw out the telling of her misdeeds. Not that she'd done anything wrong. She didn't give the stupid crutch to the dogs; they'd taken it when her back was turned and ended up enjoying it far more than she ever had.

Going to the loch had been Oslow's idea, although afterward he'd denied it, saying she'd misinterpreted his words. How could "cool water will help with the swelling" be misunderstood? And it had helped her ankle, even though she'd lost the other crutch when she'd tried to nudge a duckling in the water back toward its mother.

Lachlan stopped about six feet away from Darach and continued berating her. "To top it off, she rode Cloud whene'er my back was turned. What if that bloody, moody nag had thrown her? She could barely even hold the reins with her sore arm."

Caitlin snorted derisively. Her arm may have been sore, but Cloud had been particularly gentle with her because of her injuries. No other horse would have done that. She struggled again to get free. When Lachlan wouldn't put her down, she found bare skin and pinched.

"Ow! Christ Almighty!" he said.

Caitlin glowered at him, but inside she wore a smug smile. "Language! Do you want the devil to come-a-knocking?"

Darach nudged Loki forward and closed the distance between them. She reached up, and he lifted her onto his lap. Her body cleaved to his, arms squeezing his neck, face pressed to his skin, inhaling his familiar scent. He did the same, chest expanding against her cheek.

"By God, you smell good," he said.

His voice was thick with love, and Caitlin sighed with relief that he was here, safe. She pressed kisses all over his face until he dug his hand into her hair and captured her lips. The noise of the bailey and

Lachlan's tirade faded as Caitlin lost herself to the bliss of being kissed by her husband and held in his strong arms.

After what could have been either seconds or days, something tickled her hand and she opened her eyes. A pair of blue ones, surrounded by the softest white fur she'd ever seen, stared back at her.

She gasped, breaking the kiss. "Darach, there's a kitten on your shoulder."

"Aye." He continued to nuzzle down her neck to her ear. "That's Caitlin."

"Who?"

"I named her after you. She has your eyes, and she saved me."

Caitlin stared at the kitten. Caitlin stared back, purring loudly.

"You canna name her Caitlin."

"I already did." He straightened and nudged Loki toward the keep, then grabbed the white fur ball and held her to his chest. "She rode with me the entire way, crawled all over me. 'Tis you in kitten form. Most likely she'll drive the male cats mad with her antics."

Caitlin caressed the kitten's wee head. "They'll love her anyway."

"More than life itself."

They reached the keep, and he placed the kitten back on his wide shoulder. When he slid off the stallion and lifted Caitlin into his arms again, she was amazed to see the little angel keep her balance. Darach took the stairs two at a time.

"I thought you didn't like cats?" she asked, as he pushed through the door into the great hall. The afternoon sun streamed through the open windows that let in the warm, summer air.

"Caitlin, like you, is impossible to resist. She also doesn't understand the meaning of the word no."

Caitlin didn't know whether to be pleased or irked by his comment, so she sniffed and said again, "You canna call her Caitlin."

A holler sounded from the upper level, and they looked up to see Fergus bounding down the stairs, shouting, "Laird, Laird!" He threw himself against Darach's legs. "What took you so long? You missed the fighting, aye? They came at night, but Oslow said we were safe inside the castle. Everyone was here from the village too, and the warriors were running around. Gare was hit with an arrow, but he's all right now, and Ness's son was sick for a few days too, but he's—"

Fergus stopped abruptly as he noticed the white kitten on Darach's shoulder. His jaw dropped and his eyes widened.

"Her name is Angel," Caitlin said, "and you may only touch her if your hands are clean."

The lad stared at the kitten, then at Caitlin, then back to the kitten. Suddenly, he turned and dashed up the stairs. Darach laughed and followed at a slower pace. By the time they reached the top, Fergus was back with clean hands. Darach crouched down and the lad gently took hold of the kitten, who purred and climbed up his arm to his shoulder.

"Introduce her to the other kits and show her where the food and box is located," Darach said.

Fergus nodded and walked carefully down the

corridor so Angel wouldn't fall off, talking to her the whole time.

Reaching their bedchamber, Darach pushed inside and leaned against the door to lock it behind them. He stared down at her, that dark look in his eyes that Caitlin loved.

"I thought 'tis time for a wee prayer, Wife."

She smiled as all those interesting places in her body began to tingle. "Nay, not so wee. Surely you have many sins to confess. It may take a while."

Grinning, he walked across the room and lay with her on the bed, undoing her brooch and loosening her chemise. "I promise to worship at your altar for as long as 'tis necessary."

Caitlin giggled, then pulled his head up so she could look into his eyes. "Darach?"

"Aye?"

The adoration in his tone filled her to bursting. She traced her fingers along his face and remembered how she'd done the same thing the first time she'd opened her eyes and seen him looking down at her. "I love you so much."

He kissed her. Gently, reverently. "I love you too, lass. More and more every day."

"Even though I'm trouble?"

He laughed quietly and nuzzled her ear. "You're not trouble, Caitlin. You're a joy—my everlasting joy."

She tangled her fingers in his hair. "I'll remember you said that."

"I'm sure you will. Just promise me one thing."

"Whatever you wish." Anything he asked, anything he desired, she would do it.

He caressed his fingers over her cheeks, shaped her lips. Kissed each eyelid and the tip of her nose. Then he leaned down and brushed his mouth across hers with a sigh. She could feel his smile.

"Doona give me daughters, Caitlin MacKenzie. My heart canna take it."

Keep reading for a sneak peek of

HIGHLAND TROUBLE

BOOK #2 IN THE SONS OF GREGOR MACLEOD SERIES
by Alyson McLayne

MacPherson Castle, Loch Eireachd, Scotland

1452

FISTFULS OF HAIR FELL TO THE BED LIKE STREAMS OF molten iron. The growing pile, more orange than gold, resembled a dragon's nest, and gleamed seductively in the firelight. Amber sighed at the sight. If only it were a real dragon's nest and a beast could rise and smite all her enemies. One very much in particular.

She almost smiled at the fanciful thought as she chopped off her hair. Almost. In truth, her plan was an act of desperation with little chance of success. By all that was holy, she'd need a miracle to get away this time.

Grabbing another handful, she raised the knife and sawed off an even bigger chunk. The remaining strands sprang up to curl around her neck and ears, a light, airy feeling at odds with the heaviness in her heart.

Laird Machar Murray would come after her, of that she had no doubt. If he found her, no amount of false hexes, or curses, or threats from the devil would deter him from destroying her this time.

Her lost hair would grow back. Her lost spirit and soul could not.

The heavy wooden door rattled as a key entered the lock from the outside. It pushed open. Amber spun around to face the intruder, her heart in her throat and the knife pointed outward. Niall, the old steward, shuffled in, his worn plaid sagging below his belt. She huffed in relief and went back to cutting off her hair.

"You scared the life out of me, aye?"

"You should be scared, lass. I doona know how you've lasted this long with Laird Murray breathing down your neck. He'll turn the keep upside down to find you."

"I couldnae leave with Erin so sick, now could I? Her mother and father would ne'er recover if she died. And Ian needed me to speak for him or he would've ended up in the dungeon for who knows how long."

"You'll ne'er recover if the laird gets a hold of you—although you wouldnae end up in the dungeon. Nay, he'd lock you in his bedchamber first. And no doubt Father Odhran would consider it a just punishment for all the help you've given the women."

"He's a wee ablach, that one. The devil take him."

"The devil take them both."

Her knife cut through the last chunk of her hair and she held it in her hand, staring at it. The strands twisted and curled in long, silken waves, a last gift from her mother. Her father had loved her hair. Her grandmother had brushed it every night, singing the songs of the Highlands that Amber had so loved. Sorrow welled within her at the loss, and she squeezed her eyes shut to push it away.

Bah! Her hair had caused her nothing but trouble. How many times had she wished herself plain when some irritating man came knocking at her door, asking for her hand? Too many to count.

She tossed the curls down on the linen quilt, glad to be rid of them. She had no time for self-pity.

"Did you bring the lads' clothes?" she asked. "And the band?"

"Aye." He pulled some material from under his plaid.

Amber reached for the silver brooch that held her arisaid in place over her left breast, and released it. Niall squawked as her dress fell off, and he quickly turned around. "Lord have mercy, lass, I'm an old man. My heart willna survive looking upon the pride of Clan MacPherson in such a way."

"Is that what they call me?" She tucked up her linen shift and shook out the tautly woven cloth Niall had tossed on the bed. "I thought 'twas 'witch' and 'temptress.' Sometimes 'evil-doer,' depending on who did the talking."

"Doona be daft. Only Laird Murray and his plague of rats say such things. The MacPhersons know the sacrifices you've made, the danger you've courted for us. We couldnae be more thankful."

Amber didn't speak—couldn't speak—as his words washed over her. Her throat tightened and she had to blink back tears. Instead, she looked down and secured the end of the cloth over her breasts, trying to squash down the overripe mounds that had done naught but get in the way since they'd started jutting out from her chest when she was fourteen.

"Aye, neither could I," she said finally, her voice sounding thick. "I'll miss you all." She lifted the end of the band trailing on the floor and held it out to Niall. "Here, hold this tight now while I wrap it."

Niall grabbed it, eyes lowered, and held the cloth taut with surprising strength as she turned herself into it then knotted the band in place, flattening enough of her bust that the rest could still be concealed beneath the loose shirt. Her breath came short, her ribs compressed, but it was a strain she could bear. The bulk of the boys' plaid should hide the slight tuck at her waist and roundness of her bottom. Her legs were long and strong, and if she muddied them they should pass for a lad's. Her face, too—although nothing could disguise the startling color of her eyes. Those were an inheritance from her beloved grandmother, and had led to much trouble for that lady—as well as for Amber.

Men envied uncommon things, beautiful things, and would go to great lengths to acquire them. Luckily, the MacPhersons were good people, and Amber's grandmother an excellent healer. She'd taught Amber everything she'd known before she died, and Amber's place with the MacPhersons had been secure. They'd cherished her and she them.

Not so Laird Machar Murray. The conniving laird would as soon burn or drown her for a witch—as their good-for-naught priest wanted. After Murray tired of raping her.

Amber pulled the lads' shirt over her head, then tried to belt the plaid in place by herself. In the end, Niall had to show her how it should be done, a complicated ritual of pleating and tucking and twisting the material. He moved to a chest against the wall in the corner, and on his signal, Amber shoved the heavy piece of furniture to the side so he could crouch down and count the stones.

"This is it," he said, then pushed against the block while Amber waited impatiently beside him. Finally, a space appeared that was barely big enough for a woman. She grabbed a candle from the table and lit it in the fire before passing it through the dark hole in the wall.

"Are you sure it goes all the way down?" she asked. "When was it last used? Is it safe?"

"I doona know, lass, but anywhere is safer than here with Machar Murray."

She nodded reluctantly, then set down the candle and pulled Niall into a tight hug. "I'll miss you, you old badger. You've been a staunch friend to me, and to my grandmother before that. Our family wouldnae have survived this long without you."

Niall squeezed her even tighter before pushing her away. "Go on with you, then. And doona even think of coming back. Go find a life for yourself away from the hell of this one. Marry a good man and have plenty of fine children." He let go and lifted a bag from his shoulder. "Some food and coin until you find your new home."

After she took it, he knelt and pushed the candle through to the other side. Amber peered in and saw a narrow stairwell, barely big enough for her to stand. "When you get to the end, the bottom stone should push out. I've already loosened it from the other side. The ground is muddy. Use some dirt to darken your bare skin, especially your face. There's no hiding you're a woman without that, even with your hair shorn."

Amber knelt beside him, nodding as he talked, trying to quell that panic that had tied her stomach into knots.

"Once you're out of the keep, go to the east wall by the tanning hut. Look for a cart missing a wheel, with a rope attached. Throw the rope over the wall, then climb up the hay bales to the top. I've tethered a horse on the other side."

Amber squeezed his arm, afraid to speak lest she start crying again, afraid to even look at him. He moved over, and she wedged herself through the hole. Once on the other side, she couldn't resist and glanced back over her shoulder to see Niall's face, wet with tears, one last time.

"Be safe," he said, then shoved the stone back in place, leaving her with only her candle for company.

Lachlan MacKay, laird of Clan MacKay, lay on his belly in the scrub, staring at the pockmarked and tumbling-down walls of the once-grand MacPherson Castle. He'd counted fourteen places his men could breach the fortress, carefully noting the poorly planned circuits the guards walked on the perimeter, the easy footholds to get over the wall, the young, inexperienced men at the gate. There was a horse grazing alongside the wall, and a general air of apathy.

Surely the crafty MacPherson laird, Machar Murray, would never be so careless, so lax in his defenses? It had taken Lachlan five years to find Murray after he'd murdered Lachlan's older brother and tried to murder Lachlan himself—in order to take over Clan MacKay. Murray had covered his tracks well when Lachlan had searched for him, hiding behind silenced accomplices, false names, and convoluted trails.

So why would his home be so poorly protected? It would take Lachlan less than an hour to conquer the castle as it was. It didn't make sense.

He turned to his foster brother, Callum MacLean, laird of Clan MacLean, who lay beside him on the slight rise. He was watching the castle as well, his perceptive green eyes bright against the dirt he'd used to muddy his face and neck. He even had mud in his short, dark hair.

"Do you think it's a trap?" Lachlan asked, voice barely above a whisper.

"Maybe. I canna believe anyone would be so careless. But if it were a trap, there would only be one easy way in, two at the most. Not fifteen."

"Fifteen? I only saw fourteen."

"Aye. You always had trouble counting past ten."

Lachlan snorted and resisted the urge to punch his foster brother in the shoulder. Callum would have expected it, of course, and most likely jumped out of arm's reach, if they hadn't been intent on staying hidden.

There were five of them who had been taught how to fight—how to lead—by the great Gregor MacLeod.

Gregor had bonded the lads—all now lairds of their own clans—into a tight, cohesive unit. They did still like to provoke one another as often as they could.

It was a time-honored tradition, and both men were good at it.

"I doona need to count past ten; I'm not the one who left my betrothed behind tossing daggers and running wild in her castle. How many months has it been since you last saw Maggie? Almost forty? You can bet she'll be counting every one of them. She may use those daggers on you when you finally decide to claim her. If she'll still have you."

"She'll have me," Callum grunted.

Satisfied, Lachlan went back to studying the castle, looking for the way in he'd missed. If Callum said another existed, then it did. His foster brother was an excellent strategist, with a sharp mind and eyes that saw everything. Except, of course, the identity of the traitor in his own clan, the reason he'd left Maggie behind for so long. He was afraid to bring her home with him while his father's murderer was still on the loose.

Acknowledgments

First and foremost, to my parents, Marjorie and Jim, who fostered my love of reading and encouraged me to write. And especially to Marjorie, who brought me home a book called *How to Write a Romance and Get It Published* when I was nineteen years old. Thank you, Mom, for encouraging me to spend my summer break writing instead of getting a "real" job. ☺

To my husband, Ken, who also encouraged me to write and forgo a "real" job—although I'm sure he didn't expect me to take so long to get published! Thank you, honey, for supporting my dream.

To all the wonderful women at Write Romance (a.k.a. The Goddesses) who were the first people to read and critique my chapters: Christyne Butler, Tina Beckett, and Abby Niles. All your hard work, comments, and smiley faces were MUCH appreciated and truly helped shape the book. And I can't forget my first beta reader and awesome friend, Eileen Cook…thank you for staying up late reading my book. Smooches.

To all my amazing readers and fans at Wattpad who've left such beautiful comments about this book—my sincere and heartfelt thanks. I read them over and over. ☺

And to the awesome Cat Clyne…you left me speechless by offering a five-book deal on the Sons of Gregor MacLeod. That moment will stay with me forever. You have such an abundance of patience, kindness, and goodwill—not to mention killer editing! Thank you for such a great opportunity.

And to the other creative and organizational minds at Sourcebooks—from design to publicity, contracts to editorial—thanks for having my back!

Thanks also to my agent, Kevan Lyon, for shepherding me through the jungle. I'm glad I've got you in my corner. ☺

Lastly, to my wonderful Golden Heart class, the Mermaids. Rock stars—all of you.

About the Author

Alyson McLayne is a mom of twins and an award-winning writer of contemporary, historical, and paranormal romance. She's also a dog lover and cat servant with a serious stash of dark chocolate. After getting her degree in theater at the University of Alberta, she promptly moved to the west coast of Canada, where she worked in film for several years and met her prop-master husband.

Alyson has been nominated for several Romance Writers of America contests including the Golden Heart, the Golden Pen, the Orange Rose, Great Expectations, the Molly, and the Winter Rose.

Her self-published works in short contemporary romance include her Sizzling, Sexy, Santa Barbara series—*The Fabrizio Bride*, *The D'amici Mistake*, and *The Berrucci Rules*. *The Fabrizio Bride* was recently nominated for the RONE Awards.

Alyson and her family reside in Vancouver with their sweet but troublesome chocolate lab puppy named Jasper.

Please visit her at alysonmclayne.com and look her up on Facebook (facebook.com/AlysonMcLayne) or Twitter (@AlysonMcLayne). She loves chatting to her fans!